I'm Still Unstoppable

BOOK THREE

JADE AUSTIN

I'm Still Unstoppable

JADE AUSTIN

DEDICATION

For the book girlies who need a bestie like Abigail,
a Prince Charming like Chadwick,
a faithful gnome like Fendel,
or need to get away from a man like Florence.
This one's for you.

DISCLAIMER

This novel contains:
Entire Chapters in Italicized Font
A Bold/Capitalized Word
British Spelling and Abbreviations
Mental Health Awareness
A Man Named Chad

The following are situations or themes throughout the book.
"Major" means that it is described in more depth, while "Minor"
means that there are brief mentions or suggestions of it.

Major:
Death
Gore
Murder
Sexual Content (Consensual)
Slavery
Violence
Self Harm

Minor:
Attempted Sexual Assault
Child Abuse
Child Grooming
Genocide
Infidelity
Infertility/Pregnancy
Suicide

CONTENTS

Chapter 1: The Beginning

Unknown Woman | 1925 | Schoolyard in Germany

*T*he sounds of the school day scraped against my ears—laughter and childish energy I had never been allowed to have. Boy after boy swinging, jumping, and dashing under the hot rays of the sun while I skulked in the shadows. Their hearts pumped blood throughout their small bodies, making the saliva overwhelm my mouth, but the scent of those children diminished to nothing as the blood of another infiltrated my nose.

This smell came from a lone boy, away from the others. It was sweeter, more tempting. His nostrils flared, his fists clenched as raw anger flowed through him. His sweat seeped from his pores, saturating him like his own misery, but the salty beads did nothing to cover the smell of his blood, which called to me like a piper.

Oh, how it tempted me.

My fangs lengthened, begging me to let them out to play. But the old lady hidden within the snow-covered woods of Russia had told me a secret. She had whispered in my mind that my dreams *about this boy were sent to me for a reason. He would be important one day—too important to waste. It made the anticipation grow wild within me. Still, I'd wait until he was older before I sank my teeth into him. I'd persuade him to drink from my blood, and then he would make the most remarkable vampire.*

He kicked at the gravel, spraying it against a stone wall. I could hear his self-absorbed thoughts as they played through his head. He knew none of the other boys would bother him—none of the schoolteachers would come to see if he was all right. He was accustomed to being ignored. No one was interested in him— except me.

He was no older than eight. His hair was as golden as the sun, just like the decrepit old woman had said. Bruises decorated his cheekbone, so light a mortal could hardly see them, but my eyes could focus deeper than any mortal's.

My last dream had shown me who hit him. These bruises were the aftermath. They were in a sequence of four—the mark of knuckles—and they were from no schoolyard fight. These were the proud marks of his stepfather.

I let my toe dip out into the sunlight to feel the burn—if only for one moment—punishment for my hungry thoughts. Right before I allowed my foot to sink back into the shadows, I kicked a small rock in the boy's direction. It rolled over and over, right into his path, and his eyes became alert as they met mine. His fear reached a crescendo as he took in the woman who had so much interest in him—as he took me in for the very first time.

The beginning of something great. I could feel it in my bones.

"You're handsome, aren't you?" I asked, and he jumped. "You're going to be quite the heartbreaker when you grow up."

Stranger, *he thought, but his small feet stayed rooted to the ground. He was either too brave or too stupid to run.*

I let my eyes fall to the small pebbles, allowing myself time to think. I couldn't ruin this. Little did he know, he was destined to be part of my life. We'd be far from strangers.

After a deep breath calmed my swirling mind, I looked back up at the boy. "I travelled miles and miles in the snow to visit an old woman—a witch, some call her—and do you know what she told me?"

"That witches aren't real?" he sneered without hesitation.

I laughed at his snark. Perhaps all the joy had been beaten from him as mine had at such a young age. No matter. Soon he'd find joy again—joy in the darkness.

"Not quite," I said. "She told me I'd find a little boy with hair as bright as the sun, eyes as blue as the sky, fury hotter than fire, and named for the city his mother was born in."

His head tilted back, his eyes wide as he stared at me.

Ah, Florence. So he did know where his name came from.

He blinked at me, waiting, and I knew he was hooked.

"Want to know what else she said?" I taunted.

Florence nodded slowly, perhaps eager to keep his doubt that witches existed, but too curious to let the information slip away.

"She said that one day the boy was going to grow up to be strong—a thousand times stronger than his father," I told him, mystique flowing off my tongue. "He's going to create a war—a great war where creatures like me won't be forced to hide any longer."

The flames behind his eyes simmered, and he shook his head before casting his gaze to the floor. "That's impossible," he told me boldly, not an ounce of faith in his tone. "I'll never be as strong as my father."

I scoffed unashamedly, and his head jolted back towards mine.

I don't like this lady, he thought, and I hissed at the burn.

"Be careful with those thoughts now," I warned, but the smile still lingered on my face. "These upcoming years are going to be gruelling. Wouldn't want to make enemies with people who could be your allies."

His eyes sparked with curiosity as he realised I could hear his private thoughts, yet his arms moved, folding against his chest to protect himself from my words.

"Suit yourself, Love," I told him with a shrug. It didn't matter that he didn't believe me. He'd see it for himself. "Keep that flame you have, Florence. You and I are more alike than you know."

I winked at him, then ran so quickly that his mortal eyes wouldn't be able to track my movement.

He had nearly 20 years to start believing in monsters. But it was fun to give him a taste.

Chapter 2: Journey to the Past

Azalea | Present Day | Somewhere in Russia

I sat up straight, heaving loudly as the dream faded from my mind.
  A woman.
A boy.
Florence.
She had dreamt of him—just as I had dreamt of Noel and Leon—as Chad's mum had dreamt of me.
What did it all mean?
A sudden motion beside me caught my eye. Chad was bent down, stuffing our belongings into a sack and preparing for the night's journey. A journey to my past. Harsh winds shook the black walls of our tent—black to help shield my skin from the sun. As he packed, I breathed out, letting my reality settle back in.
"You all right?" Chad asked, his eyes still trained on his task.

I looked away from him, drawing the blankets up around me. The cold sweat that slid down my back was worsened by the frigid air that swept into the small tent.

I nodded, then added flatly, "I'm fine."

He gave a single curt nod back. "We should get going," he decided. "It's still a six-day trek to Baba Yaga."

The name sent more chills down my spine. Baba Yaga: an old witch, hidden in snow-covered woods.

The dream came back to me in a rush. I hadn't seen the vampire's face as she talked to a young Florence. It was as if I watched the memory through her eyes. I couldn't tell who she was, but whoever it was had sought out someone exactly like Baba Yaga—a woman with mystical powers that I could only dream of possessing. She could bring back memories. Was it possible that the old witch had prophesied about Florence long ago? Were Chad and I seeking answers from the very person that the woman in my dream had visited—the witch who had informed her of all Florence was capable of?

I uncovered myself from the blankets and began folding them, tempted to perform a warming charm on myself, but Eyeara's words played through my mind in warning. "You can't use magic or Baba Yaga's house will flee. You must travel on foot."

After the elf said it, I had glanced at Chadwick, wondering if he knew what it meant. But he hadn't had the nerve to meet my eyes. He was a coward. He had more secrets, Eyeara had said—secrets he wasn't willing to hand over.

"I'll go on my own," I had spewed out. "If I can't transport, I'll run. It'll be much faster that way."

The idea had been shot into oblivion.

"Her house has ears," Eyeara informed us in her dreamy voice. "It would hear you coming from kilometres away. She'd take the sound as a threat." Eyeara had straightened her shoulders and tilted her head upwards. Her stance proclaimed that there would be no argument. "Besides," she went on, "it's safer for the two of you to travel together. No offence, but a king might have more sway than a vampire-witch."

I'd swallowed down my stubbornness before a pit formed in my stomach. "What if I can't control my powers?" I asked instead, thinking of the strange old woman who could sense magic and make her house flee on command—whatever that meant. "Sometimes, when I'm overwhelmed, magic bursts out of me." I gave Chadwick a meaningful look. After all, it was his actions that had caused my last magical outburst.

But there was no excuse solid enough to convince them I could go alone—without the lying king who stood at my side.

"You're stronger than you give yourself credit for," Eyeara had deflected. "You've been gifted powers others can only dream of. Rein them in when you visit the witch in the woods, but after that, unleash them. Don't let anyone convince you to keep that strength hidden."

And it was final. Saga, the purple-eyed dragon with white scales, had flown us back to the dragon pad, and then Chad transported us to *Ypovrýchio Kástro*. Not even the fresh air from our journey or the glamorous underwater view from the Greek castle could ease my mind. How could they? I had been waiting for this moment for a year and a half—waiting to regain the memories Florence and the woman who had been with him had stolen away from me the night I was bitten. I was ready, but fear still took its usual course through me, diminishing the joy I deserved to feel.

We had transported as far as the Russian border, south of St. Petersburg, but the rest of the trip would be on foot, just as we had been instructed. Transporting closer or the use of vehicles that were all powered by magic would alert Baba Yaga that we were on our way, and apparently, she wasn't a woman who enjoyed the company of others.

Cold winds blew from the east as the snow swarmed us. The gear Chadwick had strapped to himself rattled against his shivering body. I pulled a few straps from his arms, and he let them fall so I could share the load. Throwing them onto my back, I stared at Chad, ready for his lead. Then we were off, the crunch of snow sounding beneath our booted feet.

Neither of us uttered a word. All of our energy went into each step. Our feet sank into the white ground, our muscles tightened to climb over fallen tree trunks and to avoid frostbite as we travelled by night, away from the cities where the mandated curfew was enacted. My lungs ached from the cold air they were forced to intake.

Chad stopped when the navy sky had transformed into a pool of oranges and pinks. We set up a single tent by hand, and with much regret, we piled into the small quarters. The day was spent tossing and turning and begging our minds for the sleep we'd need for six more nights of travel.

Tonight would be much the same.

We finished packing up our belongings and Chad, once again, took the lead through the forest. I couldn't fathom being a mortal and surviving without my speed or magic much longer. For once, I was thankful for the peculiar life I had been given.

With only the sounds of our heavy breaths and the occasional forest animal, my mind wandered down many paths. I pondered the possible secrets Chad held, I buckled under the burden of Florence's encroaching plans, and I tried not to hyperventilate over the memories that would soon fill my head. Before daylight shed a hint of its arrival, Chad's voice cracked over the first words he had articulated in hours.

"We should collect as much dry wood as we can and start a fire," he suggested.

It was clear neither of us had built a fire the mortal way before, but after several failed attempts, a small fire graced our numbed hands with heat. We used the little energy we had left to set up the tent, and then crumbled to the ground to warm ourselves in the final moments of night.

Chad took a deep breath, warm air spilling from his mouth. "I've been thinking a lot about how to stop Florence," he announced, his eyes fixed upon the fire.

I blinked at him, rubbing my hands together and wondering if that was the only thing on his mind. "As have I," I decided to say. Then I mirrored his deadpan expression, watching the flames that held so much spirit.

"The next time anyone runs into him or finds one of his hiding places, we *have* to steal something that belongs to him," Chad decided. "A tracking spell will help us find him—wherever he disappears to."

I fought back the bitter comment of how much he apparently loved the spell, having used it to track me down to Wyatt's house. Instead, I gave a nod and tucked my hands under my biceps. The fire focused more on my face, drying my eyes.

I was absorbed in thoughts about items I could take from Florence—if his blood would suffice, or perhaps plucking out one of his eyeballs—when Chad's voice broke through.

"I'll drop the alliance with—" He stopped, nearly saying her name, then swallowed before continuing. "I'll drop the alliance with *her*. Then I'll never speak to her again, I promise you," he insisted.

So matter of fact. So simple. Almost as though he could've stayed away from Lili all along. When in reality it had taken a year and me finding out about their kiss for him to reach that conclusion.

I rested my cheek atop my knee. "You once told me you'd run away with me—away from all of this," I said towards the dark forest. I couldn't look at him. "Sometimes I wish we had. I wish we had run before Florence murdered all those people, before the war, before you went off with Lili. I've been imagining it a lot, the two of us all alone, happy, in love…" A laugh escaped my lungs and floated into the air, the daft fantasy blowing away along with my foggy breath. "But then I wake up," I said simply, and I turned to look at him. Worry coated his face as he stared back at me, listening carefully. "That never would've worked. Florence still would've gone on his rampage, Lili still would've found some way to put her hooks into you, and you still would've lied. Now there's no way I'll ever be able to trust you. At least not as fully as I once did."

I watched his jaw stretch in a slow circle, searching for the right words to say. He blinked and a clear liquid filled his green eyes, glistening in the firelight. Then he tore his eyes away from mine. He shook his head at me, refusing to see the fated path that was so blatantly laid in front of us.

"Azalea, I—" he started, but I couldn't bear to hear his denial.

"Tell me your secrets," I cut off, thinking back to what Eyeara had said. "The 'truths' you need to get out in the open—the truths that will allow us to heal," I said sarcastically, mimicking the elf's voice. I knew it was nonsense, though it didn't stop me from wanting to find out.

He shook his head again, perhaps as pessimistic as I was that it would help. "It's too hard to say," he forced out, his eyes still shifted away from me.

I bit my lip until I could taste a coppery drop of blood on my tongue. "Well, Chadwick," I said, staring into him so intently that it redirected his eyes back to mine. "Now would be the time to tell me."

Now, while I was already shattered and spread so thin. What else could he say to hurt me?

My stomach tightened as I mentally prepared myself for the truth he held.

A deep breath flowed into his lungs and he quivered as it left, but he nodded nonetheless.

"There are three things that have been haunting me," he began. "Three more things I've been dying to tell you but haven't been brave enough to do so."

I sucked in a breath of air and held onto it, bracing myself for the unknown. "Go on," I nudged.

"I can read minds," he blurted out so rapidly that my eyes grew wide, far before his words sank in. "I'm ruddy horrible at it," he added, "but it's a gift I've possessed since birth."

I stared at him deeper, this time from confusion. "You can read my mind?" I let slip out, preliminary to my mind truly comprehending what it meant. "You've been able to read my mind this entire time, and you're just now telling me?"

"Well, it's not quite like that," he insisted, panic flooding out as he turned his entire body towards me to give me his full attention. "Remember how I told you that witches and wizards were either granted the gift of the past, present, or future?" he asked quickly.

The sound of his heavy heart pounding against his chest met my ears. I nodded slowly and he rushed on.

"My gift is the present. It's part of the reason I can produce time bubbles, the reason I can hear bits and pieces of people's thoughts, or feel waves of their emotions, but it's hazy. That's why I use my magic to help calm you. I can feel when you need help—when you want it or when you don't. I've been working on strengthening my power. If I could hear our enemy's thoughts clearer, it could help us with the war. Only, sometimes lies and panic are easier to hear than truth.

"There are others who have a clearer calling for it," he continued, much slower this time. "You, for example. You heard

Aunt Morgan at dinner that night. You hear your sister," he said eagerly as though it forgave his secret. "But I trust you. It's *extremely* rare that I try to find my way into your mind. I want to respect it."

Anger built inside me as I wondered what 'rare' moments he was referring to. Not to mention, Lili had the power, as did my sister. And Eyeara had something similar. She had called herself a soul reader. Was my mind ever my own?

"It's not something witches and wizards share freely," Chad went on. "It's private, like the colour of our magic. And I've been thinking a lot about your power. Perhaps the dreams from when you were younger were a side effect of the memory potion, not a sign that your power is focused on the past. Your ability to hear thoughts, your visions of Noel and Leon, and the way you reversed your father's death all indicate that your power resides in the present."

It was a fine theory, except the dream I had earlier that day countered his hypothesis. It had been from the past. That, or the woman was in the present, consciously throwing the thoughts my way. But if so, why?

Shivers wracked through me. I couldn't focus on it. Not yet at least. I had to encourage Chad to get everything out in the open before he wormed his way out of it.

"What's secret number two?" I forced out between gritted teeth, and Chad snapped his neck upwards, completely caught off guard.

"Right," he grumbled, pulling himself back to the original purpose of the conversation, but then he cringed when he remembered the next secret. His throat bobbed distinctly as a bit more horror filled his eyes. Every breath was forced, and every beat of his heart was troubled. He placed the palms of his hands to his face, pressing them hard against his eyelids as he half shouted, "I feel a... connection of sorts to Lili."

And the shards of glass that my heart had turned into withered away like sand.

He unshielded his face but he still didn't look at me as he said, "It's strong, and it's strange, and I don't like it, but it's there."

My lips parted in an uncontrollable gawk as he finally examined my expression—the hurt my face must have portrayed. How was there any room left to feel hurt at this point?

Promptly, I closed my mouth and looked away from him, studying the threads on my winter coat. My head nodded on its own. It fit. It all fit so bloody perfectly.

"Secret number three?" I pressed, praying it was easier to consume, something that could distract me from secret number two.

Thankfully, he took the bait.

"This one is debatably the worst," he admitted, and bumps covered my skin. Acid sloshed its way up my throat from the anticipation. "It may as well be the most horrid thing I've ever done."

I couldn't help but peek back at him. "Say it," I urged, hardly above a whisper. *Say it fast before I completely lose it.*

His tongue clicked, and his eyes travelled somewhere far away. One of his hands wrangled the other as his lips parted to utter the last truth—truths that would *not* bring any healing.

"I made a blood oath so I could find and kill the vampire who took my mum's life. Lili helped me." His face contorted with the anger he felt—anger I couldn't understand. "In order to make an oath that deals with the dead, one must sacrifice the life of another." He paused, swallowing down the grief and guilt he wore so visibly on his face. For a second, his wheezing breaths made me think he'd throw up.

"And whose life did you choose?" I breathed out, regretting the question as soon as it left my lips.

The silence in the cold, crisp air filled with the scuffling of fabrics as Chad's body shivered against the memory.

"I sacrificed my father," he said, and it was like the fire no longer existed. My body was chilled to its core.

"I didn't know my father," he continued. "I don't know if he knew about me, if he was a decent person, or if he had another family. But something came over me, and in that moment, I was so low. I didn't care about any of those things."

"And did you ever find out who killed your mother?" I asked softly.

"No," he whispered back. "And I don't think I could bear to find out. It's all so wretched—the life I sacrificed in the blood oath—the life I'm now meant to take."

I nodded as though I understood, but in reality, my mind was a blur. A hoard of thoughts crashed into my brain as it mulled over the three truths—each more terrifying than the last. Yet the thought that he had kept all these secrets from me felt like the grandest betrayal.

After a moment, Chad's voice broke through once more. "Can you at least tell me what you're thinking?" he asked. He sounded guilty as my mind crashed back to the present—from the wet snow that was melting beneath me, to the way my body shook against the cold, and the crackle of the fire.

Part of me wanted to snap at him—to tell him he might as well invade my mind to find out what I was thinking. He had lied to me for a year. But the wiser part of me knew that would be cruel. He was hurting. He was broken enough without me lashing out at him. Either way, I was at a loss for words.

"I think we should get some rest," I said, evading the question altogether. A pathetic response, but I didn't have it in me to console him the way he needed. I rose to my feet and turned towards the tent. My fingertips lingered on the zipper, searching for the right thing to say.

"I'm sorry about your father," I added, although I wasn't sure if I should be. Chad had done it to himself. "Perhaps breaking ties with Lili would be a wise thing to do—for yourself—rather than for me. She shouldn't have encouraged you to take that oath. That's not what a true friend would do."

Ducking into the tent, my chest seized at his heartbreak, but I forced myself to close the zipper behind me. He stayed out a while longer, the fire casting his shadow across the tent. He sat outside until the small fire ebbed away. Just as sunlight started to shine along the tent's black surface, Chad came in. Though I closed my eyes and didn't turn to face him—though I was still vexed with the lies—every part of me ached to hold him and tell him that everything was going to be all right.

Only, I didn't know if it would be.

Shivers coursed through me as I laid for what felt like hours, making the tent shake around us. Perhaps it was the secrets chilling me to my core, or perhaps this night was colder than the rest. Or perhaps my body was giving up on the idea of ever feeling warmth again. After all, I had gone nearly a week without it.

I pretended to be asleep. Even with Chad facing the opposite direction, I could tell sleep hadn't taken him either. His body quaked as much as mine. We lay there in silence, neither one willing to admit to the other that we were awake. But I heard the anxious pattern of his breath.

What must've been an hour later, Chad turned over abruptly. He edged closer and wrapped his arms around me. Immediately, I rejoiced in his warmth. As my muscles relaxed, his hold tightened against me and our body heat mixed together.

I wanted to shove him away. I wanted to be strong enough not to yearn for his touch, but part of me needed it—and not just the part of me that thought I'd freeze to death without it. I wanted his touch for more than the warmth, more than protection from the bitter winds, and more than for the comfort of being wrapped up in his familiar touch. I wanted his touch to heal me—to mend my shattered heart and make it whole again.

We fell asleep like that, as if we were the only two people in the world—a wordless night of holding onto one another. For a moment, it felt like things could be different—like darkness had never swept in to crush everything between us. Yet how could I have allowed that hope to slither its way in?

I'm Still Unstoppable

Chapter 3: Keys to Locked Doors

O *ne more day of travelling,* I chanted over and over—anything to keep my feet moving forwards, and to keep Chad from the other thoughts in my head. Still, intrusive thoughts kept bombarding their way in.

It was faint, but I remembered the potion—the glass they had pressed against my lips that night—my memories spilling out and spiralling down the drain. I wondered what Florence was plotting next, where he was, or how he'd respond to me getting my memories back. He had admitted he took them to make my mind weaker, to make me fall in love with him. Clearly, that hadn't worked. Would he even lift a brow or feel a spark of rage when he found out I had them back? And by now, what *was* the point of regaining my memory? Hydie was back in my life thanks to my dreams, and Wyatt and I had run into each other by fate. I could ask either of them for their perspective of my past, but it wouldn't be the same. The memories were mine. It was my right to have them.

My foot skidded across an icy patch, and my gloved hands collided with the ground to catch my fall. Chad's running footsteps drew near. His arm stretched to help me up, but before he could touch me, I righted myself. Blood rushed to my cheeks, heating them through my embarrassment, and Chad's hand paused its journey. A strange laugh left my lips, a ploy to convince him I was all right. Then, for the first time during our trip, I strode past him to take the lead. I couldn't let him touch me. Not if I was to avoid a repeat of yesterday.

Ugh. Yesterday.

It was the main thought I was attempting to banish from my mind—so Chad couldn't hear my shame for it. I had let him hold me—Hell! I had held him back. It was wrong to give him hope. As I trudged through the snow, I nearly decided to talk to him, to clarify that there wasn't, in fact, any hope. But then I cringed, realising that the mind reader was probably listening to every word of my internal struggle. Then the cringe morphed to fury.

My eyes turned red as I swung around to face him. He froze, his shoulders taut as I walked back towards him.

"How am I supposed to survive your presence," I snapped, "when I constantly fear you're in my head?"

The shock in his features turned to disdain. His eyes darkened. His jaw shifted to the side and he shoved past me, continuing towards our destination.

"I'm not in your head," he replied as I turned around in time for his irritation to ring out at me.

I let out a huff and marched through the snow after him. "How do I know?"

"*This* is why I don't tell people what I can do, Azalea," he said back, just as harsh. "*This* is why I didn't tell *you*."

"That doesn't answer my question," I barked back.

"I'm not in your head, Azalea. You're in mine. Calm your mind," he demanded. His tone made it clear it wasn't a request. "It's hard for me to hear thoughts unless you're aiming them straight at me. My mind connects more easily with chaotic thoughts."

"Chaotic thoughts, huh?" I asked, my words jabbing into him like a sharp pair of fangs. "I'm sure it was quite chaotic with Lili thinking over and over again how much she fancies you—how much she was dying to give you that snog," I let out. I didn't want to hold it back any longer. My frustration was bursting at the seams. "If only *I* had invaded your thoughts to find out you were blatantly lying about it."

Chad spun on his heels. All I could do was widen my eyes as he stormed towards me, and pushed me against the nearest tree. He held me there, fury and sadness clashing together in his eyes.

"Chaotic thoughts like your regret of letting me hold you yesterday," he corrected.

My chest tightened and my lips locked shut. *So he had been listening. Another lie.*

"It's kind of hard not to listen when you're screaming it at me," he snapped.

My teeth ground together as he held me there, bits of tree bark breaking off against my coat. How could I stop myself from "screaming" thoughts at him when it was so hard to refrain from thinking them?

"Now," he said softer. His hands on my arms loosened before he dropped them away from me. "I'm trying to block them out. I don't want to invade your privacy, nor do I want Baba Yaga to sense us coming, but you've got to do your part too. So breathe."

A heavy breath escaped my lips as I watched him walk away. I took another to try and clear my mind—as he had suggested—but it was nearly impossible. Instead, I continued after him, striding through the wintry forest with the image of a shield around my mind to block him out.

I held my tongue for hours before the thoughts were bursting from my mind once more. He could probably hear them anyway, so why not voice them and seek their answers?

"You said I was better at…" I paused, searching for a code word to use that wouldn't give away what we were. We had to be close to the witch's house by now. It was imperative that we didn't spook her or her house away. "You said I could tell what people were thinking more easily than you could. So how come I can't tell what you're thinking now?"

"Well, currently, you *shouldn't* be trying to use that side of yourself if you wish our journey to have a purpose," he said pointedly, and I nodded, knowing it'd be foolish to use my magic when we had travelled this far. "But it's like what I've said before, and what Eyeara told you. You hold the keys to several doors—more doors than either of us realised at first. You can only unlock them once you've discovered which key goes to which lock. After you've gathered the knowledge of what's behind that door, you can practise and build upon it."

I nodded absently as I took it all in. I hadn't known I was a witch, or at least I hadn't remembered. But once I had discovered it, we trained. I was already much better than I was months ago. Transporting short distances no longer depleted my energy. I could produce shields and stop skyscrapers from falling. Now that I knew I could hear thoughts and produce time bubbles, I could work on those skills as well—strengthen them and use them against Florence. Perhaps Chad and I could communicate in a way that wouldn't give away our plans to our enemies.

"Can we talk like Hydie and I do?" I asked, ducking under a low branch.

"Possibly, but it'd use more *you know what* to test it. We can try after we get back home. For now, we're getting close, so keep your voice down."

I pondered that notion for a moment. "If her house has ears," I began in a whisper, "won't it be able to hear us coming either way?"

"She welcomes weary travellers, those ignorant to her strength. Legend says she eats them and saves their bones."

Every nerve in my body seemed to tighten at that.

"Do you think that's true?" I asked. "The part about her eating them?"

How likely was it that she'd help me if all she wanted to do was devour our flesh?

Chad's step halted as if his feet had been pasted to the ground. I used my vampire reflexes to stop myself from running into him. Then I saw what had made him stop.

Just beyond a group of closely clustered trees sat a small house. Through the forest's gaps came the stench of death, and though the cottage itself looked innocent, a fence of blackened bones and skulls lined the property.

"I suppose that answers your question," Chad said, and I heard the gulp of spit that travelled down his panicked throat.

I'm Still Unstoppable

Chapter 4: Baba Yaga

With a single finger, I pushed the front of a skull, and the gate eased open. Black goo coated my fingertip, and I eagerly wiped it onto my trousers to rid myself of its feel.

"After you," Chad said with a noble gesture, and I rolled my eyes. Interesting time to regain his kingly stature.

Tilting my head up proudly, I barged through the sinister gateway. Chad followed closely behind.

Instantly, a wave of power ran over me like a wind, the smell of death more pungent than ever. It surged through me, wrapping around my legs, my arms, my core, and up into the night sky, until it was gone—all of it—the strange power as well as my own.

I flicked out my fingertips, hoping to produce a spark, but no purple lit the night. My eyes darted towards Chad, but he scrutinised his own useless hands before he returned my gaze. Though his raised brows and tense stance displayed hesitance, he shrugged. Taking away our magic must be another one of her rules—another safeguard in case other witches snuck up on her as we had. With any luck, the hold would disappear as soon as I had my memories back and we left this dreary place for good.

We stepped towards the house, careful not to appear threatening, up a short staircase, and straight to a gnarled wooden door.

I let out a deep breath, regaining my tall posture—faux bravery. My knuckles reached forwards, hovering near the door.

"It's the dead of night," I whispered, absently staring at the grains and curves within the rotted wood. "She's probably asleep."

"Then she won't be able to run," Chad replied.

I gave myself the final nudge to knock. But before the door allowed my knuckles to meet its surface, it creaked open on its own. Chilled air and stench like rotting meat brushed against our skin, welcoming us inside with a morbid taste on our tongues.

A sudden melody filled my ears as metals scraped together in a rhythmic pattern. The flicker of firelight flooded the grimy floor. Together, the sounds and the light led us down a corridor of cracked walls to a room filled with uncertainty.

I was thankful for Chad's warm breath, his proximity behind me. I could feel his strength in the air, guiding me forwards until we reached a door surrounded by a flickering orange hue. Chad placed his hand on my hip, signalling me to stop. Taking a slow, calculated step in front of me, he pushed the door open.

An old woman stood in her kitchen, turning a spoon around a pewter cauldron while a vile-smelling liquid sizzled and hissed over a fire. Above her large, crooked nose, her eyes were glazed over with white. Her withered skin and gaunt, bony features made the humming witch look frail, but the dubious smile that spread across her face as we walked into the room contradicted that.

Chad and I exchanged glances before I edged closer to the tall woman who was hunched over her work.

Clearing my throat, I announced our presence with a simple, "Hello."

The witch merely continued to smile, keeping her chin pointed towards the potion and the grin pasted to her deathly thin face.

"Sorry to intrude so late at night," I went on, "but we've heard wonderful things about your powers. I was wondering if you could help me."

The cauldron boiled, her humming played on, yet everything else around us was eerily silent.

I took a step closer, careful not to get within arm's reach. Her blinded eyes and aged features made me wonder if she might be deaf as well. She gave no tell. Or perhaps the old woman couldn't understand our foreign tongue and chose to ignore it instead.

"Do you speak English by chance?" I tried, wishing I knew Russian. "*Parlez vous français?*"

No response.

Instead, she lifted her hand, elevating a ladle from the concoction she was working on. Her eyes stared past it as she lifted it to her nose, her large, hairy nostrils widening to take in the putrid scent. An eyeball with a blue iris bobbed at the surface of her spoonful. With two lengthy fingers, she plucked the eye out and held it over the rest of the potion. Her grip tightened and goo seeped out like a last minute seasoning she was adding to her dinner. Then she lowered the ladle back down and continued to stir as she licked the remnants of the eyeball from her fingers.

Chad's stomach gave a retch, and even I, who fed off of human blood, wrinkled my nose.

"Er—Baba Yaga," I tried again, hoping the sound of her name would arouse her. "I was hoping you could help me retrieve some memories that were taken away from me."

Baba Yaga slowly straightened her back, revealing her true height. She towered at least two feet taller than me as she ladled out another spoonful and turned in our direction. Her eyes went straight through me, and as she took a step closer, I took a grandiose step back to compensate. Perhaps she could hear the fear in my step because she shook her head at me, still wearing the same curious smile. Lifting the potion closer to my mouth, she flicked her brow up, urging me to take a sip.

I cleared my throat again, desperate to find my voice— desperate to refuse the nasty potion. "Sorry, but I don't think it's a good idea for me to drink it," I told her politely, taking another step back, but her feet were quick to follow. "I'm not supposed to drink anything with blood that was taken from the dead."

She shook her head again, but I wasn't certain if it meant I'd be fine or if she didn't care about the consequences. Either way, it communicated that she could hear me.

I reversed further until my back pressed against a wall. My fingers met the cracks along it, fiddling with them, searching for the words to say to the witch. I studied the lines in her pale face, no youth left behind in them, and wondered how old she truly was. The dream of the vampire and Florence as a child flashed through my mind. If the vampire had truly come to see Baba Yaga, then it meant the old witch had to be well over a hundred years old.

"Do you remember a vampire visiting you?" I asked, unsure why my tongue was focused on information from someone else's past when it should have been seeking my own. "She would've asked questions about a boy with bright blonde hair and blue eyes. She would've wanted to know the terrible things he'd grow up to do."

I heard the fabrics of Chad's clothes shift. I hadn't told him of that dream. I hadn't told him much of anything lately. Though it was possible he read my mind.

Baba Yaga smiled brighter, but this time I could see the joy in her creamy white eyes. She nodded slowly, but her lips only parted to show her rotted teeth, not to divulge information.

As she placed the ladle against my lips, her face ignited with joy, pressing for me to take a sip. My eyes flew over to Chad, desperate for some insight. His hardened eyes tore into the woman, watching her intently, calculating something in his mind. Without removing his gaze from her, he nodded at me. He thought I should take the potion. Perhaps he found some sense of trust within the old witch—a sense of honesty that I was having a harder time finding.

I allowed my lips to part, but no taste accompanied the smell. I was unaware of the temperature, the texture, or granting the potion access to my throat. Yet a thousand scenes flashed before me, along with their woeful stories.

The empty shell of my mother.
My father's anger.
Pain.
Shielding Hydie.
My singing ghost.
Feelings of loss.

Moments of love.
Wyatt's eyes.

I'm Still Unstoppable

A cold, frigid September night.
Betrayal.
A last goodbye to Hydie.

Rain.
Hopelessness.
Red eyes.

Her voice.
Her smell.
Her face.
Telling me I was off to a place far worse than Hell.

A potion.
The curse.
Memories circling down the drain.

Florence's bite on my neck.
Invisible vines holding me down.
Her invisible vines.

Weakness.
Hunger.
Blood from his wrist.
And pain.

Searing pain.

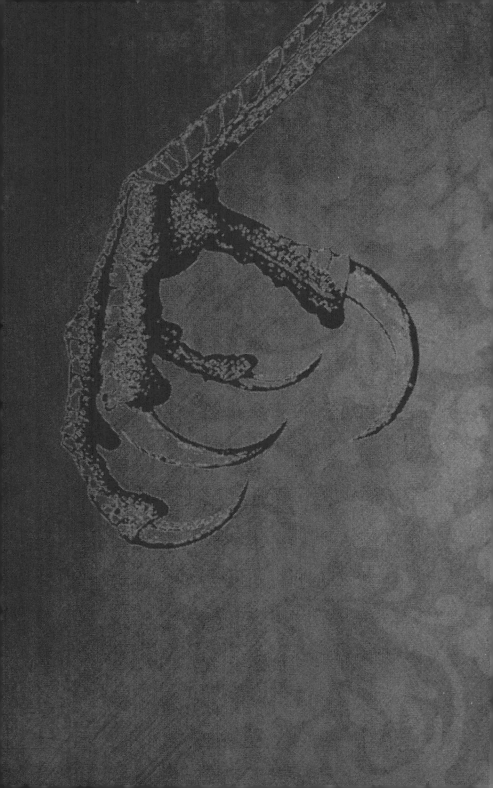

Chapter 5: Burning Hot Rage

Well?" Chad called after me, rushing to shut the old woman's front door behind him and follow me through the death-lined gardens. "Did it work?"

"Of course it bloody worked," I scoffed, knowing full well I had my own doubts but was too stubborn to mention it. "It worked *too* well."

I pivoted to meet his eyes, wisps of my hair floating around my sweat-drenched face, blood warm in my cheeks.

"I was right," I told him firmly, eager to watch his features carefully when the realisation truly dawned on him. "Lili was there the night Florence turned me. They're working together, I knew it!"

Just as I expected, his face turned stark white.

"You saw her in your memories?" he asked. His mouth remained open in either shock or disbelief.

"Yes," I replied sharply. "I saw her. I heard her. And I smelled her blood. She fed me a potion right before Florence bit me. She's the one who cursed me to forget. Fucking bitch erased all my memories!"

His raised brows grew to an even greater height, but before the self-righteous king could respond, the earth beneath our feet convulsed. The entire bone gate creaked and the dirt around it rumbled, lifting from the forest floor.

My eyes met with Chad's for a second before I took his hand, dragging him at a rate much faster than his own feet would take him. I yanked open the gate right as the ground gave an enormous lurch. Our arms waved and our feet struggled to keep balance as the ground kept rising. Before it could reach its maximum height, I took the plunge. Keeping my grasp on Chad, I pushed through the slimy gate and jumped from the rising gardens.

My feet and hand met the forest floor in a crouch, but the momentum from Chad's tumbling fall forced me to let go of him. He rolled away before his fingers dug into the snow and he pulled himself to a stop. I watched him with wide eyes, my breath coming out in panicked waves as I checked him over, ensuring he was all right, but then my gaze followed his. The spot where the witch's house once sat was now an empty square—empty except for two enormous gnarled claws. Long, crooked legs protruded upwards, strangely resembling a chicken's, before they met the dirt and roots that were somehow part of the house's foundation.

The house had grown legs.

I stood up straight, staring in wonder at the raised house as the structure began to run. As the legs worked faster to sprint deep into the forest and far away, we watched the bone gate slam shut, and the house disappeared from view.

Her house will flee, Eyeara had said, and that it had.

The trees shook from the wind that the travelling house produced. Snow fell from the branches, adding to the thick layer on the ground. Our heavy breaths and quickened heartbeats sounded through the air.

Chad swallowed through his heavy pants before looking back at me. Propped up on his forearm, his body still laid out in the snow, he huffed out, "The legends are true."

I gave him a firm nod, thankful for the gift Baba Yaga has bestowed upon me, yet hoping above all that I'd never see her or her house again.

"So she was on Florence's side all along," Chad let out, and I was grateful that he didn't mention Mrs Prophecy's name. "What are we going to do now? Seek her out? Confront her about all this?"

I felt the spark of my powers returning. Baba Yaga's hold was no longer over me. My burning hot rage was back in control. My eyes roved over the black goo that coated my hand—death from the gate, warning people not to enter the witch's house. Then my mind unlocked the door within me and my magic flowed out, vanishing the vile liquid from my hand.

"No. I think we'll wait for Lili to come to us," I declared, wondering what information we could get out of her. "There's someone else I have a bone to pick with in the meantime."

And with that, I grasped Chad's hand, pulled him up from the snow, and transported us to my first victim. One who had a lot of explaining to do.

* * *

I slapped Wyatt straight across the face.

The sound of the slap rang pleasantly through the room. He clutched his cheek, his hazel eyes returning to mine, only this time they were filled with fear.

"So I'm assuming you found out?" he asked sheepishly, and I rolled my eyes.

A puff of laughter met my ears, and I turned around to see Chad, his arms folded in a relaxed manner and a grin spreading towards each of his ears.

Wyatt let out a cough. "Er—Azalea," he started in a low voice. "Can we talk about this? Just the two of us?"

"Oh, I'm no bother. Really," Chad insisted, unfolding his arms and holding them out in front of him innocently. "I'm enjoying the show."

With an insistent wave of my hand, the front door flew open, and just as easily, my purple jet of magic forced Chad's body to slide from the room before the door shut in his face.

I stared back at Wyatt, a look across my face as if to ask if he was satisfied. Not that he deserved it, but this would be easier without Chad's eyes sparkling with joy.

"I'm so sorry—"

"I don't want an apology," I burst out, interrupting him. "I want to know why you did it—why you did it and then lied to my face the other night."

"I did not lie," Wyatt enunciated, holding a finger up to me as though he were scolding me or setting the record straight, but it was utter horseshit.

"I caught you having sex with another woman on the piss-poor excuse you call a bed," I yelled, gesturing to the futon. The very futon I had nearly let him kiss me on not ten days ago.

"It didn't mean anything. It was stupid. You weren't meant to see it!" he said pleadingly.

For a second, I was blinded by the triggering words—the exact words he had used the night it happened. Then all my anger rushed out at once in the form of a sharp zap as my finger dug into his chest. He clutched his heart, grunting through the pain. But I didn't care. I was too furious to let it guilt me—too furious to relive the depression and hopelessness that he had caused me.

"I had nowhere else to go," I told him.

"I know. I'm so—"

"And you knew that. Yet you didn't think twice—"

"And it was the biggest mistake I've ever made," he shouted back, probably trying to overpower my volume.

"Why?" I asked, the memory of that night breaking through my mental shield. Sorrow began to sweep in. I swallowed down the feeling, refusing to let it show. I didn't want to be sad. I wanted to be furious. "Why didn't you tell me?"

He knew exactly when he should have told me. He should have told me when I showed up on his doorstep—heartbroken over Chad. And frankly, I was getting sick and tired of the men in my life keeping secrets, especially when they knew full well they were the only ones to benefit from the lies.

"I should've. I know that now," Wyatt spewed out, "but I thought it was a sign!" He stretched his hands out towards me, begging with his body as well as his words for forgiveness. "I thought that you losing your memory was meant to be—that it was a second chance for us—"

"You're still trying to manipulate me!" I told him, crossing my arms in front of me. My nostrils flared. He had lied. He had kept it all from me and now he was trying to justify it?

The vivid memory of the night I was changed seared. "You don't know what that heartache did to me—the heartache *you* caused," I told him firmly, zapping him squarely in the chest again. He stumbled back. I swallowed down my hate for him. "You don't know what I faced that night, all because of you."

"Whatever it was, I'm—"

He winced as I cut him off again.

"You know the vampire you saw on the telly?" I asked. I waited with heat in my eyes. I could feel them turn red. The colour forced him to nod—fear widening his eyes. "Well, his name is Florence," I went on, "and the night I caught you cheating is the very night *he* sought me out and bit me. It didn't matter that I was a witch. I was too broken to fight back. He turned me into a blood-sucking vampire and dragged me back to his lair to be his wife. But I refused, and as a result, we're now in a global war against him. So no apology you blunder out is going to fix anything. Nothing you say will make things all right between us. There are no second chances, Wyatt."

His face was much paler than his medium complexion should have allowed. He was horrified.

"I-I didn't know," he stammered, looking down at his feet. "But fate led you back to me, and that's got to mean something. I'll do anything." His eyes met mine once more. "I'll make it up to you. Just give me the chance to prove it to you!"

His fingers gripped onto my arms and he shoved his lips against mine. Air escaped my lungs—no return left in sight as his whole face smashed against mine.

I stared at the leech, shock rattling through me for a fraction of a second before his tongue tried to burst its way through. I fought against the strength and fury I felt boiling inside me. Every instinct I had screamed to blast him into the wall and shatter each and every one of his bones. Instead, I used my taut muscles to push him an arm's length away, but that wasn't enough. Wyatt's lungs worked to suck the air back into them, but I stopped them promptly by landing a punch right in his stomach. Not hard enough to rupture his organs, but damn hard enough to get the point across.

The sight of Wyatt's tortured face as his knees crashed to the ground, and the grunt that left his throat, gave me the small burst of energy I needed to make it through this long, dreary day. His lungs tried to croak for the air they so desperately needed, and the rest of his body met the ground in an attempt to rest and restore itself from the impact of my fist. I gave him one last threatening look. His lips moved to say something, but I merely stepped over his body and placed a hand on his futon. A spark lit the fabrics, and I made my way over to the door.

"Good day, Wyatt," I told him firmly, not bothering to look back at him as I grasped the doorknob and twisted it, only to come face to face with another wanker who had broken my heart.

Chad was smirking unabashedly as he peeked past me to view Wyatt writhing on the ground and the cushion that had now gone up in flames. I firmly resolved to find a way to remove the smug grin off his face—permanently.

I slammed the door behind me and the whole flat creaked. "Don't worry," I told Chad as the smoke met my nose. "I specifically remember that he keeps a fire extinguisher under the sink—the right side. Who knew these memories would come to such a great use?" before adding, "*Ypovrýchio Kástro*." Without grasping onto him, I used my purple swirls to whirl myself off to our temporary bedroom in the underwater castle.

I'm Still Unstoppable

Chapter 6: Eviction

Chad arrived right after me, and I frowned. I had specifically neglected to tell him which room I'd be transporting to. So how had he found me so quickly? It only took one second for my frown to turn into an eye roll.

He had tailed me. That's how he had arrived at my exact location.

His smile was still pasted onto his face. It infuriated me even more.

"You think my pain and suffering are funny, do you?" I tested. "Perhaps I should cause some pain and suffering for you—see how you like it."

I stalked over to the wardrobe and threw open its doors. From within, I grabbed out two trunks and immediately started tossing all of Chad's belongings inside of them.

"What are you doing?" Chad asked restlessly, but I was delighted to see that his smile had waned.

"Making it easier for you to switch to a different room in this huge fucking castle," I proclaimed, jerking up my arms to emphasise the castle's size. "I've claimed this chamber with all my tears and heartache."

He sucked his lips in, holding back his words as I continued. Perhaps he knew how little their effect would be on me.

A song played on the other side of the room, accompanied by a buzz, and our faces changed at the exact same time. I cocked my brow up at Chadwick right as his face turned a faint shade of green.

"Answer it," I demanded, knowing precisely who was calling him—the only person who ever called him.

His eyes darted over to where the phone sat, ringing on the vanity, before shifting back to mine.

"What?" he replied with a trollish expression.

"Answer it."

"Absolutely not," he said, shaking his head. He briskly walked over to his phone and pressed the reject button.

I crossed my arms. "Why not?" I challenged. "Scared to talk to her in front of me?"

"As a matter of fact, I am," he replied, letting that fear escape through his lips. "I'm frightened of exactly that."

"Why?"

"I told you I'd cut her off, but talking to her right now will only agitate you further. I'm terrified I'm going to lose you." His eyes were wide with urgency but I ignored them.

"And what makes you think you haven't lost me already?" I asked stubbornly.

"Azalea—"

"How convenient for you to have landed on the witch who helped Florence take me down," I told him. It was almost laughable. Of course she was evil. Of course she had been using Chadwick this entire time. "Does she know I know about the two of you getting all cosy?" I asked.

He cringed at the words but shook his head. "No."

"Well you got to hear my entire row with Wyatt. I think it's only fair that I get to overhear this next conversation with *her*."

"Speaking of Wyatt, that was a very touching kiss the two of you shared," Chad jested bitterly, his tone suggesting we were even, as if the kiss hadn't been *forced* onto me. "Pity I didn't get to see that part. I only had the pleasure of hearing it through the door you so kindly put in my way."

I widened my eyes at him, livid he knew about Wyatt's kiss regardless of the wooden barrier I had placed in front of him. Yet Chad didn't stop there.

"Is there any way we could call it even now?" he pressed, casting out his anger with his tongue.

I flipped the latches shut on the trunks and thrust one of them against his chest. I ignored his *oof* to spit out, "No. How about I go snog a nice bloke and make cosies with him for a *year* behind your back, and *then* we can call it even?" I snapped.

Green magic swirled around his trunks and they landed back within the wardrobe with a *thump*. The doors snapped shut, securing his belongings within. Apparently, he was planning on staying put in this bedroom rather than giving me the space I required.

Purple sparked in my hand before I sent a flame to the wardrobe. The glow of fire seemed to eat the blue-green light from the ocean that shone across the room. But Chad flicked his wrists and a bubble encased the structure. I watched as time reversed within the iridescent sphere, and the scorch marks and fire disappeared.

I squinted my eyes at Chad, furious, yet giving up all at once. "We should let everyone know we're back," I demanded, grabbing onto his arm.

The energy inside me had whittled away. After such a long journey and the huge ordeal the day had turned out to be, I didn't have the energy to deliver myself downstairs. I needed about ten years of decent rest to catch up. Perhaps those years could be of comfort to me since the men in my life lacked the proper etiquette of telling the truth.

"And then I think we should take a nice long break from one another," I added, staring Chad dead in the eye.

"Azalea, I—" He reached out his other hand to caress my face, but I tilted my head away, daring him to touch my cheek. His hand fell as he thought better of it. His lips locked in silence. With a whoosh of green, his swirl of magic took us to a sitting room within the underwater fortress.

Chapter 7: Vines of My Own

Connor and Hydie jumped up from their spots on the sofa, standing eerily straight as they took in the sight of Chad and me.

"What the hell took you so long?" Connor asked as soon as the shock of our sudden appearance wore off.

I glared at Connor for having been so close to my sister, but he promptly ignored my look as he stared at us with wide eyes, waiting for answers.

"It was a long journey through Russia," Chad answered, peering at me from the corner of his eyes. "We also took a quick detour afterwards."

Hydie was very still as she assessed me. She held onto her arms, her chest pounding as she gave Connor a quick glance before a buzz sounded and redirected my attention. Abigail and Cristin's hurried breaths filled my ears just before they appeared next to us, their brows raised as they stared at me hopefully.

"Did it work?" Abigail asked with urgency. "Do you have your memories back?"

I nodded reluctantly before gritting my teeth at the thought of Wyatt—at the thought of Lili—at all of it.

"Turns out I was right about Lili," I told them, avoiding Chad's gaze. "She was there the night Florence turned me into a vampire. It was her who fed me the potion, cursing me to forget my past, and it was her invisible vines holding me down as the venom overtook me." I crossed my arms as my fury returned. "I mean, of course it was. She's the only witch whose magic I can't see. She's been helping him all along."

Their wide eyes stared back at me as they soaked in the news.

"Lili's working with Florence?" Connor asked, gaping.

I gave a firm nod.

"Florence kept her a secret this whole time?" Abigail asked. Her face was pale with shock. She cast her eyes to the floor, her brows scrunched in thought. "I mean, I was there that night, not long after he bit you. They've been in cahoots all this time." She looked up at Chad with jarring disbelief. "You worked with her loads of times since. You never once suspected it? You gave her intel. How much does she know?"

I nearly kissed Abigail. My stomach swelled with pride. This was why she was my best mate. She thought it ridiculous Chad hadn't realised Lili was evil, even though the witch had been right under his nose.

Chad tightened his lips, his nostrils flaring before he said, "I'm afraid not," with a stony face. Then he turned to Cristin. "What's the news here?" he asked, changing the subject away from the witch who had so easily duped him.

They all exchanged anxious looks, and a pit of dread grew in my stomach, vanquishing the joy that had occupied it.

"Not good," Cristin said, clutching onto Abigail with care. "If anything, it's gotten a lot worse."

"Deaths and missing person cases have increased dramatically," Abigail explained. "The toll is now equivalent to the number of lives taken in Japan, only they're spread out across the world."

"Florence and the pink-haired Azalea are out in the open," Hydie said hesitantly, knowing the stress my imposter caused me.

I was trying to gain the trust of the Casters, yet my look-alike thrived in undoing all my work by wreaking havoc.

"The streets are overcome with riots—worldwide," Connor added. "People are panicking. It's hard for them to deny that vampires and witches exist. Not with all the work Florence and his team are doing to prove it."

Part of me wanted to scream. The other part of me wanted to stay hidden underwater and let the world fight for itself. Either way, my mind was fried.

I felt Hydie's presence push against me, struggling against the chaos. When I looked up at her, her face drooped with worry—not only for the world but for me.

And Wyatt? she asked.

My nostrils flared with irritation. I'd have to do better to push her out of my mind. How could she read me so easily? Wyatt had been cleared from my mind. Or so I thought.

Hydie shook her head as the rest of them continued, ignorant of the conversation we held in our heads.

I didn't read it from your mind, she insisted.

I blinked at her wearily, the effects of my long journey setting in.

What is it that you know then? I asked.

She bit the inside of her cheek before glancing at Connor. He didn't notice so she looked back at me. Well... she started, Chad came back here the night you disappeared. He was a wreck. I didn't know where you had gone either. We were worried about you. Chad caught us up on everything and—

Define 'everything,' I hissed back.

She hesitated and I raised my brows to urge her on. After flickering her eyes back to Connor and the rest of them, who were still engaged in a conversation about the current events, she said, *Chad mentioned he had found you at Wyatt's flat, and then let us know that you two were off to Antarctica to talk to the elves. Then later, he said you'd both be off the radar for a bit to get your memories back.*

My teeth ground together even harder. And did Chadwick tell Connor and the rest of the world why I was at Wyatt's?

Well—she started before another anxious glance over to the rest of them. *Well, I think Connor already knew that bit...*

Knew what bit exactly?

What happened between Chad and Lili...

Already knew because of the night Chad was a wreck? I tried, but I had the dark suspicion that it was more than that.

Hydie bit her lip, her eyes once again leaving mine to glance at Connor. Heat rose inside of me. My magic sparked in my palms. Her eyes flickered down to my clenched fists. The men still spoke back and forth in hurried voices, making plans I cared very little about at that moment. Abigail's knowing eyes flashed over to me, as though she could sense I needed comforting, and Hydie winced as she took in my eyes. I could feel their colour shift to red as I held my fists tight, trying to push the magic down—to prepare myself for more fury—fury I *had* to control.

No, Hydie let out, and even in my head it sounded like a fearful whisper. *Connor said he knew about their kiss before then.*

That's when I completely lost it.

The magic flowed out of me so fast that I hardly had time to bend the sparks of electricity into purple vines rather than a shock that might kill Connor. I wanted to rampage—I *needed* to lash out at the world—not just Chad. After having a shattered heart, this was all I had left in me.

The ropes twisted around Connor's ankles, yanking him to the ground with a heavy *thud.* A yell escaped his lips, and he closed his eyes, taking in the pain for only a moment before he opened his eyes wide in horror.

I stalked over to him, towering over him threateningly, and every muscle in his face portrayed he knew exactly what I had discovered.

"Azalea," Chadwick tried quickly—a vain attempt to ease the wrath I cast towards his best mate. But I didn't have time for his input at that moment.

I looked back and cast another purple vine towards Chad, but he gripped onto my rope, twisting it around his wrist and holding onto it tightly as his own green ropes wrapped slowly up mine.

He cocked his head at me, eyeing me carefully. "Easy," he warned, but I was not a fucking horse.

I ignored him, turning my head back to Connor with remarkable speed, causing him to flinch. The werewolf held his hands in front of him, squeezing his eyes shut as he pleaded, "Okay, okay, I knew about the kiss, but please don't hurt me."

"How long have you known?" I shouted, and Connor winced.

"Right after it happened."

For a moment my mind went blank. "Right after *what* happened?" I asked, yearning for specifics.

"Right after she kissed him," he screamed out, sinking further into the floor.

I pulled the ropes tighter against him, and they spiralled further up his legs.

"And you didn't tell me?"

"Well, I didn't think it was a good idea," he said pathetically.

"A good idea?" I rolled my eyes at the lame excuse of betrayal. "You're supposed to be my friend too, you know?"

"But at that point, we weren't even that close," he spewed out. "It was before you came to babysit me that first time. You know? During the full moon. It was best you didn't know. In the grand scheme of things it worked out, didn't it? You two are head over heels in love with each other!" he yelled out, but my vines travelled further up to his belt.

"Best I didn't know?" I screamed back. "And whose bright idea was that?"

His heartbeat quickened even more. I could hear it louder than any other heart in the room as the rest of them cowered nearby, unsure if they should intervene but hovering closer in case I decided to truly hurt the backstabber.

Connor finally opened his eyes to give me his puppy-dog gaze. "Okay," he said, preparing himself. "This is going to sound really, really bad, Azalea, but I promise I meant it in the best, most humane way possible."

"Spit it out," I hissed, the vines reaching to just under his raised arms.

"Okay, okay, okay!" he shouted out, his eyes darting over to Chad as a plea. I felt the other set of ropes grow taut as Chad readied to pull me back if need be. Connor's eyes landed back on me. "So," he hesitated, "I *might* have been the one who talked him out of telling you about the kiss."

"You *what*?" I screeched out.

"If he told you, it would've ruined everything!" he insisted, his brown eyes widening even more in an attempt to convince me. "Chad wanted to tell you, but I insisted that it would stop your fates from colliding, and we both knew you two were meant to be together."

I was furious—not only at them but at myself. This stupid row shouldn't have been stealing all my attention. The war was more important, but there was no ready solution for it. At least with Connor, Chad, and Wyatt, I had a way to punish them. Even if just for a little bit.

A buzzing sound interrupted my thoughts, and I glared at the magical device in Connor's pocket. Another phone call to increase my rage.

Connor let out a sigh of relief as his hands fumbled down to a gap in the vines to retrieve his phone. "Hold—hold on," he said between huffs of air. "I have to take this," he said, furrowing his brows and nodding dumbly. "It could be important, you know?"

But I could tell from his tone he didn't think it was any more important than I suspected. A ridiculous excuse to pause my interrogation.

His finger swiped against his screen and he placed his phone to his ear.

Abigail stood, biting her lip as she and Cristin stared at me. Hydie had her arms wrapped around herself in a panicked hug, her chest moving as quickly as my own. I turned around to look at Chad, his green magic slowly unravelling from mine as he raised his hands and inched closer to me. Again, I was some beast he needed to calm. They couldn't see my magic. To them, my vines were as invisible as Lili's were to me. But they didn't need to see the power glistening in my magic. They could feel it.

I glared at Chad, opening my mouth to scold him, but Connor's voice caught my attention.

"Don't worry about it," he said into the receiver. "I'll come in and clean it up."

Guilt punched at my gut. It was as if the fire within me had been extinguished by the tears that now threatened to fall.

It wasn't Connor's fault. I was angry. And I needed to be alone.

With one last miserable look at the lot of them, my purple vines flung back into me. I transported to my temporary bedroom.

No one followed me. No one tried to soothe my erupting emotions—perhaps out of fear they'd be tied down next. And after a good, long cry, I fought against nightmares to get the sleep my body yearned for after such a long journey.

Chapter 8: Almost Mine

Unknown Woman | 1941 | Deserted Building in Germany

I could hear the hopeless man's yells and pounding fists before I could smell his blood. Salty tears streaked down his face as he drove punch after punch into a brick wall, the sweet red liquid from his knuckles spreading across it. He bore the same rage he had as a child kicking rocks at the wall, and that rage had manifested beautifully in the past 16 years.

"Still unleashing your fury on walls rather than the person who truly deserves it?" I asked, commanding his attention.

Florence stumbled back from the wall. His mouth parted, gawking at the plausibility that I was truly standing before him.

He squinted his eyes, perhaps trying to see me clearer through his pathetic mortal vision. "I know you," he said. "But—it's impossible. You can't be—"

He dropped his hands to his sides, framing his Nazi uniform. I forced myself not to wince at the symbol he bore on his arm.

"What?" I teased, raising my eyes to look at his face. "I can't be as young and beautiful as the day you met me, all those years ago?"

His brows furrowed. He knew. He knew I was different, yet he couldn't quite place how.

"What are you?" he asked, hardly above a whisper, but a laugh tumbled out of me.

"Gaining knowledge to that answer depends entirely on you, Florence." My smile widened as he flinched from the sound of his name coming from my lips. "I'm not quite sure you're ready to find out. But then again, according to the blood on this wall and the tears down your face, perhaps you are ready."

I shrugged as he hurriedly wiped his face to rid the evidence of his heartbreak. His eyes returned to mine, and fury replaced his woe.

"Make me like you," he demanded, his bravery for the unknown giving me butterflies. "Make it so I can disappear the way you do—so I can stay young like you."

He had so much to do—so much to accomplish. How could he ever manage it all on a mortal's timeline?

"Unfortunately for you, I'm completely drained, Sweetheart," I told him. "I just got through turning a young woman who was well on her way to death. Your father's men were going to murder her, but I was feeling generous. I gave this one a fighting chance."

"My father's merely following orders," he told me bitterly, his eyes falling to the ground. "He doesn't decide who lives or dies."

I shook my head at him. He thought I was daft. He thought I couldn't see right through him. "Not the piss-poor excuse you've acquired as a stepfather," I said, my irritation coming out clearly. "No—your real father. He's the one who started all of this, isn't he?"

I walked closer to Florence. My soft hands found one of his calloused ones. Keeping my eyes on his, I lifted his hand to my mouth and licked off a bit of his blood. I moaned, wishing to taste more but resisting.

"Your real father's the one who made you feel this way inside," I said, tossing salt in the wound. "Isn't he, Sunshine?"

Florence's whole body went rigid. Every pore released the scent of his fear, and excitement travelled through me.

"H–how—" he stuttered, dropping his bad boy façade for just a moment before replacing his question with a glare.

"Your father's one of the reasons I'm here," I said, trying my best to sound innocent. *"You see, in many ways, you and I are alike. I learned the feeling of true hatred after my daddy watched my mother burn to a crisp. He spread rumours about her— rumours that happened to be true—and she paid for it with her life. It left me all alone. So after far too many years had passed, I killed him."*

Florence looked shocked for a second before his features morphed into intrigue. Perhaps he was ready.

"Rumour has it, you want a bit of revenge on your old man for taking someone you loved. That leaves us in similar boats, doesn't it? Plus, I've heard he makes you feel powerless—without even a single scrap of love?" I posed it as a question. I already knew what had happened, but I wanted him to open up to me.

Florence's fingers pulled away from mine. With such focus, he studied the wall, methodically tracing the blood he had left behind.

"He killed Zena," he choked out. *"My girlfriend. He told me to do it, to prove my loyalty to him, to prove I was truly his son. But it wasn't right. I didn't care about the colour of her skin, that she wasn't part of his perfect Aryan race. All I cared about was how deeply she loved me."*

The only person who had ever loved him apart from his mother—who was also a corpse in the ground.

"That was wrong of him to do," I told Florence lightly.

His head snapped up to look at me as if he'd forgotten I was there, as if he was lost in his thoughts. But over the years I had been watching him—not every day, but from time to time. Part of me felt I knew him better than he knew himself.

"If only I had been there," I told him. I felt pity for him, just like I had with my latest creation. *"I could have saved your Zena. Now it's too late."*

Florence narrowed his eyes, taking me in so fiercely that I hoped he couldn't sense my lie. Of course I could have saved the silly girl. But I wouldn't have. He was meant to go through this heartache. He had to in order to discover his true path on this earth.

"Why are you here?" he snarled, refusing to believe I was sincere.

"I don't like what your father is doing, Florence," I said, giving my most attractive pout. "You see, my mother named me after someone famous—a famous vampire on my father's side. According to the legends of my people, she was the very first vampire ever created. And your father is hurting my people."

I let that sink in before I continued. "I have something you want. You have something I want. And it's all so perfect... How about I make a deal with you? Truly, you win something either way."

He blinked at me through his glare, listening intently but not wanting to seem too eager.

"If I grant the wish you've always wanted," I went on, "the wish to be even more powerful than your father, then you must help me kill him. Afterwards, you'll have something unmeasurable—freedom from your father and his legacy."

I could almost see the gears turning inside Florence's brain, weighing the odds, trying to envision his own future.

He was almost mine.

"You're going to make me stronger and kill my father?" he asked.

"As I said, Florence. It's a win-win situation. There are a few other things I must attend to first, but if you agree, I'll come back for you. So what do you say? Do we have ourselves a deal?"

A vengeful smile graced his lips, sending sparks through my core. "All right," he said after a single heartbeat. "But only if I'm the one who gets to kill him."

I felt my lips curl into a satisfied smile. "Done," I told him.

I turned to leave but he was quick to grab my hand, and he forced me back towards him.

"What's your name?" he asked, desperation seeping into his voice. "The name given to you from your father's side?"

It was a question he had probably yearned to know since he had met me as a child.

My eyes brightened at his curiosity. "I think I'll wait and tell you after we kill your father," I told him. "Consider it another reward for your hard work."

Florence's eyes darkened as his mischievous smile widened.

I'm Still Unstoppable

And with that, I was gone, but only for a short while longer.

Chapter 9: Her True Self

Azalea | Present Day | *Ypovrýchio Kástro*

The dream was foggy, muffled like it was playing underwater. Even with my head submerged inside it, I couldn't understand it all. What was the point of these blurred glimpses into the past? How could I use Florence's history against him?

Words of "riots" and "angry mobs" met my ears, flowing in from downstairs. After smoothing down my wild mass of purple curls and changing out of my pyjamas, I transported down to where their voices were coming from.

Abigail, Cristin, Connor, and Chad were stationed in one of the sitting rooms, the blue-green hues of the ocean cast over their worried features. From further away in the castle, I could hear Charity and Leo practising both Japanese and English with the children, and the sound of Hydie's soothing breaths informed me she was fast asleep in her room.

"Yesterday a brick came through the window. Tonight someone broke in," Connor reported, his fingers threaded through his hair as though it would help him solve his dilemma.

"Broke into what?" I asked.

Connor seemed to shudder at my sudden appearance, but still responded, "The pub."

I frowned. Mortals couldn't be responsible for either of these incidents. After shutting down the pub, more wards had been placed on the building, and at least one of Chad's guards remained posted outside at all times. Perhaps the guards' resources had run thin in our time away. It was entirely plausible that they had more important things to do than stand guard outside an empty pub, but regardless, the wards should have held against a measly rioter.

"Nigel and a few other guards are going to meet us there and scope things out," Chad informed me. "You're more than welcome to join us."

I nodded, eager to use my combat skills. It felt like a lifetime since I had been able to use my powers on a real foe, and if my suspicions were correct, Florence would get to be my target.

"If Florence is there," Chad said, most likely invading my train of thought, "we *have* to take something from him at the very least—anything to track him to his lair. If we attack him at his hideout, we can take down his followers too."

Everyone agreed before holding hands to transport to Castle on the Rocks, and I placed a mental shield around myself in the hopes that my thoughts would remain mine alone.

* * *

"We found one of our guards dead inside," Nigel shouted, attempting to prevail over the ruckus of the crowd who marched in the streets nearby, holding signs in their hands and anger upon their faces. It was well after dark. Curfew was being blatantly ignored. "She was the one protecting the place. The culprit must've fled before we arrived."

"We believe killing her was the person's only goal," another guard added. "It doesn't appear that the pub was ransacked or that anything was taken."

"Makes sense," Connor replied, still staring warily at the pub door. "It's not like I keep anything valuable here anyway."

"Not unless they stole something merely for the purpose of tracking you down," I commented, wondering if our idea to track Florence had been looted.

"True," Chad admitted. He eyed the rioters, probably equally as perplexed by them as I was. "We should double-check to see if anything's missing."

The roar of the crowd continued as we ducked into the pub, leaving the guards behind to stand watch. The windows were no longer broken, but wooden boards had been placed over them to deter another break-in. I thought back to Connor's phone call yesterday, his claim to stop by and clean something up.

Everything was in order—every bottle of liquor lined neatly on the shelf, every chair stacked atop the tables, every speck of dust untouched. Yet as I wondered how easily we'd be able to spot a small missing item, a tingling crept up my spine. Someone was watching us.

Connor and Chad seemed to deem the floor level as suitable. As they began to walk up the stairs that led up to the flat, I opened my mouth to stop them. But Abigail's hand slammed onto a table.

Everyone's eyes snapped to her. Her hip crashed into the table, freeing one of the overturned chairs. Cristin caught it in a flash and placed it back before he grasped onto Abigail's arm.

"Wh—" he started, but she cut him off.

"Something's not right," Abigail said, her face paler than I had ever seen it. I looked down to the table, the mark of sweat her hand left along its surface. Her heartrate was plummeting and her knees quivered as though they would soon fail to hold her weight. She clutched a hand to her chest. "I—I feel—"

The door to the pub opened with a bang, and none other than my face appeared in the doorway, accompanied with pink hair. My eyes darted past her to see if she had brought anyone along, but no one followed her in. The sound of every guard, every mortal in the street was muffled as the riot continued. They couldn't see her. From the corner of my vision, I saw Chad and Connor move back down the stairs, their hands sliding against the railing with a slow and deliberate caution.

The woman strolled in, and a phantom gust of wind pushed the door shut behind her. "Thanks for coming by," she said loudly, confidence radiating through her.

Bumps pricked my skin as I stood there, frozen to the ground. Who was she? What did her existence accomplish?

"Ah, I haven't properly introduced myself, have I?" She looked over to Chad, glaring at him as her eyes shifted to red. "Figure now's as good a time as any since I'm being cut off entirely."

My eyes darted back and forth between the two of them until a strange movement stole my attention. Slowly, the woman's hair shimmered, transitioning to a bright blonde. Her skin grew lighter, and her facial features shifted into another's—one who was still very familiar.

Lili, I thought, unable to even move my lips as the pink-haired "me" shed her disguise and revealed her true self.

"It's really a pity going back to blonde," she said, staring at her hair as she twirled it around her finger. "Pink was always more my colour."

Abigail's legs crumbled underneath her, and as Cristin wrapped his arms around her waist, her eyes stared into Lili as though she were seeing a ghost.

"I feel *her*," Abigail said, and the whole room held its breath.

I'm Still Unstoppable

Chapter 10: Keeping Secrets

"L ilith," Abigail breathed out, still clutching her chest.

I had heard that name fall from her lips once before, at the top of Notre Dame. My eyes flickered down to her Star of David necklace, remembering her haunting past.

"Long time no see, Sunshine," Lili said to Abigail with a bright smile. "It's been what? 80 years? But not quite as long since you've been close enough to feel that pull."

That's what Abigail could feel in her chest: a pull. And if she felt a pull, it could only mean one thing.

"She's the vampire who changed me," Abigail rasped out, and Cristin held her tighter.

"You're a vampire," I let out as I stared at Lili. Not a question, but a realisation setting in.

"A vampire and a witch just like you, Darling," Lili said in a mocking tone. She stared at me, the hint of a satisfied smile on her lips. "Only, I wasn't bitten. I was born."

"Cast out of Hell is more like," Cristin remarked, but it did nothing to faze her.

Lili laughed as though we were all blind to not see it before. "Not far off, Love…" she said. "In Judaism, there was a legend long ago about the very first vampire—Lilith. Dreadful name if you ask me. I always wanted to rid myself of my father's side and merely be a witch like my mother."

My heart stopped. The information was crashing down on me all at once. Her voice. Her name. Her father. My dreams. It was her. How had I not realised it before? She wasn't just Lili. She wasn't just the Lilith that bit Abigail in the middle of World War II. She was the vampire who created Florence. She was the woman whose head I had been in, reliving memories of a time far before I was even born. Her mother had been burned at the stake because of a rumour that was true. Her mother was a witch. Yet she was a vampire from her father's side. She was right. She was like me. And it made me sick to my stomach.

I reinforced my mental shield. It was no longer merely Chad or my sister I wished to block out, but Lili as well. She could read minds.

Lili's eyes bore into me. A pressure built in my head, weighing down on my brain, but I wouldn't let her in. I couldn't tell if she had read my mind. I couldn't tell if she knew I had discovered a way into her past. But as her heated state turned into a glare, I suspected her anger was because I had succeeded in blocking her out.

"And what exactly is it that you want, Lili?" Chad asked her, nearing my side as he spoke. His arm grazed against mine, and I could feel his warmth as he spewed fire at her with his tongue. "It seems you've wormed your way into all of our lives, and for what purpose? To win a war? To gain access to our side and feed our plans to Florence?"

"Perhaps," Lili answered with a coy shrug.

"She's the witch who's been helping you?" Abigail asked, turning her head to gawk at Chad and me. "She's *the* Lili?"

"Frightfully small world, I'm afraid," Lili replied.

Abigail shook her head in disbelief.

"What?" Lili asked, fierceness raising in her voice. "Like I'm the only one keeping secrets? I think not." She watched Abigail closely. Though her steps were slow as she advanced towards her, her words seemed to swoop in like a hawk ready to catch its prey. "There's a little thought that keeps creeping into your head, isn't there, Sunshine? You don't want it to be true, but you know it is.

They're going to find out sooner rather than later, and they're not going to take it lightly..."

The way she spoke was like a luring spell that led you straight to your death. It was coated in silk and honey, but bore a poison that was sure to sting.

"Please don't," Abigail muttered, strength fading away completely and replacing itself with pure fear.

"Why not?" Lili asked, addressing the whole room. Her voice was loud and bitter as she looked at each and every one of us. "Perhaps Abigail's secrets will shed light on Chadwick's, and then you can all have everything out in the open. *You* cast me aside," she continued, pointing at Chad this time. "We could've been everything, the perfect power couple all the Casters longed to see. You could've persuaded me to join your side, but you chose the frail little girl over me." Her eyes flung to me as though I had ruined her life when, in fact, it had been the opposite. "Glad to see that kiss he and I shared tore you apart though." She pursed her lips, satisfied with the job she had done.

But her words and anger meant Chad had done it. He had cut things off with her, though it had taken a thousand signs for him to see through her feigned innocence. He must have contacted her when I was asleep.

"So now that we're all here," Lili announced, "let's get things into the open. Abigail, do you want to explain who killed Chad's mum?"

Abigail's eyes went wide.

"And then Chad," Lili went on, "you can explain why it is that you have to kill her now."

No, I thought. I couldn't breathe. It couldn't be true.

The blood in Chad's face drained, and he stared straight ahead, unable to look at Lili, at his friends, and especially not at Abigail. I wrapped my hand around his, pushing as much strength as I could into him. The soft brush of Connor grasping Chad's shoulder met my ears, but Chad remained frozen.

"Chad, I'm so, *so* sorry," Abigail said, breaking into a plea. "It was an accident. I was depressed. I was too terrified to let the sun take me so I stopped feeding."

I remembered the times she had brought me in from the greenhouse at Loxley Lair, all the times she had forced me to drink even when I felt I didn't want to live.

Chad still couldn't bear to look her way. Beneath my shock, my heart ached for both of them.

"I was trying to starve myself to death," Abigail went on. The words came spewing out of her. She blinked and red tears streamed down her white cheeks. "And your mum, she just—it was the wrong place at the wrong time. I didn't know who she was," she said, shaking her head. Her eyes were wide, her voice hoarse as she choked on more tears. "I was too thirsty to control it. That's when Cristin found me. I was a wreck. He took me to live at Loxley Lair. Afterwards, we heard rumours that a vampire had killed the Caster queen. I didn't want to believe it was me, but I kept thinking about it ever since I found out that you were a prince—that it was *your* mum who had been murdered by a vampire—and the guilt has been eating at me ever since. I'm sorry, Chad. I'm so, so sorry."

Lili rolled her eyes. "As touching as this all is," she said, relishing in all the misery, "we haven't even gotten to my part of the secret."

My teeth gritted together, pouring every ounce of hate I held into the woman before me. My palms started to tingle with magic, but I kept the fire in so I wouldn't hurt Chad as I held his hand in mine.

"I drugged Chadwick—poisoned him slightly—into making the decision, but he sacrificed his father's life to find his mother's killer," Lili announced, pausing as a mischievous look brightened her eyes. "All while the murderer herself was right under his nose. Not only that, but he had been so close to finding his father too, yet he never even suspected it."

I frowned. What the hell was she leading up to?

Chad broke his distant, lost stare to look at Lili. She smiled like his interest was her golden prize.

"Yes, that's right. Your father. Turns out your girlfriend was looking for him at the same time," Lili cooed, stepping closer to us, but I took a half step in front of Chad to block her path. Her eye contact didn't waver. She stared straight at Chad as she neared us. "Remember that detective? Detective Harrison, was it? The one whose funeral you passed up to go on a wild goose chase for Florence? A chase I set up by the way. Well, it would appear that he and your mum had once been madly in love. Unfortunately, when she got knocked up with you, your infernal aunts convinced her it would never work—a queen and a mere mortal. He never found out about you. And he never will now that you sentenced him to death—Florence was kind enough to handle that small detail. Apparently, he was delicious."

The information shot into me like a bullet. The connections—so many connections between everything that had happened.

"Poor old man always missed your mum though," Lili went on. "He poured his whole career into taking over her obsession, trying to save a little girl from her treacherous father. Looks like everyone was obsessed with Azalea, even in those days. I'll never understand why." Her eyes glowed red with hate.

"Anyway," Lili drawled, picking a piece of dirt off her dress and dropping it on the floor, "it was all in the hope that Queen Madelyn would find her way back to him. Perhaps she would've if little Miss Abigail over here hadn't gone and drank every last drop of her blood."

Each sentence crowded in my mind, but I held the shield tight, refusing to let her in my head. It was too much for me to handle, let alone for Chad to mourn on his own.

"Oh, don't look so crushed," Lili mocked, reaching a hand out towards Chad's face.

I grabbed onto her wrist before her skin could meet his, but she didn't even flinch. She simply let out a small chuckle.

"Perhaps a kiss would make it feel better," she teased Chad, sticking out her glossy lips in a pout.

I threw her hand down in time for a purple fireball to fly out of me and crash into the side of her face. A gasp left her lips, but the sound slowly turned maniacal as she laughed through the pain. When she pulled her hand away from her injured cheek, I could see why. It was healing at a marvellous pace—just like an injury would've done on me—just like it would to the other vampires in the room.

Lili winked at me and then vanished without a trace.

For a second, the room was silent. Then Chad's body shook against me, unable to soothe itself. His lips parted as if to say something—anything—but as a whimper tumbled out from Abigail, Chad disappeared in a cloud of emerald green smoke.

I'm Still Unstoppable

Chapter 11: The Only Answer

Abigail let out a sharp cry, and her knees crumpled underneath her. Cristin gripped onto her, keeping her upright. A waterfall of blood tears streamed from her eyes as shivers wracked through her, and I stood between her and Chad's dissipating cloud of green smoke, torn in two and aching to comfort both of them.

I had known Chad's secret, but it acquired a whole new meaning when it meant he was cursed to kill my best friend. I had noticed Abigail was growing distant in the past few months, but I had never dreamt in a million years that this would be the reason why.

I reached out towards Abigail, but a spurt of anger stopped me. She had known. She and Cristin had both known and they had kept it a secret.

Agony overwhelmed me. I felt lost as I turned to Connor. He looked as though his mind was as muddled as mine. But with the eerie silence outside, I knew I should take them back to the underwater hideaway.

Weaving my hand into Connor's, I grabbed onto Cristin's shoulder and propelled the four of us into a cloud of purple. The shimmering sea danced upon our skin when we arrived.

Cristin's eyes met mine, guilt swirling within them as he studied me, but I turned away, and he took it as his cue to leave. He escorted Abigail up the grand staircase, supporting the weight of his sobbing wife with each step. Eventually, the heart-wrenching sounds of Abigail's sobs died down.

"You should go to Chad," Connor said, breaking the numb trance that had captured me. "He would want you to. I know it'll be hard for you after everything the two of you have faced, but he needs you right now."

A heavy breath left my lungs. Connor was right. As much as my mind wrestled with the idea, I knew it was the right thing to do. I nodded at the slick floors, too frightened to admit it out loud.

Connor wrapped me up in a hug, whispering in my ear, "I'm sorry," but I didn't know which part he was sorry for. Nor did it truly matter.

He let go and I tried to manage half a smile before transporting myself to the one place I knew in my heart that Chad would go—home.

Castwell Castle and all its beauty was dulled with gloom when I arrived. Though the moon glistened across the lake, though the tall towers invited me in, the entire estate radiated Chad's sorrow. He had once told me it had been his mum's favourite castle and it was no wonder why. The lake and towers, along with the enchanted maze and stables filled with magical creatures… It was lovely even in the darkest of times. But the memory of his mother was why he loved it most—why he favoured it over all the other castles he owned.

I turned in the direction of Chad's aching heartbeat. As soon as my eyes landed on the stable, the doors burst open, and a gallant white unicorn raced through. Chad sat atop its saddle. His long sleeves were bunched at his elbows, his forearms flexed and his knuckles white as he gripped onto the reins. He stared straight ahead into the forest beyond. His expression was hard and focused. It was rare I saw him as anyone but Chad, the man I met in a pub one night and fell in love with. Yet as he rode towards me, his brooding eyes—his fierce breaths escaping in time with each gallop—all I could see was King Chadwick Castwell, High King of the Casters.

Without a spare glance, he and the mystical white beauty swept past me. My breath caught as the wind from their insurmountable pace whipped through my hair. And then I watched as they wove their way through the trees, and out of sight.

* * *

I sat by the lake for two hours, dipping my feet into the warm, enchanted waters. Thoughts of secrets and betrayal swirled around my mind, no longer making sense amongst the mayhem within. Thoughts that all desperately needed to be sorted. Foremost was the image of Detective Harrison's pale, drained face, haunting my mind. The drawings and papers cluttering his small house pierced through, the sound of his phone whizzing through the air so I could report his murder—all etched in my memory forever.

Chad's father.

Whom he had killed, even if indirectly.

I wondered how Lili had convinced Chad to make the pact— if she had slipped him a potion or if it had been a spell to make him more vulnerable. But it all came back to the fact that he shouldn't have trusted her in the first place.

No longer content with sitting on the edge of the lake, I decided to take a swim. My hands worked to pull my shirt over my head before I dragged my trousers slowly down my soft brown legs. After setting my clothes neatly on the bench, I dove into the lake, hoping the warm magic within would wash away my worries. It didn't.

Bubbles led the way back to the surface. As soon as I took a breath of fresh air, I had to force back the tears. What was I doing here, waiting for a man who clearly wanted to be left alone? He had ridden right past me. Who knew how long it would be before he returned? Or *if* he returned at all…

I pushed myself up to float on my back, taking in the night sky and the milky white moon. Clouds floated about, covering most of the stars from view. Through the water that splashed around my ears came the padded sound of hooves as they slowed to a trot along the grass. Immediately, I pulled myself upright and swam towards the edge of the lake, right to where my feet could touch the bottom. I expected Chad's eyes to avoid me, just as they had when he rode past, but when I saw him looking right at me, my body jolted. He dismounted the magical beast in one swift motion, and as he turned to me, the unicorn pranced back into its stable.

Chad walked into the shallow end of the lake, his shoes still on, his clothes still hugging his body. I watched him carefully, taking in all his details as he made his way closer to me—his slow staggering steps, the mist that came out with each struggling breath, and his empty, sullen eyes. He had lost a part of himself. Water soaked its way up his clothing as he drew nearer, but he paid it no mind. He merely gazed into my eyes, and I could feel every part of his hurt as though it were my own.

When he was close enough to touch, I grasped onto his wet shirt, his dragon tattoo visible through the white fabric as I pulled him closer to me.

"I'm sorry," I whispered, looking up into his eyes. "I'm so sorry."

"It's all my fault," he choked out. "Abigail... the detective... None of this would be happening if it weren't for me."

I pulled him in closer, placing my forehead against his, and shook my head. Sorrow built in my chest, flowing up to my throat, but I willed myself to speak. "You mustn't think of it that way," I stressed to him. Those self-sabotaging thoughts would do him no good. "Lili poisoned you. She tricked you into making that oath."

"But how can you be so sure I wouldn't have made the same decision without it?" he asked, pulling back to look at me. He tilted his head down to avoid my eyes. "I've always wanted to catch the person who killed my mum. Who's to say I wouldn't have killed Abigail before I met you—before I gave her the chance to show how selfless she truly is?"

My teeth sank into my bottom lip as I mulled the idea over. "What matters is what we can do now, not what could've happened. We can fix this," I insisted, squeezing him hopefully. "What happens if you don't complete the blood oath—if you don't kill Abigail?"

"Then I'll die."

"Oh," I responded, my heart dropping. I shut my mouth, completely lost for words. My chest quivered against his.

It was either him or her. Only one could come out alive.

I swallowed down my fear and pushed away the chills that not even the enchanted waters could soothe. "We'll go back to Baba Yaga," I decided. My voice was loud as I shifted my tone to determination and my words away from mortality. "We found her once, we can find her again. She'll be able to undo it, like she broke my memory curse."

But Chad shook his head, and any optimism fled from me. "She can't fix this one, Azalea," he told me softly. "Death is the only answer. I knew that going into it. But I can't kill Abigail."

I listened to the sounds of his chest as his lungs pulled the air in and out of them, wondering how many more breaths he had left in this world. Of course he wouldn't harm Abigail, no matter who she had taken. He would sacrifice himself before it ever got to that.

The stubbornness I held forced me to give it one last go. "Isn't the sacrifice of your father's life not enough to satisfy the blood oath?" I asked.

"No," he breathed out. "No, it's not."

Scenes of Chad's death played in my mind. Ginny's prophecy. I was going to kill Chad. Whether it was truly me, or Lili disguised as me, it didn't matter *who* did it. It was going to happen. The dream had come to me for a reason. Was this it? Was this the way the oath was to be fulfilled?

Ginny's ghastly voice played through my head, telling me everything would happen the way it was meant to, but this couldn't possibly be the ending to our story. It simply couldn't.

Tears filled my eyes. Part of me wanted to push them away. I needed to be strong—for Chad. The weight of the world was on his shoulders, and though I longed to take it for him, the best I could do was feel it with him.

Chad's hands found their way to my bare hips, and the water shimmered around us. He ran his fingers absentmindedly up and down them, still staring off into the nothingness.

"I didn't know him," he said, and Detective Harrison's unseeing eyes played in my mind. "I barely knew my mum, and no matter what I do, I'll never be able to get that time back."

I nodded against him to show I understood, but something inside me begged to burst out. Slowly, I placed a hand on either of his cheeks before delivering his forehead back to mine.

Without a thought as to how I'd do it, I pushed every memory into his head that I could. The sweet voice of the ghost who had sung to me in every time of need. A vision of her hiding a book about magic from my father. Her nudges towards clues and paths that I needed to follow. Her green eyes that matched Chad's, and her soft features as she begged for my forgiveness.

Then the thoughts shifted to the mysterious man who watched over me from across the street. The way he fought to prove my father wasn't fit to keep us, and the drawings he had made of my eyes. The beautiful wreath Hydie had swirled into place with her golden magic, right after the man had been laid to rest. Memories Chad had never seen of his parents but could now hold close.

When I opened my eyes, a tear trickled down Chad's cheek. His laboured breath caught mine.

"Thank you," he whispered as he wrapped his arms around me and pulled me in as close as he could. "Thank you for showing me."

My hands sank back to his shirt as his grip loosened. Unsatisfied with the wet fabric, the sullen way he had walked into the lake, I placed my fingers on the buttons. I undid them one by one until I could properly see the top of Saga's portrait against his skin. My fingers paused for just a second as I took in her blinking eyes, and then they continued down until Chad's whole chest was uncovered.

His hand found its way to my chin, pulling it up to stare into me. All his troubles were displayed on his weary face as I looked back at him. His eyes studied mine closely before they wandered down to my lips. The overwhelming desire to ease his sorrows consumed me. I leaned into him slowly, terrified my body would push him away as it had in the last few months, terrified I was still cursed to hurt him if my lips touched his. But the curse was broken. So I closed my eyes and planted my lips against his.

I'm Still Unstoppable

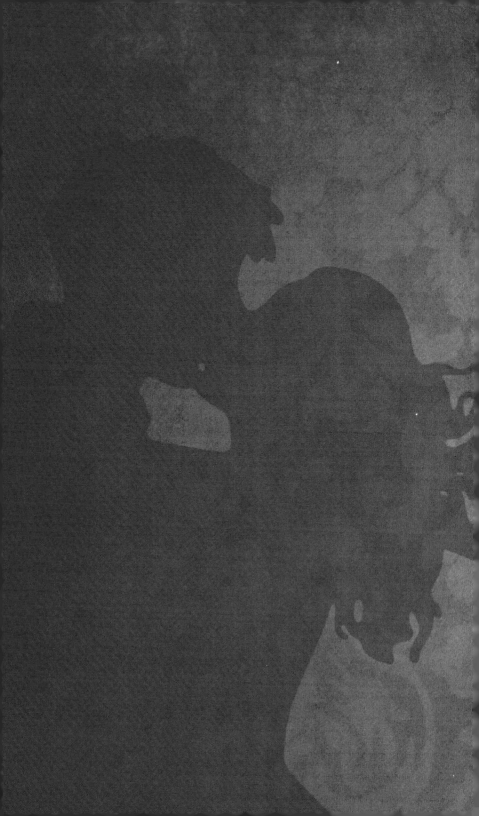

Chapter 12: To Take Away the Pain

Chad didn't even flinch. My powers didn't blast him away. Instead, we absorbed every part of the kiss. It had been an eternity since our last, yet it felt as though my lips belonged with his. I wanted to clear everything from his mind, have him focus on something simple and natural rather than the devastation. And based on the way his chest lifted to breathe me in—the way our arms wrapped around each other, anxious to hold tight—it was exactly what we both needed.

His lips parted, sucking the breath from me and leaving a pleasant chill in my mouth like the effects of spearmint. His bare chest pressed against my skin. Despite the warm waters, my shivers advanced through me as I wove my fingers up into his hair. And I let all my worries wash away as I gave myself wholly to him.

I tried to focus on his lips, the feel of them against mine, but was instantly distracted when he moved his hands to slip up my sides. My toes curled into the lake floor. His hands travelled further and further up, slicking back my drenched hair so he could grasp onto it with each and every muscle within them.

My hands slipped under his open shirt, pushing it off his shoulders, over the perfect curves of his biceps and down his arms until the shirt floated away peacefully. He grasped back onto me as though he was frightened I wasn't real, and I held him tighter to let him know it wasn't all a dream.

His tongue rolled over mine, and the closer I held him to me, the more of him I felt. I could feel as he pushed himself against me and as his hands tickled their way over the thin fabric of my bra, testing how long I could go before I invited him underneath. It wasn't long at all before I eagerly caved. I screamed into his mind, longing for him to undo the latch. As if he had heard my begging, he obliged. The straps fell from my shoulders. After he pulled my bra off, his hands brushed against my breasts and cradled them.

I let out an excited breath and nibbled on his earlobe, letting him know how much I enjoyed his touch. He lifted me into his arms and I straddled my legs around him. My body yearned to make him feel at peace—to heal him from the inside out. Before we could get lost in the night or the early spring breeze, I transported us into *our* bedroom in *our* castle.

Our wet, tangled bodies landed on the bed and I towered over him, the water from my hair raining down on him as his eyes sparkled at me. I placed my mouth on his, refusing to let the delicious taste of him get away.

His lips detoured away from mine and over to my ear. I could hear them part—hear as he tried to utter words that had no place in this moment. So I leaned back and placed a finger to his lips. I couldn't bear to hear what he wanted to say. I couldn't handle any more emotions. I pressed my finger against his lips, and the feel of his skin drove my finger into his mouth.

His teeth parted to bite lightly on my finger, the pressure increasing as a grin spread on his lips. The pain made me wetter. The rest of my fingers grasped his chin, massaging the prickles along his face as my bottom ground circles on top of his arousal. I could feel my own warmth overpowering the cold from the lake water that was still dotted across my skin, and he bit my finger even harder, his eyes lighting up because he could feel it too. He released his jaw to bite the skin below my thumb, then bit further and further up my arm as I continued to move my hips in circles against him. He felt like perfection against me.

My muscles crumbled, only able to enjoy so much pleasure so soon, and my entire torso fell into him. The new position granted his teeth access to my shoulder, and then my neck. My hair draped over us as his tongue slipped out to play along my favourite sweet spot.

I dug my nails into his sides, dragging them down until they met his pants. The button nearly jumped out of my way and his zipper zoomed down all in one go. Scooting back, I pulled down his pants, forcing his tongue to part from my neck. He lifted up so I could undress his bottom half and toss the rest of his clothes and shoes to the floor. His member pulsed excitedly as I ran my hands back up his cold thighs. I indulged him with a teasing lick as I locked eyes with him. Without skipping a beat, I grabbed onto it as I pulled myself up to his level and gave him several long strokes. My hand brushed up against my panties as I did it, aching to feel him against me. I repositioned my hand so that his full length could rub against me instead.

Chad's hands grasped onto my hip and the back of my neck as he moved his body up and down. A long grunt left his lips as I moved faster, but then broke away to press his tip against the fabric, right against the warm opening of my body.

The hand he had on my neck swept up into my hair, tightening around the base of my strands, and he drove my lips back onto his. The pressure and movement of his lips and his tongue as they caressed my mouth drove me mad, pushing me to finally pull my underwear to the side, and allow him full access.

He slid all the way in, provoking a sharp gasp from my lips, and he took it as a challenge to do it again and again and again. My lips suctioned away from his so air could rush into my lungs. I sat upright, raising and sinking into him, pulling at his hair, unable to open my eyes as I enjoyed every motion. I felt as Chad's hands slid up my sides until he held me tight, his thumbs massaging circles into my nipples.

My release was coming closer and closer, and I *had* to feel my chest against his.

I dropped down, pressing my breasts into him. Nuzzling my face into his neck, the urge to taste him sparkled in my mind. My fangs lengthened. They dug ever so lightly into his skin, and two small, tempting drops of blood dripped their way into my mouth—sweet as candy. As he let out a loud grunt of air, I could feel the added warmth as he came into me, and I rode him and rode him until my vision turned to stars. My legs quivered against him as I let out a scream of pure pleasure. I was melting into his arms as my body convulsed ceaselessly. The rocking of our bodies slowed, but his throbbing pulse continued to satisfy me until every bit of energy had drained from my body.

"Fuck," Chad breathed out, his arms wrapped around my back as he kept me tight to him.

I smiled at the word—the only word I'd allow him to have for the rest of the night.

It took several moments to catch my breath, but once I did, I licked his neck clean. It was the perfect combination of sweet and salty as the blood mixed with his sweat. My mind lingered on the taste, his scent, the feel of him against my skin and inside me— the way our bodies fit together so flawlessly as we breathed in sync.

And for one blissful moment, the thoughts of everything else vanished. It was just us. Only for a small fraction of time, but the best moment either of us could have with everything that was trying to keep us down.

* * *

My body was numb. Every muscle within me had gone towards Chad's pleasure, and every part of him had gone into mine, so it was no wonder his panting quickly transformed into long, steady breaths of slumber.

Even though my eyes longed to close, my mind dangled dangerously over the thoughts of what would come next. Panic infiltrated its way into my chest. I didn't know what would happen between us if we woke up next to each other—what we would say or what my heart would convince me to do. Nothing had been resolved, nor could it with so many different emotions blurring our view.

So I left.

Swirls of purple wrapped around me, and where Chad's warmth had once cradled my skin, a chilled, empty air replaced it. I was back in my bed at *Ypovrýchio Kástro*. With shaking hands, I cast a spell over myself. A spell Chad and I had done several times. A "witchy" spell, as Abigail used to call it, to ensure the intimate moment wouldn't grow into something more.

I ached as I forced myself to move. I didn't want to think about the horrifying events that had led up to our moment together. I didn't want to relive all the things Lili had forced into the open. So instead, I fought against the memory, tossing and turning in bed. I didn't know whether I truly fell asleep.

A few hours later, the sound of Chad's heartbeat startled me up. His hesitant breaths reverberated from the other side of the bedroom door.

For a moment, a swirl of excitement clouded my judgement. Part of me yearned to touch him again, to let him run his hands all over me and whisper promises that everything would be all right. But he didn't.

A glow appeared next to me, and my magical sage green purse shimmered on the bed. The soft whoosh of air flooded outside the door, and my heart clenched as I realised he had transported away. I let the sounds of the whole underwater castle flow into my ears, but there was no trace of him anywhere. He was gone.

Perhaps it was my thoughts that had scared him away—my uncertainty pushing and pulling him apart. Or maybe it was the silence that scared him. Maybe my thoughts weren't screaming out at him this time. Maybe he had tried pushing against my mental shield but couldn't break through—a tally he couldn't add to the times he had tried to break into my mind. Secret number one.

What if he thought I was being too stubborn? Lili was a spy. She had been working with Florence, so she would no longer serve as a wedge between us. Though that took her out of the running to be Mrs Prophecy, it didn't take away from the fact Chad had admitted to being drawn to her—to the strong connection he felt with her. Secret number two.

But I supposed it could be his own wounds that had stopped him from coming in further. He had a dilemma to face, a choice between who should live and who should die, thanks to his blood oath. And that would be harder to do under the same roof as the vampire who had murdered his mother. Perhaps his leaving was all due to secret number three.

A light grew, protruding out of the seams of the purse. I opened it and reached in to find a letter, the envelope addressed with my name on it. With a single finger, I traced over Chad's neat scrawl before opening the parchment.

Should the urge to talk strike you.

I let out a deep breath. I would respond, but not yet. It would be foolish to let him think that sex made us better. We had both needed it in the moment, but now the moment was over.

Falling back onto the pillows, I clutched the letter to my chest. The numb feeling seeped over me, nestling itself in place once more and spreading to my mind.

I'm Still Unstoppable

Chapter 13: Maybe

Lilith | 1952 | Cottage in South Africa

*Y*ou have no idea how incredibly hard it is to find you," a voice boomed, coming from nowhere. But I knew that voice.

My hands froze on the canvas, paint coating them. I ground my teeth together, already irritated by his presence. "On the contrary, Florence. I know exactly how hard it is, as it's I who has made it that way."

His eyes flickered down to the portrait I was creating—a self-portrait that would hang on my walls in its rightful place. Not here in this ridiculous cottage. No, in my real home, a true fortress that Florence would never stumble upon.

His eyes scrutinised my art. His nose wrinkled in disgust before trying to tear into me with his words.

"You deserted me," he blundered. "You turned me into a vampire and left me on my own."

"Of course I did. That's what I do," I enunciated as I vanquished the paint from my hands.

I stood soundlessly from my chair—as graceful as my mother had taught me—and turned to give him a proper look. He was exactly the same as the last time I had seen him; beautiful, strong, and filled with rage. Yet I always left my creations. And why not? It was better for me to leave them before they could leave me. It meant I was in control.

"The world announced the end of the war—the death of your father—"

"Yes, but—"

"—so tell me," I snapped at him. In an instant, I was inches away from his face. "What would've been the point of me staying? Did I, or did I not complete my end of our bargain?"

"Not exact—"

"I turned you into a vampire and your father is dead. So did I, or did I not have every right to leave?"

"I've been searching for you for over seven years!" he yelled through bared fangs—fangs I gave him.

"And after this lovely conversation, I'll disappear even longer," I snapped back.

The mortals had killed Hitler before Florence had the chance, and according to the prophecy, Florence wouldn't start his own war until we were well into the 21st century. I didn't need him until then. I would not allow him to stick around.

"He's still alive," Florence announced firmly, and though his claim was impossible, my muscles froze.

"Who's still alive?" I sneered, forcing the words through my lips.

"My father. He's still out there."

I blinked once before laughing in his face. "Those are rumours," I said through my smile, picking my paintbrush back up and making to sit down. He was a gullible idiot. He was taking the rumours far too seriously.

But before I could sit, Florence shoved his face back into mine, my reflection glistening in his eyes as they shifted from blue to red. I planted my feet to the ground, raising my brow. He couldn't scare me. I'd created him.

"It's the truth," he spat out fiercely. "He's still out there, and you owe me. You promised you'd help me kill him."

I stared at the man, the veins at his temples pulsing wildly. His temper was as grand as I remembered from all those years ago. If anything, he sounded like my father, the lord over all vampires in his time. I watched Florence's chest rise and fall quickly. He was waiting for me to react—for me to become as equally enraged as him—but instead, I let out a calm breath. If it was true, of course his father couldn't live. He couldn't be granted the mercy of thinking he was safe. Not after all the lives he had taken from my people.

Shrugging my shoulders with the mask of indifference, I asked, "And where do you suppose we look?"

The tension in Florence's body began to ease. As he took a step away and rattled on about his suspicions, I studied him carefully. Maybe he was different from the others I had changed. Maybe he wouldn't leave me.

Chapter 14: Defence

Azalea | Present Day | Library Within *Ypovrýchio Kástro*

Y ou think we can use the dreams against her?" Hydie asked, excitement blooming in her voice.

We had just been dissecting my latest dream when the idea popped into my head.

"I think so," I said cautiously. "There's something about the way Lili looked at me that tells me she doesn't know I've seen into her past. Perhaps there's a way I can sift through which memories I invade. Then we could use the information to get to her and Florence."

"That's brilliant!" Hydie exclaimed before averting her eyes and staging a sly attempt to pry. "And have you told Abigail this bright idea of yours?"

I shook my head, sure to throw up my mental shield—for practice more than anything. It had been a week since our little run-in with Lili or Lilith or whatever the hell her name was. I hadn't talked to anyone much besides my sister. I knew it made me a horrible friend, a horrible whatever I was to Chad. I hadn't even spent much time with the children like I'd promised myself I would. All around, I was a horrible person.

"I haven't told her," I replied, avoiding Hydie's eyes. "But I was hoping perhaps you could communicate all the work we've been doing to everyone else—for a bit longer at least." So I could continue to be a coward and evade all of the problems that didn't directly involve the war.

"This conversation would be a whole lot easier if you let me into your mind," she whined.

I shook my head at her. "You know I have to practise if I'm to keep Lili out of my head."

"I know, I know," she said begrudgingly. "It just makes me miss you."

I took Hydie's hand in mine and looked her straight in the eyes. "I'm right here, Hydie, and I'm not going anywhere."

She gave me a small smile, and though her expression implied she wasn't fully satisfied, she dropped the matter, and we set back to work.

While Chad and Connor were out of the castle for the bulk of their work, Hydie and I explored the library within *Ypovrýchio Kástro*. Chad and Eyeara had said I was more powerful than I gave myself credit for—that I had keys to doors I didn't even know existed. And though it was important to find time to practise my mindreading and search for these so-called keys, we figured it was best to focus on our defensive strategies first and foremost.

We brainstormed a list of every technique Florence and Lili had already used against us. To combat Lili's mindreading, I spent hours a day working on my mental shield. To withstand Lili's and Florence's liberal use of potions, Hydie and I dedicated part of our time searching through these magical books. We found a potion to test all of our meals and drinks for poisons and trickery. Although it took us three batches before it was properly brewed, we eventually found success with it. The other advantages our enemies held were their secret location, enchanted mushrooms, and handcuffs that could block my magic.

"The handcuffs will be the easiest to try and solve next," I decided, without having any clear evidence to prove it. The mushrooms I could handle. The handcuffs were a puzzle. "Then with any luck, my dreams will help narrow down Florence's location."

We searched through nearly fifty more books before we found any information on the pesky silver cuffs.

"I've got it!" Hydie squealed as she cradled a book and ran towards the table where I sat. She slammed the heavy, aged text down with a thud before pointing to the page. "It's the same exact thing: a cuffing spell. 'The wearer of the cuffs will lose their powers until they're allowed out of them'," Hydie read.

"Or until they use their vampire strength to break free of them," I added, but that would be useless for Chad, Hydie, and any other normal Caster. "Does it list a counter curse?"

"No," she said, flipping through the next few pages, "but if we could get our hands on a pair of our own, perhaps we could make them stronger so Florence and Lili couldn't break through them."

I gulped. It was a shame Lili was a vampire-witch. She had all the same tricks I had, only decades—if not centuries—more practice.

I nodded back, hoping that Florence's side wouldn't try the same thing now that they knew I could break through the cuffs, but then pushed aside the unease. "Plus, we can use them on any other witches and wizards they've managed to recruit," I added.

"Only trouble is, it doesn't say how to make them. This book merely informs us that they exist. You could ask Chad if he has any already. If he doesn't, maybe he can point us in the right direction on how to get them."

I let out a single short laugh. I was not talking to Chad—not after *that* night.

"That sounds like a job for you, as my official communicator," I jested with a small smile.

"Did you two sleep together?" she pressed, her eyes wide with intrigue, her tone far too invested in my little love affair.

My face fell. Bollocks. Am I really that predictable?

Hydie winced. "No, you let down your shield for a second."

This is why I needed the practice.

I hastened to strengthen my shield before grimacing at how easily Chadwick could distract me, even when he wasn't here.

Purposefully ignoring Hydrangea's question, I gave her a stern look before shoving my book towards her. "I don't know if it'll work, but I found a list of ingredients for making an unleashing powder," I said, pointing to the illustration. "It's possible it only works to unlock mortal contraptions, but once we have the magical handcuffs, we could test it out. If it fails, we can make modifications on the powder until it does work."

An hour later, I was in the potions room at Castwell Castle, working diligently on the powder. I added some purple mushrooms and used a mortar and pestle to grind them in with the other ingredients. Hydie's breaths signalled her arrival just before she came bustling in, silver flashing in her hand before metal clanked against the countertop.

"It turns out, any pair of handcuffs will do," she let out, panting from transporting all the way here. "Chad says we should put the cuffing spell on them ourselves and then try the unleashing powder."

Oh, did he? I asked rhetorically, and as Hydie gave me an all-knowing grin, I slammed my mental shield into place.

"The powder's almost ready," I deflected, using a knife to scrape a bit of dried ectoplasm off a Bunsen burner-like contraption and into the mixing bowl. His name gave me goose pimples I simply didn't have the time to interpret.

The cuffing spell was easy enough. It was the powder that caused us problems.

I pursed my lips, staring at the powder as it sat uselessly upon the cuffs around Hydie's wrists.

She shrugged, accepting it hadn't worked. "Trial number two?" she asked, and I nodded.

A whole 18 trials later, I sat in a huff, having sent Hydie back to *Ypovrýchio Kástro* to practise her defensive spellwork, the silver cuffs trapped onto my wrists instead.

I had tried everything, yet nothing had worked. Glancing around at the hundreds, if not thousands of potions that lined the walls, I let out a defeated breath. Chad had made all these potions. I wanted to get better. I wanted to embrace the witch part of myself and figure out how to break out of these chains, but I was starting to lose hope.

My eyes lingered on a phial with a pink and violet potion shimmering and swirling around—a love potion.

I blinked away the memory of drinking that potion—being drugged with it—and kissing Florence's lips. *Never again,* I told myself. Never again.

A breath in the doorway caught my attention and I turned, expecting to see Hydie, but I was sorely mistaken. The sight of Chad caught my breath as he slowly strode in, his hands in his pockets, and his eyes on the mess in front of me. He moved along the walls, and over to a glass jar full of flowers, not uttering a word or sparing me a glance.

My body became so still, I could've been mistaken for a gnome in their porcelain form. Yet as I sat bone straight, rooted to the chair, Chad casually took his hands from his pockets and removed three pink flowers from the jar—azaleas. He crossed the room, back to the muck I had in front of me, and placed the flowers in a new bowl. His hand moved over the flowers, wilting them with his green magic, before he crushed them up and added them to my powder. He gave it a good stir and then slid the bowl in front of me, until it rested against the cuffs between my hands.

My eyes travelled from the bowl to his green eyes, accelerating my heartbeat as I realised he was already staring at me. His eyes shone as he looked at me, not daring to let a sound slip from his lips. And without a single word, he ambled out of the room.

It was a good ten seconds before I could breathe again—before I could pick up a pinch of the powder and sprinkle them onto the handcuffs. They shimmered in the faint light and then clicked open.

My jaw dropped. It worked.

I moved to collect a bottle and a cork for the powder. With adrenaline I didn't know I was capable of possessing, I transported straight to Hydie to tell her the good news and forced away the tingling sensation that had come over me—the tingles *he* had given me.

We spent the rest of our time researching the tracking spell and trying to find solutions for the rioting mortals—any way to reinstill the peace Florence had set to flames.

"A hair will work," I declared after reading for nearly two hours in twelve different books on how to enact a tracking spell. I'd finally found a book that wasn't so vague on the types of items you could use for it. "Blood also works, which would've been useful to know after Japan. But hopefully a quick rendezvous with Florence won't bring about any more bloodshed."

"A quick rendezvous?" Hydie blurted out. "What are you on about?"

Honestly, the idea had only sprouted an hour ago, but the more I thought about it, the more productive it sounded.

"Well, think about it," I rushed to explain, hoping she wouldn't think I was completely mad. "Nearly every time I've faced Florence, it's him who instigates it, and we show up unprepared. We never know his plan or what he's doing until he's there, and then we get blindsided and he demolishes an entire country. But if I set up a meeting with him on common grounds, I can distract him long enough to get a piece of his hair so we can track him."

"*You* as in you alone?" she gawked.

"Yes. Him and me. One on one."

"And you think he'll honour that idea instead of ganging up on you?" she questioned with a raised brow.

"Not exactly," I admitted, my stomach squirming at the idea of being alone with Florence, "but I can set up the location to ensure only he and I go in. If he wants to bring people he trusts to stand guard outside, I'll do the same."

"And what bargain will you use in order to lure him there?" she asked.

"Well," I started, shifting in my seat, "I think we should try to focus on breaking apart his team. And with Lili being the main aggressor, we should start with her. We could tell him that we have information he'd be interested in knowing, and I have the feeling he'd be more than happy to meet if he knew I was the one who'd be telling him. Then when he's there, I could plant a seed of doubt about Lili in his head to weaken their union."

"All right," she said, making it clear by her tone that she was sceptical. She absently flicked the pages of the book with her thumb. "How will you get his hair?" she tried next.

A smile crept onto my face. "By using my feminine wiles," I told her, half joking, half not. "Not enough to make him suspicious, but enough to get close."

I took a deep breath. Suddenly it was refreshing to hear the plan aloud rather than strictly in my head—refreshing yet terrifying.

"And there's something else I want to try in the meantime, to help us get ahead of the mortals," I continued, not wishing to overwhelm her, but her face paled at the idea of more risks. "Don't worry," I said quickly. "This one's far less dangerous. It's a way that we can find out what the mortals are planning *and* for me to try out an offensive strategy."

I scooted in closer to her, dropping my voice to make sure none of the Night Crawlers in the castle could overhear.

"I want to go to a riot in disguise—hear what they have to say—get inside their minds. It might give us an idea on how to show them that not all witches and vampires are evil."

"And by disguise you mean…" Hydie asked, her eyes squinted with interest.

"Exactly how Lili's been able to shield her identity," I told her.

"Hence the offensive strategy part," Hydie replied, and I gave her a nod before sitting up straight again.

"Only, I think we should keep all of this between you and me. At least, until the plans are more concrete," I said quietly, letting down my shield so she could feel my fear. Part of me still doubted it would be worth it to meet with Florence, and I knew my friends would think it unwise for me to do any of this on my own. But a part of me ached for the risk—the danger—the distraction. Not to mention, I had to learn independence if I was to gather the strength I needed to win this war.

Hydie nodded slowly, letting me in her head to feel her hesitations. "All right," she agreed, scrunching up her nose. "But when you're ready, you'll have to tell *these* plans to Chad on your own."

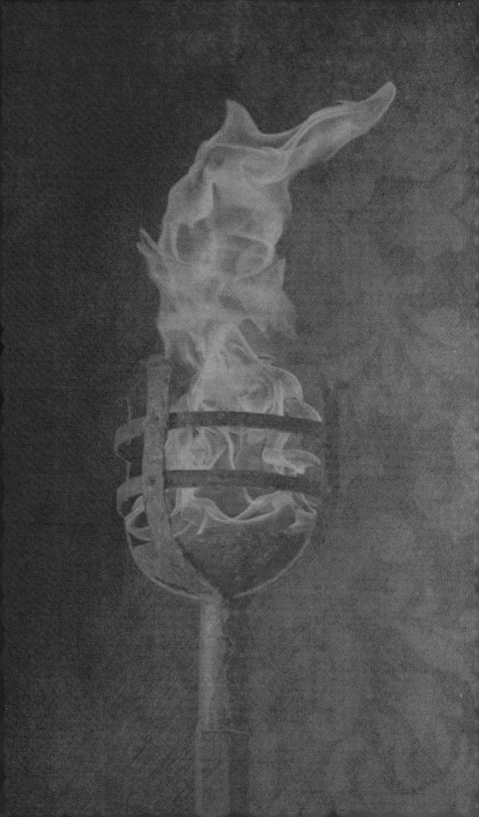

Chapter 15: Riots and Revelations

Of course I could do it. If Lilith could change her appearance, then why shouldn't I be able to? It had only taken a day to master. It had been simple to change my hair colour to purple, and I had done that ages ago, before I knew that door existed. Now it was unlocked. Changing the rest of my appearance wasn't too different.

I stared at my new reflection one more time, thankful there were no magic mirrors in *Ypovrýchio Kástro*, only perfectly normal ones that didn't allow others to travel through them. I had transformed my skin to a lovely, darker shade of brown, my eyes to their original chocolatey brown colour, and my hair to match. After tweaking several other features such as my height, my cheekbones and my general build, I deemed myself entirely unrecognisable.

As soon as I transported to the woods near Castle on the Rocks, I peeked through the trees to see a boisterous crowd. The full moon shone brightly on their faces, and I realised they were rioting when most werewolves would be out roaming the night.

The mortals were so ignorant to the world they were so vehemently against.

Despite Hydie's suggestion, I hadn't told Chadwick my plan. At least not yet. He would've merely tried to convince me to bring him along, but I ached to be on my own. Whether it was a stupid idea or not to surround myself with my enemies was outweighed by my need to get that man out of my head. And what better way to do so than to submerge myself in danger?

I slithered through the trunks and snuck my way into the crowd of at least four hundred outraged people. A hooded jacket helped shield me from the night's breeze—that and the heat given off by the mortals. Bodies knocked against me as I shoved my way through, eager to blend in rather than stand on the edges. There were demands written on poster boards, most insisting that "mythical" creatures should be destroyed—their lives taken as retribution for all the mortals who had died by their hands. And as jeers and calls for punishment were shouted into the cold air, I pushed past their thick skulls to try and pry my way into their minds.

I heard fragments of their panic as they all bombarded my head at once—hundreds of voices coming from the people who had no clue as to what was really happening in the world around them. Both internally and externally, they yelled about creatures they didn't understand, and grouped us all into one category: murderers. I tried to focus on one mind at a time, to tunnel my way in so I could discern any plans or prevent any prejudices, but the crowd was too vast and their thoughts too scattered. So I pulled out of their heads and walked on, hoping to find whatever it was they came for.

Then all at once, a name floated from their mouths over and over in chorus. I joined in on the song as a middle-aged man with dark skin and a sensible suit climbed onto a low cobbled wall. He looked like the very definition of a politician—clean shaven, tall, important—and though his stance was firm, a sense of friendliness warmed his features.

"Welcome," the man greeted, sure to keep his balance as he towered over the crowd, allowing more of us to see him. "And thank you for the fierceness with which you fight to keep mankind safe."

The fervent cry of the crowd grew louder as if to prove his statement correct before it simmered down to hear more of his speech.

"For those of you who have yet to meet me, I am Garick Reeves, and I fight for justice. The murder going on out there is unjust. Our families and our friends will be next to go. Ask former Prime Minister Alastor if you don't believe me."

I followed the heads of the crowd as they glanced behind us. There, in the very alleyway his daughter had died, sat what had once been our prime minister. Shadows draped over him. My eyes focused to take in his swollen eyes, lined with darkness. His beard had grown longer since I last saw him, and his wrinkles deeper as though he had aged ten years in the span of mere months. He looked utterly empty.

"Due to the tragedy he and his family are facing," Reeves continued, drawing our attention back to him, "Alastor has stepped down from his position. I've been placed as the new prime minister."

A few people at the front of the rabble began to weave their way through, passing out flyers with a photograph of Reeves. I studied his picture, wondering if his heart was as kind as his face. Was he another enemy, or someone who would listen if I had the chance to speak with him?

"Our enemies were hiding," he resumed, making his campaign focus clear, "but now they're out to seek revenge on us. Let's ask ourselves, revenge for what? What have we done to deserve the deaths they've caused?"

The crowd began shouting out replies, and though it was difficult, I could make out a few.

"We haven't done anything!"

"They envy us!"

"They're killing for fun!"

"Now it's their turn to die!"

I resisted the urge to fight against their mob mentality—to call out that we weren't all like Florence. Some of us were working hard to fight against him. The mortals wouldn't be able to win on their own.

"They're making a game out of it!" a woman called out.

"Exactly," Reeves replied, pointing a finger at the woman who had referred to Florence's tactics as a game. "They're making it into a game we will not lose. Our ancestors believed in them, yet these creatures went underground and fooled us, convincing us that they didn't exist. Think of the multitude of deaths they caused when we thought these monsters only belonged in stories. Now that we know they dwell among us, we will find their weaknesses and use them against them. We'll guard ourselves with stakes. Driving them into the vampires' hearts will kill them—"

"What about the witches?" someone shouted.

"Our ancestors have answered that question for us," he responded. "We'll set fire to them and watch them burn. We'll burn down the whole world if it keeps innocent humans safe."

I was conflicted between scoffing and fearing Reeves' tactics. Stakes would do nothing against vampires. That was a myth. Putting weapons in the hands of scared, untrained civilians would produce more mortal casualties, and fire would endanger more mortals than it would the witches who could easily transport away.

It was ironic. They were so furious, even towards witches, though each of these rioters held a magical phone in their pocket—stood under the magical glow of the streetlights only to go home to their houses filled with things they called science and engineering. They held up signs produced by magically powered machines, not mortal-made torches and pitchforks like their ancestors had in the past, but gifts witches had convinced them were technology rather than the work of witchcraft.

At that moment, an idea sparked in my mind, straightening out the defeated crook in my neck. An idea to show the mortals that not all of us beings of power were murderers, and that I could point them towards the ones who were.

I'm Still Unstoppable

Chapter 16: Someone Like Her

Lilith | 20 Years Ago | Hidden Fortress

*F*ind me someone like her," Florence demanded. His voice was fierce, full of rage, but we had known each other for far too long. He couldn't hide his mourning from me. That was one of the things I liked best about him. I didn't have to read his mind to know what he was thinking.

"Find me someone who looks exactly like her—someone who will make my life less dismal."

He couldn't even say the dead woman's name anymore. It was as if her name was taboo even more than 60 years after his father had taken her from him. Yet he still fixated on her flawless brown skin and curly dark hair instead of the perfect woman standing in front of him.

It was disgusting.

His body was slumped into a dining chair, a leg lazily dangling over one of its arms, not realising that his words cut through my heart like a dagger. But I wouldn't let him see. I'd never let it show.

Putting on my usual seductive smile, I stood between him and the table. I dragged my fingers along his bare chest, watching as his hair stood from my touch. His body was aroused. It wanted me even if his mind didn't. One touch from me and he'd take me right here on the dining table. But not this time.

"Not now," he hissed, slapping away my hand. "I'm serious. I need someone, someone my father would've detested. Someone witty enough to keep me entertained."

I knew exactly what he meant. Someone who wasn't blonde, blue-eyed, and poised. Someone who wasn't me.

We had tracked his father together, all the way to Brazil where he hid like the Nazi scum he truly was. We slaughtered him—tore him apart piece by piece—the man who yearned for a powerful Aryan race. No wonder Florence despised me deep down. My appearance was everything his father stood for, even if he had been against my lineage.

"Are you even listening, Lili?" he growled, snapping his fingers in front of my face.

For a second I fantasised about snapping his neck in response. Why the fuck had I let him find me? I was fine without him in the years since we killed Hitler. But after a while, I had let loneliness prevail. I allowed Florence to seek me out—let the pull lead him here to my ancestral home—and for what? For him to walk around as if he owned the place? For him to sit and sulk about the love of his life? Now I'd never get rid of him. He'd always be able to find me here.

"Yes, my love. I heard you loud and clear," I replied, fighting back the urge to use a bitter tone. "You want me to find a girl like Zena."

He winced at the name, shifting away from me.

"Exactly like her," he grumbled, but with much less bite than he had before. "And this time I won't let anyone take her away from me. We'll be married right away, and she can help me with my plan."

I rolled my eyes, not even bothering to correct him. It was our *plan. Hell—my plan if anyone's. I had gone to Baba Yaga long ago for the damn premonition. It was my goal to allow Casters and Night Crawlers to walk out in the open. It was unfortunate* that I needed this prick to help me, and even more unfortunate that he was so damn beautiful.

"And what will you be doing while I'm out searching for Miss Perfect?" I purred, hoping he'd let me touch him, hoping he'd reconsider. But no.

"I'm going to go speak to Elizabeth Downy—put some of my charm on her. Perhaps she'll reconsider the offer to join me."

My teeth clenched onto the inside of my cheek until I could taste the blood—salty but sweet. Same as every time he mentioned that insufferable wench. But Elizabeth was the least of my worries now.

"And when I find this wife of yours—what then?" I asked, digging my claws into my arm to prevent my rage from coming out fully.

"We'll follow her, make sure she's perfect, and then we'll change her."

As if it were that simple. As if the pull would work any better for him than it had for me. It wouldn't make her love him. After all, I was the one who changed Florence. He was drawn to me, yet he resisted the idea of taking me as anything besides a temporary lover. He wanted more.

"And what if she doesn't fall for your charm as easily as I do?" I asked, teasing him like it was a game, one I wouldn't admit I was losing. "What if she insists on going back to her old life?"

His eyes met mine and he smiled his mischievous grin that always stirred something inside me. Something hungry. The table was pressed up against my backside as I stood before him. My hands gripped it and my chest rose up and down, ready for him. He stood from his chair in one fluid motion and placed a hand on either side of my hips. There was a stirring between my legs as he leaned us both backwards onto the table. I let out an eager breath as his lips brushed against mine.

"Then I'll kill her and we'll move onto the next," he breathed into me, and I couldn't hold out any longer.

I grabbed onto his hair, bit onto his neck, and let him take me right there on the table.

Just as I had wanted.

Chapter 17: Letters to an Insufferable Idiot

Azalea | Present Day | Bedroom Within *Ypovrýchio Kástro*

*Z*ena, I thought, blinking out of my trance. That's why Florence had sought me out, or rather Lili had for him. I looked like the woman who had once loved him. Though I would never be able to replicate those feelings towards him authentically, perhaps I could use the knowledge to fool him.

I had done it. After hours of trying to force my way into Lili's past without a dream, I had finally managed it. I had unlocked the damn door. Although I had tried to find her mind in the present rather than her past, and was sickened by the act Lili and Florence had been about to perform, this memory would have to suffice.

I practically flung myself out of the bed, strode across the room to grab my green purse, and sat at the desk. A pen and a blank scrap of parchment were waiting patiently inside. I hadn't written to Chad after he and I had been intimate. He had told me to write when I was ready, but the brief in-person sightings of him were challenging enough. Neither of us tried to talk about it.

Blinking at the paper, I strived to make this conversation light but also business driven. Hydie had filled him in on my last few Lili dreams, so I'd come back to my latest vision. First, I had to tell him about my idea from the riot.

> Chadwick,
>
> Sorry to bother you, but I want to keep you updated on my wicked plans. I went to a mortal riot to hear them out. Don't worry, I used Lili's trick of shapeshifting so I wasn't recognised. Anyhow, I came up with an idea that may help the mortals come to our side. Do you have time to discuss it?
>
> - Azalea

Sixty seconds later, his reply came.

> You went to a riot? With who? You should've told me. I would've sent Nigel with you at the very least.

Was that truly all he wrote? He ignored everything else to go straight into overprotective mode. I squinted my eyes at the parchment, half tempted to use magic to try and reveal any invisible ink where he might have responded to the rest of my letter. Did he really have no interest in my new talent or my brilliant plan? And what would sending one royal guard do? Get us caught because Nigel couldn't shapeshift?

> I was perfectly capable of going on my own, thank you. As I said, I was in disguise. Besides, the mortals think a stake to the heart and fire will kill me. They have no real strategy, only fear and hate for all vampires and witches. I don't think they care about the

other creatures that exist, or at least they see them as less of a threat, which leads me to my plan.

You once told me that mortals couldn't be too furious at our presence, not after everything that witches have given them. They don't know that electricity is magic. So let's take it away from them. Let's show them how hard life would be without it and see if they come round. I want to enact a worldwide blackout.

My heart hammered as I waited. The plan was not complete codswallop. It would work.

This reply was slower—his writing neater. Perhaps more thought than fear had gone into it.

That's brilliant, Azalea! Honestly. We can discuss the details and then I'll arrange a meeting with the Casters to inform them.

I blinked at the letter a few times, wondering if there was a catch. It was nearly *too* easy to convince him. A worldwide blackout would be massive and possibly even catastrophic if the mortals didn't take it seriously. Was he merely agreeing to avoid a row or did he truly concur?

I watched as his words vanished from the parchment before placing my pen to it.

Perfect. Thanks.

Tapping my fingers against the table, I tried to plan out the phrasing for my next idea—how to talk about meeting one-on-one with the murderous man who had tried to rape, attack, kidnap, and poison me multiple times—but in a light, business-like way. My heart jumped out of my chest when his next reply came.

I'll come by after I visit the London library. I keep going to look into the orbs, but the future's been consistently blurry.

Tell me about it, I thought to myself.

For me, it's the present I'm having difficulties with. I managed to look into Lili's past on command, but even when I try, I can't look into her present. Perhaps she keeps changing her mind about something so her path isn't set in stone, or maybe she has a way to block others from seeing her fortune.

Now that I think about it, I wonder if it's because she's a Gemini. Blimey. I can't believe I didn't see she was up to something before.

I blinked, my mind completely perplexed as I tried to figure out his connection between the two and why my protests against her hadn't been enough.

What does that have to do with anything?

The Gemini symbol is the twins. People born under that constellation often have a hard time showing their true selves or lead two different lives. I was blind to not see it.

I couldn't believe my eyes as I stared at his writing. Was he truly that much of an insufferable idiot to not decode how his words made me feel? After scribbling down my next reply, I shoved it into the envelope.

So we're going to completely ignore the millions of times I told you she was evil?

Well, that too but the stars are more concrete.

"Concrete? The everchanging stars?" I huffed aloud, though I knew no one would hear it.

The other reason I had decided to write to him swung back into my consciousness. It was up to me to gently inform him of my plan since Hydie refused to. Perhaps he'd be so overwhelmed by his dazzling astrological sign theory that he wouldn't be bothered by the next part of my plan.

In the vision I just had about Lili, she and Florence were talking about that lady named Zena again, the love of his life, and apparently, I resemble her. That's the reason they changed me—to become her replacement of sorts.

I've decided to use the knowledge of Zena against Florence. I'll meet up with him and remind him about her when we're alone. It'll let me get close enough to get a piece of his hair.

Subtle. Light, business-like, and very subtle, I thought as sweat accumulated on my palms.

An anxious puff of green magic marked Chad's sudden arrival to my room. Before a word slipped from his lips, he dropped down to his knees, grasping my hands in his as worry coated his face.

"You can't be serious," he scolded, yet his eyes were full of fear. "Going to that riot on your own is one thing, but going to Florence by yourself? That's suicide. That's asking for him to kidnap you!"

I snatched my hands away from his and stubbornly busied myself with the task of moving my purse aside—as I would no longer be needing it.

"One," I snapped, "he's not going to kill me. In Japan, he was much more interested in taking me with him. And two, if worse comes to worst and he does kidnap me, then perhaps he'll keep good on his promise to stop all this, or at least slow down. People are dying. We might as well try everything. Besides, I don't think it'll come to that. I think he'll be interested in the deal I have to offer."

"How can you be so naïve?" Chad spat out, ignoring my glare. But his tone wasn't harsh—it was a plea spilling from his lips. His hands clutched onto my hips instead. "He poisoned you with a memory potion, his own venom, and a love potion. How could you risk that?"

"Hydie and I have been working on strategies to use against him," I reminded him, but the speed and urgency in his voice rejected my statement, deeming it futile.

"He's hurt you before, Azalea. He's tried to *force* himself on you."

"And I won't let that happen again!" I yelled out, triggered. My body became tense. The thought of Florence on top of me had compelled the words to come out in a rush, to block it out, to try and forget it had ever happened.

Chad closed his mouth tight as if he understood that bringing up that memory was going too far, but he stared at me intently, begging me with his green eyes to change my mind.

I looked down at his hands as they clutched onto my clothes for dear life and took a deep breath before starting again.

I let my eyes crash into Chad's once more. "I'm going to meet with Florence," I told him, firm yet gentle at the same time. "I'm going to meet with him, and pretend to make a truce, and get something from him to track him to his hideout."

Slowly, Chad pushed himself up from his knees, and a shaky breath left his lips.

"How would we contact him?" he asked, as if forcing the question out.

My eyes lit with excitement. I knew the answer, already having solved that question. Only, Chad wasn't going to like it.

"The same way we're going to announce the blackout," I said smugly, "and the same way Florence reached out to us: the telly."

Chapter 18: The Ultimatum

I sat in a tall, ornate, wingback chair as Eyeara fluffed my hair, setting every curly stand into place. When Chad had informed the other Casters of the plan, she insisted on being a part of it. Apparently, this didn't merely extend to her elven magic and her ability to translate the broadcast to every mortal language in the world. It also meant playing dress up with me.

"The mortals would be stupid not to heed your warning. You look like a proper princess now—or a queen," she told me, straightening the icy crown she had placed on my head.

I looked down at the light blue fabrics she had dressed me in. If anything, I looked like an elf.

Abigail sat nearby, observing us anxiously from the corner of her eye before she caught my gaze. She was instantly on her feet, moving several metres away. The memories of her standing in Eyeara's place, helping me get dressed for important events, didn't help ease the awkwardness between us. I still hadn't talked to her, nor had Chad, and based on her eagerness to run away, she was still ridden with guilt.

"It's perfect, Eyeara," I said, gently pushing her hand away from my head. "Thank you for coming today. You've been so much help."

The elven princess smiled softly as she studied me, no doubt reading whatever my soul had to tell her.

A gust of wind took her eyes from mine. Chad popped in amongst a green swirl of smoke, allowing four others to join us in the underwater castle: Fendel, who sported a bright smile as his eyes landed on me; Poppy, fluttering in with her green wings and tiny frame; Nigel, clad in his silver armour; and Mia, a manananggal from Loxley Lair whose organs were casually dangling out of her severed torso.

A stool magically appeared next to me in a cloud of rainbow dust. Then Fendel waddled forwards and began to climb up a mini, rainbow-coloured staircase he produced in order to sit on the tall stool next to me. Wrapping my arms around him, I welcomed him to *Ypovrýchio Kástro* and thanked him for coming. The others took their places next to my chair. Chad, Eyeara, Hydie, Connor, Abigail, Cristin, Noel, Leon, and Leo also gathered on either side of me, closely followed by Charity and the tiny jorogumo, Kana, who both stood in their spider forms. Vampires, witches, wizards, jorogumos, a werewolf, a manananggal, a gnome, a fairy, and an elf—a mosaic of different creatures—all to stand at my side and represent our united front.

Chad floated a camera in front of us, then met my eyes patiently. Nodding, he said, "Ready when you are."

I let out a calming breath before nodding back at him. "As ready as I'll ever be," I decided.

And before I could change my mind, Chad flicked his wrist. The shutter of the camera unveiled its glass through a cloud of green smoke, and I opened my mouth, ready to either devastate the mortal world or to claim them as my allies.

"Good evening," I said into the camera. "Many of you think you've seen me before—on every screen in the world. However, it was my enemy you saw, disguised as me. Those enemies, who are your enemies as well, are full of lies and deceit. Now it's time for you to hear the truth.

"My name is Azalea, and I do not work with Florence, the man responsible for the destruction of Japan and so many other horrors. In fact, I was a witch living as a mortal until Florence bit me. Now I've been condemned to crave blood, but I don't give in to that pull. Instead, I drink a potion so I don't have to take anyone's life."

I looked around at my comrades, thankful they were there.

"Not all vampires, werewolves, witches, elves, and other magical creatures are evil. Most vampires only feed once a week to keep themselves alive. Several werewolves lock themselves away during the full moon so they won't be tempted to harm you. Mermaids maroon themselves in hidden fortresses, only striking down the humans that dare to enter their territory, and though witches hide so you don't burn them in fires, they still find peace in their hearts to help you every single day.

"Witches and wizards have secretly shared potions and powders disguised as medicines to heal your sicknesses. They've given you things that you call technology, electricity, and science, but truly, it's been the gift of magic you've been using all along. That's how we've been able to tap into every device in the world tonight. That's how you've been able to communicate with loved ones, seek knowledge that's outside your grasp, and find entertainment during your free time. But what's been given can also be taken away."

I stopped for just a moment so the billions of people I held as my audience could understand the truth of my words. Sweat and chills mixed across my skin, but I used everything within me not to let my fear show. I wanted them to trust me. I wanted the world to believe we could do good. It wasn't fair to label us all as evil.

"We've lived amongst you for the past few centuries, hiding to protect both you and ourselves. And although it could be a paradise to live with you, out in the open as our true selves, Florence has a sadistic, morbid way of introducing us to the world—a way we wholeheartedly disagree with. He is collecting followers who no longer wish to remain hidden, ones who crave death, and he's begun a war. *They* are the enemy, not us.

"Now we're down to two options," I said firmly, then I gestured to the magnificent creatures by my sides. "If we were to disappear again, we would take everything we've given you with us—the internet, the electronics, the medicines—the magic that has transformed your generations and helped sustain the human race. We'll take it all back and you can fight this war against Florence on your own." I paused to let it sink in—truly sink in so they could see how useless this plan would be. They didn't know how to kill us, and I wouldn't tell them how to destroy us if they meant to use it against creatures with good souls.

"Or," I resumed, my tone lighter, "you can join us in our fight against Florence, and help us capture the people who'd rather put you in submission. Then we could live with you in harmony."

I counted to ten slowly, waiting for the people I couldn't even see to make the right decision before striking with my ultimatum.

"To help you decide, we're going to enact a worldwide magical blackout," I announced. I held my head high though I felt sick to my stomach. This was it. My version of a bomb. "This blackout will allow you to experience the first option I spoke with—a life without those who could be your ally.

"In one week's time, on 1 April, the blackout will begin. We will go into hiding, taking our magic with us, and let you fight on your own. This will last as long or as short as you let it go on. We'll be in touch with the mortal leaders to see what you decide.

"On 1 April, do not fly, do not drive, don't do anything to put yourselves in harm's way. Don't operate any machinery or you'll be putting yourself in grave danger when it all comes to a stop.

"We've come to an agreement that the only exception to this rule will be hospitals, as we don't want any more death on our hands. It's your job, however, to protect the hospitals from greedy mortals who will come to seek the power within."

I clutched my hand with the other. It was shaking ever so slightly because I knew what message I had to deliver next—to whom I would be saying it.

"Florence," I breathed out, his name tasting putrid on my tongue, "wherever you are…" The image of his cocky grin as I spoke to him bogged down my mind, but I pressed on. "Before the blackout begins, the two of us are going to have a chat." Each word was enunciated. Each word made it clear I was in charge, and I wasn't going to live in fear of him. "I have information you'll want to hear—information that I will tell you when we meet one-on-one, face-to-face." My gaze bore straight into the camera lens as if he were truly in front of me—as if it was only him and me. "Meet me on 31 March, as soon as the sun sets," I said in a dreamy voice, knowing it would lure him in. "Meet me in Germany, at the same abandoned building we found you at before. If you come alone and play nice, then I will too. Let's settle this like adults."

It was a dare. A dare I knew he couldn't pass up.

I looked over at Chad. A warmth crept through to my bones, the shivers and shakes vanquished. I had infiltrated the mortals' fears and given them their ultimatum. I had slithered my way into a meeting with the villain—a meeting where I would throttle Florence's perception of Lili and take a piece of him—a piece that would lead us to their hideout.

Chad's eyes gleamed with hope as he stared back at me. He shut the camera lens with a satisfying *click*, allowing the mortals their time to prepare. Now it was time to plot.

Chapter 19: Nothing Like Me

Lilith | A Year and a Half Ago | Street Outside a Row of Terraced Houses

*T*he young woman walked across the street, no quickened heartbeat, no sweat marking her trepidation—only the whisper of a smile across her face. It was as if she had no fear for the darkness—no fear for a red-eyed stranger lurking in the night.

She was exactly like the others. Number ten on the list of girls I had found Florence in the past years. Her hair—long, brown, frizzy curls that could suffocate someone. Her skin—several shades darker than my pure white tone. And her eyes—brown but they'd turn to a vampire-blue when Florence was done with her. And based on his description of Zena, he'd fall hard and fast for this one. Just as he had with the others. Only, they hadn't lasted long. They hadn't fallen in love with the cold-hearted man with a longing to prove himself.

I watched from the street as my latest prey stood on top of a rubbish bin, clung onto the gutter, and then climbed up the side of an end-of-terrace house. Her limbs moved with an eerie ease—so easily it seemed impossible. I squinted at her curiously as she made her way to the second level. She pushed up a small window and slipped inside, all while keeping the faint smile on her perfectly plump lips.

I rolled my eyes. I knew exactly what that childish grin meant. She was head-over-heels for some lowly mortal. Disgusting. She was weak to fall for someone with no power, but that was pish posh—nothing I couldn't erase from her mind with a strong draft of memory potion.

My fingers brushed against the petals of an odd hedge that sat in her gardens, sharp tingles meeting my fingertips. It was too cold for September. Yet despite the frost that threatened to freeze the other plants, these flowers were in full bloom—azaleas and hydrangeas mixed together as if they sprouted from the same roots. Though some were my favourite shade of pink, something about them set my nerves on end. Suddenly, I longed to be home, among the black lilies in my courtyard—the only plants I allowed to live on my land.

Inside the house, the stupid woman, who was about to gain everything I had ever wanted, flicked on the lights. Instantly, a sharp scream fled from her lips. I dropped down to the ground, hiding behind the flowering hedge, but as a voice from another seeped out the open window, I realised it hadn't been me who had given her a fright. It was someone else.

Perking my ears, I focused on the small room, the vampire hearing I inherited from my father coming to use. A man spoke to her, such anger rattling his voice as he forced his volume to remain low.

"Get out," he hissed. He sounded older than the young woman, colder, and full of hatred like my father had been.

"I'm sorry, Azalea," another young, feminine voice called. "He came in and wouldn't leave and—"

"You're an abomination. You're going to Hell and you're never coming back," the man interrupted.

A harsh slap sounded, followed by a whoosh of air and a heavy thud as the man's body hit the ground.

Goose pimples prickled over my arms, yet it wasn't from the cold night air. It was from the cause of that whooshing sound. I *could feel it as if it were a part of me, and in a way it was. It was the same power I had—the power that people like my mother could pass down to their children.*

I looked down at my fingers, still tingling from the hedge, and it slammed into me what that feeling was. It was the feel of magic—magic keeping the flowers in their prime—protecting them from the frigid air.

The woman was a witch.

For the smallest fraction of a second, pity poked at my heart. She was like me. She was a witch—soon to be a vampire too. She was cursed with a father—a man who was kicking her out of her home—like my father had done to me. He had called her an abomination—he was against the woman's magic as though it was something we could choose.

But I had heard the crash as his body hit the floor. Thrill pumped through my heart. Perhaps there was hope for the weakling yet. Perhaps she killed her father for the pain he inflicted upon her.

She backed up towards the window, her shoulders rising and falling as though something strong was building within her. My breath raced, waiting to hear to see what they'd do with the dead body. Would they bury it beneath this hedge? Let the flowers hide the stench of his decay?

But then the most atrocious sounds met my ears.

A laboured breath.

Another heartbeat.

And I knew it had been too good to be true. She had let him live.

I scowled. I had been right before. Of course she was too weak to end him. Another reason to resent this woman for the rest of her breaths.

"Help me drag him down to his chair," the witch whispered to the third figure in the room. "Perhaps he'll wake up and think this was all a dream."

My warm, defeated breath mixed into the September night air. No. She was nothing like me. She was pathetic—a soft fool. But perhaps it would play out to my benefit. Florence may grow sick of her sooner once he discovered she had powers but no itch to kill. And then maybe he'd let me dispose of her.

Chapter 20: Cuffs

Azalea | Present Day | Bedroom Within *Ypovrýchio Kástro*

*T*hat night…

The vision of Lili stung as I tried to force it aside. It wasn't my past I was trying to see, it was her present. But just like my last attempt, it hadn't worked.

I remembered that night—the memory of attacking my father and staging it as a drunken nightmare—the smile that had been on my lips as I thought about a future away from my father. A future with Wyatt. But everything had gone wrong. Days later, that dream had been corrupted. Wyatt had stomped on my heart, and then Lili and Florence had dragged me away.

The memory of the bite—the venom flowing through my veins—the pain—all of it sent flashes of horror, blinding me. I didn't want to see Florence tonight. It was ironic how I had fought to have my memories back only to realise I wanted every moment with my creator erased—and to never see him again. But that wasn't how my life worked. There were precious moments before I'd be seeing my red-eyed demon again.

My hands quivered as I sat in front of my vanity, combing out my curls. I pushed away the past, giving everything I had to the present. It was all aligned. Connor had Chad handled. He'd be keeping the wizard busy while I went to Pasewalk, Germany on my own. There, I'd use my tricks on Florence, snatch a greasy blond hair, and be one step closer to destroying his plans.

I stood up from my seat to stare at my pyjamas in the mirror, my fingers tingling as they resisted the work they must do. Closing my eyes, I pictured the dress in my memory—one I had worn for Florence long ago. It was a tight, black turtleneck dress that showed off way too much of my thighs. "Wear something all black and sexy," he had demanded, and this outfit had been my compromise, yet it still held a thousand stories. I had worn it the night he forced me to come to Downy Lair. It was the very dress he had torn later that night as he pinned me to my bed—ready to steal the rest of what he had taken away from me.

When I opened my eyes, I was wearing the dress, and I had to blink hard to wipe away the memory. Swiftly flicking my wrist, a pocket appeared at the side of the dress. As the purple smoke dispersed, I pocketed a few pairs of handcuffs and a bottle of powder to unlock them, all primed and ready to use against Florence if it came to it. My hands gripped tightly onto the dress I loathed with so much passion, shifting it around as if it would become more comfortable, but I knew I could never find it so. In the end, the dress might be worth it. It might trigger a memory within Florence's mind of the time he got so close. It might make him more susceptible to my ruse.

A cyclone of green played in the mirror's reflection before it revealed Chad. Spinning on my heels, I propped up the shield in my mind and cursed Connor. He had one job. *One,* yet Chad was here anyway. A sinking feeling settled in my stomach as I realised I'd have to use plan B.

"I'm coming with you," Chad demanded, grasping onto my hand as though the very words would cause me to flee. "I tried to accept that you'd be going on your own, but I can't. I'm not letting him take you."

His worried eyes darkened as they fell to my bare brown thighs and then climbed my outfit, conflict behind them as he likely realised who I was wearing it for.

This was precisely why he couldn't come. His eagerness to protect me alongside his fear would drive Florence away. The vampire would see right through the false information I needed him to focus on.

I wiggled out of Chad's hold, forcing my hand not to quiver. "Chadwick," I said, inserting a calmness to my voice, "you're not in the right mindset to come with me." He'd ruin everything.

But it wasn't enough. As I backed away from him, he stepped towards me. My legs met the vanity behind me. His arms moved to either of my sides, caging me in as he stood above me, staring me dead in the eyes.

His green irises were saturated in a mixture of determination and denial. Placing my chin in his hand, his thumb brushing against my bottom lip, he replied, "I won't let you go alone."

Each word was crystal clear. He stared into me as my eyes flickered back and forth between his. The intensity within them begged me to cave in. His lips hovered inches from mine, close enough to touch but not daring to. His breath cascaded along my skin. My heart pounded as his thumb went back and forth, back and forth across my lip. Part of me wished for him to lean in—to make the next move.

Thoughts of that night at the lake pushed their way into my mind, swirling with memories of a time not too long ago when he had more than satisfied me in the armoury. He had lured me there, insisting we were there to train, only, he made it quite clear that training was not on his mind. After handcuffing and pleasuring me, he froze my chains to the wall. He had left me there half-naked—declaring that I'd have to free myself as my training. I clutched onto the edge of the vanity, remembering how much I craved his touch. But it was not him who would be doing the seducing.

"I won't be alone," I breathed out, very conscious of the way my breaths brought my chest closer to his. "I've arranged for your guards to keep watch nearby."

Chad scoffed, breaking the hold he had over me. His arms rose with fury. He stepped away, spitting out fire as his voice grew harsher. "So my guards are allowed to come but I'm not?" he asked.

I clicked my tongue. He was so stubborn. Did he want a hair from Florence or not? Did he want to track down our enemy or allow them to keep winning?

"Your guards," I snapped, losing my patience, "aren't emotionally distracted by the mission."

"Risking your life doesn't hold as much heartache for them as it does for me," he retorted without skipping a beat. "You aren't their fated mate."

His bold words slashed across my heart, deep enough to draw blood. My brows shot up. Sweat congregated on my palms as I clutched the vanity behind me, threatening to reveal the stress he was putting upon me.

He had never called me that. He had alluded to me being his fated mate, but he had never said it outright.

He stared back at me, waiting for my reply, but what did he expect me to say? How did he expect me to react? Sentimental, surely—yet nothing but contempt flowed from me. It boiled down to the fact that he could say it—could be so certain the stars were speaking about me—now that Lili had proven it wasn't her.

I clenched my jaw and forced myself to take three steady breaths. The stars didn't matter right now. What mattered was that plan A had failed, and Chad was clearly too attached to come.

"I have several pairs of handcuffs," I said, trying to sound level-headed. I patted the pocket in my dress so he could hear them *clink* together as proof. "Hydie and I have tested them. They're too strong for a vampire to break free from them, and I'll use them if I suspect Florence is going to kidnap me."

It was not the reply he wanted to hear.

"Let's just go there and kill him," Chad suggested quickly, but he wasn't thinking.

"And find their hideout how?" I countered, leaning towards him as if to better hear an answer I knew he didn't have. "You can't track a dead man."

"All right," he replied, plainly unconvinced as he folded his arms across his chest. "Suppose you go to Pasewalk on your own and Florence shows up to have a little chat. How, exactly, do you plan on getting close enough to steal one of his hairs?"

I took another deep breath to calm myself, even though I knew it wouldn't help. I had specifically left that part out when I had told him the plan. Only, there was no evading it now.

"I'll seduce him," I said plainly, arching my brow as I waited for him to challenge it.

Chad blinked at me twice, giving the words time to sink in.

"Your plan is to seduce him?" he asked as though it were the most ridiculous idea he had ever heard of.

A laugh escaped my lips. Surely dangling myself in front of the murderer would suffice as a distraction.

"You don't think I can seduce him?" I asked Chad, trying to mask my smile with a stern voice, but it came out too light.

Pushing on his chest, I drove him back until his legs bumped into my bed. A puff of air escaped his lungs as he sat, half falling onto it.

"I think you could seduce anyone," he rushed, "but—"

"But you don't think I can protect myself?" I pressed further, trying to uncover the root of the problem.

His muscles tightened as he gripped onto my duvet. Perhaps he regretted letting the statement roll off his tongue as an insult, but I was far from hurt. I knew he wanted me to stay safe. I was merely enjoying the game.

"No," he spoke clearly. "I know you can protect yourself, I just think—"

"You could do a better job?" I teased.

I lifted my brows, daring him with my eyes to insinuate that I was weak. I watched for a second as he squirmed, then I rested my legs against his and wrapped my fingers around each of his wrists. He was taking me far too seriously, but I could use this…

His lips moved with the intention to say something, but I pushed against his wrists to lay him down across my bed. He promptly shut his mouth as I climbed on top of him, spreading my legs to straddle him. His eyes widened ever so slightly as my hair fell over my shoulder and he looked up at me.

"So let me get this straight," I resumed, guiding his arms so they were raised above his head, resting close to the posts of my bed. "You think I could charm Florence long enough to take his hair, and that I could protect myself, yet you still won't admit it's not necessary for you to be there?"

His throat bobbed as he stared at me. I let my fingers slide up to intertwine them with his. As his lips parted once more to reply, I placed a light kiss on his neck and his eyes closed. Any words he was about to say morphed into a light moan. My thoughts pondered what he was thinking but not enough to slither my way into his head—not without permission.

"I want to be close," he finally let out, "in case he tries to take you away."

"What's the point of having your guards around if they can't protect us?" I asked, releasing his hands to trail mine lightly down his arms and back to his wrists. My fingertips tingled from the delicate touch.

That's when I let the metal click into place. Plan B.

His eyes darted up to where the cold wrapped around him, cuffing his wrist to one of the posts on my bed. In the blink of an eye, I was back on my feet. A purple frost spewed out of my hands, freezing the handcuffs tightly to the bed.

Chad gawked at me as soon as his eyes had caught up to what had happened. It was the exact opposite of how we had been in the armoury. This time he was locked up and I was in control, only the finale was much less pleasurable.

"Don't worry," I said, summoning up the same sly manner he had used when he tied me up. "I already told Poppy. She has strict orders to come and set you free if you're still stuck here in an hour."

The same words he had promised me. And then I transported away.

I'm Still Unstoppable

Chapter 21: Double Agent

The building smelled like death—quite the paradox seeing as it had been deserted for several years. We had researched this place long ago—before we knew who Florence's father was. It had once housed hundreds of German soldiers through both the world wars—a military hospital where Hitler himself had come to heal. Florence had been out in the gardens when we had arrived, the pull yanking me towards him as it always did. As soon as his eyes had fallen onto us, he had run. We had chased after him, Chad throwing blasts of green magic after the vampire. Only, something had protected Florence—something unseeable. An invisible force had redirected Chad's magic away from his target and off into the trees. I hadn't understood it at the time, but Lili had been there that day, saving Florence arse, ruining our attack. This time, however, we'd be safely indoors, and I would be seeking to ruin her.

I sat atop a counter, studying the grime and peeling paint on the walls. The faint shimmer of the wards glistened around me, letting sounds in but denying their escape. I could hear each breath that the guards took as they stood outside, less than a hundred paces away. My fingers tapped across the countertop, tiny echoes bouncing off the walls. I faced the main entrance, waiting for the feel of the pull to click into place—waiting for *him*. I relaxed my shoulders, refusing to show my fear, and crossed my legs, allowing the hem of the dress to hike further up.

I could do this.

I could face him.

The pull nearly jerked me off the counter as it announced Florence's arrival. A series of buzzes sounded through the air, growing louder, synchronised with the feel of the pull. He hadn't come on his own, nor had I expected him to. But his mates would have to wait outside.

There was an ache in my heart as the pull begged me to draw closer to him, but the rest of my body froze in place. The buzzes stopped. A single set of footsteps approached at a mortal's pace before there was a loud tug on the door handle. Even as Florence pulled vigorously, showcasing his strength and hubris, the lock refused to give. He let out a loud scoff and then hammered his fist on the door.

I flicked my fingers and the entrance swung open. My purple magic subsided to reveal the man I loathed most in the world— the man who had killed millions to sully my name and lure me to him.

His gaze lingered over me from the bottom up, just as hungry and pathetic as I remembered. He took in every part of me as if he owned me—as if my body was his to stare at. It wasn't until my magic slammed the door behind him that his eyes met mine and he spoke.

"You were supposed to come alone," he said, a hint of humour in his sultry voice. He kept his distance as if I was a snake ready to strike.

I graced him with a light smile. "As were you."

His laugh echoed through the room, bouncing off the wards that prohibited anyone else from hearing us. I wondered if Lili was out there—trying but failing to eavesdrop. Or was Florence such a coward that he had sent her in his stead? She had so easily worn my skin. Was the shapeshifter wearing his now?

His cold gaze sent shivers down my spine. "But we both know you're more trustworthy than I am," he said, the intent to tear me down gleaming in his red eyes.

"Yet not nearly as foolish," I quipped.

His face fell. His utter pride coupled with the feel of the pull convinced me it was truly him standing before me, not Lili in disguise. Either way, I had to be careful not to push too hard. Beneath his tough exterior was the same shattered boy I had seen in Lili's past—one who hid behind a mask of fierceness but was broken from within.

"What is it that you want, Azalea?" he growled. "Obviously not to join me, so why call this meeting? To distract me while your men lower my numbers out there?" he asked, throwing a hand to a boarded-up window.

I hopped off the countertop, closing the distance between us by mere inches. "My guards will not fight, and yours won't be able to harm them. They're protected from each other with wards and a strong willpower not to demolish the scum you brought along," I told him firmly.

"Then what is it that you want?" he asked, his face scrunched up with a century's worth of mistrust.

But I didn't dare to step closer. His tight stance told me he'd bolt if I moved in on him. He thought it was a trap. If I wanted to get close enough to steal a hair off his head, I needed him to come to me.

"I told you," I replied, doing my best to sound bored rather than on the attack. "I have information for you. I want to warn you of something—or someone."

He stared at me from two metres away, his eyes shifting back and forth between mine. "Who?" he breathed out simply, and I smiled once more. He was sceptical, yes, but interested.

"Tell me," I said, prepping my tongue for a series of half-truths, "are you aware that Lili is still working closely with Chad?"

His shoulders slumped ever so slightly at the thought of such betrayal. Was he really so fragile and broken inside that he'd throw out decades of partnership with the vampire-witch after hearing one lie slip off my tongue?

Delighted, I continued.

"Lili came forth months ago, telling us of her alliance with you. She begged Chad for his forgiveness. She's told us all sorts of information against you. Of course, I still don't trust her," I said, chancing a step closer to Florence, "but then again, neither should you."

He shook his head, sure to stare me down as he did it. "I don't believe you," he snarled. "She's been loyal to me for—"

"Several decades," I finished for him, drawling as though it were old information I was already privy to. "I know. Or at least it seems that way. She was led to you by a prophecy and introduced herself to you when you were a young boy. She turned you into a vampire and helped you kill your real father when the whole world believed him to be dead. She's done a lot to try and prove her loyalty to you—even showed you her grand fortress where I suspect you hide now."

I watched him carefully, taking in the smallest widening of his eyes before he squinted them at me with stubborn disbelief. So he *was* at Lili's hideout. If only I could pinpoint where that was.

"Don't worry," I added quickly, "she still hasn't told us where that is, but the truth is, she's got you hooked. You have the right to know. It's all very convincing. But she is what she is, Florence. She's a double agent, playing both sides, though she'll only ever be on her own team. She'll drop you the second you've fulfilled the prophecy."

It was the stillest I had ever seen him. His eyes were focused as if the gears in his head were turning too quickly to allow time for a blink.

"How do I know you're not lying?" he asked between gritted teeth.

"You won't," I replied simply. "Not until you go and figure it out for yourself."

His features softened, but I knew I had to keep at it if I was going to reel him in.

"She's torn between you and Chad, you know," I told him lightly. "She fell in love with you first. She knew I was a witch when she found me but she wanted you for herself. She knew I could never love you the way Zena did—"

I could sense his rage before I felt the air around him as he pummelled his way towards me. Without a second's hesitation, I put up my purple shield and he slammed against it, throwing daggers with his eyes as his heated breath fogged the shield.

"Don't say her name," he threatened, baring his fangs at me.

There it was—proof I had the upper hand.

I nodded, watching him closely, waiting for his breaths to ease back to normal. When they did, I let my shield disappear, embracing the closeness he had delivered.

"But now Lili has moved on," I told him softly, ready to chain him in handcuffs if he made another abrupt move. "It appears Chad and her got a lot cosier than I thought," I said, homing in on the hurt I still felt from their kiss—true hurt that I hoped would be convincing enough to Florence.

The anger eased out of his eyes, replacing itself with desire. "Ah, yes. I heard about their little *tryst*," he said, leaning in with stark curiosity. "And how are the two of you handling this lover's quarrel?"

I lifted my chin proudly, playing my own smile behind my eyes and not letting it reach my lips.

"Wouldn't you like to know?" I dismissed, fluttering my eyelashes playfully.

He smiled back but there was no joy in it, just a thirst for power.

"You know," Florence said, looking around the room, "this is a special place." His eyes landed back on me.

I gritted my teeth. What was he on about now?

"How so?" I forced out, playing along. I didn't care why it was special—why he had been here the first time I found him in this city. What I cared about was plucking one of his hairs.

"This is where my parents met," he replied.

He drew farther away from me to take slow, calculated steps towards the most distant part of the counter. I could feel him slipping away. I leaned up against it to show him I wasn't afraid, but my heart betrayed me. As he ran his fingers along the edge, getting closer and closer to where I stood, my heart hammered out of my chest. A smile played across his lips. He could hear it. He could hear my fear.

"My mother was one of the nurses taking care of my old man," he went on, reminiscing as if it was a lovely childhood story he had been told several times. "It was right after he was injured in the war. 'Temporarily blinded by a mustard bomb,' they say. You Brits are to thank for that. It was back when he fought in the First World War. My mother nursed him back to health."

His fingers drew dangerously close to my arm as I propped myself up against the countertop. I watched him out of the corner of my vision, but it was his red eyes that I was trained on. Joy started to seep into them. He was right in front of me, right where I needed him. And though I ached to transport away, the pull danced wildly within me. It was as if the pull wouldn't be satisfied unless his skin touched mine.

"I was conceived under this very roof," he said, his eyes widening as his finger left the counter to graze my stomach.

Sickness swirled within me. For him to talk about his conception as he touched my stomach—I wanted to run as far as I could, but I didn't allow myself to flinch. His eyes glistened as he felt the fabrics of the black dress. I was supposed to be seducing him, yet all I had to do was let his own imagination run wild. And it was about to pay off. I just had to time it perfectly.

"I remember this dress," he breathed out, his eyes pasted to the black fabrics. "Correct me if I'm wrong, but I believe there was a bit of a mishap and I tore it."

He thought I was part of his game, but really, he was playing mine.

I pushed off of the counter to lean in towards him, my nose nearly touching his. "Such fond memories," I lied. "I couldn't bear to give it up."

I bit my bottom lip to ease the urge to kill him then and there. I wondered the best way to do it. Burn, crush, poison, or flay. Which one shall it be?

It won't help, I reminded myself. It wouldn't stop the plans he had already set in motion. Even if he died, Lili could easily carry on their mission, rallying his followers behind his death.

"We could re-enact that bit," he threatened, grasping onto the dress, the thirst to tear through it again probably fresh on his mind. "I could pin you down to this counter, and thanks to your wards, there'd be no one to barge in and stop me."

And there was the perfect moment.

My hand grasped tightly onto the back of his blond hair, jerking his wandering hand away with it. As I put on the brightest smile I could manage, I led his lips closer to mine, keeping him eager for more. He needed to know I was in charge.

"Forcing your hands on me has never won me over, Florence," I told him, staring him dead in the eye. "It appears you're just as blind as your daddy."

His body was rigid as I pulled his head back, the vein in his exposed neck pulsing. His breath deserted his lungs as he stared back and forth between my eyes. I couldn't tell if he was afraid or merely too stunned to speak. Either way, he knew he would not be doing anything to me atop this counter.

Drawing my hand slowly from his hair to release him, I felt a few silky strands cling to my fingers.

"Now, here's my offer," I said. I put the hand with his hair behind my back, and with the other, I reached out to touch his face. Each nerve in my body was an anxious ball of fire. Memories of every time he had ever touched me triggered terror within me, but I didn't let it show. He flinched as my skin met his again. Perhaps he was afraid I'd hurt him—but he let my fingers cradle his chin. His face was perfectly smooth—not a single hair pricking me. "If you stop killing people," I continued, "I'll ensure that creatures like us won't have to hide. Of course, you've made yourself a known threat to the world, so remaining above ground can't extend to you—at least not for a century. After that, we can make a deal with the Casters to let you come back around, and erase any evidence from the mortals so they won't recognise you as the man who killed their ancestors. If you agree to all that, then I'll help you get your revenge on Lili."

He scoffed and I dropped his chin. "As I remember it," he said, "last time we met, *I* was the one giving *you* an offer. Pity you didn't take it in time."

He smiled, his lips parted as he pressed his tongue against the roof of his mouth, waiting as he egged me on. Screams from that night played in my head—screams of the millions he had killed. He had offered to stop the bomb from exploding if I went with him. I had injured him, and the woman who I now knew was Lili had transported him away. It was unsettling to think of the pink-haired version of me as Lili, but it had been her all along.

"As *I* remember it," I mimicked, "Lili saved your arse and you ran away before you could hear my answer."

It was so easy to take away his smug smile. His face dropped again.

"I had you handled all on my own," he snapped. "You would've come with me if she hadn't pulled me away."

I shook my head. "Only, we both know you would've killed all those people anyway," I told him.

As I said the words aloud—as he didn't deny them—the weight from the guilt slipped off my shoulders. I hadn't taken those lives, nor could I have stopped their deaths. But now that I had these precious hairs, I could stop him from the next attack. It was time to create that tracking spell.

"Have fun working with your blonde-haired, blue-eyed traitor, Florence," I said, placing my hand behind my back to join the first. "Think of my offer. Let me know what you decide."

But Florence's eyes widened. I could hear his heart pumping quicker. He shook his head, not wanting me to leave so soon, and reached his hand out to grab my arm, but I gave him a reproachful look. His hand fell, giving up on the idea of touching me again.

"Where are you going?" he spewed out, all confidence evaporated. He was a scared little boy, terrified I'd abandon him. He scrunched up his nose and rolled back his shoulders to erase the terror in his voice. "Back to your Prince Charming?" he let out quickly, disgust flinging off his tongue. "It's never going to work between the two of you."

A pang of woe stabbed into my heart as Florence declared one of my fears, but I had what I came here for. I didn't need to stay and listen to his desperate attempt to keep me in his company.

"Goodbye, Florence," I told him sternly.

His words poured out with as much malice as he could muster. "Before this is all over," he threatened, leaning into me, "your witch-boy will die. And then you'll be in a pretty white dress, ready to spend the rest of eternity with me."

Not in a million years.

I shook my head. His distress brought a grin back to my face.

"I'm really going to enjoy killing you, Florence," I told him, ready to transport away.

"So do it!" he encouraged, shouting out the dare. He lifted his arms violently as if to ask why not. "Kill me. What's stopping you from doing it now? Don't tell me that after all this time you've come to feel something for me."

I wanted to prove to him how wrong he was. I wanted to tear him apart, limb by limb, but something told me this wasn't the way he'd die. His death was going to be delicious. It was going to be everything I thought it would be. But for now, it was time to go.

Behind my back, I twirled his hairs between my fingertips. I didn't owe him even a second of my time.

"Wait—" he said, reaching out towards me.

But I couldn't stand the thought of his touch. Not again.

Before his skin could meet mine—before I let another word penetrate my ears—I transported away.

My feet touched down to the dirt ground, right outside the hospital. Nigel and the other guards looked at me, waiting for my cue, but as a loud, hostile roar rose from the building, our eyes travelled there instead. I could still feel the pull as it tried to tug me back towards my maker—back towards the sound of furniture crashing to pieces—but I planted my feet firmly against the ground.

I hated that bloody pull.

I was going to sever it one day.

I flinched as glass shattered inside the building. He still had the same rage that had filled him as a child, and Lili was right. It had manifested since.

Looking back at Nigel, I gave him a firm nod. I didn't want to hear any more of Florence's tantrum. He nodded back and placed his hand on my arm, and his burnt orange smoke surrounded us.

We disappeared from Pasewalk, Germany to land on luscious green grass, on the border of Austria. Atop a large cliff of monstrous boulders sat one of Chad's castles, one I had seen before. This was the true castle on the rocks, the one that gave the English version of its name to the pub: *Schloss auf den Felsen.*

Wind whipped through my hair as the other guards appeared next to us. Taking in a deep breath, I advanced towards the castle, shaking the touch of Florence off of me. Phase one was complete. Now it was time for phase two.

Chapter 22: Course of Action

Screams haunted my head as I sat in a chair rocking back and forth, trying with all my might not to crush the glass phial in my hand. Screams of whom, I did not know, but they invoked terror all the more. My eyes darted around as the guards' magic swirled in a chaotic clash of colours, providing more wards on the Austrian castle, when a puff of green smoke made me jump.

"Did you get it?" Connor asked. His feet had barely touched the floor next to Chad and Hydie when the words flew out of his mouth.

Though Hydie and Connor were staring at me avidly, Chad's gaze was pasted to the floor of his castle. I rolled my eyes, irritated by Connor's question, by all the movement around me, and by Chad's heated glare at the floor. Making sure my mental shield was intact, I studied the crease in Chad's brows and the tautness of his jaw as he rubbed his wrists. Ah, so the king had managed to get out of the chains—but was it on his own or with help?

"Does everyone really have such little faith in me?" I asked as my eyes flickered back to Connor. "Of course I got it."

I raised the phial to reveal ten golden strands of hair within it. Nigel had brought me the glass as I was too afraid to let the hair leave my sight. With Lili as such a convincing spy, it gave me little faith that Chad possessed the ability to judge if all of his guards were trustworthy.

Hope sparked in Connor and Hydie as they smiled, but Chad's jaw remained tight. Apparently, he was still furious I had left him tied to my bed rather than let him tag along. But his expression suddenly softened. His cheeks flushed as he ran his eyes over me—all the way up the infernal black dress I had worn for Florence.

"And did he hurt you?" he asked, searching for damage. "Did he lay a finger on you?"

I flicked my fingers to transform the dress into a full-coverage blue one to hide my body from Chad. Not only that but to dispose of the horrid dress Florence had liked so much.

"I'm fine," I growled back. "Now teach me how to make this tracking spell that makes it so easy to stalk your prey," I suggested harshly, still peeved he had used the spell to follow me to Wyatt's house.

Chad's anger returned to his face as his eyes boldly met mine. His body straightened and he crossed his arms with defiance. "First, tell us how it went with Florence."

I gritted my teeth but when I saw Hydie and Connor's eager looks, I decided to tell them the story. Their faces slowly morphed into shock as I told them what little had happened other than gaining Florence's hair.

"And you'll let him go into hiding if he helps us?" Hydie asked, furrowing her brow at me.

"Of course not," I huffed out. "I'd never let him off the hook after all he's done. I fully intend to kill him, but he doesn't have to know that. He needs to think I don't completely hate him in order for his plan to crumble, and for him to unknowingly lead me to their lair." I wiggled the phial before to her as proof that at least part of the plan had gone off unhinged. The rest we had yet to see.

"What if they have something of ours to track us?" Connor asked.

"That's pretty likely considering the fact that *you* used to live with Florence," Chad said, thrusting a finger towards me, "and I used to work closely with Lilith."

"Ah, yes—too closely, some would say," I remarked bitterly.

"So we should only travel between safe locations," Chad finished, ignoring my statement, but his green eyes didn't meet Connor's as he answered the question. They stayed glued to mine—trying to provoke me. "What's next in your master plan?" Chad sneered back.

"After we create this tracking spell, we'll build up our army," I replied without hesitation.

"Have we not been trying?" Chad asked, eyeing me as though I had forgotten all the hard work he had put into it.

I hadn't forgotten. Nor had I forgotten how his attempts had mostly failed.

"Go through everyone again," I demanded. "Every Caster, every Night Crawler who's ever refused our alliance has now seen what Florence is capable of. They'd be idiots to think they're immune. We'll seek them out and show them that fighting against Florence is our only chance at hope. We'll really need to drill in the fact that Casters and Night Crawlers can work together. We can coexist without murdering one another. Isn't that right, Chadwick?" I asked, as if to say he better watch his temper or we'd be proven as hypocrites.

"And if they still refuse?" Chad asked.

"Then they'll rue the day they turned us down," I replied without missing a beat. "We could offer them a fortnight to decide if they're joining us. If they decide against a union, they'll have to protect themselves."

"There's no telling what Florence could do in that time," Connor said with a wince.

"We already told the mortals they're on their own until they agree to a peace treaty. We'll do the same with the Casters and Night Crawlers. If they ask for protection, we'll put them into hiding—protect whoever will let us."

"You should start with the Day Walkers in Egypt," Hydie suggested. "They're close with Abigail and Cristin, but they don't want to pick a side. Perhaps if they met you, they'd come around."

I nodded at her before looking at Chad. His eyes were cast towards his guards as they finished the last of the wards.

"You and I can try to talk them into joining us," I suggested to him.

His eyes shot back to mine and my stomach dropped as I realised I had suggested the two of us go alone.

Before he could answer, I rushed on, eager to show him that it was a meaningless gesture.

"For now, we should put these hairs to good use. Hydie, come with us to work on the spell," I said firmly, refusing to be alone with Chad again, Not after our sex escapade that started in the lake, and how easily he had let me seduce him into those handcuffs. "You need to learn how to make it as well," I added to Hydie, trying my best to sound innocent.

But Connor and I were going to— she began to insist.

I bore my eyes straight into her, making it clear it was not a request. Besides, what were she and Connor going to do on their own? They didn't need to be alone just as Chad and I didn't.

Fine, she snapped back.

And we set off to work.

I'm Still Unstoppable

Chapter 23: And So It Began

The clock struck 12 on 1 April. Lights from all over the world flickered off as the magic fled from them. We watched from afar as the world came to a halt, on a screen only a Caster could manipulate. No mortal would be able to use electricity unless they were at hospital. And though there was no broadcast to show the mortals the intensity of the choice they had made, we saw the devastation as the blackout commenced.

The magic they had unknowingly been using for generations was wiped away with one strong gust of air. Planes plummeted from the skies, cars crashed, fires erupted. There were images of shops that had been looted and destroyed beforehand as panic swept the human world. People wept in the darkness, lit only by the small sliver of moon that hung in the sky.

And so it began.

A chorus of screams echoed through my head—of the people who had died in Japan—of hundreds of young voices. The mortals hadn't listened. They hadn't heeded my warning. They hadn't taken the blackout seriously. Now there were more deaths. And it had been my choice.

I shook my head, fighting back the war of anger and pity that raged in my mind. I swallowed down the guilt in my throat and rubbed at the chills that crept up my arms. I prayed that most of the mortals had stayed home, safe from injury even as their lights and heat died out, bearing witness from their windows to know I had spoken the truth.

Connor was back at the underwater castle to inform the others how my meeting with Florence had gone. Chad's guards milled about the Austrian castle, placing yet another round of protective spells on it. That left Chad, Hydie, and me alone in a different room within *Schloss auf den Felsen*, staring at the screen. And although the tracking spell was complete, I fiddled with the tiny jar of remaining blond hair, eager to find Florence's hideout and put an end to all of this.

Chad flicked his wrist and the screen disappeared. His eyes stared into the space where it had sat as though he couldn't unsee the tragedies it had shown.

"Some of the mortals have begun raiding cemeteries," Hydie told Chad, breaking his focus away from the empty air. "Abigail said the Loxley Coven doesn't feel safe. When she went to visit them, they asked for your protection from Florence. They want to know if you can relocate them."

He nodded in reply. "We'll bring them here," he decided. "It'll serve as a safe house for any Night Crawlers wishing to escape the war."

"I've been practising my transportations," Hydie added, glancing back and forth between Chad and me. "If you were to make me a Holder, I could not only help transport people here, but it would help me strengthen that skill even more."

Her lips scrunched to the side, awaiting our answer to her plea. She was asking for more freedom. Other than *Ypovrýchio Kástro* and *Schloss auf den Felsen,* she hadn't been anywhere else in ages. As much as I wanted her to stay safe, she was an adult. She had the right to make her own decisions without her older sister hovering over her.

"It's all right with me as long as you promise to be careful," I replied. I looked to Chad for his approval of the idea, but his eyes didn't meet mine.

Of course she'd be careful. She was very bright and it was about time I let her put her training to use. Besides, if I didn't have to deal with transporting people, it would give me more time to focus on the next stages of our plan.

"Yes," Chad told her. "It would be good practice."

And with that, we each retired to our separate rooms, while the rest of the world seeped into chaos.

* * *

Two nights later, Chad and Hydie worked to deliver the members of Loxley Lair to the Austrian palace. Nearly the whole coven had arrived, but I wasn't sure how long it would take for the rest to get here. I greeted them in the foyer, groups of them landing in puffs of green or golden smoke depending on which Holder brought them here. Each of my old covenmates stared around the castle with doubt dimming their eyes before they were shown to their new chambers. It was a suspicion I didn't understand considering it was *them* who had asked for *our* help.

"War always brings out suspicion and secrecy, doesn't it?" Irma asked in her thick German accent moments after Hydie transported her and Ingrid there. "What was with the black invitations that King Chadwick was handing out?"

I smiled, knowing they had each proven themselves trustworthy if Irma and her wife had passed our test. Irma stared at me patiently, waiting for an answer, while Ingrid was a step farther from me. It was just like Irma to talk to me without a second's hesitation, and just like Ingrid to stand silent, watching me, apprehension weighing down her otherwise beautiful face and strong German features. Their blonde hair glistened under the enormous chandelier that hung above us as most of the other members of the lair started to make their way out of the grand foyer.

"Apparently, it's something he's been working on—a way to determine who we can trust and who we can't," I told them. "The ink was charmed so only those who are against Florence can read it. If you could read the ink, then it means you're on our side— against a world where innocent people's lives are the cost. And if you believe that, then it's less of a risk to share this location with you. We'll do the same for anyone else who needs to stay here. It helps keep everyone safe."

Both of them blinked in surprise at discovering they had passed a test they'd unknowingly taken. Irma was right. War did bring suspicion and secrecy, but those sentiments weren't always necessary.

"Which brings me to the next thing..." I hesitated, embarrassed to show the error in my ways but knowing it was past due.

They both eyed me curiously. Ingrid sucked in her lips, quiet as she always was around me, and Irma bounced ever so slightly on the balls of her feet as she waited to hear what I had to say.

"I owe you both an apology," I blurted out. My gaze shifted back and forth between the two of them. "I haven't been very kind to either of you. You've both been close to Abigail but I wasn't as trusting. You see, a while ago there was a woman who gave me a letter from Florence. She didn't let me see her face but she had long blonde hair like both of you. I was convinced that it was one of you who delivered the letter, that you two were spies working for Florence, but I know now that you aren't."

I heard a series of clicks as Irma fidgeted with her nails before her face dropped into a frown. Their heartbeats slammed against my eardrums—almost as if guilt was driving the acceleration. Irma pursed her lips to the side before they parted.

"Well, actually..." she began slowly, but the typically silent vampire next to her cut her off.

"It wasn't us who gave you the letter, but I did make a deal with Florence," Ingrid said, pausing to let the information sink in.

And it did. My heart rate increased to match theirs as I was blindsided by the confession. I hadn't heard her say a word since right after I had met her, since I had grabbed her arm and received a vision of Florence destroying their old coven. After that, she had been afraid of my touch, perhaps afraid I had Caster blood if I could see visions, or afraid I'd see more. But Irma had always been the opposite. She was eager to touch my hand or embrace me in a hug as though she had nothing to hide. So which was it?

Ingrid cleared her throat to continue. "After Florence murdered everyone else in our coven," she said, the memory pushing woe into her voice, "he told me the only way he'd let Irma and I live was if we promised to seek out Loxley Lair—if we took shelter there and became his spies."

"We weren't allowed to tell you," Irma filled in, wringing her hands together. "He had a witch seal our lips from telling you, but when we realised we were safe at the lair—safe from him—we stopped feeding him information."

"Not that we had much to share anyway," Ingrid added.

"I was hoping that if I touched you—your arm or gave you a hug—you'd receive a vision of the truth," Irma announced, a soft plea in her voice. "Then it could break our vow to Florence. I prayed that you'd see Ingrid only made the agreement to protect me. But we've been thinking a lot the past few months and we're ready to fight with you and truly stand up to Florence."

All the times she had touched me, and not once let her muscles flinch away from me like Ingrid would, she was trying to get me to have another vision?

I shook my head, closing my eyes for just a second to help my brain compute it all. "But if a witch, presumably Lili, put a spell on you, how is it that you're able to tell me all this now?"

Both of the blonde vampires exchanged glances before giving me a shrug.

Why would Lili's spell no longer work on them? Why was I suddenly dreaming of her past?

I thought of the truths Ingrid and Irma had told me and their ability to see the ink on the black invitations.

"You've both proven yourselves as honest," I decided, "so let's put all of that in the past. You're here now, and I assume you're ready to fight?"

"Yes," Ingrid said in a stony voice that still seemed so foreign to me.

"Is there anything we can do to help?" Irma asked, her pitch raised slightly with hesitant hope.

I glanced around the room before nodding. "Actually, there is," I responded, a picture of my best friend blossoming in my mind. A friend I hadn't spoken to or given the benefit of the doubt. One who was frail and was going to need the strength to fight, regardless of the mistake she had made over two decades ago by killing Chad's mum. "Abigail has been rather down lately," I said, hoping they wouldn't require elaboration on the matter. "She should be here soon. Perhaps you could meet the kids and cheer her up a bit."

"We'd love to," Irma said.

As if on cue, Chad, Hydie, and Abigail appeared in a cloud of green smoke. As soon as they touched down, Chad and Abigail recoiled from each other. Abigail looked around at anything else in the room. Chad placed his hands in his pockets, suddenly interested in the floor, while Hydie bit her lip, but they were accompanied by no one else. Nearly all of the Loxley Coven was here, but not all of them. What had happened with the rest?

Irma ran over to greet Abigail, already beginning her mission. I was left with Ingrid for only a brief second. Her lips curved upwards ever so slightly, the closest thing to a smile I had ever seen on her, and then she joined Abigail and her wife.

Hydie strode over to my side.

"Charity and Leo want to move into *Schloss auf den Felsen* as well, to stay with the coven. They plan to bring Kana too," she told me. "But Abigail and Cristin have requested to stay with us at *Ypovrýchio Kástro* a bit longer. They think it'll be best for Noel and Leon since they're Casters—at least for now."

I looked around at the Night Crawlers as more of them made their way back down to the foyer after getting settled in their bedrooms. Gnomes tip-toed around, joined by fairies delivering blood duplication potions to vampires and rare meats to the werewolves and manananggals. Chad's guards stood, awkwardly attempting to mingle, but their stances communicated anything but a relaxed atmosphere. They mirrored the straight backs and jumpy stances of the Night Crawlers, each terrified by the other, yet trying against all odds to coexist.

"Perhaps you could speak to Chad about it and make sure he's all right with Abigail and the others staying at *Ypovrýchio Kástro*," I told Hydie. Although, he hadn't kicked them out yet.

But instead of nodding, Hydie placed a careful hand on my arm.

I think it's about time the two of you began speaking again— without others around, she added as I opened my mouth to interject.

She was right. I had done my best not to be alone with Chad. Fear kept steering me away, and although I was not ready to discuss a future between the two of us, I could at least woman up enough to ask him this.

Hydie gave my arm a squeeze before departing, and as I looked back over at Chadwick, I dug my nails into my palms. His gaze flew over to Abigail for only a touch of a second before he glanced away, as though horrified they might make eye contact. His gaze landed on me—perhaps fate's cue for me to go over to him.

I took him in. He looked pale—thinner than usual, like stress was eating away at him. There was too much on his shoulders.

I took exactly two steps towards the man before his expression crinkled into a scowl. I could hear his teeth grinding together as he took me in, and without a word, he stormed past me.

As a last-ditch effort, I reached out to him, my hand brushing his shoulder only for him to jerk away from my touch. My eyes tracked him, taking in the stubborn pride in each stride until he rounded a corner and disappeared from view.

My stomach tightened in anger. The prick was still cross with me.

Chapter 24: Doors Bursting Open

I pursued the sound of Chadwick's heartbeat, hunting him all the way to an office on the eighth floor of the castle. The double doors crashed into the walls beside them as I burst my way through, but the loud clatter did nothing to distract the wizard from the papers he was bent over. Not even a glance was spared in my direction as the doors slammed shut behind me.

"You're still pissed off," I hissed at him, tempted to scream but forcing my volume down. "All I did was prevent you from coming to a meeting that you would've ruined."

In lieu of a prompt response, the tosser merely ran a finger down the parchment, his gaze fixed to it. He didn't quiver against my wrath. Instead, he took a long sigh and positioned his hands to hold his weight against the table as if my question had stolen all his energy. "Not at all," he spoke calmly. "What would give you that impression?"

My mouth fell open. Was he serious?

I stepped up to the desk, placing my hands against the table to mirror his stance. "How about that sneer you wear on your face, or the way you completely brushed me off downstairs?"

"Has it occurred to you that I just didn't want you to touch me?" he asked blankly, staring into me like he was daring me to fight back.

I shut my mouth. No. It had not occurred to me. But why was a comforting hand completely out of the question when he hadn't rejected my touch at the lake or in my bedroom? He was still seething, so why deny it?

Chad waited for my reply, a brow cocked with arrogance. I wanted to punch him. I wanted to scavenge his head and force out the truth like he might try to do if he were in my position.

"Let me into your mind," I blurted out before I could stop the words from spewing out. If he wouldn't tell me straight then perhaps he would let me hear his thoughts—feel them. I refused to push my way into his mind, not when I knew firsthand the invasive feeling of him ravaging my mind, but perhaps he would allow me into his head if he would not explain aloud.

"No," he said simply, shutting down my hopes. His wrist flicked and he produced a pen out of thin air before scratching down something irrelevant onto the papers before him.

My brows shot up at his obvious defiance.

"No?" I repeated.

"No," he confirmed, his eyes blatantly refusing to meet mine. The stubborn git.

Never mind that he had not once asked to read my thoughts. Never mind that he was lying to my face about being cross.

I strode around to his side of the desk, nudging him aside so I could read the paper he was so absorbed in. Different clans and covens were written upon it, some circled, some crossed out by an angry hand.

"It's the list of groups who have agreed to work with us," Chad explained, ignoring my shove except for a slight tightness in his voice.

"Yes, I can see that," I snapped back as my eyes lingered on the question mark he had added next to Loxley Lair.

"And we're still on for visiting the Day Walkers tomorrow?" he asked plainly.

I let out an aggravated sigh. "If I can stand to be in your presence by then," I countered, and he met my eyes once more.

A smile peeked out across his lips as though something I said was funny. Part of me fought the urge to invade his mind anyway, to see what was so comical, while I bit my tongue to keep it from saying something to wipe the smile off his face.

"What?" I scoffed instead.

Chad shook his head. "Nothing."

I bit the inside of my cheek to help rein in my temper—to move on from the conversation he simply wasn't willing to have. "Why is there a question mark next to Loxley Lair?" I asked instead.

He shrugged in response. "When I was talking to them, they seemed more inclined to stay hidden than to fight."

It brought me back to what Irma had said about suspicion and secrecy. "They were hesitant to live in a Caster's home," I explained, "not hesitant to join us. They're already on our side."

"If you insist," Chad said with a ring of indifference in his tone.

He took my hand and delicately uncurled my pointer finger to guide it along the paper. The soft brush of the parchment tickled my hand as he rubbed my fingertip against the question mark, green magic seeping through, erasing the symbol from sight. His hand was warm against mine, almost mesmerising, until I felt his body inch closer, and I became startled as his hot breath met my neck. My jump only succeeded in pressing me closer to him.

"What do you think you're doing?" I asked as I spun on my heels to face him, my nose nearly crashing into his as he stared down at me.

Both of his arms blocked my exit as he leaned into me, his hands now on the table to cage me in.

"You won't let me comfort you with a gentle hand, yet it's okay for you to hold mine and then capture me?" I asked.

"'Capture' is a sizable word for a vampire who's ten times stronger than me."

"Fifty times, *at least*," I quipped, "but still not a fair excuse."

"Then it should be easy to get out," Chad parried.

"Or you could be a gentleman and move out of my way," I proposed, unashamedly coming off as bitter.

His nose moved closer to mine until they were touching. For a split second, butterflies fluttered around my stomach. His breath was warm against my face, his eyes a forest of green I could get lost in. Then reality snapped back into place and I realised what he was doing. He was trying to tempt me—tempt me the way I had done to him in my bedroom. But why?

I glared at him, shaking my head as I pondered that exact question.

"If you're so desperate to read my mind," he breathed out, "why don't you just do it?" He was teasing me, daring me to do it.

I placed a hand on his torso to push him away lightly, a task made difficult by my urge to hit him instead. He merely leaned in closer.

"I told you," I replied curtly, my voice growing faster as I went. "I won't do it without permission. It's invasive and rude, not to mention, something an enemy would do. If I want to read your mind, I'll ask. If you don't let me, that's your choice."

Chad shrugged it off, aggravating me even more. "It's not my fault you would scream your thoughts at me," he insisted with a nonchalant tone.

I huffed out. "But it is your fault that you kept that knowledge from me, making it easier for our enemy to—"

"Something I already apologised for—"

"—read all my thoughts—"

"—so perhaps it's time for you to get over it," he interjected, and I shut my mouth with a snap. It was as if he had struck me across the face with his words.

Fury was boiling over to the point I was going to explode if he didn't take back those jarring words. I could feel my eyes turn crimson and my fangs threatened to take their next meal.

Get over it.

I couldn't comprehend the demand, let alone accept it. How was I supposed to get over him snogging a person—one whom I had told him for months was an enemy? How was I supposed to ignore the fact he had kept it a secret from me—sharing the information with Connor behind my back? He didn't trust my instinct. He didn't trust that we were meant to be together if he could so easily sweep all his secrets from me under the rug, and now he expected me to get over it as if it were merely a minuscule roadblock?

Without thinking, I went to shove him. I was too perplexed to form proper thoughts or a verbal response, but his hands were already on my wrists to stop me. Green magic flowed out, binding my arms in place. So I did the next best thing. My knee lifted into his groin, and instantly, his magic shot back into his hands and his breath left him as a pathetic whimper. His own knees crumbled ever so slightly. His thighs clenched onto my leg. His tortured face brought a smile to mine, but then he cocked his head at me and the hint of a smile shone on his face. It only lasted a second before he grunted out again and then lunged forward, burying his face into my neck. His jaw tightened onto my skin and he bit down hard—perhaps to help relieve his pain—perhaps as revenge.

But, oh, that was my weakness, and the damn wizard knew it too.

My muscles relaxed as Chad bit down harder, his tongue massaging its way along the skin he gripped with his teeth. He pushed me onto the table until I melted against it, extinguishing the fire that had raged inside of me.

With one hand wrapped around me, he used the other to grip my thigh and pull my leg up. His soft hand was heaven against my skin. Pulling back to stare into me, he let his nails graze against me, up and down my thigh until they drew closer and closer to another sweet spot of mine. Shivers erupted across every inch of me. I knew he was seducing me, but still, I longed for it. Let him seduce me, let him tempt. Let him win me over and make me his.

I sat back up with impeccable speed, and his breath surrendered itself to me as it left his lungs once more. With a swoosh of wind, I pushed him the metre it took to reach the stone wall behind him and pounced, kissing him anywhere my lips had time to kiss, and touching him anywhere my hands dared to touch. Soon, his hair, his lips, his torso, and the massive bulge in his pants were all mine. I pressed myself against every part of him, wanting to hurt him and love him and punish him all at once. His warmth and the fiery passion behind his lips became my own. I was furious with him, yet the anger drove every part of my body to push into him harder, to kiss him harder, to hate him harder.

He picked me up in one swift motion as my hands massaged roughly against the stubble on his jaw. His feet took one broad step until we slammed back into the table, and he threw me on top of it. I could feel the table shake underneath me. I burned with impatience as he slowly climbed his way above me, my body bending parallel to his until the cool surface met my back. I grasped onto his shirt, tearing it open as he hovered above me. He reached to pull up my skirts but he froze when I plunged my hand into his pants. I gripped onto him, massaging his warmth in my hand and staring into his eyes. A gasp left his lips. I felt my way around, teasing him gently. His eyes flickered as I rolled him within my hand, pulling him closer to me.

As if he suddenly remembered the path his own hands were taking, he moved with haste to push my dress up to my waist, and pushed my knickers aside. I grasped onto the back of his neck, pulling his mouth to mine, and as he thrust a finger inside of me, I bit down onto his lip—hard.

Blood trickled into my mouth, and I fought the urge to suck harder, rub him faster. His finger made its way in and out of me, leaving only to work circles against me and to add two more inside. I could feel the pressure within my core building, so I jerked my hand from his pants. My mind struggled to focus on unlatching his belt, to push his pants off over the tight muscles of his bottom, and then to grab onto him again to put him inside of me.

But fate had another plan.

The doors burst back open right as Chad pushed himself inside of me, forcing a whimper from my lips—both from his thrust and the sudden shock to my heart. Our heads whipped over to the doors to see Connor stumbling in, his hand covering his eyes as he fumbled to close the doors behind him.

I heard the latch click just as Chad pulled out of me with a speed too pleasurable to put to an end. Still, we flung ourselves off of the table, away from Connor, moving at the speed of light to cover up any skin that was showing from our impulsive act.

"As welcoming as your angry shouts and lust-filled cries of passion are for everyone else in the castle," he said harshly, taking a careful step towards us, "perhaps we could figure out important business first. Then you two can go off to a *different* castle where everyone's hearing isn't as crystal clear as ours."

My lungs struggled to steady themselves. Blood rushed through my heart and up to my cheeks as the embarrassment truly set in.

He was right. Connor was *exactly* right. What was I thinking, having sex with Chadwick? That was the last thing that should be on my mind.

"Anyway," Connor continued on in a sing-song tone, chancing a peek between his fingers before dropping his hand away completely. "I was sent to see if you two were still going to Egypt. Abigail and Cristin wanted to offer their insights."

I turned towards Chad and was met with an intense stare, like he was waiting for my response, or perhaps not waiting at all. Possibly trying to read it for himself. His green eyes bore deeper into mine, his chest rising and falling, heaving to catch up on air. I threw up a shield in my mind but his face became completely unreadable as he stared back at me, wiping away the small stream of red that oozed down his chin.

I glared at him, taking the opportunity to straighten out my dress better. This entire *thing* was completely his fault. He was trying to rile me up—trying to make me so furious that I would lose all sense of what truly mattered—not mindreading, not our stupid, continuous row—but finding a solution to winning the war.

"Change of plans," I told Connor, glancing down to the wrinkled parchment that I had just been laying on. I quickly found the words "Day Walkers" smudged upon it and then looked up at the werewolf who was very right to break apart my interaction with Chad.

Unfortunately.

Before I could truly think it through, my lips parted and the words fled from them.

"Connor," I said firmly, leaving no room for discussion. "You're coming to Egypt with me instead."

Chapter 25: His Precious Little Azalea

Lilith | A Year and a Half Ago | Hidden Fortress

*F*lorence burst through the front doors, heat practically steaming around him.

"Those fucking Day Walkers won't join us for anything," he spat between his gritted teeth. "They're going to regret their insolence."

I tried to conceal the joy on my face as I set down the map I was looking at. "Relax," I cooed, well versed in his tantrums by now. They did nothing to raise my blood pressure, only to spark my curiosity. His fury often meant he'd be up for some fun. "I'm sure they'll come to their senses. Especially once they see what happens to Japan."

"They better. I need—argh! I need something to calm me, someone to calm me."

And there it was—the fun he needed. My heart lifted but part of me despised the feeling. He needed someone. Why did my body ache to be that person?

Slowly, I walked over to him. Circling around him, I took in his tense muscles, the agitation that shook through him—something his precious little Azalea loved to cause in her first few weeks at Loxley Lair—not soothe as I did.

Placing myself behind him, I rubbed his shoulders, relishing in the way the tension relaxed at my touch. My fingers could win over anyone.

As his body leaned into me, completely entranced, I let one of my hands trail over his shoulder and down his torso, descending as low as I dared. I expected him to melt—to sink further into my touch. Instead, his body jerked violently. He pulled away to face me with a disgusted scowl—a buzz vibrating the room from his sharp moment—no hunger left in those beautiful blue eyes. My heart jumped as his gaze pierced into me.

"Oh, don't seem so desperate," he snarled, a twist of the knife he had stabbed into me. "I know what to do," he continued happily, his eyes now lost in a fantasy.

I took a step back, forcing an indifferent smile on my face—to pretend I wasn't broken. "What's that, Sunshine?" I asked, imagining the ecstasy I'd feel if I ripped his head off instead.

Only, he didn't skip a beat.

"I'll make Azalea come with me to Downy Lair," he said as though the idea was oh so clever. "Perhaps forcing her to have some fun will do the trick."

Fun. The word made my insides boil. Downy Lair was a piss-pour excuse for any entertainment. Their brutal vampire orgies were the opposite of that. And for Florence to think he could have any fun with Azalea... No, the stubborn girl wouldn't allow it.

He flicked his brows mischievously as though it was some brilliant, devious plan, but all I could feel was anger. The night he had turned her flashed across my mind—his hunger, his thirst, the heat he felt as he bit into her and she sucked the blood from his wrist in return. The night he unknowingly turned the witch into a vampire, making her more like me.

My own voice from that night filled my head. I had told her we were taking her somewhere far worse than Hell, and I wasn't wrong. I had fed her the memory potion and used my magic to strap her to the ground. As she screamed for mercy, I had seen myself screaming for my father to stop his punishments—his hate against me from such a young age. We were so alike, Azalea and I, yet all Florence wanted was her and not me.

"And what makes you think that bitch will play along?" I asked lightly, testing Florence's pride. Azalea hated him. She wanted nothing to do with him.

He didn't snap at my insult. He merely grinned in response. "Don't forget, my sweet Lilith. I have her identification card," he said, a scheme in his eye, a sick thrill in his tone. "Once I dangle information in front of her, she'll be begging to come along."

For the millionth time, I gritted my teeth at the fact that I had let him stick around. But if all he was going to talk about was her, then there was no point in spending this much time with him. We would have to work together from a distance or I would slit my own throat.

"Perhaps she will," I replied with a grin, masking the feel of what could only be defined as jealousy as it coursed through me. It was a foreign, disgusting feeling that I wanted to claw out. "What an excellent idea."

Chapter 26: Check and Mate

Azalea | Present Day | Chadwick's Office

I t was a game of chess.

"And how will you get all the way to Egypt without me?" Chad taunted, killing off my pawn. "You've never been there."

But it was as if he had forgotten my power—as if I hadn't transported all the way to Japan before, and that was even further. Although, that time I had felt a pull to help Kana. This time there wasn't a child that needed my help, only stubborn, fully grown vampires I needed to convince to help our cause.

I rolled back my shoulders, ready for the fight. I didn't want him to come.

"I'll use the mirrors in Castwell Castle," I said boldly, making it sound more like a set plan than a suggestion.

Striking down his bishop.

"Last I heard, you blasted them all apart," he retorted, ignoring the fact that his bloody kiss with Lili was the very reason I had blasted them.

"Then *fix* them," I spat out, enunciating the words so he couldn't misunderstand. It was not necessary for him to come along. Connor was perfectly capable of helping me with the Day Walkers.

"I can't always clean up after your messes," Chad sneered, moving to demolish my queen.

"Nor can I with yours," I snapped. If his involvement with Lili wasn't a huge mess, then I didn't know what was. "And if you're incapable of fixing the mirrors, I'll go to your aunts' and use one of theirs," I resolved, determination thick on my tongue. "If you don't want to help me get to Egypt, then shove off."

"Ruddy chance they'll let you use a portal without me there to escort you," he countered.

"They don't have to like it."

"I'll follow you to Egypt then," he claimed as if it was all so simple, as if he had my king surrounded, and I rolled my eyes at his childish attempt to force his way along. "I'll go through the mirror right after you."

"Ah," I said smugly, flicking my fingers at him, producing a small flame in my hand to remind him of my powers. "But I can just 'blast' it apart after Connor and I go through." It was his king that was truly cornered.

Chad effortlessly blew out the fire in my palm, then his lips tightened as he took a deep breath in through his nose. His eyes were cold. If vampire blood ran through his veins, his eyes would've turned red from the fury.

Check and mate.

Connor stood awkwardly next to us, shuffling his feet as Chad and I stared at one another in a heated silence.

"We'll meet you at your aunts' castle in Lancaster," I told Chad after a few beats, stabbing through the quiet with a dagger, "where you will act as a mediator. Bring one of the magical letters so I can show it to the Day Walkers and see if they're trustworthy. Then you can go look for something else to muck up."

My tone was as vicious as my venom. Then I transported away before he could argue. I was going to need a good night's sleep, especially if I was to deal with his attitude for even a fraction of the next day.

For once, the dream of Lili and Florence revived a bit of positivity rather than the negative effect my dreams usually had. Ignoring Florence's obsessive behaviour over me, he and Lili had mentioned one thing that might work in our favour. The Day Walkers might be adamant not to join us, but at least they rejected the dark side at some point. There was hope yet.

Connor was tasked with speaking to Cristin and Abigail to find out who to contact and where to go once we arrived in Africa. I wasn't in the mood to face anyone—not after letting my guard down enough for Chadwick to get to me.

A few hours after the sun had set over the Mediterranean Sea and made its way past the Lancaster horizon, I collected Connor to begin the journey. Transporting to Lancaster was a complete waste of time and energy when *Ypovrýchio Kástro* was already so close to Egypt, but I still wrapped my fingers around Connor's arm, and off we went.

We landed outside a ward and looked up to where Chad waited in the front gardens with his two wicked aunts. He lifted his hand and the ward shimmered, allowing us to step through.

Their castle was just as gaudy as I remembered, gold and mirrors covering the entire exterior. And even though the two witches knew Lili was fighting a war against them, they still kept the gardens full of lilies—all the azaleas uprooted to spite me. At least they hadn't added anymore imprisoned gnomes. It was all a perfect display of their vane personalities. Only, today it worked out to my advantage. Who needed an attic full of mirrors when his aunts' castle was bloody made out of them?

The two women glared unashamedly as we approached, red magic hovering around their fingertips, while Chad stared at us, his hands casually in his pockets and a look of indifference on his face. I wondered if the hags knew Chad and I were amidst a row. But the disgusted expression they gave Chad before flouncing back into their castle and slamming the door behind them confirmed they were in the dark. They'd be far too jovial if they suspected something was amiss.

When we reached Chad, his gaze turned harder. I held out my hand expectantly, tightening my lips and raising my brows before he growled under his breath. He flicked his wrist as though helping me was an excruciating task. A single black invitation appeared from a puff of green smoke and slammed into my chest with vigour. A fake smile brushed his lips as he squinted his eyes and boiled my blood. So bitter. Suddenly, I felt very justified in my decision to bump him from the Africa trip and replace him with Connor.

I took a threatening step closer, ready to snap back at him, but Connor quickly intervened. He placed his fingertips on both of our chests, his whole body between us as he gave us each a small shove.

"Whoa!" he called, driving us apart. "As much as I'd *love* for you two to get on again, I'm pretty sure that this back-and-forth bickering is what got you all hot and frisky yesterday, and I really don't want to be an audience. *Again*," he added as a reminder.

I was too furious to feel any sense of shame, but Chad, on the other hand, took a step back. The tension eased ever so slightly but the scowl stayed pasted on his face.

"Remind me why I'm no longer invited to speak to the Day Walkers," he commanded.

An exasperated huff left my lungs in a hurry. "Obviously it's not wise for the two of us to be alone together," I told Chad. "We can't be in the same room without wanting to rip off each other's heads."

"Or your clothes," Connor added unnecessarily.

I narrowed my eyes at the werewolf, and he raised his hands in surrender.

"You're not helping," I snapped at him. "Besides," I added, turning back to Chad, "I need to be away from you. Think you can give me space, or do I need to handcuff you to my bed again?"

Chad's jaw ticked before his eyes landed on Connor, but I stared into him, directing the Caster's attention back to me.

"We have the mirrors," I said, gesturing up to the putrid castle, "now you can leave. Perhaps you can put yourself to use by grabbing that list of yours with all the people you've failed to get on your side and set up a meeting with them so I can rectify those unions as well."

I looked away from Chad, not wanting to see his sour expression, but before going through the silvery portal, I chanced one last look at him. He stared back at me, his face showing no emotion. It was merely blank and unreadable. Then he gave

Connor a look, some unspoken language travelling between the two of them before they each nodded firmly, and Connor grabbed my arm to pull me towards the closest mirror. My mind itched to read theirs, to find out what they had agreed upon.

One of these days he's going to infuriate me so much that I'll lose my moral code and invade his mind, I thought to myself. And then Connor spoke our desired destination and we plunged ourselves into the unknown.

Chapter 27: A Million Grains of Sand

A wall of dry, warm air hit me as we crossed over into the deserts of Egypt. The darkness welcomed me like an old friend, and the sand beneath us wrapped around our feet like a hug.

Connor's eyes met the moon as it hung in its place, his muscles taut as he stared it down. I closed my eyes. Guilt tugged at my stomach. I hadn't even stopped to consider the moon's cycle.

I felt as it shone down on my face. A full moon. Why did I always subject my dear mate to the worst situations?

I opened my eyes and watched as a flood of bumps rushed up his arms, raising his hairs and travelling across his skin. He could feel it. The itch. And even though Chad's magical potion protected him, I knew him well enough to sense his urge to burrow under a stack of blankets rather than blackout and turn into something other than himself.

I turned my head back to the mirror in time to watch it shimmer and disappear like a mirage.

"It's okay," Connor insisted, and my eyes flashed back to his. He gave a brave smile. "I can deal with the moon. Let's just hurry up and find these Day Walkers so we can go home."

Resting a caring hand on his shoulder, I gave him a firm nod. "Let's get this over with," I agreed.

He returned the gesture, and we set off to our destination.

Although the Day Walkers wouldn't be able to sense my magic like Baba Yaga could, Cristin told Connor they'd be able to hear the buzz if I sped towards them, giving them enough time to flee from confrontation. So, instead, we went at a mortal's pace. Silence between us, tall hills of sand surrounding us. Sand spraying in every direction with each step we trekked through it.

The circular moon cast shadows across the hills, marking the direction we should travel to reach the city. As we clambered over the hills of sand, the moon glistened on our skin, feigning innocence as though it didn't cause Connor harm, and as if it wouldn't switch places with the sun in a few hours—a sun that would scorch me.

"I'm sorry I didn't tell you about Lili and Chad," Connor said suddenly.

My breath caught and I felt my eyes turn red before I blinked the anger away.

Connor hurried on, fear creeping up his throat and seeping into his words. "I swear I would've told you if it had felt significant at the time, but everything you and Chad have shared since has been so much more powerful," he said. "Chad's meant to be with you. Lilith's a nobody."

A bit of empathy swirled around me. I gripped at my shirt, not wanting to feel the pain. Lili was *not* a nobody, regardless of Connor's words or how Florence pushed her aside. She was clever, powerful, and beautiful beyond comparison. No wonder she followed Florence around. No wonder she had stuck by Chad's side for as long as she did. No one saw her true worth.

"Don't worry," I said, glancing at Connor from the corner of my eyes. "I've come to realise it's not completely your fault, so I suppose I can forgive you."

The ends of his lips spread into a grin, but then his expression morphed into a wince. "And is there any of that forgiveness left for Chad?" he asked hesitantly.

I pivoted my head to widen my eyes at him but kept walking all the same. I wasn't there yet. Chad and I had too much to handle without me throwing my indecisive heart troubles into the mix.

"Look," Connor said quickly, "the next time Chad screws up and fesses it up to me, I'll be sure to knock some sense into him, and then come straight to you with the details."

I laughed, my body momentarily forgetting its woes. "You sound certain he's going to mess up again," I said pointedly.

"Well, he's a man," Connor said with a shrug. "We can't help being stupid sometimes. It's in our blood."

"Perhaps if I suck out all his blood—to rid him of his stupidity—it'll ensure he makes wiser choices," I teased.

"Word has it, that might just happen," Connor replied morbidly, and the light-hearted feeling in my body vanished.

My whole body cringed at the memory, the dream, the prophecy. Whatever it was loomed closer. I blinked. No words came forth. I shouldn't have said it so lightly. Chad's death was no laughing matter.

"We still haven't figured out Ginny's prophecy," Connor went on, "but at least now we know it's probably not you who kills him. Lili can shape-shift."

More guilt sloshed around my stomach, making me feel ill. I shook my head. If only it were that simple.

"It was my hair in the vision," I breathed out, hardly able to utter the words. "I could feel everything—taste everything. It's going to be me, not Lili," I admitted. As much as I'd like to think I couldn't do that to someone—anyone, let alone Chad—it didn't feel right to lie.

"Yes, but Hydie says you feel the same way when you dream about Lili, like you're actually her, not just watching."

"That's different," I insisted, looking down at the sand.

"Is it?" Connor asked, but I couldn't tell if it was hope in his voice or denial.

Either way, I shrugged my shoulders. "Let's hope not."

From beyond the next hill, I could hear signs of life. When we finally reached the hill's peak, an entire city bloomed into view. Even draped in the darkness from the night, Cairo was more beautiful than anything I had expected. The green trees, and bright blue pools, and the multitude of tourist sites were enough to make the town look like a paradise. Yet there were two things that came crashing down into my consciousness like a meteor, vaporising the soothing feel that I wished so badly to soak in. Tall buildings lined the streets, reminding me of the ones that no longer existed in Japan, and millions of flickering candles made the reality of the blackout a sharp sting.

Magical tools had made all of this: the lights that stood empty, the buildings, the roads. And now the magic that helped keep the city lit and alive had evaporated.

I tore my eyes away from it all to scan the skyline, and there, far in the background, was an enormous pyramid, marking the location of where we'd soon be unwelcome guests.

Connor gave what sounded like a fake cough from beside me before opening his mouth to spew more nonsense. "Don't you think it's about time you two fixed things?" he asked.

I slumped my shoulders. How could the werewolf possibly ponder that with everything else that was going on?

"We're fine," I grumbled, taking a step either to resume our walk or avoid the conversation, I hardly knew. "Great actually."

"Great?" he asked, doubt saturating the word.

"Yes," I spat out between gritted teeth. "Chad and I have an unspoken agreement."

"To what?" he asked with a cruel chuckle as he jogged to catch up to me. "To fornicate like bunnies just to avoid a grown up conversation? To continue hurting one another until you both break?"

My body froze from his words as they shot into my heart like a silver bullet. "No," rushed from my mouth before I could think it over. "To—" To what? I couldn't think of a fitting response. I couldn't move my lips to form a lie because he was right. That's exactly what Chad and I were doing.

I let a deep breath flow in and out of my lungs. What were we going to do? "To not discuss things that have no place in the middle of a war," I decided.

"Well, I don't think you can survive much longer," he spilled out, "and I *know* he can't."

I frowned before turning to face him. "Rubbish," I uttered. Complete and total rubbish. This was good. *We* were good. Sure we were arguing seemingly nonstop but it didn't matter. We were surviving. We were still alive and that's all I could ask for.

"He can't live like this," Connor pressed anyway.

I rolled my eyes. Where was my fun, goofy mate Connor? The one who always held a smile and oozed boyish humour. Where was he when I needed him the most?

"The king seems more than fine to me," I fought. Chad always had a snarky retort for anything I said, and he was still managing everything he needed to get done as the king of Casters.

"No, he's a wreck," Connor said bluntly, "—and yes, because of you," he added as I opened my mouth to insist it was because of the war.

I shut it promptly.

How was Chad a wreck?

"You're all he ever talks about," Connor blabbered on. "He's always on about how stupid he feels for messing things up with you, and he's not eating and—"

"Make him eat," I gasped out, remembering how pale and thin he had looked. Of course he was going to act off if he wasn't eating.

"I try!" Connor yelled out. "He's depressed. He loves you, Azalea. And for now, he's trying to cope with this weird, random, scream-at-each-other-until-you-have-sex type of relationship because it's the only thing you'll give him, but if he goes on like this much longer, he's not going to have the strength to fight the battles he needs to."

I swallowed down the miserable feeling inside of me, but sadness caught in my throat. "That's not fair," I told him firmly as my stomach clenched on all the stupid, pathetic guilt it held inside. Connor couldn't place that burden on my shoulders. Not when it was one I couldn't bear.

My eyes fell to the grains of sand at my feet. It was me who had seduced Chad at the lake. Me who had told him to hush, to not talk about his father's death or his mum's murderer and just let me touch him. It was me who had run my hands along his arms, convincing him I longed to kiss him before chaining him in my bedroom, and it was me who went screaming after him only to end up on the table he worked at, ready to use his body as a distraction.

179

"'Nothing's fair in love and war'," Connor said, stealing me away from my morbid thoughts. I looked up at him, my mouth shut tight. "What can he do to fix things anyway?" he asked. "Kill Lili?"

I rolled my eyes. How would that change anything? "No! Of course not," I spat out. That was farcical. "If anything, I want to be the one to kill her. And Florence."

"Then what?" he barked back. "Make you his queen?"

"What?" I screamed out, my heart pounding insanly from the idea. "No! Don't be ridiculous."

"Then what?" Connor pressed, his gaze intense as he said it. "He can't go back in time—"

"I know he can't!"

"—and you know he would if could—"

"I know," I groaned out, my heart speeding out of control.

"—he *loves* you."

I couldn't take the pain anymore.

"Stop!" I shouted out into the night, loud enough for the whole city down below to hear, and Connor shut his lips.

I knew—I knew all of it but it didn't make it hurt any less. It didn't fix anything, and it sure as hell wouldn't save Chad's life for me to admit I still loved him too.

Connor and I each took a deep breath before I broke away from his stare to look down at the beautiful city below. Suddenly, I didn't have the energy to face the Day Walkers. How could I when I didn't even have the energy to face my own feelings?

"Look," Connor started, his tone a bit lighter as he nudged me playfully. Playful. The playful Connor I needed just then. "You're like a little sister to me," he said. "I have to protect you, even if it's from yourself."

A laugh flew out of me at the absurdity. "I'm a year older than you," I reminded him, but he brushed my comment away with his hand.

"That's completely irrelevant, Azalea," he drawled out, and I let out another laugh—a real laugh that lifted my heart. "You know," he continued, "Chad's not so bad if you think about it. Look how smart he is. He's not even thirty and he's leading an entire war. He invented a blood duplication potion for vampires like you, *and* my very own potion to stop me from turning into a werewolf. Not to mention, he's romantic, and good looking," he added, flickering his brows.

"You're more than welcome to date him yourself," I countered, holding my chin high, and he let out an exhausted huff.

I shook my head, fighting off a grin. Sure, Connor was obnoxious, but I was only hurting myself by burying my feelings. Either way, I didn't have long to think about it, for as soon as I started, a shuffling sound behind me drew my attention.

"What was that?" Connor asked, hurrying to turn and scope out the area.

I shook my head once more. "I don't know," I breathed out. "But let's move."

As soon as the words fell from my lips, sand shot into the sky, not ten metres away from us, interrupting the thought. The sand crashed back down, too close for comfort.

I met Connor's eyes, my body tightening as I gave him a sad look. It had to happen. He had to change his form—give into the itch if we were going to be fast enough—if we had any chance of escaping whatever it was that had sought us out. Fear grew in his eyes as he realised what must be done.

Another blast of sand came closer before several more joined it, forming a full circle around us.

"Run!" I shouted. Then I took off, without the chance to assure him that everything was going to be all right.

A ripping sound came from behind me, followed by the sound of Connor's paws spraying sand in his wake as he ran after me. But the bursts of sand didn't grow distant in my ears. They followed after us as we ran towards the edge of the city, stalking us like prey. I could feel my heart clash with my ribs as I ran, panic taking over.

"Keep up!" I shouted behind me, but right as I glanced back to make sure Connor was safe, the ground in front of me erupted. I jolted to a stop but it was too late. A hand wrapped in tattered clothes sprang from the ground and attached itself to my ankle. My whole body fell forwards, smacking into the sand with a thud. I scrunched up my face as it collided into the ground, coating my tongue in its gritty texture.

A whimper sounded from somewhere else as another hand reached out to grab me. A creature's clawed hand scraped against my skin as more and more hands tore out from the ground to clench onto me. Without so much as a thought, I sent shots of purple magic at each of them, sitting up quickly to defend myself from more of them, but a thunderous roar filled the air. Looking back, I watched as ten fully fledged mummies with hollowed eyes swarmed Connor. He was hunched over as a werewolf, biting, tearing, and attacking them back, but for ancient skeletons dressed in rotted cloths, their strength was overwhelming. They screeched loudly, speaking words I couldn't interpret. As I sent my magic over to help him, the mummies rising from the ground around me took advantage of my distracted state.

More partially wrapped skeletons emerged from the ground, grasping wildly, ripping my clothes. Purple fire flew out of my hand, igniting a mummy who had its arms around my waist. I didn't feel the burn as it shrieked, finally letting go of me to sink back into the depths where it had come from. I threw more fire at the other mummies but it only pissed them off. Fuelled by anger, their pace quickened. I compensated with my own speed. Grabbing one of their heads, I used it to smash into another one before I crunched its skull in my palms. Only, more rose from the ground to attack.

I had to get over to Connor. I had to grab onto him and transport away—to anywhere but here. If I accidentally took some of the mummified corpses with me, at least I could handle a small number without more sprouting from the ground. But with every attack, it became impossible to locate the werewolf.

Sending out a purple force field around me, I used my other hand to set more of the attackers aflame. My ears perked, searching through the night for sounds of Connor without taking my eyes off of my enemies. I heard his teeth chomp down onto bone, no flesh to muffle the sound. Keeping the shield around me, I sent a purple vine out of my other palm in Connor's direction, hoping it would grasp onto him. Something at the other end tugged back. I chanced a look over.

The vine had wrapped itself around Connor's massive form, along with three mummies that had their bony fingers in his fur. The fur shrivelled down to brown skin as he shifted back into his human form.

"Just go!" Connor shouted as a horde of more mummies burst from the ground, roaring and chanting in a language I didn't know. "Go, Azalea! You have to transport without me. I promised Chad I'd keep you safe."

My mind froze for half a second before I understood. Their unspoken language. Chad had made his best mate promise to keep me safe at whatever cost if he couldn't be there to do it himself.

But I couldn't leave Connor there.

I tugged at the vine, moving the whole group of them closer to me, but it didn't help. Connor's yell called out into the night as the smell of his blood slithered into my nose. His body hit the ground with a thud, but it didn't stop there. I stared in horror as the mummies pulled him down, his captured limbs grasping at handful after handful of sand to stop himself from sinking. But in the blink of an eye, the top of his head disappeared into the sand.

It had eaten him.

The earth had swallowed him whole.

The shield around me snapped into nonexistence as I blasted the mummies away. I transported to the spot where Connor had disappeared. On my knees, I desperately tore at the sand, digging madly, aching to pull him out. A panicked sob left my lungs as the sand seeped back into place. There was nothing. He was gone. He had just been there and now he was gone.

"Connor!" I screamed, my lungs heaving, my throat clamping. My only reply was the roars of the creatures behind me.

A wall of sand cycloned around me. I flicked my fingers, sending a blazing orb of purple light around me. Through it, I watched as a face appeared in the sand, hollow and fierce like the other mummies yet intensely more haunting. It let out a scream, its mouth lengthening. All the sand around me started to suck into it. And just as chills began to cover my skin—just as my instinct to flee took over—the monster in the sand stopped me mid-transport, and I sank into the ground.

I was buried—buried alive.

A million grains of sand consuming me.

I couldn't see, I couldn't feel, I couldn't taste, I couldn't hear anything past the sand for one terrifying moment before a breeze blew and gravity tempted me towards a deathly fall. I was no longer in the ground. Instead, I could see the beautiful city with its bright blue pools and orange candle lights, but from far above. Brick after solid, golden brick sat beneath me as I clutched onto them, about to fall off of what I realised was nearly the topmost point of a pyramid.

I caught myself, pulling away from the edge without any idea how I had sunk through the ground only to be up high with winds bursting past me. I should've been thankful to be free of the sand, but fear pulsed through me even more. I jerked my body away from the edge and came face to face with another mummy.

Its bony fingers grasped at the fabrics of my clothes, and it dragged me away from the cliff, over to a pitch black hole formed at the very tip of the pyramid. Terror stabbed into my stomach as I realised he was going to let go. His mouth fell open to let out a fierce roar, and spit rained down on me. I reached out for anything to stop me from dropping into the belly of the pyramid. I felt as my sweaty fingers rubbed against the mummy's wrappings, but as he let go of me and I plummeted into the darkness, his unravelling, aged cloths did nothing to slow my descent.

My scream echoed on as my body cascaded downwards until there was no air left in my lungs. The horrid sensation of falling overtook all my senses. Thoughts of dying plagued my mind before light flooded back into view and my back collided with a pile of sand.

Frantic shuffles and a high-pitched ringing met my ears. Connor's terrified face came into view above me, but with blurred vision I saw three of him. His hands wrapped around my arms, yanking me up, but my whole body felt numb. I crashed back down to the floor, and Connor threw my arm over his shoulder to hoist me back up. Ever so slowly, and as white flashes of light obscured my view, the ringing sound transformed into a deep, eerie chant.

The song was captivating, almost haunting as the nonsensical lyrics crashed against my eardrums. The mummy repeated the same string of foreign lyrics until a familiar sensation flowed through me—as part of me was ripped away—exactly as it had been at Baba Yaga's house. Only then did I realise it wasn't only my magic that was trapped, we were trapped too.

Thin streams of sand fell all around us in an ever-flowing motion as though they were bars of a prison cell. Adrenaline poured into me, giving me the strength to stand, and I pulled away from Connor to storm through the falling sand—to escape. Yet as soon as my hands touched the tiny grains, they turned as solid as metal.

Over and over, my hands crashed into the sand, the sand that looked so easy to penetrate but simply refused passage. Beyond the bars, the walls were covered in hieroglyphics. Several dark tunnels led away, and a single pair of hollowed-out eyes stared back at me. The mummy that had dropped me from high above stood in the shadows, watching my panic as if he was feeding off of it.

"Let us out!" I demanded, fear racking through me. "We're here to speak to the Day Walkers. Let me speak to them!"

But if he understood me, he made no move to indicate it. He performed no act to set us free. Instead, he sank back into the darkness until not even my vampire eyes or ears could detect if he was still there, watching.

I unleashed everything I had on the enchanted bars, the power of a hundred men flowing from my arms, the strength of fifty beasts, but nothing bent the unbreakable bars. Standing back, I flicked my fingers over and over, but it was no use. My magic was gone.

"Azalea," I heard Connor breathe from behind me, but I kept going. I kept banging and pulling and fighting to find a way out.

"Azalea," he called again, only this time in a whisper. When I turned around to face him, he wasn't looking at me. He wasn't trying to join in my feeble attempts to break out. His attention was drawn to the opposite wall, where instead of dark corridors beyond the bars, there was the navy blue sky and the circular frame of the full moon.

The light from the moon shown in, casting the shadow of the striped bars along Connor's sickly face. I watched as his cheeks began to twitch. His body started to contort as I had seen it do before. It was torturous—a stark contrast to the times he shifted by will.

"The magic..." he sputtered, "the potion... It's—it's not working."

My lips parted in horror. My magic wasn't working, and the potion inside of him, helping him to stay in control of himself was failing too.

I took in three panicked breaths before lying. "It's all right," I told him. "Just breathe. You can fight it!"

"Azalea!" he said again in warning, his voice crescendoing until it morphed into a fierce howl.

My eyes grew wide as I stepped back. My whole body pressed into the bars behind me, my fingers clenching the suddenly solid sand before I turned around to bang my fists against them.

"You don't understand!" I screamed out into the darkness after the mummy. "You have to come back. You can't leave us in here."

Ripping sounds filled the air, taking me back to when I had seen Connor's skin break apart, dark fur protruding out angrily. So different—so painful compared to his new way of turning.

Howls reverberated around us, threatening to drown out my cries for help. Connor's body grew, expanding up to the low ceiling, stretching his skin and veins.

"We're here to talk!" I screamed even louder. "We need to speak with the Day Walkers—the vampires. We're not here to harm you. Cristin and Abigail from Loxley Lair sent us."

The bars around us merely buzzed with excitement as I pounded against them.

"You have to unblock our magic," I tried again.

I looked back toward my mate, hoping to instil some finally reassurance, but he was no longer himself. His brown eyes were that of a stranger, and soon, it'd be my strength against his. There was no telling who would come out alive, if either of us.

I turned back to the dark corridors, squinting my eyes to search for any movement.

"He needs magic to stay himself!" I screamed out, blood crashing through my body uncontrollably fast. I tried again to pull apart the bars, bend them to my will, but even my strength and speed as a vampire were no match for them. "Please," I begged, calling out into the darkness. My voice was hoarse. "He needs it to stay human. He needs the magic!"

A shimmering sound added to the chaos behind me, and I turned to see that a new set of falling sand had appeared right between me and where Connor had once stood. Only, this time I came face to face with a pair of glowing yellow eyes. There was no kindness left in them, just hunger. It was no longer my mate that stood in front of me, but a ferocious, rampant animal, ready to attack.

With nothing but the falling sand in his way, an ear-splitting scream left my lips as he lunged towards me and his jaw snapped shut.

Chapter 28: The Name of a Flower

Lilith | A Year Ago | Lancaster, England

*T*he guard stared at me, his jaw open like a bloody fool before his gaze fell back to the five vampires who lay dead in the black mud.

"How did you—" he stumbled.

I fought the urge to yell at him—to tell him how useless he was as a Caster, let alone a royal guard, if he couldn't kill those vampires himself. But I held my tongue. I had a role to play.

"Please," I said, mustering up a girlish innocence within my voice. I looked around into the night, hugging myself and shivering as if I was frightened, but I had never been afraid of the dark. I was a creature of the night. "Please, sir," I stressed. "These monsters were speaking of an attack on our prince. There's bound to be more of them. The Prince of Casters needs to be warned."

The guard let out his shock in a series of ridiculous grunts before he finally responded.

"*Of course. Yes,*" *he flustered, thrusting his palm out at me. His magic must have jutted out because my stylish pink heels became rooted to the ground. "Stay put. I'll send them here to speak to you.*"

He disappeared and my lips curled into a smile.

Incompetent. That's what he was, but it was working out in my favour. It was too easy. He had said "them." Perhaps tonight I could hit three birds with one stone.

It was Florence's idea really, perhaps the first clever idea he had come up with in months. Either that, or the only one I allowed my ears to take in. Then another trip to Baba Yaga revealed the perfect way for me to infiltrate the royal family. A prophecy.

Get close to the Casters, *Florence had ordered.* Keep Florence's friends close but our enemies closer. *The first part I had failed, judging by the blood that spilt out of the vampires at my feet. I had never cared for Florence's friends anyway. Keeping the Casters close, however, was an idea I could get behind.*

The blood of the vampires leaked out ceaselessly. Wasted, yes. But I wouldn't let it tempt me. Drinking from them would make me physically stronger, but it would disrupt my healing speed—something Florence was daft enough to risk, but I would not.

I pointed a finger down to my feet, freeing them from the hold the guard had placed on them. This time, real shivers crept up my spine as I waited. Shivers of excitement.

The prophecy was of our *war, Florence's and mine. It was told that we'd lose, but only if the king of all Casters married his powerful flower. So I had a choice to make—convince the king I was that woman to steer him wrong, or join him to become part of the winning side. But why choose when I could have both? And seeing as the Casters had no king who ruled over them all, I devised a trap for the very person who stood next in line.*

My heart beat faster as the seconds ticked by. Any second. Any second and I would come face to face with the man himself.

Part of me craved a man's attention. It had been weeks since I had forbidden Florence from coming to my home. He had tried to come back when the Loxley Coven had tossed him out, but if he insisted on raving about Downy Lair all the damn time, then that's where he would stay. He had been moaning on and on about his insufferable new creation—as if she was finally the one—as if she could soothe all his pain, if only she'd succumb to him. She was special. He knew she was different, but only I knew why, for not even she knew what she was.

A twig snapped somewhere in the thicket, the wind carrying the scent of a rabbit and the sound of its paws. It irked me. When would they come?

This is why I was still alive. This is why I had found Florence. Killing his father was far from his only purpose. This is why that stupid old hag in Russia had seen him in my future. And it all boiled down to these moments when our plan was finally manifesting. When we would convince the other side to trust me before we tore the world apart. Then the mortals would discover creatures like me existed. And they'd worship at my feet, precisely as I deserved.

Another wind wrapped around the night, but this time it carried the scent of eye of newt, toe of frog, and, best yet, Caster blood. Three sets of feet touched down to the ground. Two old women blocked the third figure. Their taut stances only tightened as they took in the scene before them. One witch pointed her finger out into the night, and I knew better than to assume she hadn't produced a force field around them. The second witch, nearly identical to the first, froze before her glare tore into me. She was so sluggish. I watched in agonisingly slow motion as she pointed her bony finger at me. I could feel as her invisible stream of magic jetted towards me. And as every nerve within me itched to fight it off, I stayed still, letting her think she had a hold over me.

My mental shield flew into place, protection from the powers they might possess, in case telepathy was a gift they held. Two of them were old. Time allowed them to strengthen their skills. Older than me in looks, though in truth, I was far older thanks to the blood my father had passed down to me. But they were royals. They had resources. I couldn't risk letting them into my mind and capturing my plan when it had barely just begun.

"Please!" I shouted, falling to my knees to bow like I was a simple peasant. "My Lord, My Ladies, it's not like me to kill, but I had to. These creatures—they're vile. They were going to hurt the prince."

"And you slayed them?"

"On your own?"

"Five vampires to one witch?"

"Who were they?" the witches asked before I could answer their other questions.

What a dreadfully overwhelming pair they were.

I took a staggered breath to continue my ruse. "I did what I had to. They were vampires,*" I led, stressing the word with my wide eyes and trying to ignore how much I disliked the two women already. Part of me itched for them to move over—to let me see the prince—to know exactly what I was working with, but they refused to budge. "They attacked me," I said, glancing down at the dead men. "I did what I had to in order to survive. But I can undo it... If that's what you wish, I'll undo it."*

They frowned in unison, the witches each dragging their feet mere centimetres forward as if to get a good look at me. And that was when I caught my first glimpse of the prince.

He was stunning. His attire was fit for royalty: expensive blue fabrics with intricate silver embroidery. His dark hair was laid in neat waves, meeting a short, well-kept stubble around his face. He had dark lashes and a natural dark lining around his eyes, and while his aunts prowled closer to me, their nephew was far more cautious. He scanned the wood around us before his green, sceptical eyes fell back on me.

Dreamy, yes, but also wise to be wary.

"Undo it?" one of the witches asked.

"Undo it how?"

I stared back and forth between the two women. It was them I must convince. They were the iron doors of a gate, intercepting my path. My lies were the key, and directly past their blockade was the prince. The one the prophecy spoke of. The one who'd win a war against Florence if I let him. The one who needed the most powerful sorceress alive to aid him. And if I had any chance of being freed of the secrecy the mortals forced upon me, it was I who had to keep the prophecy from coming true.

"Yes," I told them, faux desperation coating my face. "I have the power to unravel time, to send it in reverse. I will do it if Your Majesties ask it of me."

A bluff. I could no easier bring these vampires back than I could the life of my mother. My powers of time bubbles only extended to small matters. But it was a game. A game I knew I could win.

"Undo death?" one witch asked.

I let my eyes dart over to the silent prince, his unwillingness to trust me shining through before I looked back at the women.

I nodded. "Do you wish my attackers to live?" I asked in a quivering voice. I tightened my body in a cringe I hoped was believable.

One witch flared her nostrils in disgust. To bring back a life as lowly as a vampire? They had hated that half of me far before one of my creations had killed their sister. Now, they thought of us as abominations.

Of course they wouldn't ask it of me.

"Don't be ridiculous," one snarled while the other spat at the ground.

"Death is their rightful place. Isn't that right, Chadwick?"

The prince's eyes stayed pasted to mine as he gave his aunts a heavy nod, as though he was fighting through tar to manage it. Only, his gaze into me spoke of more than mere curiosity. I knew that look, that concentration. He was trying to reach into my mind—to find the truth—yet he was frustrated I kept him out.

His gift was of the present as mine was.

I kept hold of the shield, thankful I had conjured it in the first place.

"You can read minds," I breathed out.

He shifted his weight as his aunts simultaneously slid in front of me to obstruct my view of him once more. Shutting their gate tightly.

What a coward he was to hide behind them. A beautiful, brilliant coward.

"How could you possibly know that?" one witch hissed at me.

I looked away to give the appearance that I was shy or modest or whatever they wanted me to be. Then I looked back to tell them my secret. "I know because I can read minds as well."

The creak of their gates creeping open.

Mindreading was rare, even among witches. It had taken me hundreds of years to crack the code—years normal witches didn't typically have.

I studied them, testing how hard it would be to steal into their minds.

Truth potion, *a witch muttered in her head.*

I shook my head, trying my best to seem polite as I did so. I was not going to drink a bloody truth potion, even if they shoved it down my throat. It was too risky. I'd have to earn their trust slowly.

"That won't be necessary, Your Highness," I tried. "Anything you want to know is yours. I have nothing to hide."

She stared at me with suspicion in her eyes while her sister glanced back and forth between the two of us. I didn't dare look at the prince. I didn't dare let him in to read the truth.

"Who are you?" the witch who had captured me with her magic asked.

"What's your name, girl?"

A name. A name only my mother had ever called me would leave my lips, setting the stage for our future. They wanted a name that the skies told them was of value. They didn't want my birth name. They wanted a name that brought hope. The name of the stars. The name of their chosen queen.

"My name is Lili."

The name of a flower.

The brows of the witches rose at once. A loud crack sent the invisible rope around me back into the witch's finger, and a flame seemed to burn eagerly in their eyes—the eyes of both witches but not their nephew's.

Prince Chadwick took the slightest step back, so small a mortal wouldn't have noticed. His broad shoulders fell at my words and his lips parted as if to deny the name.

"You can't be," he said.

And even though I knew I wasn't the girl from the prophecy, even though I knew it was all an elaborate hoax, I couldn't help but feel the ache in my tortured heart as he shook his head.

He didn't want me.

He didn't want me to be his fated mate.

But why not?

I'm Still Unstoppable

Chapter 29: *From a Seasoned Queen to a Young One*

Azalea | Present Day | Prison Inside a Pyramid

I jerked awake, sand spraying past the shadow border and into the creeping sunlight as I pushed myself back against the bars. How long had I been asleep? It couldn't have been long. The sun was a foot closer than had been. I hadn't meant to let my guard down, not when it could be my last moments alive. Moments that were instead filled with dreams of my enemies.

Looking down at the flesh of my hands, I yanked down my sleeves. I rubbed the fabrics against my cheek, feeling the burn of my tugging skin as I went. Slobber that the mummy had showered upon me haunted my face—covering it like a plague of boils even though it was likely I had gotten it all off hours ago.

The dream of Lili was pointless. So she wasn't the girl of the prophecy. What did it matter if I died in an Egyptian prison cell in the centre of a pyramid? The knowledge was useless, just like all the superfluous acts that had occurred in the hours since being futile. The darker, unaware part of Connor had dug madly at the sand to try and attack me, to no avail. The sand had merely replaced itself over and over, making it impossible for him to break through the barrier. For hours, he fought with a hunger-induced rage to reach me.

I sat in the corner of the cell, the furthest point from where Connor had crashed against the bars, shoving his snout through as far as he could to get a whiff of my scent, and digging endlessly to cross the barrier only to find more sand. If it weren't for the bars the mummy had placed in the way, I would've been scraps of meat. Now, as daylight approached the edge of my cell, I was doomed to become a statue instead.

There was a time when becoming a statue was preferable to the life I lived: lost, cornered by Florence, trapped without a memory. Yet as I sat there, fighting for an escape, I realised I was finally at a place where I wanted life. My frantic attempts to use my magic, to dig my own way out by hand, to move the sand by any means possible—they all failed. And every scream for help went unanswered. Still, I wanted to live. I didn't want the sun to stop me.

There was so much I had left to do. I couldn't let Florence or Lili win. I couldn't let the mortals burn the world down or my enemies to conquer it. I couldn't become a statue only to abandon my sister, to leave things with Abigail on the rocks, or things with Chad dangling high off a cliff. Perhaps I could wake Connor, tell him my goodbyes for everyone, especially since there was still a chance he could make it out alive.

I rubbed methodically at my neck, my vocal cords scratchy and sore. The part of the sand bars I leaned up against was as solid as steel against my back. The rest of the bars still flowed down as if I was no bother to them. Soon I'd be forced to stand since the sun was mere inches away from my boot.

A snore sounded from the cell next to me as Connor sprang up out of his slumber. Scraps of clothes still covered him. His skin was back to its furless state, but bruises and bright red cuts decorated nearly every inch of it. Out of instinct, I tried to sink deeper into the bars, but he was no longer of any harm to himself or to me. He looked around wildly, his fingers gripping onto the sand to ground himself to his location. When his eyes finally landed on me, I flinched.

"Azalea," Connor breathed out, panting heavily. "What—what—"

He didn't have to ask the full question. His face soured as he realised exactly what had happened. His throat bobbed as he looked around the cell, taking in the supernatural bars that trapped us in, the line between the darkness and the light on the floor. His gaze flew to my arms, and then to whatever exhausted, petrified, sand-covered expression was on my face.

"Did I hurt you?" he asked.

I shook my head, ready to conceal the fear I was giving off. "No," I told him, the hoarse words clawing their way up my sore throat. "Of course not."

His heart rate slowed for a mere second before the reality of our situation sank back in. It started pounding against his chest as if to break out of both his body and this cage. He stood up, adrenaline pumping through his veins as he took hold of the bars and shook at them.

"Has anyone come? How long have we been down here?" he asked, peering into the dark.

I shook my head. "No one," I replied dully. "I can't hear anyone. I can't smell anyone. I don't think there is anyone."

The panic within him exploded. His face turned red with heat. Gripping onto the bars, he tried with all his might to pull them apart, a growl escaping his lips, but no sign of his werewolf strength lit through.

"Hey!" he called out into the void. "Anyone! Let us out! Come let us out now! She can't be in the sunlight! She'll die!" he yelled, standing on his toes in an attempt to see further, but even with the daylight spilling in, the tunnel remained pitch black.

I looked back to the line of light, now an inch away.

"I already tried all that," I told him. "Save your breath."

"The mummy—the chant he was saying," he said, turning back to the cell only to pace back and forth. "It must've been a spell or something to keep the magic out."

I nodded, having gathered as much already.

The sun moved ever so slowly yet so quickly towards my doom. I pushed myself off the ground, my back sliding against the bars on my way up. This was it—my end. My moment to pick a pretty pose before the sun turned me to stone forever.

I swallowed hard, the spit causing my throat to ache as the heat of the sun met my skin before its light could.

"Connor," I said quietly, shivers breaking through the heat. "Promise me something."

"What?" he asked, his eyes focused on our escape rather than what fate lay so plainly in front of us. He stood with one hand gripping the prison bar, the other pushing his hair back.

"Promise you won't let my sister see me," I whispered, the sun bathing the tip of my shoe. "Or Chad. Don't let them see me like this."

"Like what?" he asked, furrowing his brow, but when his eyes landed on me they widened. "Azalea—" he said urgently.

"When the Day Walkers come," I cut off, "tell them our mission. Show them this," I said, placing my hand into my pocket. My fingers gripped onto the black card, then lifted it out to creep along the bars towards him.

Out of the corner of my eye, I watched him shake his head.

"No," he spat out. "Azalea, it'll be all right. We'll get out of here. *Both* of us. We just need to—"

"Connor!" I screamed at him, a sharp pain burning into my toes. I shook the black page, urging him to take it. "Take the damn letter."

I could feel it. I could feel the burn.

He snatched the letter out of my hand before turning away. In the back of my mind I could hear him shouting. I could feel the bars against my back as he shook them, as he called out for someone to come—anyone. But soon my screams drowned it all out.

The sun felt like a thousand fires as it touched me. I looked down as my arms slowly shifted to grey, cracks sprouting up as the sun covered more and more of me. I couldn't stop the screams from coming out as all the pain in the world began my demise.

Abigail's voice sounded in the back of my head. She said my medium-brown skin would help protect me for a short time compared to the other vampires, the ones with fairer skin. But would lasting longer under this torment be better, or would it be worse?

I turned my head towards Connor and saw the fear radiating in his eyes. My reflection glowed in his pupils as my skin slowly hardened, as it turned greyer. His lips moved but I couldn't hear the sound that came from them. A sound louder than his voice— louder than my screams—conquered. And the foreign voice of the mummy was back.

There was a tug over my whole body, and when I blinked, the prison had elongated, leaving the sun's light a foot away. The burn eased, and as I held my hands in front of me, the grey and cracked skin slithered away, replacing itself with the brown skin I had before.

An arm, darker than mine, burst past my side, past the gaps in the bars, and I jumped away from it.

"What a touching moment," a voice said from behind me.

I whirled around to come face to face with the man to which the arm belonged. His brown chest was bare but his body was adorned with golden paint and antiquated jewellery. His head was held high, displaying his power. Gold shimmered off his headdress, the bands on his arms, and his loose pants even though the light had not yet touched them. His expression was cold against the heat of the day.

"Your blood is poisoned by the pale mortals," he said, staring at his hand as it glistened in the sun, the smallest trace of smoke emitting from it. His accent was thick as it rolled off his tongue. "If your blood was purely from Africa, you would've lasted longer before you started to crack."

Every part of me stood still as I stared at him and he stared back, egging me on to reply. Not even Connor stirred in his spot.

"You speak English, I presume," he stated, as if he hadn't been eavesdropping on our conversation—as if my language was the reason I hadn't replied.

I nodded, bumps covering the skin that had just been on fire.

"Then speak," he commanded, tilting his head up so he could look down upon me. "Or shall I command *them* to send you back towards the sun?"

His fingers snapped and the darkness shifted behind him, finally breaking my paralysis. A horde of at least twenty mummies marched into the room, their feet booming against the ground as they surrounded the perimeter and blocked the exit.

Shadows washed over their dirty cloths, sand clinging to the once light fabric, and I wondered if these were the same mummies that had pulled Connor and I through the ground. How many decrepit, lifeless creatures did he possess? They pulled to a stop, pivoting abruptly to face me. It had been their spell that had saved me from the sun, but with a simple phrase uttered in their ancient Egyptian language, they could send me right back into the scorching heat.

Connor growled at the clothed figures, the werewolf inside him still prominent even in the day. My gaze shifted back to the man in front of me, the Day Walker who had just threatened to have his mummy guards continue to test my fate. I didn't know how to play my cards—whether I should argue the state he had put Connor and me in or whether to play nice. What was there to say to the vampire who held you hostage in a cage where only his mummies' powers could work?

I looked back at the Day Walker's arm, still sizzling in the light, the faintest shade of grey tinting his beautiful skin, before I spoke.

"And what is it you'd like me to say?" I asked. He had all the cards in his hand now. "Beg for our freedom? I did that all night long and it went ignored. You know I'm not your enemy yet you choose to be mine."

"'Not your enemy'," he mocked with a grin. His smile grew to reveal his fangs, white as the snow he had likely not seen in some time, not while hiding in his pyramid, trapping people who could be his allies. "The world is my enemy after everything they've taken from my people—pillaging, raping, enslaving—erasing our culture because they believed theirs was better. I don't need the British, or anyone else claiming to be my friend."

"I'm not asking you to forgive the horrid things of the past," I told him.

"We're here to ask your help to prevent more evil from happening," Connor added, gripping tightly to the bars as if he wished it was the Day Walker's neck in his hands.

"The answer is no, and it always will be," the man sneered. "You think you're the first to try and pull us to a side? Well, you're wrong."

"I know I'm not," I told him bluntly. "Cristin and his wife, Abigail, have come several times. Even Florence has given it a go, but thankfully he, too, failed to persuade you." He knew precisely who I spoke of. There was no use explaining further.

"You're ignorant to think we'd help you," he roared, pulling his hand out of the sun. He paid no attention to his skin as it healed. He inched closer and closer as grey smoke left his skin, advancing on us, his rage near its maximum height. "The men in Europe have done nothing but attempt to ruin us. And you," he said, turning to me, his eyes red with hate. "Your kind is no better. You've let them win by mixing with my kind."

"We agree," Connor said, and the Day Walker leaned back ever so slightly, caught off guard. "The people of Africa have suffered far too much. You shouldn't forget that or leave it in the past, but you should fight to make sure it doesn't happen again."

"The pale-skinned Night Crawler, Florence, will leave us alone," he growled back.

I tightened my fist. What was with these arrogant males like him and King Eyeron that made them think they'd be safe when the rest of us rotted in the ground? Heat ignited in my core like magma.

"He'll leave you alone until it's no longer convenient to him. If you choose not to help our cause, then you're equally as guilty as those who are against us."

The man opened his mouth to fight back but the voice of a woman cut him off.

"Silence, my dear Pharaoh," the voice said. "The vampire-witch speaks with reason."

It was my turn to be caught by surprise as a beautiful woman with shimmering bronze skin stepped forward. Her black and blue makeup highlighted her blue eyes, coming to a sharp point at the ends. A golden headpiece wrapped around her head with an ornament coming down between her dark brows, matching the gold of her neckpiece that spread over her breasts, leaving her stomach bare. She had golden lines that covered her face in a geometric pattern that matched her husband's, and a long tan skirt that trailed down to the ground in a flawless array.

"I'm Sadiq, Queen of the Sand and Pyramids, Mother of the Day Walkers," she introduced herself. "I've heard so much about you. Forgive my husband. He's set in his ways, but lucky for you,

I don't always follow his lead. I set my own path. Cristin and Abigail are dear friends of mine."

She turned her head to signal the mummies. With a whisper of his breath, the one nearest us spoke a chant. Then, as if the sands of time had finally run out, the last grains that had been flowing between us crashed down with a whoosh.

I still didn't feel entirely free with an army of mummies and the pharaoh there. Connor and I exchanged glances before I took a step further from the sun.

"Thanks," I told her anyway, and she gave a nod.

"Look, I know you've heard the spiel several times over," I said, glancing over at the pharaoh's hard glare then back to Queen Sadiq, "but we need the Casters and Night Crawlers that we can trust to help us, and you are high up on our list."

She studied me carefully, pursing her lips, her eyes scanning over me with precision, the same way a Caster might if they were attempting to read my mind.

Her lips parted to shed more of her beliefs. "Sometimes it's best to protect your own people, and them alone," she told me sternly, and my heart fell. "From a seasoned queen to a young one, know that there are times the whole world cannot be saved."

Her words took me aback, and I shook my head at her. "I'm no queen," I told her. I didn't hold that power. It would be unfair to pose as one. "But everything in my soul tells me that fighting against Florence is the right thing to do, and that's what I have to follow."

"'No queen,'" she repeated, raising her brows. "Our tellers say the stars speak to the contrary. If anything, you're the acting queen, and if not official, then you'll become a queen soon."

Fortune tellers.

I took in the feel of the title she'd given me—a word that should frighten me given my current relationship status with Chad—but for some reason the word didn't bring shivers to my core or fear in my heart. Something about it felt right.

There was a light scraping as Connor's feet shifted against the sand.

"We didn't come to threaten you," he told them. "We want your help as well as to protect you."

"We don't need your protection," the pharaoh glowered. "We don't need your help, or your money, so you'll find you have nothing to offer."

"Perhaps after you read that letter," I started, angling my head towards the black envelope in Connor's hand, "you'll see we have something else of value to offer."

Connor held the letter out to the queen, but with a buzz through the air, the pharaoh snatched it from his hand. His neatly trimmed nails clawed at the envelope, tearing it open and grabbing out the parchment within. He froze in confusion before letting out a growl. Flipping it over with vigour, he looked at the back and then thrust his hand at me.

"There's nothing on this," he yelled, shaking it angrily.

Ah, not a surprise.

"Only those who truly believe in our cause can see it," I replied.

Before my fingers touched the page to retrieve it, his queen took the letter from him with a gentle hand. Her eyes scanned back and forth over the letter, taking it in with a light smile. Then they flew up to return my gaze.

"It seems he is blind but I offer you my ears," she said. "I'll meet with this king of yours. It just so happens that your gift is exactly the thing I seek."

She held her hand out to shake on it and I took her delicate hand in mine.

"What is it?" the pharaoh demanded. "What is the gift?

But she ignored the question, looking only at me, and my heart lifted, knowing the answer.

It was friendship. The queen of the Day Walkers was going to listen to our plea in the name of our new friendship.

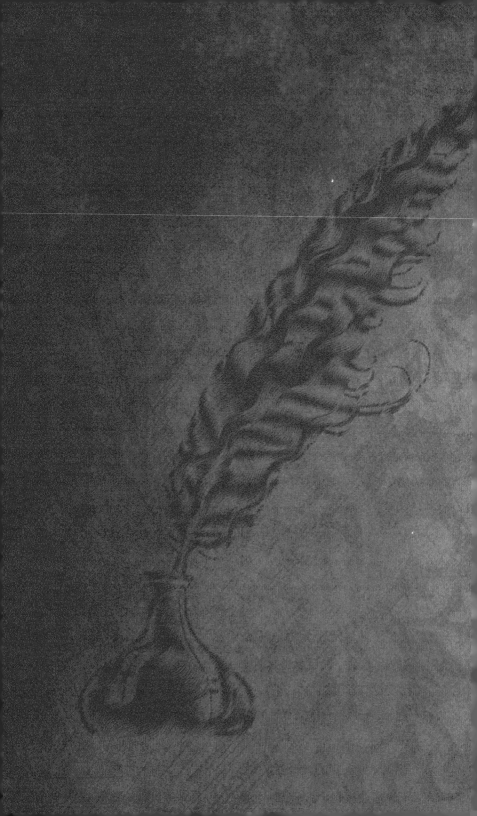

Chapter 30: Invitations

I followed the sound of Chad's heartbeat and the smell of his
sweet scent up eight sets of stairs, right to the office I had
found him in last. He stood at the same table with a straight
back, a quill in his hand as he wrote with magical ink atop more
black parchment.

A flood of fairies and gnomes fell into the room, weaving their
way around it, balancing stacks of black envelopes with their
magic, and then exiting once more. Names were written upon the
envelopes in silver swirls, one of which spelled out "Queen
Leira."

"I heard about Egypt," Chad said, hardly slowing his writing.
"Nearly killed by mummies, a werewolf, and the sun in just a few
short hours."

I held back a laugh. I knew precisely what he was getting at.
He wanted me to admit I needed him. But I was too stubborn.

"Yet I'm still alive," I replied instead.

"That you are," he admitted, dotting an 'i' with more force
than the others. "Though you're going to have a hell of a time
stopping me from coming with you on your next suicide mission,"
he rubbed in.

I rolled my eyes, not bothering to mention there was nothing he could've done in that Egyptian cell, not once our magic had been blocked. But it didn't matter what I said. It wouldn't deflate his ego.

"What's all this about?" I asked, gesturing around to all the chaos.

"We're having a meeting," he said shortly, glancing up from his writing to gesture towards the fairies and gnomes before his quill set back to work.

I stared at him blankly. "We are, are we?" I asked, taking a better look at the small creatures milling about. There were hundreds, if not thousands of letters.

What meeting exactly?

"Yes, a meeting with all the Casters and Night Crawlers I— what was it again? 'Failed' to bring to our side?" he asked, posing his brows quizzically at me in conjunction with the rhetorical question.

Only problem was, would my words come back to help me or bite me?

"Sounds pleasant," I said, concealing for only a second that I didn't mean it. "A big meeting where all the creatures who wish each other dead meet in one grand location, ready to make that dream come true."

"Did you have a better idea?" he asked. His green eyes finally met mine to drill into my soul. "Perhaps you'd like to hop up here to discuss the matter further?" he posed, running his hand along the wooden surface of the table—the table we had nearly had hot, angry sex on not 48 hours ago.

Heat crept up my cheeks as I stared back at him, eager not to look at the small magical creatures that fluttered about. I watched his lips stiffen as they fought off a grin.

What an arrogant ass.

"How did it go with the Day Walkers?" he asked, slicing through the tension with a knife. "You know, *after* they took you as their prisoner?"

Something he was clearly not going to let slide.

I held up my chin. "The pharaoh was still opposed," I said, remembering the defiance he wore plainly on his face, "but the queen could see our message. She's agreed to listen to you."

"Splendid," Chad said cheerfully, shuffling a stack of finished envelopes before handing them off to a gnome. "I'll send an official invitation off to Queen Sadiq as well."

But there was something else that didn't sit well in my core.

"Where will this meeting be held?" I asked.

"Here," he replied simply, picking up his quill once more to finish where he left off. Silver ink flowed effortlessly from the tip, never in need of a dip in an inkwell.

"Here?" I asked, surprise stricken across my face. "At *Schloss auf den Felsen*, where we just brought most of the Loxley Coven?"

This plan couldn't possibly run unhinged. Yes, the Loxley Coven was growing used to Chad and his Caster guards, but inviting countless other Casters into their new, temporary home would be more than overwhelming.

"Yes," he said with a nod, lazily crossing a 't' as if this conversation was of little to no use to him. His voice turned to a whisper to be more discreet. "They weren't very happy about it, but what choice do they have?"

"You already discussed the idea with them?" I asked, a bit gobsmacked that so much had happened while I was away. The plan was already set in motion.

"Yes," he replied, returning to his original volume.

"And were they appalled?" I pressed, clenching my jaw at the shortness of his response and his tone.

"Yes, and some of them are still a bit peeved with you."

I blinked at him. "With *me*?" I burst out. What the bloody hell did I do?

"Yes," he said brusquely, and my fists tightened at the simplicity of the short word he kept spitting out. "It was your idea after all."

"My—" I rolled my eyes. My idea, yes. My sarcastic, stubborn proposition to make Chad feel a sense of failure. Not a real idea.

I took a deep breath to steady myself, and my eyes fell to his hands as he carefully folded a letter into thirds. Green smoke lifted it into the air and into a matching black envelope before sealing itself away. Chad's fingers plucked the envelope out of its floating position and set it back on the table to write "Princess Demriam" on the front. My brows furrowed. He had already written to the queen of the mermaids. Why write to the princess too?

"I figured I should write a more personal letter to Demriam, given our history," he explained.

"Ah, lovely," I countered. A flood of images that the mermaid had sent to me of the two of them in the throws of floppy fish sex clouded my view.

A smile played purely in the whites of Chad's eyes, and I put up my mental shield, remembering to block him from my thoughts.

"You should stop doing that," he said, flicking his wrist to frisbee off the letter to a fairy who caught it in midair before rolling it up tightly, placing the message into a bottle and then corking it. Chad then picked up a fresh piece of parchment and began writing another letter. "Perhaps we should start letting each other into our minds rather than rejecting the other altogether. It might come in handy down the road."

"When will this meeting be held?" I asked, promptly ignoring him. I didn't want him in my head, nor did I want to be in his.

Rather than voicing his answer, he halted his writing and handed me the letter. I took it, eyeing him suspiciously before glancing down to it.

If you can see this message, then you can be trusted. And if you're on our side, then we need your help.

You are cordially invited to a Caster and Night Crawler meeting to discuss a possible union. Should you choose to accept the invitation, it's imperative that you only bring guests who can see this writing.

The rest of the letter went into the details of the meeting, including the date.

I looked back up at Chad, my mouth gaping. "That's in two weeks' time!" I exclaimed. It was so soon.

"Ah. So you can see the ink," he announced slyly, letting his smile shine through this time. "I suppose I can trust you to come along then. Good thing too, as you'll be leading it. It was your idea after all."

I shook my head at the wizard, raising my brows. He was insufferable. "Now I'm beginning to understand why I kill you in this vision of mine," I told him, not bothering to feel any guilt.

He smiled back, looking into my eyes with a gaze both playful yet fierce. "And I'm beginning to understand why I let you."

I explored the features of his face, trying to find a tell for what he meant, but the more I read him, the more I realised that was his game. He wanted me to reach inside his mind. He wanted to let me in.

* * *

Chadwick addressed a formal invitation to Queen Sadiq while I took to writing an invitation of my own. Later that day, after the sun had set, I transported to England, a black envelope clinging to the sweat in my hand.

This one was personal. This one had to be hand delivered.

Castle on the Rocks Pub came into view as I walked the rest of the way, my feet slowing to a stop. Plywood still boarded the windows, eerie as the moon cast shadows of the building over the otherwise dark street. It was quiet tonight. No rioters lining the pavement, no electricity flickering within the street lights, no hum of magic anywhere besides the magic I held in my fingertips. Quiet except for one other heartbeat.

Nearing the alleyway, I focused my eyes on the dark and my ears on the heartbeat. It quickened as a man looked up at me, skipping a beat as hope flushed his face. He took me in with squinted eyes, and that hope faded away.

"Oh," he said sombrely. "I thought you might be…"

His voice trailed away as he looked down to his hands, rubbing them together as his arms rested on his knees, sitting against the dirty stone wall. He faced the wall that still held traces of blood, a scent the mortal couldn't smell—a colour now faded away. The blood of his daughter.

I placed each foot carefully in front of the other as if I would frighten the man away. How many visitors did he get here? How many people tried to speak with him—convince him that waiting here for her was a lost cause? I wondered if I would be the last.

Finding a spot about a metre away from him, I sat down on the hard ground, the cold seeping past my dress and sending a chill through me. I forced my eyes to scan the wall—to remember the way Florence had pressed the woman against it—her blonde hair, the scream that escaped her lips as he took a bite from her neck, a scream so short before it was replaced by the cracking of her skull.

It was one of my very first visions. A scene that played in my nightmares for weeks after. It was one of the many reasons I would hate Florence forever, and one of the many reasons I pictured killing him on a constant loop. He came to Loxley Lair, not for their ideals and peaceful way of life but because of their diversity. Other covens like Downy Lair didn't mix with creatures who weren't vampires. But Leo and Charity invited the other Night Crawlers in. He was there to build an army, and after some members of our coven hadn't been able to see the writing on the black paper, it would appear he had succeeded. He didn't have the ideals of peaceful people. He didn't have the good morals to let innocent people live. He had the motives of a killer.

The man shifted next to me, his dark blond hair rustling against the stone, hair he had passed on to his daughter. I took in his discomfort, the way he cringed away from me, knowing I was only going to make matters worse.

"I saw your daughter the night she disappeared," I said softly, easing into it. He didn't flinch. I doubt I was the first to say it to him. The pub had been so busy that night. "And I'm not a parent myself," I went on, "but I do have people I hold dearly—people I never want to have a last breath—people I'd fight to the death to save and never believe were gone unless I saw it with my own eyes. Because of that, I owe you an explanation for what happened to your daughter."

The former prime minister's head jerked up so he could stare at me with wide, haunted eyes, and my chest clenched against the woe I was about to cause him. I swallowed, bracing myself for his heartache.

"Do you know where she is?" he asked, his hope tearing me apart. "Do you know where they took my little girl?"

He was going to close himself off when I told him. He was going to hurt so much more when I took the hope away, but it was false hope. It wouldn't help for him to hold onto it.

"It was over quick," I told him, the crack of her skull smashing into my ears. "It was over before she knew what he was."

"Who?" he asked, his voice cracking on the word, disgust on his tortured face.

"You've seen his face," I told him, shaking my head as I looked back at the wall. "I think everyone's seen his face—the vampire who's trying to take over the world."

I could feel his heart rip into shreds.

What could I say to him? That I would've stopped the vampire from killing her? From drinking her blood? How could I? It was my first hunt—the night I had first met Chad—considered taking his life so I myself could have a meal. If I had, there would've been two bodies to bury that night.

"His name is Florence," I decided to say, "and he's vile. He hunted me in the middle of the night. However, instead of using me solely for blood, he used me in another way. He bit me, and he turned me into a vampire as well."

The former prime minister studied me before realisation dawned on him.

"I've seen your face on the news too," he said. "You work with him."

Apparently, he hadn't seen my attempt at taking over all the screens in the world. Either way, he didn't run. He likely didn't care for life now that his daughter was gone.

I shook my head. "Contrary to popular belief, the woman who's working with him used magic to disguise herself as me—something I'm working to prove but is serving difficult. I hate Florence and I'm going to kill him one day. I'll kill him for me, for your daughter, and for every other innocent person he's hurt."

"Why should I believe you?" he asked, sneering as if he thought I was lying. But I could hear the hurt behind his mask.

"I know where your daughter's buried," I told him, swallowing down the shame I felt.

His arm slipped from its resting place. He squinted his eyes against the dark.

"I know where she's buried because I helped lay her there," I finished. I had to tell him the full truth. My conscience would eat away at me if I kept it in.

I reached out to hand him the letter—the letter that held the information he dreaded most—information that would lead him to his daughter's remains. He stared at the letter like it was a poison to put him out of his misery, tempted yet terrified. I shook it slightly and his hand gravitated towards it like a magnet.

"The instructions to find her are in that envelope," I told him, then I let out a long sigh. "I know you have no reason to trust me, but mortals like you can help us defeat Florence once and for all. In that envelope, written in normal ink are the directions for finding your daughter's body. Go to her. Give her a proper burial." I took another deep breath, steadying the quiver in my lips to let out the next part. "Under the directions is an invitation, only you might not be able to see it. You see, it's written in magical ink, so only people who are trustworthy can see it."

He kept his mouth shut, but I could hear his breathing change—the way he had to force his lungs to work.

"You can't bring your daughter back, but you can help avenge her. So if you can see the message, and if you want to come to our meeting, then we'd love for you to be a part of it."

I stood up and brushed the dirt from my dress.

"I'm really sorry for your loss," I told him. "And I really hope you come."

He didn't give a response, nor did I expect him to, but as I walked away I heard him choke on a sob. My chest tightened, feeling but an ounce of his pain. A moment later, I heard the envelope tear open, and that was all I could ask for.

Chapter 31: Temporary

I sat in my room—my room at *Ypovrýchio Kástro* that was meant to be temporary. I was supposed to go back to my bedroom in Castwell Castle, back with Chad, but the longer I was here the less temporary it felt.

My fingers curved around the air, purple magic flickering from the tips as I tried to unspill a glass of blood. Broken glass glistened amongst the red liquid, a stream slithering its way across the vanity. On my third try, I watched carefully as the liquid worked in reverse, as the glass crunched back together within my time bubble. After the last piece clicked into place, and it looked as if the spill had never occurred, I picked it up and smashed it again.

If I was going to have any luck reversing Chad's death, and producing a time bubble on command, I was going to have to practise every day. Lili was no longer a viable Plan B, and there wasn't anyone else.

After two more successes and the idea to try something larger the next day, I let my mind wander. It focused on the prime minister, on what it would be like to lose someone I loved, and I prayed I'd never have to feel that hurt. Only, it was inevitable. I was a vampire. If I survived this war, if everyone I loved survived, it was still likely I'd outlive Chad, Connor, and Hydie. They'd live longer than a mortal but not as long as I needed them. The thought crossed my mind that Abigail could keep me company in my old age, but it faded as quickly as it had come, sinking with guilt.

It was either Chad or her. One of them had to die. And even if by some miracle, they both survived, why would Abigail keep me company when I hadn't so much as checked on her in her time of need?

I listened as someone's breathing turned from distant white noise to a more steady and local sound, and as the person approached my door, rapped their fingers against it, and waited for my response, the guilt inside me grew even more.

Clutching tightly to the handle, I turned it and pulled the door open. Cristin stood in front of me, just as neat and well-kept as he always was, and it hit me how long it had been since we'd had a proper conversation. His crisp blue Oxford shirt complimented his dark skin, and his khaki trousers still radiated with heat from being ironed, all while I stood with my hair in a mess and sweat dripping down my brow.

He gave a closed-mouth smile as he rubbed the back of his neck.

"Hey," I said as a lame greeting. I should've opened with an apology or grovelling for forgiveness that I hadn't come to see him and Abigail and the children. But an informal greeting was all that fell from my lips.

"Hey," he said back, still wearing a small smile that didn't quite match the awkward expression he held in his eyes. "How was Egypt?"

A repulsive snort pushed its way out my nose.

"You mean after the mummies pulled us through the sand and dropped us from the top of a pyramid into a cell where I almost got turned into both a werewolf and a statue?" I laughed, and Cristin's smile grew ever so slightly at the sarcastic humour. "After that, it was quite peachy. Queen Sadiq came and it all went uphill from there."

He let out a light chuckle. "The pharaoh and his soldiers have always been one for dramatics," he said. "I should've gone with you. I didn't expect him to go through all of that."

I shrugged, happy I was at a place where I could joke about my near-death experiences, safe in an underwater fortress.

"I suppose in times like these, you can never be too careful," I admitted, excusing the Egyptian king's behaviour. "I'd probably drown any sorry tosser if they discovered this hideout," I said, gesturing around us. "But I'm fine. There's no lasting damage, just temporary."

Temporary. That word again. It was all just temporary.

The cold metal of the door knob was still in my hand. I let go of it, not wanting him to think I longed to close him out.

"How are you? And Abigail?" I asked softly. I had to know.

"Oh, ashamed would be a good word for it," he admitted, letting a deep breath out with the words. "But you know Abigail. She appears strong for Noel and Leon, but the guilt is hitting her hard. She worked really hard to forget... *it,*" he settled on, "and that makes her feel even worse."

I remembered the first day I met Abigail, the way she took care of me, bathed me after Florence's bite. She had listened to my pain. Consoled me. Told that my memory loss wasn't the curse I believed it to be.

"Some find that it's easier to not remember the past, so perhaps we should just let it be," she had said. *"There are times in my life I'd give anything to not remember."*

I closed my eyes, breathing in the memory before looking back at Cristin.

She had been talking about taking Chad's mum—taking her life. Madelyn, Queen of the Casters, my singing ghost. Abigail regretted it—for herself—for Chad. It's one of the many things that made Abigail a good person.

"I've been meaning to come by," I told Cristin. "Meaning to and failing. I'm sorry I haven't."

"Trust me," he said, "we understand."

Even though I knew he meant it, it didn't make it right.

"How's Chad handling it all?" he asked, trying to sound upbeat but failing miserably. His shoulders fell. "I mean, he already had too much on his plate as it was."

My misery didn't curtail. "As horrible as it sounds," I said, bracing myself for the truth, "I haven't checked in on him either. Not since the day we found out at least."

Surprise flashed across Cristin's face before he washed it away. He shook his head. "I'm sure he knows you still love him," he replied, placing his hands behind his back like he was a soldier at my door, telling me my loved one had passed away in the war.

A laugh fell from my lips as my cheeks heated, but I nodded anyway. "Yes," I said quietly. "Perhaps he does."

Cristin pivoted his head to look behind him, and I wondered why he was really here. Was it to find out about Egypt? Was it to see how I was doing? Or was it something else?

"I know you're probably busy," he started again, "but I was wondering if you could help with Leon."

He looked back at me, a plea in his eyes that brought worry to my chest.

"Yes," I spat out automatically. "Of course. What is it? Is something wrong?"

I was so out of touch, even with the children. I had been neglecting my duty of teaching them magic—even protective spells they may need one day soon.

"Well," Cristin continued, "Noel said he's been having nightmares. He won't go to sleep. We've tried silly mortal methods like melatonin and lavender soaps to try and soothe him before bedtime, but they haven't helped," he said, the wear of a long day of parenting plain on his face. "And I know you have a bit of experience with bad dreams, so I was wondering if there was anything you could try to ease his mind."

Ah. Nightmares. Yes, I was quite familiar with those. Cristin once had the luxury of waking me up from one when we all lived at Loxley Lair.

I gave an encouraging smile. "You and Abigail are doing an amazing job with them," I told him. "Yes, let's go see how Leon is doing."

As we neared the children's bedroom, the gentle scent of the lavender soap wafted past, and I resolved to take a hot bath myself later on. Kana's spiderwebs mapped out a game across a corner of the room. A small, dimmed light floated in the air, lighting the space just enough so I could make out the figures that lay there. Soft snores came from Abigail, Noel fast asleep next to her, wrapped in her arms. In bed next to them sat the small boy, the blanket drawn tightly up to his neck, and fear in his eyes. His shoulders relaxed a bit when he saw me. I stepped lightly through the room and sat on the edge of the bed.

He had his own room. He had his own bed. But the few short years he had lived on this earth had left him afraid.

I spoke to him the way I always did.

Hi, Leon, I thought towards him with a warm smile. *Cristin said you've been having nightmares. I was wondering if I could have a look.*

I hovered my hand over his head, waiting for his permission. As usual, no words came from his lips—just a small nod.

The instant my hand touched his forehead, screams filled my mind. A thousand screams, a thousand tiny faces, a thousand nightmares.

My hand flung itself back, but even as the room came back into view, and as my lungs struggled to catch their breath, I could still hear the echo of screams—the echo of children.

I fought to put on a brave face and noticed Leon studying me carefully, waiting for answers or perhaps waiting for a remedy. But it hit me. He wasn't even four years old. Not even four, yet he was still burdened by dreams of torture, as if he hadn't already suffered through enough. Suffered into silence.

His small hand wormed itself into mine, and he squeezed it as if telling me I'd be all right. I squeezed it back.

Have I ever told you about my dreams? I asked him.

He shrugged his shoulders.

I used to have dreams or memories of how horrid my father would treat me. Then I started having dreams about you and Noel.

He nodded, squinting his eyes in wonder, waiting for me to continue.

Chad once said there was a reason I was having my nightmares, I told Leon, *and as much as I hate to admit it, he was right. They led me to my sister and they led me to you. And you know what?* I paused, his eyes staring at me with wonder. *I think those children in your vision need to be found too. Perhaps that's why you're having them—perhaps you were meant to show them to me.*

He furrowed his brow, and I shook his hand gently.

If it's all right with you, I'd like to try and take these dreams of yours. Perhaps I can help those children, and you can get some sleep?

Leon's eyes wandered over to his sister and Abigail as they slept peacefully, to Cristin as he leaned against the doorway, and then back to me before he nodded.

I leaned my head against his, and thought back to the way Chad took away my dreams when we were in America—the way he took away my nightmares to protect me from the wendigo that lurked nearby, threatening to enter my dreams. I channelled that same calm into Leon's mind and in return, the screams seeped into mine. They pleaded and cried so loudly as I watched tears flow from their eyes.

I blinked, and my own tear fell. Leaning away from Leon, I wiped the blood tear away and took in the relief and exhaustion that now coated the little boy's face.

There, I thought towards him. *Now you'll be able to sleep.*

A small smile formed on his lips, and I returned it immediately before giving him a stern look.

Have you and Noel been practising your transportations in case of an emergency? I asked.

He shrugged, a bit of playful guilt causing him to shrink down.

It's important. You have to practise. How about the shields I taught you? Have you been practising those?

This time Leon nodded. He moved his fingers in a circle above him, and though I couldn't see anything, I could feel a tingle of magic.

His magic was invisible.

Before I could give it more thought, Leon opened his mouth, and for the very first time, I heard him speak.

"Goodnight, Azalea, " he whispered in the sweetest voice before turning over and closing his eyes.

My eyes widened before they flew back to Cristin, who smiled at me.

"Thanks," he mouthed, and I nodded back, a smile on my face as I got up and we both left the room, closing the door behind us.

"We want to bring the children to the meeting tomorrow," he said, and I stared back at him, the dim light in the corridor casting shadows across his face.

I wasn't sure if it was safe, but I knew they'd have several people there to protect them.

I nodded. "It'll be good," I decided. "We have to show the others that Night Crawlers are capable of loving Casters, and not just in a romantic way but real familial love. Besides," I added, "I know you and Abigail will protect them like you always do."

He gave me a warm smile.

"Goodnight, Azalea," he said. "Don't be a stranger."

I watched as he walked down the corridor away from me. I thought about the screams, about Florence, Abigail, and the meeting, and a wave of fatigue washed over me. Making my way back to my temporary bedroom, I decided to pick out an outfit for tomorrow and then get some rest. Unfortunately, the task was far more daunting than it needed to be. After narrowing the choices down to two dresses, I tapped my foot anxiously, staring down at them as they lay across the bed. They were both long and beautiful, but one was black, Victorian-styled, and gothic, while the other was light, whimsical, and cheery.

A whoosh of magic filled the air, and I turned to see Chadwick, his green magic swirling around him.

"Azalea," he greeted with a nod as his shining green eyes soaked me in.

My stomach leapt. I missed those eyes. I missed his voice. As much as he frustrated me to no end, it still lifted me up. It had been days since I had seen him. We were both busy preparing for this meeting, yet we still had no clue how it would turn out.

"It's good to see you," he said, full of warmth as he stared into my eyes.

I shook my head, a smile forcing its way onto my face. "As much as I hate to admit it," I challenged, "it's good to see you too."

His smile grew but his jaw tightened, a failed attempt at hiding it.

"The mermaids have agreed to come," he informed me, a pinch of cheer added to his tone.

"My, oh my," I teased, picking up both outfits from the bed and walking over to a full-length mirror. As I took turns holding both of them in front of me, I added, "That must've been some letter to Demriam. A declaration of love to persuade her, perhaps."

Chad shook his head, his grin interrupted by his ajar mouth as he looked at me with disbelief I could be so cheeky. I watched his reflection as he took a few steps towards me until I could feel his warm breath across my cheek. His eyes flickered back and forth between mine.

"You know there's only one woman I'll be in love with for the rest of my life," he dared to say, and it was my turn to be stunned into silence.

I let my eyes fall from his, flustered as blood rushed to my cheeks.

"What do you think?" I asked, looking back to the dresses, eager for a distraction. I put the light one under my chin. "For this grand meeting, shall I dress as a witch, or as a vampire?"

Slowly, he reached around me, his arm grazing mine, and he held onto the fabrics of the dresses. Green magic swirled around them, and both dresses vanished from my hands to be replaced with a shimmering teal gown and a silver crown.

Then his eyes met mine in the mirror once more, his lips brushing lightly against my ear.

"You shall dress like a queen," he whispered, and I prayed he couldn't read my mind.

I'm Still Unstoppable

Chapter 32: Invisible

*T*he doors burst open and my mental shield locked into place out of habit. I turned around to see Prince Chadwick as he strode in. A smile lit his green eyes, a slight hop in his otherwise strong and steady steps.

"I just finished the guard briefing," he said cheerfully. "They've heard rumours that the people wishing to start the war are in New Zealand. I have a hundred men travelling there as we speak to scope things out."

False, I thought to myself, making sure my mind was completely closed off and safe from his talents. His enemy lay right before his eyes. He was just too blind to see it.

"That's wonderful," I chimed in, knowing full well it would be a dead end.

He immediately set to work, reading the list I had been working on. The years I had spent on this godforsaken earth provided a wealth of knowledge. Enough to make it seem like I had connections. Enough to keep him and his aunts interested in me.

I studied the lines on his face, the way they morphed from a giddy charm to pure focus on the information before him. Even with an impending war, he embodied kindness and warmth. Would the war steal that from him? Would he kill me if he discovered who I truly was—what I was? Or did his kindness make him weak?

"This is brilliant, Lili," he told me, grinning over the paper, his eyes locked to it.

"Cheers," I replied, pink flushing my cheeks.

A compliment.

How rare it was for Florence to give me one. The sound of it flowing off Chadwick's tongue sounded foreign to my ears.

I glided over to a floating map, hoping to shield my face—trying to harden my heart. I didn't need compliments. I needed to gain his trust.

"Each of these points on the map is one of my contacts," I told him before pointing to a few of them. "There's a powerful elder witch in Russia, the Witches of the West, separate from the AWC, then there's the Greenland Genies, and the Warlocks of the South," I said, moving my finger to each of them in turn. "We could go to them together if you'd like. Once you speak to them, I know they'll have as much faith in you as I do."

Chadwick let out an unconvinced laugh, joining me at the map. "I wish you were right," he replied, "but it's hard to convince the world a war is coming when the only major signs of it are mortal disappearances and the stars." He shook his head as if it were a pipe dream. "Not every Caster studies the stars and even less choose to believe them. Half will think I'm mad. The other half will think I'm hunting for glory."

"But you're not," I said firmly. "And they'll see that, I promise."

I lifted my hand to hold his, and the feel of it shocked me. Warm. So warm, soft to the touch, gentle... Florence's hands were the opposite. They radiated frost and rage.

Chadwick squeezed my hand tightly, his eyes shining as he smiled down at me, and for a second, I wished he wouldn't let go. I could hold on, I could savour that touch—the touch of someone who didn't want me purely for what I held in between my legs or the power that came with hundreds of years of life.

But all too suddenly, the prince let go of my hand. The smile faded from his eyes, and like a spell, the pleasantness that had filled my chest vanished. He moved over to a tall bookshelf and let his fingertips trail along the spines before lifting out a book he found favourable.

Envy filled my chest. Envy over a damn book.

Chadwick cleared his throat. "We have access to the future," he said loudly, "which means we have the chance to stop the enemy before they've begun. How many Night Crawlers can say that?"

Oh, you'd be surprised, *I thought to myself. Me, being one. Or did I count as a Caster? Neither side had ever accepted me.*

Chadwick spoke of the future like it was a clear path, yet it was not. Yet even with the infamous prophecy looming over, the future was dark, it was foggy, and its winding road led to even more uncertainty—like who he himself was destined to be with.

Even with all the information I had fed him, he made no move to proclaim me as the woman from the prophecies. Perhaps he didn't think I was good enough to lead the Casters. Not special, not important enough. Who knew? I was meant to get close to him, convince him I could be his queen, but I was getting nowhere, and I couldn't figure out why. It was easy to make Florence lust for me. It was easy to make him touch me, pleasure me, even with his stupid little vampire-wench in the picture. But Chadwick? No. He was always just out of reach.

With one hand, I plucked an open book from one of the surfaces, ready to busy myself elsewhere. With the other, I felt as a stream of clear magic left my fingers, just as invisible as I was as it forced the parchment I had been writing on to roll up into a scroll.

My mother once told me every Caster had their own colour, their own swirls of magic. I still remember the pale expression she gave me when I had whispered I didn't have one—the red tears I spilt over being different in yet another way.

I wondered what colour Chadwick's magic was. If it was blue like a calm sky or yellow like the warm sun. If I had a colour, would it be black like my soul? Or perhaps red like the blood I fed on? I hoped it would be pink. I liked pink.

"My aunts say you must stay for dinner," the prince commented lightly, but in a way that made it seem like it was a question rather than something he'd actually force me to do.

My stomach dropped at the idea. Atrocious. Not again. Chadwick I could handle, enjoy his company even, but his aunts were as putrid as the mortal food they expected me to eat. Last time I barely ate, chalking it up to keeping my figure, but how many times could I use that excuse before they saw right through me? I preferred, a thousand times over, to drink their blood instead. But of course, I had to give in.

"That's awfully kind of them," I said, mimicking the way his fingers had held his book, keeping my eyes glued to the cream pages. "The duchesses have been nothing but kind to me."

"They rather like you," he informed me.

My eyes shot up and my insides fluttered as I noticed he was staring straight at me. He was telling me what his aunts thought, and nothing more. I decided to push.

"And what do you think of me?" I asked, tilting my chin to the ground but staring up at him as I edged my way closer.

His face fell ever so slightly and I fought against the sadness in my heart—the sadness his expression forced me to feel. He didn't want me. Would he ever? Could I convince him?

"I think you're brilliant, Lili," he said, looking away from me. "I do, I just—"

"Don't trust me?" I guessed. What the fuck was it?

He shook his head. "It's not that," he replied simply, but his lips shut as though he couldn't explain further.

So I pushed once more.

"Perhaps you don't think the stars are talking about me," I suggested, shame coating my face as I took another step towards him.

"My aunts think—"

"But what about you?" I asked, cutting him off. I was now close enough that I could touch him if I wanted—if I was so inclined. "What do you think I am? Part of a prophecy? Or a distraction from your true fated mate?"

He stood in silence and I hated him for it.

Speak, *I wanted to scream into his mind, but I couldn't risk letting him into mine.*

I reached out and placed my hand on his chest, my heart racing as if it were a dare.

Only, it was more than a dare. It was fate at its finest—fate interrupted. If this didn't work I'd have to try a love potion on him. Or was he wise enough to know better than to fall for it?

He lifted his head, showcasing his learned pride from being a royal, but I knew a rejection when I saw it. I'd have to take the answers from him. I'd have to steal the reaction I wanted if he wouldn't give it freely.

He went to take a step back, but I knew his guard was down, and I seized the opportunity. I gripped onto his shirt before he could leave me.

"Then perhaps a kiss could give us the answer," I told him, staring straight into his green eyes, and before he could voice his rejection, I pounced.

My lips crashed into his and I could feel something inside me. Not a thirst for his blood, nor a hunger for his power, but a deep wanting—a longing for him that I didn't even know I had.

For what felt like an eternity, he stood there in shock. I couldn't tell if he hated having my lips on his or if he wanted more. The mystery left me terrified to my core. But then in one swift motion, my doubts were washed away as his hands grabbed onto my waist, and he pulled me into him.

He was kissing me back. He was kissing me, and the world around us, with all its troubles, was melting away.

But just as I thought I had him, I felt him grow cold against my skin. He jerked back, and our connection was broken.

"Lili, I'm sorry. I shouldn't have done that. I—" He stopped. Horror struck his face. His beautiful face that had just ran his lips all over mine but was now marred with regret.

I could see the answer on his face, the reason he had pulled away, and if I wanted to, I could've infiltrated his mind to confirm it all, but a knife twisted in my gut as he displayed the truth so clearly.

He would not fall in love with me.

He was in love with someone else.

The thought choked me. I was frozen. I couldn't ask him if it was true. All I could do was crumple up and die as he stared at me with pity—pity because he would never want me the way I wanted him.

"Lili," he said, but his soft voice was a grain of sugar amongst a sea of poison.

He took my hand in his, ready to force-feed me the reality of it all, but I yanked my hand away. The rough movement wasn't proper—it wasn't a fit response when the Prince of Casters was trying to apologise, but I couldn't help it.

He dropped his hand. His mouth shut as he placed both hands politely behind his back—a perfect gentleman taking the hint that I didn't want to be touched. But his gesture made it hurt all the more.

Touch me again.

The shield in my mind sprang a leak, water bursting past a rock barricade, ready to flood straight into Chadwick's mind, but I quickly plugged it from spraying out. My breath caught as I let it out, coming across as a crazed laugh, but there was no joy in my heart. No joy for knowing I was unwanted by yet another.

"I should explain," he said, his arms still tucked behind him, his posture perfectly straight yet softened as though his whole body were apologising.

I shook my head, praying against all odds that he wouldn't. Keep it in your head, *I pleaded.* Lock it away and I'll pretend this was all a dream, *I thought, but the thoughts crashed against my shield, keeping them as my own. Thoughts he'd never get to hear.*

"Your Majesty," I said quietly, giving him a faux smile. "You of all people don't have to explain yourself."

"A leader, of all people, should explain their actions," he replied, a correction in the most gentle fashion.

My lips tightened as my gaze fell to the floor before looking back at him.

He took a step closer to me as if no longer afraid I'd latch onto his lips.

"I think I'm in love with someone else," he said, as soft as a feather brushing against my skin.

And there it was. The words I didn't want to hear.

I felt as my heart plummeted 50 stories. Why was it that every man I opened my heart to already had theirs taken?

I forced out another small laugh, as genuine-sounding as I could bear. "A man as handsome as you, Prince Chadwick?" I asked, innocently batting my eyes at him. "It shouldn't surprise me, should it?"

His lips shifted to the side. The words spilled out of me before I could stop them, false optimism clawing its way out with them.

"So, what's her name, this lucky lady?" I asked.

For a moment, his mental shield slipped. Thoughts of him wanting to pat my shoulder, to comfort me in a strictly platonic way, flowed into my mind before he realised his error and slammed his shield back into place. But patting my shoulder would happen over my dead body. Instead, I turned away from him, my hand trailing along stacks of useless papers and information I had planted to distract the Caster from my plan. When I peered at him out of the corner of my eye, I saw his expression wither cowardly as his lips parted to admit...

"Her name," he said, "is Azalea."

My heart stopped. My legs failed me, halting me far too abruptly.

You have to be fucking kidding me. A flower.

I could feel him trying to fight his way into my head—to feel my reaction—but I pushed out my shield harder than ever against his magic.

Azalea. It was impossible. There was absolutely no fucking way it was the same girl—the same Caster I had hunted—the same Caster I had given to Florence—the same Caster he had made stronger with a single bite and the blood from his body.

My lungs were capsizing.

I needed to escape. I needed to get out. But I had to make sure...

"A flower," I breathed out, and the gallant prince nodded.

"I'm sorry," he whispered, but I would not take his fucking pity.

I shook my head, my face scrunched into something ugly to hold back the flood. If he saw the red tears, he'd know I wasn't merely a Caster as I claimed.

"No," I told him firmly. "You do not need to be sorry—Your Highness," I added as a clumsy afterthought. I swallowed hard but my spit burned my throat. "Tell me everything," I forced out in a cheery tone, joy wringing my throat like the liar it was. "What's the future queen like?" I asked, emphasising the word.

I could die. I was a fraud. I was a joke. But Prince Chadwick let out a laugh of relief as though he couldn't see through me. That, or he didn't want to read the hurt that was so clearly etched into my soul. The fool was blinded by the love he had given to the wrong girl—given to someone who wasn't me.

"Queen," he laughed, rubbing the back of his neck in a sickeningly adorable fashion. "Well, it's a bit too soon for that, but honestly, she's lovely." He breathed it out like he could hardly believe how god damn perfect she was.

"She's witty, and kind, and far too selfless for her own good," he told me, his gaze lost as if he could picture her there in the flesh.

I forced my lips into a friendly grin as he looked back at me.

He continued to go on and on about how he fancied her, but he wasn't sure if she felt the same way about him anymore. I could only stand to listen to half of his bullshit before being swallowed by darkness.

This was complete and utter codswallop. Florence had mentioned that his Azalea was messing around with a Caster, but the prince of all Casters? I couldn't possibly be so unlucky that it was the same girl.

"And what does this Azalea look like?" I asked, cutting him off. My tone was so buoyant, so friendly as I feigned a lighthearted curiosity. My mask was working in overdrive to hide my spite.

"She's beautiful," he said, looking off into the distance again. "She has these stunning blue eyes, long, dark curly hair, and golden-brown skin that's tan enough to make anyone envious."

The sound of his praises slowly trickled out of my consciousness as I realised how blind I was this entire time.

I had started this. The prophecy spoke of a flower and it was me who was pushing the prophecy into existence. I was the reason Chadwick's fucking flower was going to blossom into the most powerful sorceress of all time. I was the reason she would become a queen and I would lose a war. All this time I was planning on *distracting Chadwick from fulfilling the prophecy. All this time I was trying to get him to believe the prophecy was about me, all while I created the woman myself. It was me who had found her, convinced Florence to change her, even though I knew she was a witch. I was guilty for making her stronger, all so I could make Florence see it was me he was meant to be with. But I had failed. Now, not only was the vampire-witch irresistible to Florence, but she had Chadwick in her clutches too, and she was destined to be the Caster queen.*

The potion to wash away her memories, to make her fear the thought of love or even the colour of the very liquid that would sustain her, it was all for not. She had won the prince's heart. She had fought through it all. I had to toil harder if there was any hope left.

I had fooled myself into thinking I could be the one, the one the stars spoke of. But how could I ever be anything more than the stupid, pathetic, weak girl I was born to be?

Chadwick rambled on joyously. "She's stubborn beyond belief," he said with a hoppy tone, "but it's one of the things I love about her," he finished, and I knew I had to get out.

Love.

He used the word love.

But perhaps there was a chance... I had cursed Azalea to fear the feeling from the beginning. Perhaps she hadn't broken my spell. Perhaps she couldn't reciprocate his feelings for her.

"I'm going to go for it. One last shot at my Valentine's Day ball," he announced, and my eyes flew up to him. "Which you are, of course, invited to—" he added.

"What?" I asked, blinking my way out of my haze.

"You're invited to the ball," he repeated.

"No," I corrected, "the bit you mentioned before that."

"I'm going to ask her to be with me one last time that night," he said.

I forced my shoulders not to slump. Of course he was. He was going to sweep her off her feet and the bitch was going to say yes, curse or not.

Suddenly, I decided to be very busy the night of 14 February, and far away from Chad's stupid ball.

"But I fear that making her my queen might be a lost cause," he said, sadness suddenly seeping into his voice, but it put a ray of sun in mine.

"Why is that?" I asked, perhaps a bit too eagerly.

He shook his head. *"Nothing,"* he replied vaguely. *"Either way, it doesn't matter. I'll let her make the choice."*

But then it hit me. The one reason that truly kept them apart. The same thing I had been hiding from him about myself. One small word trickled into my head.

"Because she's a vampire," I breathed out. He knew.

Chadwick's entire body froze. The blood drained from his face as his warm breath left his fallen jaw.

"How—" he stammered in disbelief.

I shook my head quickly, my eyes trailing away from him and down to the floor.

"Forgive me, Your Highness," I spewed out quickly. *"I didn't mean to invade your mind. It just—screamed out at me."*

Lies. His mind was locked shut against me. I couldn't read it if I pried it open by hand.

His eyes widened but the effort was a waste. What did it matter now if he thought I was powerful? The prophesied queen was already at his fingertips. Perhaps my presence would confuse him a short while longer but he'd see through me soon enough. I didn't matter.

"You'll still stay for dinner, won't you?" he asked suddenly, and my insides shrivelled.

So I endured dinner.

I endured his aunts.

And I endured the bitter feeling in my heart, all while wearing a smile.

Later that night, I found myself in the bath, the water around me cold as the night turned into the early morning hours. I was too frozen to move. So, instead, I stewed in my own misery.

I pondered over all of it—over whether or not Florence knew which Caster Azalea had fallen in love with—over if I should be the one to tell him—if I could've stopped this all from happening if only I had paused to listen to the vampire drone on about her. Instead, I hadn't seen past my own jealousy.

I shook against the glacial waters, staring down at my wrists as I rested them over the edges of the bath. Turning my arms over to reveal the blue of my veins, I surged my magic towards them until a line of blood, ten centimetres long, puckered out of both arms.

Invisible magic.

Just as invisible and insignificant as me.

I watched as the vampire part of me took over, healing the skin quickly, too quickly to allow me to feel all of the sting.

Over and over, I forced my magic to make more cuts into my pale skin—deeper each time—longer—harder—cursing myself for not drinking the blood of the other vampires—cursing myself for not allowing it to slow down the healing processes that my body performed so easily.

Only to watch the cuts heal again and again.

Rage took over the hollowness I had succumbed to. I screamed, scratching and clawing at any part of my skin, the water—red—splashing around me and onto the floor. I stood abruptly from the bath and stalked over to the mirror. In the reflection was the hideous image of myself, the person no one would ever come to love. I watched my features slowly shift out of place and into the woman who had it all.

The exact image of Azalea blinked in time with me, and as I stared at my transformed self, I vowed I would not let Azalea have everything I had worked so hard for. I vowed she would not win.

Chapter 33: Blue

Azalea | Present Day | *Schloss auf den Felsen*

I stood in the meeting hall of *Schloss auf den Felsen*, my hair woven around a modest crown of thin, silver leaves, the teal dress Chad had transformed wrapped around me. Yet I felt nothing like a vampire, nor a witch, nor a queen. Instead, I felt sorrow. I felt as gravity pushed upon my shoulders and pinned me down.

I hadn't tried to see into Lili's past—it came to me in the form of another dream. It floated through my mind as an unwelcome guest, but the sadness within me wasn't due to the kiss. It wasn't a side effect of the hurt and hate I had felt towards Chadwick and Lilith. No—it was empathy for the latter, though she was supposed to be the villain.

The aisle leading to where I sat on a large, extravagant throne was blue. Blue like Lilith's eyes. Blue like mine. One of the many things we had in common. My fingers scratched at the wooden armrest beneath them, moist from the anticipation. Soon, hundreds of people would sit before me—hundreds or perhaps none at all. Perhaps no one would come. Yet even though the idea was daunting, I couldn't focus on the meeting. All I could see was the blue.

There was a shimmer in the empty throne beside me, and I didn't have to look to know Chad had appeared. I didn't have to pivot my head to know green magic swirled around him. All I could feel was Lili's pain as she cut deep into her skin with invisible magic—invisible—just like Leon's, just like I suspect mine used to be. After I had been turned, before I knew I was born a witch, my powers came out in different ways. In the form of candles burning my bedroom ceiling at Loxley Lair. In the form of dreams. Was it our inability to see our own strength that masked the colour of our magic, even to ourselves? Or the depression our pasts held that weighed down on us?

I blinked and looked at the hall around me—formal, grand, fit for the royal Caster king. It was the perfect location for the meeting—owned by Casters yet the current safe house to Night Crawlers—common ground for both worlds to join together and hear what we had to say.

Finally, I looked over at Chad to see him peering at me, studying the lines of exhaustion I no doubt wore on my face.

"Nervous?" he asked in lieu of a greeting, but his voice was soft, worried.

I hardly knew the answer. I could no longer differentiate between all the troubles that suffocated my lungs.

I thought about it as I stared back at the blue carpets. People were still dying. Florence continued to hold the upper hand, and the mortals were still trapped in a dark world without magic. It didn't feel like the word 'nervous' embodied it all.

I lifted my shoulders in a shrug before the weight forced them back down. "The world is so heavy," I replied, not expecting him to understand what it meant, but he placed his hand over mine, stopping my nails from carving into the wood.

"It is," he said, and I looked into his green eyes. "But if history has shown us anything, it's that there's nothing you can't survive, Azalea. You're unstoppable."

The words crashed into my consciousness like thunder. My stomach tightened as if it wished to reject the idea, though part of me absorbed it anyway. I had survived my father, Florence's bite and his wrath. I had survived my own thoughts of suicide, and my shattered heart. I had withstood the sun, the mermaids dragging me deep into the icy waters, mummies sprouting from the sand, and everything else that had tried to end my life. Then it dawned on me. Chad was right.

I was unstoppable.

My hand flipped over and I returned his grip, the feel of his warm hand foreign, yet home all at once. He had lied, yes. He had kept secrets, he had broken me, but as I held his hand, anger didn't rush through my veins. Perhaps it was the dream dulling my other emotions, or perhaps it was the passing time, but the animosity seemed to be washed away. In its stead was something worse, only I couldn't quite place what the feeling was.

A buzz sounded from outside the castle, and I straightened my back as my ears focused. Seconds later came the whooshes of magic and the chatter of low voices.

They were arriving.

Chad took a deep, steady breath from beside me but panic flooded my nerves.

"You should be the one leading," I blurted out. I looked back at him with wide eyes. "You're the king. They don't want to hear from me. They want to hear from you."

"You'll be fine, Azalea," he said, his thumb grazing my hand. "I'll be right here if you need me."

I shook my head as a pit in my stomach formed. "It's not the same," I waved off. "I'll look like a fool if I stop to ask you for help."

Only, instead of support came a light chuckle.

"If only there were a way we could speak without anyone else hearing," he said mockingly.

I stared deep into his eyes, biting my cheek as I considered it. He wasn't wrong...

"I'll let you in my head if you let me in yours," I bargained. If only this once.

He lifted my hand and placed a gentle kiss upon it. *You already have my mind, my hand, my heart...* he said into my head, and blood rushed to my cheeks, though I prayed he couldn't see it.

That was the feeling I had in my chest, right in the place I thought was shattered and then hollowed out—the feeling far worse than anger. It was love. And the thought of reopening that door sent chills up my spine.

The large wooden doors in front of us opened and I grasped onto the distraction. A downpour of water sprouted from the top of the entry, blocking the view to the entrance hall, and magically disappearing as it crashed onto the tile floor. A second later, Hydie, Connor, Abigail, Cristin, and the children walked through it, not a drop of water soaking their clothes.

Chad's body tightened beside me. His eyes were focused away from Abigail as if he were pained to be in the same room as her, but he stayed silent. Not even his thoughts were slipping my way.

The plan ran through my mind on repeat to ease my worry. I was in no danger of the people who were about to enter through that doorway. The waterfall would act as the invisible ink in the letters had. Only those who truly wished to help would be allowed in.

Hydie was in charge of watching people's auras, to see if they changed or were at risk for starting an uprising. Eyeara, the reader of souls, would be using her own skills similarly. Connor, Nigel, and the other guards were strapped with holy water, and Abigail and Cristin were in charge of getting Noel and Leon to safety if need be. Charity and Leo would watch over Kana, the gnomes were in charge of ensuring the identity of our guests, and the fairies would keep watch from perches up above. Every precaution for safety was in place.

From outside, there was a strong gust of wind that rattled the castle's windows before the thuds of large beasts touched down to the ground. A familiar roar informed me exactly who had arrived. The water parted again, this time to reveal Eyeara. She glided through, closely followed by her mother, Queen Aria, Icaron, and a few guards, all a lovely shade of blue. Icaron gave me a nod before each of the elves found their seats.

Soon, the fear that no one would show vanished. Person after person, creature after creature walked through the waterfall unscathed. People who would hear us out. So many faces, both familiar and new—the Loxley Lair members, the vampires Charity worked with in France, Queen Sadiq and a few of her mummy guards, more vampires I didn't know by face or name. Werewolves, manananggals, and gnomes. Several women with eight spidery legs crawled into the room, and a movement in the corner of my eye caught my attention. It was Kana, squeezing Charity's hand excitedly. Jorogumos, just like them.

Koda and his wife walked in next, followed by what had to be at least ten other representatives of the Native American witch tribes. I let out a breath of relief. He had told us they wouldn't help, but they were here. At least they were going to listen.

That's Victoria of the American Witch Council, Chad informed me, tilting his head towards a witch with long black hair. He looked me over as if trying to get a read on whether or not I was open to conversation. When I nodded, he continued on. *The one whose house we broke into when we went to America.*

I remembered it well. *Did you ever free those gnomes in her front garden?* I asked, rather ashamed of myself for not asking sooner.

Of course I did, he said, sounding insulted I would believe otherwise.

Good, I let out, but I said it too quickly. He had to know I meant it. *Thank you,* I added.

It was the right thing to do, he replied. *It's wrong to keep them as trophies, but...* He paused to give me a stern look. *Let's not tell her it was me...*

I grinned at the secret—a secret that helped bring peace to our otherwise conflicted world.

Chad tilted his head towards the next group.

That's the British council, and the Chinese one next. He frowned, his eyes flickering through the crowd as if he realised a vacancy. *I don't, however, see the Witches of the West, nor the Greenland Genies, and the War—*

Warlocks of the South, I finished, staring off to the distance as if I was lost in a trance. Lili's list played in my head. I had just dreamt about it.

Yes, Chad thought slowly, eyeing me with care. *They're the ones I had to speak to the night—*

You were supposed to come with me to get my sister, I finished for him, *only instead, you went with Lili to speak to them.*

Chad's face fell but I smiled smugly.

No hard feelings, I told him, holding up my chin. *But no, they won't be coming.*

Chad furrowed his brows as he waited for me to continue.

I looked down at my hands before returning his gaze.

I had another dream about Lili—and you, I told him, taking heed of my phrasing. I didn't want to think about the kiss, not now, not ever again. *You were looking at a map with all her contacts—a 'powerful, elder witch in Russia', the Witches of the West, the Greenland Genies, and the Warlocks of the South. They're all her contacts. I don't think any of them can be trusted.*

Chad nodded slowly, the memory playing in his own mind. *What about the old witch?* he asked. *Do you think she was referring to Baba Yaga?*

It was my turn to nod, only I didn't fully understand it. It must be Baba Yaga. Lili had referred to her before in these dreams, but if the old woman was on Lili's side, why would she help me? Whose team was she on? Or was she on her own?

The gnomes filed into the room, and immediately, sour faces appeared on many of the Casters. Witches and wizards stared down at the gnomes, scrunching their noses as if they were filth. The gnomes didn't cower. They didn't turn into porcelain as they normally did amongst the witches. Instead they stood as tall as their short bodies allowed them, showcasing their newfound bravery. Even Fendel, who caught my eye from across the room, gave me a wary look, but he sat in a chair that a witch was about to take. He gave her a dirty look as she swept her skirt away from him and was forced to take a different spot. Oh, how far he had come. It was the Caster's turn to take the next step.

There was an uproar of excitement and panic running rampant through the air as more of them filtered in and sat upon the chairs. The room was bursting with colours, skin tones ranging from as dark as night, to browns, to peaches, to green, to blue, all the way to the pasty-white skin of the eldest vampires and milky-white transparent ghosts. It was beautiful, but chaos was sure to ensue.

A gaggle of mortals walked in next, the same fearful look on each of their faces as though they had voluntarily walked into the lion's pit—only far worse. They clung together as if it gave them a chance against the rest of us. The first few I recognized from Castle on the Rocks Pub. The next were both the new prime minister and the old. But after them was a mortal I was nowhere near prepared for.

Wyatt.

I turned sharply to behold Chadwick, trying with great difficulty to mask the anger on my face, only he was determined to avoid my gaze.

Why, exactly, is Wyatt here? I hissed over to Chad.

The stupid king merely shrugged at me before thinking, *I expect it's because he got an invitation.*

Chad was lucky we were in a room full of people I needed to convince I wasn't a killer.

A task you *were in charge of,* I fired back instead of wringing his neck.

What? he asked, feigning innocence before he finally looked at me with a smug smile. *We need mortals on our side. He's a mortal. And thanks to you, his number's in my phone.*

I looked back at the crowd, too furious to meet Chadwick's eyes. When I had run into Wyatt, I got his number to help me remember my past, not to involve him in this new life.

Knowing full well the answer was no, I asked, *And is my ex the only mortal you know?*

Him and my old barmen, he replied lightly. *I think I'm starting to warm up to Wyatt after you tried to burn his whole flat down. Besides, I figured I invited my exes. It was only fair to bring yours.*

I clenched my jaw, doing my best not to scream at him aloud. *And did any of your exes cheat on you and indirectly get you turned into a vampire?*

He hesitated ever so slightly before admitting, *No.*

I settled back into the throne, removing my hand from his to resume clawing at the armrest. *Well then, Chadwick,* I said without looking at him. *I think next time I'll be in charge of invitations.*

From the corner of my eye, I watched as his posture loosened ever so slightly—heard a small chuckle leave his throat as if I had told a joke. *Seems appropriate, My Queen,* he jested.

I felt as my eyes turned red, and I closed them to shield them from the Casters down below. After taking a deep breath in through my nose and out through my mouth, I felt my eyes shift back to blue and reopened them.

Call me that again and I'll gouge your eyes out, I told him calmly, half meaning it.

Which truly would be a shame because I'd no longer get to see how beautiful you are, he told me lightly.

And although I could see he was facing towards me in my peripheral vision, I didn't give him the pleasure of meeting his eyes.

Poppy zoomed through the air, bringing me back to my mission, and whispered into my ear at a magical decibel that only I could hear.

"That's everyone," she said.

My heart sank lower, but I gave her a nod, and she flew away.

The mermaids? I asked Chadwick, scanning the room as if I had somehow missed them, an affair that was not very likely. *I thought you said they'd be here. Is it possible they couldn't get through the waterfall?*

I looked at Chad, his eyes narrowed as they took their own sweep through the hall.

Not likely, he said slowly. *I just hope Florence and Lili didn't find a way to hold them up.* Then his face contorted into what was meant to be a comforting smile, only it wasn't. *No matter. We move forward. It's time to begin.*

Before I could respond, he was up on his feet. The whispers in the crowd died at once. The fearful faces turned to Chad, waiting to see why they were all there and if it was worth it.

"On behalf of those who have put this meeting together," he said loudly, "I'd like to thank each and every one of you for being here. We know the reservations you have, and are thankful you came anyway.

"For those who don't know me, I am the High King of the Casters, Chadwick Castwell, and I'd like to introduce my counterpart, Azalea Kroge," he announced while gesturing in my direction. "She will be speaking tonight."

I tried not to flinch at the last name—my father's—a name I hadn't gone by since I entered this dark world of blood and war.

My body jolted up into a standing position as if I were plagued with sudden stage fright.

It's all right, Chad cooed into my mind, and for a moment I let his soft voice take over my nerves, soothing them before I fully faced the crowd. My lips parted, but a voice from the crowd erupted out before mine had the chance.

"Sorry we're late," a woman said, having just flowed through the water in the doorway. And instantly, I recognised her face— the queen of the mermaids.

Chapter 34: Three Worlds in One Room

Queen Leira walked fluidly into the room, at least twenty mermaids following her. Any fidgeting in the crowd ceased at once—every movement stilled. Not a single breath fell from the Night Crawlers or Casters alike. These women needed no introduction, not with their green-gold skin that morphed into scales, and the way they held their heads high, unashamed of their naked bodies. Though their tails had transformed into long legs, it was clear everyone had either heard the legends or was wise enough to keep quiet as they felt the power radiating from the sirens, even without their song.

Eyes explored every inch of their bodies as they drew closer, and Queen Leira's face split into a proud smile. She took in the Caster nearest her, her eyes eagerly washing over his handsome features.

Annoyance filled my chest as I looked at their appearance—so bold it was unbearable—but then I looked over and saw Cristin cover Leon's eyes and Noel scrunch up her face in disgust, and I had to stifle a laugh. What an absurd show.

"It's been many moons since we've been on this soil," Queen Leira said dramatically, "and there are so many treats that our bodies can't resist."

The man, whose attention she had so thoroughly captured, reached towards her, his arm moving on pure impulse. And though the woman beside him pulled him away, there was a wave through the crowd as nearly every man leaned in their direction. It was like a silent mating call that the mermaids projected everywhere they went.

I watched Connor's eyes glaze over before his face contorted with jealousy. His gaze flickered down to the man's hand, still held tightly by the woman he had come with—like some primal instinct was urging him to attack the man if he tried to touch the mermaid again—like it was a competition.

Unlike the others who had walked through the waterfall, the queen and her court stayed wet as they had already been drenched in water before they arrived. Their salty scent met my nose, reminding me of the ocean water that I had vomited up repeatedly the last time I saw them.

Demriam, princess of the enchantresses and Chad's former lover, flicked her long green dreads over her shoulder to reveal her bare breasts. Her eyes flew directly to Chad, who gave her a firm nod in greeting. He quickly exchanged looks with me, and I didn't have to read his mind to know their appearance made him on edge. His features displayed it clearly.

"Sirens," a jorogumo called out, appalled as her eight hairy legs cringed with disgust. Her eyes met mine, coated with betrayal. "Witches are one thing, but sirens are far worse."

"Why?" Princess Demriam asked in a confident voice, just as smooth and tempting as her mother's, and I realised it was the first time I had ever heard it. She carefully placed one foot in front of the other, drawing deeper and deeper into the crowd, a line of other mermaids slithering after her, parting the way like a giant eel. "Afraid we'll sing you a little lullaby?"

"They're our guests," I said loudly, hoping to ease the tension, but the idea was immediately rejected.

"They're dangerous," another Night Crawler corrected.

"Only if you're not on our side," the Queen Leira taunted, arching a single brow up at the creature.

"Which we are," I said pointedly, "so why should any of us have anything to fear?"

"Why are you even here?" a voice snapped. I followed it to a short man with long black robes and a white beard. A Caster, of course, and he was staring straight at me. "We saw you on the telly the first time. Showing up a second time to announce that was an imposter doesn't make it true. Why should we believe you?"

"You're here because you read a letter in invisible ink," Chad said sternly to the man. "The only people who could read that letter are people who are against Florence. Every single person in this room, including Azalea, has seen the ink. That unites us. We're on the same side whether you like it or not."

"What side exactly?" a manananggal asked, casting a dark look across all the Casters in the room. "As far as I'm aware, the Casters don't want us on their side. That's why they created the division between us in the first place."

"A side that promotes life rather than death," I said directly, and it was as simple as that.

"That's rich coming from someone who drinks blood to stay alive," a male Caster replied, a bitter expression pasted to his face.

"Don't claim to know my story," I replied darkly, "unless you have walked in my shoes."

The man's face stayed sour, but he shut his lips, and I continued.

"Lilith and Florence have banded together to create a world where Casters and Night Crawlers are no longer in the dark—where mortals know we exist. The secret's out. That knowledge is irreversible, but that's not where Lilith and Florence intend to stop. They've gone too far. The death toll is in the millions worldwide. They want to punish mortals for making our kind stay hidden for the centuries. The only reason we've stayed hidden is because mortals have a habit of turning violent towards things they can't understand." I looked across the crowd before meeting eyes with the prime ministers and then Wyatt. Quickly, I looked away.

"Whether it be witches or vampires, or even other mortals with different viewpoints and opinions, they do not ask questions until after the harm has already been done. Instead of helping them learn about our kind, Florence wants to keep them as slaves. His father was Hitler. We've all heard of the hell he created. Well, Florence's sole purpose in life is to outdo his father's work. And it's up to us to stop him."

"That's all great," a witch said from down below. I recognised her as one of the people Chad had mentioned was from the British Witch Council. "But how can you expect us to work together? I refuse to work with the likes of them," she added, casting her eyes over to Vincent, the warden of the Loxley prison, who bared his fangs in return.

Connor, who was apparently over the queen's entrance, responded by taking a threatening step forwards. "If a Caster king can befriend werewolves and vampires, and invite all of us into his home," he said, "then you can follow your king's lead."

"He is an anomaly," Victoria of the American Witch Council reciprocated.

"How about the children then?" I said, waving my hand towards Noel, Leon, and Kana. "Two Caster children have become best friends with a jorogumo. Is that an anomaly too, or are grown adults, such as yourselves, simply ignorant and incapable of loving someone who's different from you?"

"Perhaps they've been brainwashed," she suggested, squinting her eyes angrily at me.

"You know, I can't help but notice there are far less Night Crawlers in the room than there are Casters," someone who must've been a wizard sneered back. "If the other Night Crawlers have joined Florence, perhaps the rest of you are next."

"There are less Night Crawlers here because this castle belongs to a Caster," Chad answered. "Florence is killing anyone who won't join him. People are scared for their lives. Of course more will join him. But it's not only Night Crawlers, it's Casters too. Florence's numbers are growing at an exponential rate. Perhaps some are following them out of desire, but a swarm of *people*," Chad stressed, as it was not just Night Crawlers, "are joining his side out of fear. Fear brings forth weakness and uncertainty. Unity will make us strong. If we fight amongst ourselves, we'll be the ones letting them win."

I nodded in agreement. He was exactly right. "What we've asked you to do by coming here tonight is to stop identifying solely as Night Crawlers, or Casters, or mortals," I added, "and think of us as a team that wants to keep peace in this world and humanity alive. We're all against the world Florence wants, full of death and torture, and that's what unites us. As King Chadwick said, the invisible ink proved that. So did the waterfall."

"That doesn't mean *they* won't put a spell on us," a jorogumo said, scrunching her nose at a witch, probably haunted by the memory of one turning her into the creature she had become.

"It's witches who forced us even further into the darkness," a vampire pointed out. "Years ago, we were a team, united against the mortals, staying hidden together, but you broke that alliance."

"Because your kind are killers," a wizard accused.

"Casters aren't so innocent," Charity said defensively. "Nearly every Night Crawler was once a mortal. And yes, it was mostly Night Crawlers who turned them, but it was a witch who turned me into what I am—all because she thought I wasn't good enough for her son."

"As a punishment for your behaviour, I'm sure," a witch replied, as if it justified the cruel action.

"Because I fell in love?" Charity asked, furrowing her brows at such a conviction. "There should never be a punishment for love."

"Your kind literally eat us and mortals," a mermaid sneered.

"Yet we're supposed to trust a bunch of slave keepers?" a werewolf from Loxley Lair asked, pointing at a gaggle of witches in the seats in front of him. He knew full well how afraid the gnomes were of witches.

"They're pests," a wizard spat out, glaring at the gnomes nearest him.

"What about *them*?" Queen Sadiq of Egypt asked sceptically, nodding her head towards the queen and princess of the oceans. "One song and those sex-obsessed breeders could control all of us."

"How tempting," Queen Leira taunted, her eyes flickering with fire as she stood even taller. "Let's give it a try."

She opened her mouth and a sweet melody spilled out as the room erupted into even more chaos. I felt something tickle my ears and the world became silent. My eyes met with Chad's and I realised he had used his magic to stop their song from meeting my ears or his, just as he had done on the ship. There was a blur of movement as vampires hurriedly covered their ears. A mummy stepped in front of his queen, his mouth stretching unnaturally wide, and I knew he was singing his own curse. The mermaids didn't even flinch. About a hundred colourful shields bubbled into place over the Casters who tried to protect themselves, including a purple one that Noel cast over Cristin, Abigail, her brother, and herself. A golden one that Hydie produced was large enough to surround her, Leo, Charity, Kana, and Connor, who began to claw at the forcefield in front of him. He tried desperately to escape before realisation dawned on his face that he had fallen for the spell. Everyone else who hadn't protected themselves fast enough stood with milky eyes before they dropped down to their knees, their hands raised above their heads to bow down to the sirens.

Queen Leira stalked over to Connor, a cruel smile on her face as she sang and swished her hips back and forth. Her fingers hovered closer to the werewolf and the shield around him. Connors eyes morphed from a grounded awareness to a hungry longing as the queen tested the golden magic's hold. Yet just as her fingers were about to touch the shield, right over Connor's cheek, the plugs in my ears melted away and I opened my mouth to speak.

"That's enough," I said firmly.

And just like that, the song ceased.

Hands clapped to the ground as the hold over the bowing crowd was released.

My eyes were red once more, only this time, I didn't care to conceal them. A shot of surprise blasted through Queen Leira's features as she looked at me, but it vanished, and was quickly replaced with her smug grin.

"You've more than proven your point," Chad said sternly, taking a step forward.

Her eyes flickered over to Nigel and the other guards as they stepped towards her as well, ready to react if needed, but the sly woman raised her hands, posing with a faux innocence. "That's all I wanted," she said with a shrug. Then with one last wink at Connor, she glanced away. "I don't know how we got roped into being part of the Casters anyway. If it were up to me, there wouldn't be any of this Caster-versus-Night Crawler business. It would be the Land Dwellers versus the Ocean Rulers, and you would all leave us alone."

"Good riddance," someone muttered.

I cleared my throat, hoping to ease the tension as several people took their seats once more. "The mermaids are valuable beyond belief. Yes, their song can control you, but they can also put images in your mind," I informed the crowd, trying not to picture the scene of Chad and Demriam that I'd been forced to watch. "The vampires have speed, the witches have magic, the elves have their own powers, and some of the mortals who are here have influence. We're all valuable in our own way. We could be unified. We just have to learn to trust each other."

"Your kind killed our queen," a witch spoke out, as though an alliance was not possible.

My heart froze as my eyes snapped up to Chad so quickly. The breath he took sounded forced before he looked back at me. There was a brave expression on his face but behind it was pain. How could I not have seen this topic coming up—been smart enough to think of an aversion? I wanted to freeze time—reverse it so Chad didn't have to hear those words—so he didn't have to relive his mother's death in front of everyone.

"And who's to say she didn't deserve it?" a vampire I didn't know asked, and just as I thought it couldn't get any worse, it did.

"I am," Abigail said softly, yet there wasn't a soul in the room who didn't hear it. Her big blue eyes shot up to the vampire. She stood from her chair and said loudly, as clear as day, "I can say she didn't deserve it because I'm the one who killed her."

Chapter 35: No More Hiding

Abigail's words paralysed the entire hall. There was a deafening silence. For a moment, I questioned if I had actually heard the words come from her lips. How could she say it aloud? How could she admit it here in front of all these people? The silence clawed through me before Abigail broke it.

"I killed the High Caster Queen, the mother of your king," Abigail said, her voice breaking past the tears she was struggling to keep down. "So I know above anyone that she did not deserve it." She moved closer, taking small, precise steps towards the witch, her sincerity coating her face like a painting. "I took a mother away from her son, and a queen away from her people. It's a sin I will bear for the rest of my life. A sin I would die to erase."

"That can be arranged," a wizard said darkly, not a beat later, as the rest of the room stood in silent disbelief.

"It will not," Chad replied gravely, staring the wizard square in the eye until the man looked away sheepishly.

"She belongs in jail," a warlock claimed softer, knowing Chad's pain.

"She deserves the death sentence," another Caster shrieked.

"That's not your decision," I announced angrily, my fangs threatening to lengthen. Abigail hadn't killed Chad's mum on purpose. She hadn't wanted any of this.

Chad stirred next to me as if he was contemplating what to say. My heart ached for him.

You don't have to defend Abigail. Not here, I told Chad. *The two of you can discuss this away from everyone else.*

But he gave me a sad look and didn't respond.

"She was our queen—" someone blurted out.

"She was *my* mother," Chad interrupted, "so I'll be handling matter. Not you."

Chad's heated gaze made the Caster look away, but someone else picked up where he left off.

"I don't see your aunts here," Princess Demriam said, staring straight at Chad. "It's almost like they weren't invited. Or were they, and they couldn't see the ink?"

Though I could've slapped the siren for being so forward with Chad when he was clearly hurting, she was right. Mallory and Morgan weren't here. Why?

His reply was calm yet full of authority as he said, "They think the Casters can fight Florence on our own, but they are wrong."

"If your own aunts don't agree, and you're on the side of the vampire who murdered your mother, and dating one of them, why should we fight for you?" one of the members of the Chinese Witch Council asked, far too boldly for someone who was speaking to their king.

"If I can come to peace with all that," Chad replied coolly, "then you should be able to as well."

I took a deep breath. Chad shouldn't have to deal with this. "Besides, it was Lilith who bit Abigail and gave her that unquenchable thirst," I told the man before turning to the rest of them, "and Florence who sired me. We have reason to hate them just as much as anyone else in the room—if not more."

"How many have you killed as a result?" a wizard asked roughly, presumably waiting to hear some grotesque number.

"None," I replied firmly, staring him down, ready for him to challenge it. He didn't.

"We've heard rumours of covens who breed and feed on their own children if they're born as mortals," a woman said. "People don't change their inner urges just because someone tries to force them into it."

"We have connections with one of those covens," Chadwick said.

"The night of King Chadwick's coronation," Eyeara spoke out, "he led a rescue mission that saved several of their lives from Florence. I'm sure they'll be open to a discussion."

"We'll strike a bargain with them," I told everyone. "They can keep breeding if they give us the children who are born as mortals. We'll re-house them. There are children around the world who need our help, including Caster children," I added, gesturing towards Noel and Leon, but as soon as I said it, I knew I shouldn't have.

Abigail, who was back in her seat, tightened her arms around the two kids as members of the crowd revolted.

"*You* are raising Caster children?" the same witch asked.

"I'm not a bad person," Abigail cried out. "Their Caster father died and their mortal mother tortured them."

The witch turned to face Chad. "You're letting the woman who killed your mother raise two little Casters? Perhaps we should question your sanity."

"Again," Chad said between gritted teeth. "Anything dealing with my mother is my concern, and my concern alone. Your opinion is not necessary. The children are in far better hands with these Night Crawlers than they were with their mortal mother, physically and emotionally."

Noel nodded her head eagerly.

"The point is," I went on, raising my volume above the murmurs of the crowd, "not all Night Crawlers are evil. Sometimes our bodies force us to do or crave things we don't want to, but Abigail doesn't let her hunger get to that point anymore. The holy water has proven that not all of us are evil. There's a line between good and bad that we haven't crossed—regret being one of the things that keeps us from crossing to the other side. We've made a choice to save people from Florence's way of life. That's why each of us could see the invisible ink. That's why each of us could enter through the waterfall. Not only can we coexist, we can work together."

"Every group in the world isn't represented tonight," a Night Crawler noted, glancing around doubtfully. "Even if we all agree to fight, would we be enough?"

"No," I said, calculating Florence's army against ours. "But it would show others throughout the world that we can live together in peace. Time is of the essence, and time is running out. We have no option left but to join ranks as quickly as possible."

"I apologise that many of you feel anxious," Chad added, "but we are not always given the gift of time during a war."

I thought back to all the screams I had heard in my head—from Japan, from Leon's dreams, and from God only knew where.

"What about the mortals?" a ghost asked, his voice echoing eerily through the hall.

"How are we going to stop them from trying to hurt us?" a manananggal asked.

"Let's ask them," Eyeara suggested, looking over to the group who had sat entirely silent this whole time. Not that I could blame them.

Wyatt's eyes met mine, holding the same plea he had worn the last time I had seen him, just before I lit his flat ablaze. I quickly glanced away but came eye to eye with the former prime minister, whose woes of having lost his daughter still weighed heavily on his shoulders, and I decided I couldn't quite look at him either. So I turned to look at Garick Reeves, the current prime minister and found that he, too, was looking at me, only he didn't have regret or sadness in his eyes. His brown eyes bore a stark curiosity that chilled me.

I stood taller, ignoring the bumps that appeared on my skin. "Last I checked, the mortals aren't taking the discovery of our existence very well," I started, thinking back to the riot he had led. I stared down at him, raising my brows to magnify the information I held. "There was talk about burning us on pyres and driving stakes in our hearts. Has anything changed?"

For a split second, his curiosity shifted as a bit of blood left his brown cheeks, and he cleared his throat. Perhaps he was used to holding the spotlight amongst a crowd of mortals, but he was not used to being surrounded by creatures who were quite different from him, especially ones who were aware of his plans against them. Yet he was standing in this room, unscathed by the waterfall, having seen the ink, so something inside him made him trustworthy.

"Well, everything has changed," he said, only a fraction of his boldness from the riot still intact. His eyes anxiously drifted to the people around him and then back to me. "Since you started the blackout, we humans have come to see that witches, and such, are... well... Your powers are somewhat of a gift."

"Somewhat?" I questioned, and he quickly rectified his words.

"An *immense* gift," he corrected. "And though we still fear a world where some of you could control us, or change us, or kill us, it's fair to point out that humans—or mortals as you say—can do those things too."

The room seemed to relax a touch as he admitted this. All eyes were on him as we waited to hear what the mortals had to say.

"Go on," Chad said from beside me, sitting back in his throne with his own curiosity plain on his face.

Reeves went on, his voice more confident. "I've been chosen as a spokesperson for my kind. We're interested to know what life would look like if this Florence fellow was, in fact, defeated. What would it mean for mortals if we wanted the technology back? If we made a treaty with the paranormals, what would become of humanity?"

Chad and I exchanged glances. What would it mean to coexist? What would it look like?

It's up to you, my love, he said through our connection. *You're in charge of this new world.*

I tilted my head to scold him ever so slightly. When, exactly, had I signed up for that?

Turning to scan my eyes over the crowd, I found that several audience members had followed Chad's gaze to me. The goose pimples that covered my skin stayed in their place.

"It would look like freedom," I answered, staring back at Reeves. "Freedom, inclusion, truth, and collaboration. We'd have to put several laws in place, and it would take time, but it's been done before with other diverse communities. And knowing what we all know now about our histories, we can evolve with our growth."

This time, there wasn't a single person in the crowd that cried out to reject the idea or deny the possibility. Instead, I could feel an overwhelming sense of hope, a strange desire to see this new world at work. As my eyes scanned over them once more, I could feel my heart lift into my throat. Was this world possible? Was there truly a future where we could all form a single partnership?

One face in the crowd, however, shifted from hope to wariness. Former Prime Minister Alastor's expression scrunched up with the pain of a broken heart as he became torn.

"I want this man dead," he said, his voice breaking on the words, "perhaps more than any of you. But who's to say more humans won't be killed in this 'new world' you speak of? Who's going to protect more lives from being taken once vampires can roam the world freely?"

"We'll show the mortals we're not all like the man who took your daughter from you," I told him, my tone soft and gentle. I wanted him to know I cared. "Witches, vampires, werewolves— all of us have been living underground for hundreds of years. That's our proof that we can live in the same world as humans. We don't have to go extinct for you to be safe. Most deaths have been from humans—human shootings, human wars, human illnesses. If anything, working together will help sustain mortal life. We can help prevent all that from happening."

"That still won't mean we're safe," Alastor said quietly.

"No one will ever be safe," I told him, "but we can do our best. We can set the laws—forbidding creatures such as ourselves from turning mortals into jorogumos, or vampires, or anything without consent. We'll do our best to make everyone abide by them. Then we'll set laws that pertain to our diets—"

"So what will the vampires do once these new laws are in place?" a French vampire interjected. "I'm all for a world with peace, but how peaceful can we be if human blood keeps us alive? Are we expected to starve to death?"

"You sleep in a coffin," a witch commented bitterly. "How alive can you really be?"

"Drink animal blood," Cristin suggested, ignoring the witch's comment. "I've been doing it for years."

"It's not the same," Queen Sadiq told her friend patiently, shaking her head.

"Then you can feed the way I've been feeding for over a year now," I announced. "King Chadwick has invented a blood duplication potion. With one drop of human blood, we can feed a whole host of vampires. It's just as good as the real thing and it'll keep you alive."

"What about us?" a manananggal who wasn't from Loxley Lair asked. "We need more than blood. We need flesh—organs."

Wyatt flinched at these words.

"We have a prison for those who refuse to abide by the mortal laws," Charity commented, addressing the manananggal. "You can eat from there."

"That's barbaric," a wizard gasped.

"Do you have an alternative idea?" Chad asked harshly, and though the wizard made a face that announced he preferred manananggals to not exist in the first place, he hushed up.

"One prison isn't enough to sustain all the Night Crawlers in the world, even if most of them drink this blood duplication potion," a person pointed out.

"So we convert more of the prisons," Leo suggested. "Surely there are enough criminals in the world to go round."

"And who knows?" Connor said. "Perhaps it'll deter people from committing crimes if a violent death is the price they'd pay."

"What about their families?" the new prime minister asked. "Even prisoners have loved ones."

"Not all of them," explained Vincent, having worked with the prisoners firsthand.

"And some of the prisoners have families who know they deserve death," Hydie put in. "I, being one of them, would know."

"Then we'll enact a death sentence," Charity proclaimed. "Anyone who takes an innocent life, regardless of what type of being they are, will have a trial. If a crime is found to be grave enough, then they'll be sent to the prisons to give their life."

"Murderers… abusers… rapists…" I added, Florence's red eyes penetrating my mind.

"All right then," Eyeara asked in her powerful yet soothing voice. "Anyone disagree?"

The crowd looked around, considering the details and whispering to deduce what it meant for them. Then Queen Leira flipped her long green dreads over her shoulder.

"And what does this mean for the mermaids?" she asked. "If humans know where to find us, they'll decide to do some fishing."

"Our kind will slaughter and shipwreck anyone who tries to hang our corpses in a museum," Demriam threatened, and I fought not to roll my eyes.

"Then we'll put laws in place for you too," I said. "Perhaps when mating season comes around, you can let a few ships slide. I'm sure the men will come lining up."

The siren princess let out a laugh. "I could get used to that," she decided, looking around at all the men that could sustain the mermaids' existence. Then her eyes landed on Chad. "We could hold a competition of sorts for those wanting to donate their seed."

"Sounds pleasant," I inserted, interrupting the lovely thoughts I'm sure she was having about her ex-fling.

She turned her heated eyes to me, and for a moment, I was sure she was going to obscure my sight with more scenes of her and Chad's past, but instead, my sister's voice filled my head.

Don't worry, Hydie said, sounding amused. *I'm blocking all the lovely visions she's been trying to cast your way.*

Cheers, I told her.

"Alright," Chad said abruptly, standing up once more. No doubt trying to interrupt the little reunion between Demriam and me. "Any other questions about life here after?" he asked the crowd.

There was some murmuring, but then it morphed into a silence that brought joy to my ears. They were content with our plan—at least for now.

"So how do we win?" a witch from the British Witch Council asked quietly, but her tone, hesitant as it was, showed she was coming around.

Excellent question, I directed towards Chad, but I knew it was my turn to speak. I had to be the one to put the first step into motion.

"We have several plans," I said, not allowing my voice to quiver, regardless of the reaction I was about to provoke. "For one, any Caster with a gnome in their possession will need to free them immediately."

"What?" a voice erupted from the crowd.

"They're vermin," a wizard called. "Why should we?"

"Because it's hereby illegal," Chad announced, his expression as firm as his voice. "Worldwide."

"Those gnome statues have belonged to my family for generations," a witch cried, no hint of remorse for the creatures in her clutches.

"That makes your case worse," I said pointedly, "not better."

"You have no place—" someone tried to snap at me, but Chad cut her off.

"It's non-negotiable—regardless of whether or not you help our fight," Chad demanded. "The gnomes are living creatures and you will not treat them as slaves or statues. It would be an injustice to continue turning a blind eye. We need them. They've already done so much to help us in this war."

"Then what?" Icaron asked, knowing the freedom of gnomes made no difference to his kind. I had never heard the elf speak. He spent all his time silently judging my actions, yet he was somehow on my side. "How do we stop Florence?"

"I procured one of Florence's hairs," I said, "and we made a tracking spell to lead us to his and Lili's hideout."

The crowd paused to take it in. They paused because for once, they were given a glimpse of something concrete that we could work with.

"We're going to send in spies to map out the lair," I continued. "Once we know everything about it—how many people he's working with, how many people he's taken prisoner—once the size of our forces are adequate, we'll attack."

"How many do you think we're dealing with?" a Night Crawler asked.

"We don't know," I told him honestly. "But we suspect that his stunt in Japan has scared millions more into submission."

"Besides us, who else can we get on our side?" a Caster asked.

Queen Sadiq answered that. "I have an army of mummies under my command," she informed everyone. "The other countries in Africa are waiting to hear my judgement, but once I give it, they'll likely join. In contrast to your cultures, we don't divide ourselves based on how we were born or what we became later in life. We stand together as a continent."

"Abigail and I have priests all over the world working to bless more holy water," Cristin announced hesitantly, perhaps wondering if the mention of her name would draw out more criticism.

"It would be immensely tricky, but if enough elves worked together," Eyeara began, "perhaps could we make the holy water rain from the clouds."

"That's brilliant," I said, my heart rate accelerating with excitement.

"What if they hide inside their fortress, away from the water?" a werewolf pointed out.

"Then perhaps we could cause a flood," Charity endorsed.

"We wouldn't want his innocent prisoners to drown," I said, thinking back to the children's screams.

"Is it true they have wendigos on their side?" Victoria from America asked. "They can attack us by accessing our dreams."

I found Koda in the crowd and gestured to him for an answer.

"No," he said firmly. "Wendigos work independently."

Victoria nodded, likely as thankful as me that the creatures weren't allied with Florence.

"There are also legends of mud creatures in Judaism," Abigail said, staring at the ground, but then she put on a brave face and looked up at the crowd. "Legend has it that they'll help in times of great need. Some of the fairies and gnomes are helping me locate them."

I tried not to look surprised. As the main leader, I should've known this, yet my communication with her had been more than lacking lately.

We waited for more questions, more fears, but it was a moment before anyone spoke.

Blonde hair shimmered as Irma twisted a few strands absentmindedly around her finger. "After this war," she said quietly, "nothing will ever be the same again."

It was true, and though I should've been scared, a flutter in my heart told me it would be all right. "Perhaps it'll be a blessing rather than a curse," I said kindly.

"No more slaves," Fendel piped in with a brave, longing look in his eyes.

"No burnings at the stake this time round," said a rather old-looking witch.

"Silver to the heart," a werewolf mentioned.

"Or pretending our powers are anything less than gifts," Chad added, and several people nodded.

No more hiding.

"You think laws will be enough?" the prime minister asked tentatively.

"They'll have to be enough," I said. "We don't have another option."

"We have laws at Loxley Lair," Leo said.

"Your laws are upheld because your members agree to them before living there," a French vampire from Charity's clothing company pointed out.

"Then we'll have to change the world," Chad resolved.

"Many more people will die," Ingrid said sadly in her strong German accent.

"But even more would die if we chose not to fight," I replied.

"And wars can last years," Queen Aria said, looking at Eyeara.

"After what I do to Florence and Lilith, there will be no one left to lead them," I answered, longing to make it a reality.

A silence swept across the room as every head turned—every eye landed on me. Only this time, there was no doubt. I could see in their eyes that they believed in this future.

Eyeara looked at her mother, wrapping her hand around hers, and then her eyes moved to mine. She let out a deep breath. "The elves will join your fight," she declared, "as will our dragons. My father is no longer fit to rule if he chooses to stand on the sidelines while the world burns. The other elves and I have met in secret, and it's been decided that we'll fight in King Chadwick's name."

"You know we will," Leo said, holding Charity and Kana closer to him.

"As will Africa," Queen Sadiq announced, waving a hand to include her mummies. "The pharaoh won't have a choice."

I nodded, grateful, and looked around, hoping more would join in, but no one else was as eager.

"How much time do we have to decide?" a Caster with a Spanish accent asked.

"You can decide now," Eyeara announced, eyeing the Caster unapologetically, "or you can let more innocent people die. The choice is yours."

Several people, Casters, Night Crawlers and mortals alike, looked away, guilt evident in their eyes. There was a pause that lasted an eternity, but in that time, I decided Eyeara was right.

Giving them time would merely provide them with an easy escape—a coward's exit from the war.

"All right," Reeves said, speaking for the mortals. "I'll tell the other humans I think we should join, but only if you promise to put the laws in place and end the blackout."

I nodded and Chad spoke up. "We give you our word," he said, and Reeves nodded back.

I gazed across the crowd, watching as some averted their eyes, but I knew if fear was keeping them silent now, it wouldn't be long before fear would make them reach for help. We could work with this. We could win them over without any more thought.

"Keep your mirrors uncovered," I told the crowd. "We'll need a way to contact everyone when it's time. Whoever chooses not to stand with us will be on their own."

At once, members of the crowd stood from their seats. Cries of "Wait!" and "We've reconsidered!" broke out through the full hall. My eyes linked with Hydie's.

Their colours? I asked her.

Hydie squinted, taking in the chattering crowd. "Yellow," she said simply, describing the aura she could see cast around the outer edges of each person.

I smiled at my sister. She had sat down with me when we were younger, taught me all the colours, and we had talked for hours about what they must mean—a memory I was thankful to have back. Yellow meant the crowd was optimistic. They knew we stood a chance.

My heart lifted. I spotted Eyeara in the audience once more, and she gave me an affirming nod. The reader of souls. That was all I needed.

Warm skin wrapped around my hand and my eyes flickered down to Chad's fingers, then to his kind smile and his green eyes. He squeezed my hand in his, and the joy within me was so vast, I had to look away.

We could do this.

I'm Still Unstoppable

Chapter 36: His Fingers

We plotted for hours, those three worlds in one room, now starting to resemble a single team. There were so many variables, so many obstacles, yet there were so many things to inspire hope.

The instant the meeting was adjourned, I fled. Too much delight swirled around my stomach to chance staying a second longer. I wouldn't linger to wish anyone a farewell—not when there was the risk of running into Wyatt, or Demriam, or anyone else who could extinguish the high I felt. I wanted to be on my own to fully soak in the moment. So I transported to my bedroom at *Ypovrýchio Kástro*, only I didn't get the chance to be alone. There was already someone in my bed.

Chad reclined on the pillows, the faintest dusting of green smoke around him as if he had known I'd escape the second I was allowed. And I should've realised he wouldn't let me.

"Off so soon?" he asked, puckering out his lips as if pondering why I'd want to leave.

I clucked my tongue at him. "Apparently, I'm not that lucky," I teased. What I wanted was to take off this sweltering dress, lay down, and stare at the ceiling with a dumb grin on my face. We were finally getting closer to ridding the world of Florence.

"Cheeky," Chad dished out. "Well then, if you don't want me here, I won't tell you how brilliant you were tonight."

I snorted, most unattractively. "I was brilliant?" I asked. I started to shake my head, but I thought better of it and decided to accept the compliment. The Casters and the Night Crawlers were coming together to fight my greatest enemy. Perhaps we had done something right after all.

"Fine," I said, trying my best to conceal my smile yet failing. Taking a few slow, calculated steps towards Chad, I kept my eyes trained on his. "Don't tell me. And I won't tell you that you killed it out there. It may give you a big head. Now, help me out of this dress."

A demand, not a question.

Turning away from him, I reached to my back and began to work the laces of my dress, loosening them quickly. There was only a short, hesitant moment before the creak of Chad slipping off my bed, and then I felt his hands cover mine. He took over, untying the laces, but much slower—gentler. His fingers traced up my sides before he delicately lifted my hair over my shoulder. Then his hands trailed up my hair, stopping when he reached the crown on my head.

"I see you took my advice," he whispered, the warmth of his breath caressing my neck. "You dressed like a queen, and you wore the title well."

I gave him a scolding look from over my shoulder, even as the idea of what it meant to be his queen sent shivers down my spine.

"Stop pushing it," I warned sternly, and I pivoted my neck away once more, but not in time to shield myself from his smug smile.

He liked the way he made me squirm.

His fingers wove their way back down my arms, zigzagging through the maze of goose pimples that his touch had sprouted. The dress sagged, signalling it was loose enough to remove, but Chad stepped into me closer.

He turned me around to face him. Once again, his warm breath played dangerously across my skin, weakening my legs. His arms wrapped around my waist, and he nuzzled his face into my neck.

I allowed myself the luxury of basking in his warmth, of letting my hands explore the curves of his arms, but then he pulled back to run a thumb along my bottom lip. He stared at my mouth, hunger fighting its way out.

"Perhaps we could get together tomorrow to trade notes on how our meeting went," he suggested. "Just the two of us... on my desk..."

I was weightless. The memory of him laying me out across his desk flooded my mind, and I glanced down at his lips.

Yes. I need that desk. But not tomorrow. Now.

His whole face creased as it shifted into a giddy grin. It wasn't until that moment that I realised my guard was down. He was in my head.

He let his thumb run once more across my lip before I whacked him in the stomach, and his hand fell. A grunt left his mouth but it did nothing to wipe the smile from his face. What a dirty, rotten trick seducing me like that. A trick that rivalled my own.

I scowled at him, but before I could shut off my mind to him or scold him for stirring feelings within me that I didn't want to admit, he whispered something that froze my anger in midair.

"I have to leave," he said, and I jerked away, separating our bodies so I could see him properly.

He most certainly could not leave. Not with his desk calling out to me with such urgency.

He stared at me intently, his smile merely brushing his lips, his eyes eager as if he was trying to read me. But I put my mental shield back in its place.

"Leave to where?" I asked, the annoyance I felt clear in my tone. Why wouldn't he stay? Why wouldn't he keep his arms around me and find ways to celebrate the outcome of the meeting?

He squinted his eyes ever so slightly, glancing back and forth between mine. If he felt any hurt at being pushed from my mind, he didn't voice it.

"It's about time I reconstruct all those mirrors in Castwell Castle, don't you think?" he asked, his fingers finding their way to my bare shoulders as I held my loosened dress in place. "You told everyone at the meeting to keep their mirrors uncovered. I suspect there will be loads of people trying to get in touch with us soon."

Why were my words coming back to haunt me again? And of all the moments—when his fingers were so warm against mine, tempting me to give in. I couldn't bloody well lay down and smile like a fool up at my ceiling now, could I?

"Unless you give me a reason to stay…" he suggested, his eyes digging into me hopefully, but I would not take the bait.

"Go," I said shortly. It was the lightest tone I could manage before deciding, "The mirrors have been broken for far too long. Besides, I'm leaving too."

Chad's fingers paused as he lifted a brow to encourage an elaboration.

I thought back to our suggestions of how life could be after the war, and though I agreed wholeheartedly, there was one loose end I needed to tie.

"I'm going to go to the Loxley Prison," I announced, casting my eyes over to the wardrobe. "Seems as good a time as any to say farewell to my father—properly this time." Before he became someone's meal.

Chad's eyes shot over to a clock that ticked on the wall, spirals of blue and green circling it like a magical typhoon.

"It's nearly sunrise," he pointed out, but it was irrelevant.

"I'll be quick," I replied, enunciating each syllable to display my stubbornness on the matter.

"All right," Chad said, moving his hand up until he held my chin, angling it up at him. "Do you want me to go with you?"

I stared into his green eyes, noting the sincerity that played within them, but then I shook my head. "No, you're right about the mirrors. And meeting with my father is something I have to do on my own."

Chad nodded before he pulled me in for a hug. I could feel his heartbeat against my head—slow, steady. His heart was full of care. He truly was a good person.

He pulled back, holding my chin once more. "Will I be seeing you soon?" he asked.

It was a fair question. Lately, we had been going days at a time without seeing one another.

"Yes," I told him. "To… *debrief* that meeting," I added, letting the true meaning of my words dance out. I had a feeling we wouldn't get much talking done.

He let out a small chuckle. "I can hardly wait," he said softly, stealing my breath.

I shook my head at him as I watched the green smoke surround him and take him away. "Tosser," I muttered under my breath, though I knew he wouldn't hear it. One day we'd have to stop teasing each other and let our bodies give in—a day when we weren't clouded by sadness or anger and when no one would be around to interrupt. Unfortunately, that day was not today.

I turned towards the wardrobe, ready to pick a sensible outfit and face my wretched father, only to come face to face with Chad's mother.

Chapter 37: Mother and Father

My breath caught and I turned back round to try and catch Chad, but there was no use. He was gone, his mother filling in his vacancy.

Letting out a harsh breath, I met the ghost's eyes, eyes I had seen all through my childhood and into my adulthood. But why?

"Why are you here?" I asked her, harshness lapping off my tongue like a whip. As if the idea of meeting with my father wasn't challenging enough. "Your son was literally here not two seconds ago. He's the one you should be seeing, not me."

I walked through her image, to make a point more than anything, but I immediately regretted it.

Fucking freezing, I thought to myself. Ghosts were so fucking cold.

For a moment, I couldn't shake off the feel of her icy body. As soon as the paralysis subsided, I rushed to the wardrobe, shaking the shivers off of me, and slipped off my formal dress to put on a simpler one. Then I grabbed the first pair of shoes I found, praying she'd be gone when I looked back. I wasn't that lucky.

She was still in my bedroom, floating centimetres off the ground, staring at me as if I were the one to be pitied, as if I were dead and she was alive.

"What?" I barked, shaking my shoes at her, hoping to ward her off. "Madelyn, was it? You can leave now. I don't have time to follow you through the streets of Germany into a trap, or up to an attic to face Lili and pictures of children who have been abused. I don't have time for whatever it is that you're here to show me this time—and with no explanation whatsoever," I added abruptly. She could take her grey skin and melancholy face somewhere else.

I stormed past her, diligent to avoid her icy soul this time, and plopped down onto my bed. As I shoved my feet into the shoes, however, I could still see her from the corner of my eye.

"Your son told me he hasn't seen your ghost in years," I snapped at her. "Go haunt him instead. Unless you want to open your damn mouth and actually tell me something useful this time. Perhaps sing some helpful information in one of your blasted songs?" I suggested, but she merely looked at me with her tragic eyes.

"I'm going to see my father in his prison cell," I said as I stood. "You know? The man who tortured me for years? You remember. You were there, watching, singing, hiding books about witchcraft so he wouldn't see. For what purpose? I'll never know. Perhaps it began with you wanting to help me. Did you suspect I was part of your son's prophecy, or is that when you decided to turn on me and lead me to Florence's hideout as a trap?"

My heart pounded as I stared at her, waiting for an answer I knew wouldn't come. Just her ridiculous despondent expression.

The ghost reached towards me, and the thought of her icy touch caused me to jolt away. But when her translucent skin followed after me to touch my cheek, I closed my eyes. And for a second, I felt her warmth.

When I opened my eyes, the ghost of Chadwick's mum, my singing ghost, was gone, and I was left with tears in my eyes.

* * *

I stood in front of the iron gates, the buzz of electricity in my ears, the feel of the pebbles beneath my feet. The white building towered above me, a faint light only touching the tip of the tallest floor. The spiked fence crackled with gnome magic and bars shielded every window, but through the glass, the interior was pitch black. Even the mortal prisoners felt the effects of the worldwide blackout, even if the magic still worked to keep the criminals caged inside.

A breeze swept across my skin and through my hair, not warm yet not quite cold. It brushed up against the tiny bumps that had gathered along my arms—chills from staring at the prison. Part of me wanted to transport back to my bed. Part of me wanted to hide from my father, hide from ghosts, hide from reality. But if luck was ever to befall me, this would be the last time I ever saw him. Soon, this prison and others all around the world would become feeding grounds to a far larger crowd than just Loxley Lair.

Vincent gave me a nod as I walked past him. Apparently, I wasn't the only one to get straight back to business after the grand meeting of Casters and Night Crawlers.

Even through the faint light of dawn, my eyes focused on how extraordinarily white everything was—the magical cameras that turned to follow me as I walked past, the walls, the floors, even the ceilings that housed the unlit bulbs. Together, they served as a pathway to the beating heart I had grown to hate with all of my own. I didn't need a room number. I didn't need an escort to find him. All I needed was the sound of the heart that I had once pulverised into a million blood-drenched pieces.

Perhaps that's why my singing ghost had come to visit me. Was she trying to discourage me from going to see my father? Or it could've been my conversation with Chad that prompted her visit. Was she no longer satisfied that he and I had been torn apart? Did she fear I was getting too close to her son again, as her insufferable sisters did?

It felt like I had been punched in the stomach. I could still feel her hand against my skin, warm like a memory. Warm like she loved me as her own child. How could I think she didn't? How could I think she despised me like her sisters did when the trap in Germany was the exception, not the rule? I hated that I couldn't understand it.

My feet stopped just outside a checkpoint, two sets of bars preventing prisoners from escaping as others came and went. A guard stood to the right in position. To most, he might've been cloaked by the darkness, but my extraordinary sight granted the ability to focus in on his familiar face.

"O'Brien," I greeted, smiling over at him.

He didn't return the smile. Instead, he looked at me with sad eyes, just like the ghost had moments ago, just like he had the night he walked in on Florence attacking me.

"Azalea," he replied, giving me a nod.

"I didn't see you at the meeting," I said lightly, making for conversation.

He shook his head. "Nah, I didn' go. It's my nigh' for guard duty here. Ginny was there though."

"Oh good," I answered automatically, and then I crinkled my face. Good? Why had I said that?

"Er—You're not abou' ta go in and talk to your father, are ya?" he asked me, tilting his head towards the door, and suddenly I understood his gloomy demeanour. "I know he's your family 'n' all, but he's a wicked piece of work. Better left alone, I mean."

A dull laugh left my lips. "That he is," I agreed, "but I have some things I'd like to get off my chest."

O'Brien's shoulders lifted with indifference, though his brows spoke another story as they furrowed with disapproval. "If you're sure…"

He took a key from his pocket and began to slide it into the door. "He's not sedated anymore, but we have the cuffs on him so he can' use his powers. I don' think he'd do it even if he wasn' though. He's always screamin' 'bout how much he hates magic and everyone who uses it." The lock turned and the first gate clicked open. Then he gave me a sympathetic look over his shoulder. "Especially you," he added.

I let out a breath. "I know," I replied. It hardly mattered. "But I can handle it, I promise." I knew what I was even if my father refused to accept himself. Though he wouldn't be able to physically harm me, I knew what he was capable of doing to my heart. Lucky for me, there was hardly any of my heart left to break.

Together, O'Brien and I stepped through the first gate, then the second, placing ourselves closer and closer to the man who had caused me so much trauma as a child—memories that were now crystal clear thanks to Baba Yaga. Somewhere behind these white walls coated in darkness, Noel and Leon's mum also resided. Hatred flooded my veins. I hoped she was rotting away for the harm she had caused her children. How many more young witches and wizards were out in the world, suffering the same fates our parents had given us?

O'Brien escorted me down a long corridor. Several small, orange lights danced across the floor, mingling with the darkness. As we passed the other cells, the other heartbeats, the other breaths of the caged prisoners, each orange glow of candlelight flickered in their eyes. I saw their wonder as they watched me, unaware why I was there, unaware as to what the new world would turn this prison into. I remembered hearing the prisoners' stories the first time I had been there, the way an infuriated ghost had told me they didn't all deserve death. Now, seeing them again, I resolved to hold a trial for each of them after the war was over. Perhaps between mindreading, auras, and soul-reading, we could decipher who *did* deserve to be eaten.

O'Brien stopped and pointed farther down.

"Three more cells 'n' then you'll find 'im," he told me in a whisper. "I'll be back past the gates if you need me."

I gave him another smile, not bothering to tell him I could already feel where my father was. This time, O'Brien returned my smile before his footsteps echoed back down the corridor, and the clicks of a key led him back past the gates.

Three cells away, the heartbeat pattered in a slow, steady rhythm, its tempo calm, but it quickened as I drew nearer. When I reached his cell, I gazed in. Past the bars, I saw him sitting next to a candle, his brown eyes piercing into mine. The heartbeat faltered for just a second. Then it began to pound against his ribcage, equally as trapped as he was in this cell. He glared at me with pure malice.

"Come to finish me off?" he seethed. His nostrils flared in disgust as he took in his eldest and most hated offspring.

"Not *yet*," I said, staring back at him to emphasise each word's meaning.

I half-expected him to yell at me—to scream obscenities and unleash all the animosity he held for me. Instead, he was calm—collected even—as he leaned back in his chair. One of his arms rested against the table beside him, his other arm on his lap, his wrists connected with silver chains—magical handcuffs to bind the power he possessed.

"I hear they no longer have to poke and prod you with injections to suppress your magic," I taunted, waiting for his usual response.

On cue, his entire body seized at the word. Tiny droplets flew out as he spat, "I hear there's a group of people against you and yours." His eyes flickered down to my hands before they met my eyes once more. Hate filled him—his eyes, his lungs, his posture—yet no denial of his powers fell from his lips.

Progress.

The candle flickered, causing the shadows of the bars to dance across his face. It felt good to be on this side of the bars, not trapped as I had been in Egypt.

"There were actually two groups against me, if you must know," I told him. "One group was of mortals who believed the world was better without creatures like *us*," I stressed, to let him know they had been against him too. "But now that they've seen the benefits of an alliance, they're starting to come around. The second group, the one who's still against me, is filled with creatures who believe we should come out into the open. They believe we should collect mortals as slaves—treat them as lesser beings." I paused and gave my father a pitying look. "I'm afraid you fit in with neither."

He leaned in closer to me, the chains rattling. His eyes widened enough for me to feel the heat behind them. "When I get out of here, I'm going to fight against you. I'm going to fight for the life you've taken away from me—not just these past few months, but from the moment I realised what you were."

I couldn't help but smile as I shook my head at him. He was delirious. How could someone blame a child for what they were? He was beyond help. He was beyond seeing the truth. And he could live out his days in this prison, as numbered as they were.

As I leaned towards him, his pathetic hope of escape rang in my ears. "You won't get the chance to fight," I whispered, relishing in the thought of it. "You'll be stuck here, forced to hear the whispers of my victory. And though I doubt that any of that will bring you to your senses, just know it'll bring me joy. You're the monster, not me. You're the one who gave Hydie and me these extraordinary powers that will help save lives, and while you'll be stuck in here until the day you die, we'll be out there living our lives."

"I gave you nothing," he replied stubbornly, his eyes shifting away from mine. Even as he looked away, I could see fear flash within them.

Perhaps his progress was not as I'd thought.

"Tell me," I said, placing my hand on the cold metal bar, my fingers sliding down the smooth texture. "Why is it that you tortured me all those years for having magic? How is it that you denied your own for so long?"

"I said," he growled behind gritted teeth, "I didn't give you anything." His temper was rising rapidly, synchronised with his volume. "It was all beaten from me before you were conceived— beaten out until there was nothing left."

Ah, I thought, heart racing. We were getting somewhere.

"My parents saw the devil within me when I was a child," he explained, his jaw no longer clenched. "They forced it out until nothing was left. I had to do the same with you."

"Do what?" I asked, shaking my head at him. "Force your childhood trauma on me?" He was despicable. I tutted at him disapprovingly. "Unfortunately for you, and my grandparents, that's not how it works."

His eyes darkened with both hatred and curiosity. But even if he was beaten, even if he was drowned as he had done to me, or boiled as Leon's mother had done to him, the man before me had made his own choices of how to treat his daughter. He didn't deserve the life I had given back to him. Why had I reversed his death?

I cleared my throat, breaking the harsh silence between us. "Do you know there's far more than just witches and mortals who live in this world?" I asked him.

He grunted, unimpressed. "One hears whispers."

"Well, several of those creatures just held a large meeting, discussing how the world is going to change after I win this war. We're going to model other prisons after this one—to allow creatures of your worst nightmares to come feed on the inmates," I said, clicking my tongue to allow the vision to set in. "Perhaps you should be the first to die."

The cruel man didn't flinch. He stared back at me with a fierce heat in his eyes. Hydie said she'd be fine with him dying, and though his original, barbarous death had been accidental, this time it would be intentional. I wanted him dead. He was my father—my own flesh and blood—but I craved it no less. The way he stared into me made me want to kill him then and there, but I couldn't. I needed so badly for Florence to be my first true kill.

I turned abruptly, ready to leave before I ripped my father's head off.

"You're going to Hell!" he called after me, words he had uttered many times. Words I had let haunt me for far too long.

I didn't give him the satisfaction of turning back toward him. If I was going to Hell, then I prayed he was going somewhere far worse.

I stormed out of the gloomy prison, nodding a farewell to O'Brien and then to Vincent as I passed. Though I longed to abandon the wretched place, I couldn't help but glance back, the light of the sun shining further down the exterior. I watched as a werewolf greeted Vincent, ready to switch posts, and an inhale of fresh air later, I transported back to my bedroom in *Ypovrýchio Kástro*, my heart pumping vigorously all the while.

As soon as I felt the floor beneath my feet, a light caught my eye and I turned to see my purse glowing. My breath left my lungs in a stubborn huff.

What now?

I grabbed the green purse and pried it open, wondering what Chad wanted to talk about when he was the one who decided to leave first. It's not like I'd be any help making the potion to dip the mirrors in, nor did I want to do it. But as my eyes scanned Chad's neat writing, my shoulders fell.

I fixed a single mirror and Eyeron's already demanding we meet with him. Is there any way I could tempt you to come?

The thought of the elf king, with his judgemental stare and inability to respect women, infuriated me. Another incompetent parent to deal with. One would think I had met the quota in the last hour after dealing with Chad's mother and my father, but apparently not.

And to have to deal with Eyeron in the attic of all places? That attic was one of the last places I wanted to be, ranking no more than a centimetre above the prison that held my father. My last visit to the tallest tower of Castwell Castle plagued my mind— every shattered, aching piece of my heart haunting my chest, the memory of the glass that had pierced through me, cutting my skin…

The only thought that filtered over to the bright side was that I'd at least be at the castle I called home. And oh, how I missed it.

I pulled out the pen that lived within the purse, adding my own message to the page.

Perhaps I could be persuaded…

Chad's reply came within seconds.

Will grovelling on my hands and knees suffice?

I laughed, surprised I was capable of doing such a joyous action after who I'd just faced, and who I was about to.

Yes, I believe it could. Unless you have a better offer?

It was worth the try, if only to stall a little longer.

I have just the thing. Only, it'll have to come after you help me. Think you can be patient?

Did he know me at all?

Patience doesn't exactly sound like me. Does it? Will I particularly enjoy this surprise?

No.

The word caught me off guard. What sort of an argument was that? Either way, he won, and I found myself outside the attic door, wondering if this visit would be as traumatic as the last.

I'm Still Unstoppable

Chapter 38: Only One

Y ou had the largest meeting in our history without me!" the elf king roared through the mirror. If it weren't for the glass between us, I'd swear I could feel the heat of his breath, rivalling the fiery breath of his dragons. "Thousands of people yet *I* was not invited."

I didn't bother correcting him. It had been hundreds, not thousands, but perhaps it would soon grow to that number.

"You aren't part of our alliance," Chad replied sternly.

"I am King Eyeron of the elves, lord over the frozen continent and all the Casters who live here, and you would dare to hold a meeting of this importance without me?"

His roar echoed through the attic, bouncing off of the mirrors that were whole once again. The glass unshattered, each piece back in its rightful place, and no reflection of Lili this time, or the kiss she and Chad had shared. The broken glass and image of Lili wasn't the only thing absent. The chest Chad's mother had led me to was gone too.

Eyeron forced a breath out through his bared teeth, seething and boiling. The last time the elf had spoken to us through a mirror, he had insisted upon keeping an eye on me, as if *he* should fear *me*. He gave me a frosted bracelet to track my movements, one I had thrown at him after he broke our agreement. This time, however, he was past fear and straight to fury.

"You *were* King of Antarctica because I allowed it," Chad reminded him, "but I'm no longer letting you rule. You received an invitation like everyone else. You didn't see the message, therefore you are not to be trusted, and Casters who are not to be trusted are committing treason. You are hereby relieved from your title."

"Re—" Eyeron choked over the word as if it scorched his tongue. "Relieved?" he asked. "You *cannot*—"

But Chad didn't let him finish. "I can, and I am."

"That's preposterous!" the blue elf spat out. "No one will allow this. No one, I tell you. My men will stand by me."

"Your people see through your craven ways and have already pledged their allegiance to me," Chad countered.

"Says who?" he screamed.

"Says them," Chad replied with an air of calm. "You see, *they* could read the invitations, so they were allowed into the meeting."

"And who is going to take my throne? My brother, Eyetronus? Or my Hand, Icaron? The Warlocks of the South?"

"No. Someone far more qualified," Chad said with a proud smile. "Eyeara."

"Eye—my daughter?" the elf sputtered out. "What have you poisoned her with to turn against me?"

"Your sexist behaviour over the years has served as the poison, and now she is the antidote. She'll take your place, and you can stand trial for treason against the High King of the Casters," Chad said pointedly.

"I will not allow this. My wife will talk reason into Eyeara's head—"

"The wife you've belittled for half a century? No," Chad challenged. "I'm afraid she won't speak for you. In fact, she's one of the several elves speaking against you at your trial."

Eyeron opened his mouth to protest, but Chad held up a hand, and the elf was silenced.

"Now, Eyeron," he said as if scolding a child. "I've heard your complaints and the requests you made have been denied. I no longer have any use for this conversation."

Chad waved a hand and a puff of green smoke erased Eyeron's blue face from the mirror, replacing it with our reflections. It was then that I realised the shocked expression I wore, clashing with the hard, annoyed look that swallowed Chad's whole body.

A long, weary sigh left his lips, his shoulders rising with the inhale and falling with the exhale, and then the tension in his body seemed to disappear, replacing itself with irony.

"One mirror," he laughed, holding up a single finger and turning to face me. "Only one mirror fixed and we have to deal with this."

I shook my head, stepping closer to him until I could feel the heat radiating off his body. "*You* dealt with it," I corrected, having been far too entranced to butt my way in. "My presence was not necessary. You dealt with it quite nicely, if I do say so myself. Almost like a king," I added, wishing to pay him back for calling me a queen. Only, it didn't pack the same punch.

He breathed out a light laugh. "Cheers," he said, rolling his eyes at the backhanded compliment. But then worry washed over his features like a rogue wave, and his hand gently lifted mine until my palm was at the perfect height for him to study.

"How was it with your father?" he asked, running his soft thumb along my palm, tracing the lines with care and sending a light shiver across my skin.

My usual reaction of shutting down and pulling my hand away from him evaded me. Almost as if I needed his touch.

I took a deep breath to begin my response. "Precisely as one would expect, I suppose," I said, watching in admiration as his thumb worked its way along the surface of my hand.

What was he reading? What could he tell from the lines that hadn't shifted?

"You know," Chad started, his voice soft but true, "it wouldn't be such a shame for your father to leave this world for good."

My heart tightened at the memory of having killed my father once before. I had used my teeth to scrape the taste of his blood from my tongue, right after I had deflected his spell and it crashed back into him. His magic had exploded him into a million pieces—a spell that was meant for me.

I closed my hand to clutch onto Chad's. He looked up at me, a clouded storm of thoughts lost in his green eyes.

"I know," I told him, and in all honesty, I was ready to let go of my father. Apart from taking back the horrid way he had died, I don't know why I had made the decision to keep him alive.

Chad squeezed my hand, his other finding its way to my cheek, his forehead resting lightly against mine. He closed his eyes and inhaled, and without any of his calming green magic, he stole away my sorrow. That is, until he froze against me.

Something was happening.

Both our minds unlocked in unison to let the other in.

What is it? I asked, but I didn't have to. His power was bursting through in a panic. His gift was the present. He could feel that something was wrong. But if he could feel it, I could see it as clear as day. My mind took over, and a series of visions pushed their way in.

Children screaming.

Bars surrounding crowds of imprisoned people.

Tubes attached to bodies, red liquid flooding through, leading their way to dark ceilings of a tunnel.

The scene disappeared in a blur, pulling me to another location. The setting shifted endlessly, as if travelling a vast distance, before it stopped abruptly on Florence. He grinned at a familiar man with red eyes, blood-stained teeth, and sandy-blond hair that was greased back into a low ponytail. They stood together in a forest, several other men with them, watching eagerly from the cover of the trees as chaos unfurled.

People poured out of a tall building, the sun nearly blinding as it reflected off of the bright white paint. Countless mortals sped past the electric fence—the gate ripped clear off its hinges—the buzz of gnome magic gone. They ran across blood-splattered pebbles, past statues that felt so out of place, and into the forest where Florence and his followers waited for them.

Loxley Prison.

"The prisoners are escaping."

The words were out of my mouth before I realised they were mine. From what felt like kilometres away, an alarm went off at a near-deafening pitch. The siren from the face recognition software in the library was screeching at top volume. I held tighter to Chad's hand, the ever-forming pit in my stomach growing with the thought that this could be another trap. My mind raced with the possibilities of what I could do to help, what I shouldn't do...

"My royal guard is on it," Chad uttered, and I felt my head nod as though the action didn't quite belong to me.

"Did you see the children?" I asked, wondering if he had seen my vision through the open gateway. "I think they're somewhere else but they're trapped."

"Yes," he said, his throat sounding tight as he forced the words out. "And the man with Florence—do you know him?"

I paused for two heartbeats before nodding. Yes, I knew Benji. So insignificant, yet I would never forget his face. I had seen the vampire before, when he lived at Downy Lair with Elizabeth, and then again at a New Year's Eve ball at Loxley Lair—as Florence's guest.

Saliva clawed its way down my throat as the memory seeped in. Another bad memory amongst thousands. The man's red teeth—red eyes as he played a game of questions—asking if I'd save a midnight kiss for Florence. O'Brien had cut in, taking me out of the equation for just a moment before panic overtook me and I ran. I ran up the stairs, through the trapdoor, and into the woods, but Florence had come after me. That night was the closest I had ever been to killing Florence—a stone to the head— knocking him out cold. How had I not killed him in the time since?

Chad squeezed my hand tight, bringing me back to the present and to the realisation that I had let him into my thoughts. Only, this time I didn't mind.

He tilted his head down at me, a look in his eyes as if to tell me everything would be all right. And I wanted to believe him, I did, but from where I stood, everything appeared grim.

The past.

The present.

The future.

The thoughts in my head kept colliding, moving as quickly as my vampire blood allowed them to. I couldn't think straight. I looked around at all the mirrors that still needed to be dipped into the magical potion. Only one was fixed. Only one fraction of the problems around us mended amongst a thousand problems that kept multiplying.

I looked back at Chad, and as green magic surrounded us, the children's screams plagued me. What else could possibly go wrong before things began to get better?

The smoke cleared, but we weren't surrounded by screaming children, or white walls, or chaos. We were in the stone castle that balanced precariously upon a stack of rocks.

I looked to Chad, whose lips were already parted.

"This is where Nigel will come with the report," he explained, and not a second later, a swirl of orange tornadoed into view.

The morbid look on Nigel's face said it all.

"It's not safe for you to go," he panted.

A mix of emotions ran through me, everything from stubbornness for thinking I could handle whatever Florence threw at us, to uncertainty, to relief for not having to go.

"What's happening?" Chad asked, his voice low and steady. No hint of fear, just purpose behind his words.

"Florence is attacking the prison," Nigel began, his shoulders back as he delivered his report. "He and about ten others—a mix of Night Crawlers and Casters—have broken inside. At least a thousand more are waiting in the forest outside, waiting for us to retaliate, but—" He broke off suddenly, and shook his head, and his gaze dropped to the floor. "They're impenetrable."

I felt nothing but dread as I listened. *A thousand* beings? We knew Florence's numbers were high, but I couldn't breathe as the image of so many vile creatures together in one place made my entire body tremble. Despite that, a question burned in my throat.

"What are they doing with the prisoners?" I demanded of Nigel, trying to stifle the quiver in my voice.

Nigel's eyes flickered over to me with a sadness swimming in them before he opened his mouth once more.

"Some, they're killing," he said, but it was a tone that made it feel like the worst was yet to come. "And others, they're turning."

Turning, I thought. He was biting them, changing them, siring them, making them feel the pull.

I closed my eyes, the same visions attacking me once more, before opening them to ask the question that most eagerly begged to come out.

"And what's happened to the people we know? The Loxley Coven members who are standing guard."

I didn't have to say their names. He already knew.

I watched with bated breath as Nigel and Chad both inhaled, the sound of the air passing between us like ghosts.

"O'Brien," Nigel said firmly but quietly, "he's gone missing. Vincent and your father—" He stopped and pity coated his features. "They're both dead."

Chapter 39: Fun

Lilith | A Few Months Ago | Her Bedroom

*Y*our hair is getting longer," I said, my own blonde hair draped over Florence. I sat on top of him, riding him up and down, up and down—just as vigorous and rough as he always liked it.

His hands slid off my bare waist to yank my hair with one hand and squeeze a breast with the other—punishment for speaking. I let out a stunned breath, but I shouldn't have been surprised. Causing me pain was precisely the thing that got him off.

He tugged my whole head down to him, the ridge of his brow nearly bruising mine as he pushed it against me. The movement broke the steady rhythm of my hips.

He gave another violent tug like he wanted to rip all my hair out. I tried to believe that wasn't true, but I was a fool not to accept it. He wasn't into blondes. They served as his meals or his favourite victims to aggravate his dead father.

I dragged my tongue up the side of his cheek, tasting his salty sweat, and his grip loosened on my hair. His nails dug into my breast as he used it to anchor me up or down or wherever he wanted me. Then he struck me hard across the face, and I was left with the sting before he grabbed onto my hip once more.

I was all for the aggression, but he never did it the way I liked. There was never any meaning behind the pain, no true passion, just the pent up anger he was trying to get out. It's not as if he ever caused me any true pleasure, nor was he trying to. He wasn't thinking of me anyway. He was thinking of her.

His eyes glazed over, and I knew his mind was on Azalea before he uttered the word.

"Shift," he demanded, grabbing onto me until my skin cracked under the pressure. "Turn into Azalea. Now."

I fought hard not to roll my eyes. He'd take my attitude out on me if I let him see it, and not in a good way. So I shifted. From the corner of my eyes, I watched as my straight blonde hair transformed into long, dark curls. I clutched onto his chest as my hands and arms shifted to a soft shade of brown.

God, I hated being in this body.

"Tell me you're proud of me," he growled. "Tell me we attacked Downy Lair so fiercely that you're going to cream all over me."

My stomach tightened. Downy Lair—its coven demolished.

"I'm so proud of you," I repeated, if only to shut him up and get it over with.

What was once Florence's favourite getaway was now ransacked and ruined. There had been a time when he'd raved about the ten other vampires he'd had sex with all at once—the lovely orgies—the way they drank each other's blood, and tore into the slaves they kept there. It was barbaric, but I had never been one to tell him not to go. He loved it there. He loved the way Elizabeth swooned every time she got her wrinkled hands on him. He loved the way Miss Perfect had squirmed the time he brought her there, and most of all, he liked the way he could read the jealousy on my face when he talked about the place. But now, Downy Lair no longer existed.

Florence stared up at me, a smile on his face as he grunted over and over, completely immune to how I felt about wearing someone else's face.

In one swift motion, Florence flipped us over so he could hover above me. He kept pumping in and out, in and out, but it wasn't enough to satisfy him. He grasped my neck with all his might, and my mind flashed back to the Downy Lair—Florence holding Elizabeth's neck so tightly that her skin cracked like stone. She had clutched at his hand, but all the vampire blood he'd drunk these past months had made him stronger than her.

Her wide eyes stared to the side, watching as our followers tore her coven to shreds, drinking their blood and dropping them into the large fountain, tainting the fresh blood with that of the dead. Her followers, or what was left of them anyway, sped around, trying to fight us off. Their black clothes were a blur, making them look like mere shadows. Her prisoners ran, screaming for their lives—some with a glint of hope in their eyes—but death would be their only form of freedom. We weren't there to leave survivors. We were there to send a message.

When Elizabeth Downy could take no more, she let go of Florence's hand. She forced her face to turn in his direction.

Only, when she looked up at Florence, there was something besides fear in her eyes, something besides pain or woe. Something I knew all too well. It was a deep, hopeless love for the monster.

"It's been fun," Florence had told her, sounding as if it truly had been.

Fun, I thought as I watched him cast the acid across her face— heard the excruciating sizzle along with her bloodcurdling scream.

Fun was what they shared, and it had all been tossed away so easily.

He'd pushed her away roughly, and she stumbled back, right up against the fountain where she crumbled. Florence turned from her, heading back towards the long stairwell that led several flights back up to the crypt with Elizabeth's name on it. She watched him stalk away from her, her hand clutching her face, in too much shock to plead or move. But then I blinked and her eyes bore into mine. The shock had left her face. In its stead wasn't pain or hate or jealousy. No, instead there was pity—a pity I couldn't understand.

Florence rode me harder, bringing me back to the present. As he pressed my head deeper into the pillow, I held my breath. He was close.

Suddenly, he jerked himself out and he came all over me, leaving no part uncoated. And as he whipped his cock around, a bit flew towards my eye. I squeezed my lids shut right in time to avoid it. He never trusted me enough to finish inside me. He knew I had a spell that would stop me from getting pregnant, on the off chance my vampire half let me. But I didn't think it was because he thought I'd be able to trap him into being with me. I had no doubt he'd leave me and whatever child we bore. I suspected he was afraid of leaving any offspring, because it would make him more like his father, and that's the part that disgusted him most.

He swung his body to the side, dismounting me like a horse, and plopped down next to me.

"Well, that was fun," he said, kicking the blankets off himself before hopping out of my bed.

He put one leg after the other into his trousers and buckled them closed, but my mind still lingered on the three-letter word.

Fun.

A word he used all too freely to describe both sex with me and when killing his old ally.

Then it hit me—harder than the slap to the face. I knew what the look Elizabeth had given me meant. It meant I'd be next. There'd be a day when Florence no longer needed me, and I'd be cast aside, regardless of how much I loved him.

I sat up, not bothering to cover my naked body—Azalea's naked body.

"Until next time," I said coolly.

He let out a laugh that was neither warm nor inviting.

"Until next time," he replied, and then he left.

I'm Still Unstoppable

Chapter 40: To Die a Thousand Deaths

Azalea | Present Day | Bathroom Floor

Vomit plummeted into the toilet. He was vile. Florence was a vulgar man and I never wanted to touch him again, let alone be in Lili's head, living through sex with the man who hurt me so thoroughly inward and out.

My skin was raw—raw and red from scrubbing and clawing his feel off of me in the shower. Yet it wasn't enough. My stomach lurched again, emptying what I hoped would be the last of it. After flushing and wiping my mouth, I fell back against the wall, hugging my towel around me and letting the water from my hair leave a mark on the stone. I was drained of everything.

It was pathetic, really. People had died—more turned into monsters—and I was sick over something that had *nearly* happened to me. I was sick over the thought of Florence touching me—the memory of him straddling me and unbuckling his pants. Only, I should've left those horrid thoughts in the past to focus on the present.

Vincent was dead. I had seen him yesterday. Thrice—at the meeting, coming into the prison, and then again when I came out. I hadn't uttered a word, only an impersonal nod, and now he was cast into stone.

Nigel had told us how it happened—how Vincent and the others tried to fight back—how they were injected with serums to weaken them, then dragged into the sunlight and pinned down by creatures who could withstand the sun. He didn't tell us the details, but I could imagine how their skin sizzled and scorched against the rays of light until their writhing ceased and their skin hardened into grey stone. Scenes flashed before my eyes, so vibrant, until I could smell the burning of their skin and feel the heat of the sun on my own.

Then there was O'Brien.

He had been with me moments before the prison attack. He was standing guard right outside my father's cell block.

"Missing?" I had asked Nigel blankly, the word not quite registering. "What do you mean he's missing?"

"As far as we know, he's gone with them," Nigel announced. "He's not amongst the dead or the statues, but I don't know where else he'd be."

"Do we have more eyes out there now?" Chad asked in the commanding voice of a king.

"Yes," Nigel replied, "but not nearly enough. So much is happening at once, and they know there's nothing we can do about it."

The cameras that had followed me down the white corridors flickered in my mind, followed by the memory of the alarms blaring. Florence's face had triggered them.

"Have you checked the prison security footage?" I asked, but I feared it was too soon for that. I ached to transport there, to go help whoever I could, but it was impossible. They had an army. Our army was only half-assembled—at best.

"The cameras went out," Nigel said apologetically. "It appears they still have a stock of mushrooms."

It was a punch to the stomach. The gnomes had worked so hard to retrieve all of the magic-blocking mushrooms and keep them away from Florence and his followers.

I scrunched up my face, trying to make sense of it all.

"How did the injection they used on Vincent work then?" I asked. "Isn't that magic?"

The royal guard shook his head. "Potions are different. Mushrooms stop active magic from a being or device. They don't affect the magic in potions."

I swallowed hard, fear building in the pit of my stomach. We needed to hurry. It was rash to go and confront an army we weren't prepared for, but I couldn't just stay there.

"We may not have the numbers, but it's cruel to stand here while people are dying," I told Nigel and Chad. "We can gather who we have and go fight."

"That's suicide," Nigel replied bluntly and I gritted my teeth.

This was nothing compared to Japan.

"I've seen worse," I snapped.

"We'll choose our battles wisely," Chad said steadily, "and this one is not worth it."

"And what classifies a battle as worthwhile?" I asked stubbornly.

"It's a prison, Azalea," he said softer, knowing firsthand the temper I possessed when I believed in something.

"So?" I replied, folding my arms. "The very first time I visited that prison, I listened to the inmates talk from behind a two-way mirror. I heard their stories. They're not all bad. Some are cursed with misfortune and bad judgement."

"It's still—what? A couple hundred criminals?" Chad pointed out. "They would've been turned into meals for the Night Crawlers anyway."

I sucked in my lips, remembering the pact I had agreed to at the meeting. But I couldn't give up just yet. "Where was this reasoning when we went to stop Florence from attacking Downy Lair?" I asked, giving it one more go. "They were horrible people, yet you showed up to try and help *them*—"

"I showed up to help *you*," he said pointedly.

"So what do you suggest we do while my friends get kidnapped and turned to stone, and others are getting turned into *vampires*?" I asked, my voice rising to compete with my accelerated heartbeat. "Sit and have a spot of tea while the bad guys win?"

My whole body shook thinking about it. And my father—I didn't even know what to think. He was gone—gone for good this time. Did it matter how it happened? Did it matter that it was Florence's followers?

Chad took a step closer, vanishing the gap between us, and placed my hands in his. "We study them," he said even softer. "We study them until we know exactly what they're plotting, until we know their plans better than our own. And then we'll strike."

Staring into his green eyes, I watched the wisdom that flashed behind them, and bit the inside of my cheek.

I hated when he was right.

So we did. We studied them. Nigel transported in and out to deliver more news from the royal guards—more tales and tallies of how many were dead, changed, or missing. Fairies and gnomes would follow the tracking spell, then travel in secret to map out Florence and Lili's hideout. Chad stationed himself at the library to watch the orbs, and everything was in motion for hours before I fell asleep only to be woken by that nightmare of Florence.

The bathroom floor felt cold underneath me, my hands shaking, my stomach still tight. I hated every part of the man who sired me.

The door to my bedroom opened, and I smelled Chad's familiar scent before he appeared in the doorway. Worry strained his features as he took in the sight of me.

"Someone said they heard you were sick," he said. "Are you all right? What's wrong?"

I stared up at him with urgency in my eyes, urgency to make it all go away before I unlocked my mental shield and threw the images at him. I had no words, only the memory I wished to scrub from my mind just as I had scrubbed my body.

Chad jerked back, a jarring look on his face before disgust overwhelmed it.

"Revolting," he said, walking over to slump down the wall and join me on the floor.

He stared straight ahead into nothingness before he shook his head and looked at me. I could feel the warmth of his body. He lifted an arm as though he was going to tuck me into his side but stopped abruptly.

You probably don't want anyone to touch you right now, do you? he asked, placing his hand into his lap instead.

An intense, incomprehensible feeling came over me.

He was letting me in again.

Shaking my head, I slouched down and placed my head in his lap.

I need your touch, I thought, pushing my way into his mind. *You're the only one who can erase the feel of him.*

Closing my eyes, I felt as Chad's fingers ran slowly over my hair, the tickle of his magic as he stroked his hand over my cheeks, and all at once the misery in my stomach and the thoughts of Florence's hot skin on mine vanished. Chad had whisked it all away.

I rolled over to look up at him, and he smiled his warm smile that had brightened my day so many times before. His green eyes relaxed as his thumb rubbed against my cheek. I placed my hand over his, wishing it would never leave my skin again.

But then sorrow flowed into his eyes and he glanced away. I felt the gates to his mind shut, locking me out, and my energy depleted. He was closing himself off, and as much as I wanted him to stay open, I could hardly blame him.

I placed the shield back in my mind, not knowing what I'd think or what he'd hear if I let him stay inside. And perhaps it was better to figure that out on my own—how I felt about him and everything else—before letting him overhear the jumbled mess that inhabited my mind.

"I have bad news," he said quietly.

I sat up to look at him properly, my damp hair falling over my shoulder. My fingers gripped anxiously onto my towel.

"The gnomes and fairies have followed the tracking spell," he said, my stomach tightening as I awaited the news. "They followed it all the way to Romania, and they're working to get us a full layout of the castle Florence is hiding in. So far they've gone undetected, but it's worse than we thought."

Not ten minutes later, I was dressed and in the entrance hall of *Schloss auf den Felsen*, on the edge of a small crowd of people who used the castle as their temporary home. I made my way past Ingrid and Irma, their blonde hair shining in the light, past women with severed bodies and bat-like wings that flapped cool air across me, their lower halves elsewhere in the castle. I walked past eyes of brown, blue, and red, past ancient faces and faces that were frozen in youth until I found the middle of the crowd.

Fendel stood atop a stool, bent over an enormous, floating, three-dimensional map. Its magical surface was composed of golden dust, and it was four times my height in both length and width. At the centre of the golden map was a glittering fortress that towered at least two metres high. It reminded me of the world map Lili had shown me during the agonising tour she had taken me on—through the room in Mallory and Morgan's castle where she and Chad had shared their kiss.

Leo shook his head from his spot by the model's grandiose front doors. "If this is what I think it is, then it's remarkable," he said, studying the map with fascination coating his face. "No one's been able to find it for centuries."

"What do you think it is, exactly?" Chad asked, slowly edging past the Loxley Coven gnomes, manananggals, werewolves, ghosts, and vampires to stand by the model.

"It's not possible," Irma said in her German accent. Somehow she knew precisely what Leo meant. "It is a legend."

"It's no legend," Leo replied, shaking his head grievously.

"What else would it be?" Charity asked Irma, her voice kind yet perplexed. "The location fits."

"What legend?" I asked, making my way around the map. My hand hovered over the golden curves and angles, entranced by its beauty.

"Dracula's Lair," Leo said, and my body came to a complete stop as my eyes left the model to stare at Leo.

"Dracula's real?" Chad asked, curiosity stark in his voice.

"*Was* real," Leo corrected. "He's long gone now."

Something tugged at the back of my mind—a memory. Abigail had mentioned his existence long ago, on the night of my first failed hunt, the night I met Chad. I knew the vampire was real, yet I couldn't fathom it. He still felt like a myth. He was even part of a joke Chad had once told me in our lake. But there was something else, something I couldn't quite place.

"It's said," Ingrid chimed in darkly, "that he was a descendent of the first vampire, Lilith, born thousands of years apart."

The strange something that had tugged within me clicked into place.

"Lili," I breathed out. I stared at the ground, squinting my eyes as the pieces connected together. I could sense every eye on me, but I didn't look up until I heard Chad's voice from beside me.

"What is it?" he asked.

I swallowed hard, gazing up at him. "Lili is also a descendant of the first vampire. That's who she was named after, remember?" I asked Chad. His brows furrowed in concentration as he nodded. "I think Lili might be Dracula's daughter."

The room filled with whispers.

"She can't be," Charity said. "It means she has to be—"

"Hundreds of years old," I finished. "But is that really so odd? She's half vampire. She's immortal."

I looked at Chad. *In my dreams, she mentioned it was her ancestral home,* I told him, not wanting to tell the others about my connection to Lili. *She said that her name came from her father's side—that he was a powerful vampire—that she has been alive for hundreds of years, and that that* castle, I said, using my eyes to gesture towards it, *had once belonged to her father. Then she killed him. That must be when this lair became hers.*

Chad nodded slowly, taking it all in, but as he looked around, perhaps to see if anyone was paying us any mind, he kept his thoughts to himself.

I parted my lips to speak to the others.

"Where is it?" I asked sharply, wondering where our tracking spell would take us. "Where's Dracula's hidden fortress?"

"It's located in Transylvania," Fendel squeaked in his high-pitched voice, "at the centre of Romania." He used his finger to circle a spot at the edge the fortress, near a tree. "It goes underground several stories. That's where they're keeping the slaves for the bloodfall."

"Bloodfall?" a manananggal asked. "Is that—"

"Exactly what it sounds like," Fendel interjected grimly.

I sucked in my lips as I looked at the spot. This was Chad's bad news. This was what made their hideout worse than we had originally thought, for there wasn't simply a three-tiered fountain of blood as there had been at Downy Lair. No. There was a "bloodfall" as Fendel called it, where thousands of gallons of blood crashed down into an indoor pool—blood that was being taken from countless men, women, and even child slaves as we spoke. Florence didn't just *do* evil things. He personified them.

My eyes closed, memorising the part of the castle Fendel had pointed to, and my magic focused on its depths. Glimpses of the real castle came like sharp jabs of a knife.

Humans—masses of naked humans attached to tubes—crimson blood flowing out of them. The vision blurred, dragging me elsewhere. The next sight was worse. Children—the children from Leon's visions. A sea of them shivering in cold dark cells. Florence was collecting them all, keeping them as trophies and worse, bleeding them dry to show off his power.

The scene blurred once more as the force yanked me down corridors, around corners, and up, until I was jerked to stop, standing on steps I had stood on before—not in flesh but in a dream. A crowd jeered around me. Florence's anticipating stare slammed into me. The rustling and squeaks against the black floors as a body was dragged towards me.

Chad's body.

This was Ginny O'Brien's vision.

I watched in slow motion, knowing precisely what was about to happen. I was locked in a trance, a slave to its every whim. I tasted, once more, as I drew the blood from Chad's neck—felt his body shake under my tongue. I heard his breath quiver in his lungs and release into the air one last time. As his body fell to the floor, my eyes clashed with the other me, the one with pink hair—Lili. I blinked and we were outside, white orbs, tall hedges surrounding me, floating parchment, and then a raging fire as Florence's cruel laugh rang out into the night.

The scenes—connected yet disjointed at the same time—played over and over in my mind. I felt a tear trickle from my eye and down my cheek as I watched Chad die a thousand deaths.

As quick as a snap, *Schloss auf den Felsen* rushed back into sight.

It felt like my blood had drained from my entire body, leaving me cold and empty. I fell onto the hard floor. Before I knew it, warm hands wrapped around me, pulling me back up. But as Chad held me tight, as his worried face took in mine, his lips moved soundlessly. I couldn't hear anything around me. Instead, a single word erupted in my head.

Soon.

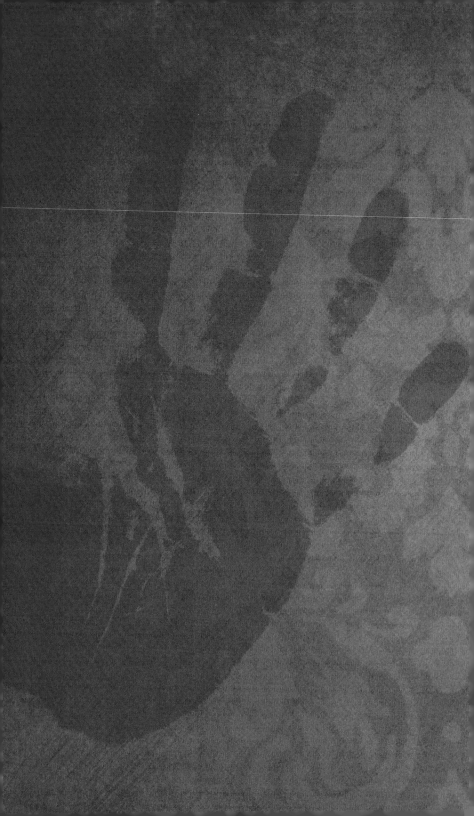

Chapter 41: Panic

The word screeched in my ears, deafening, melting my insides.

Soon.

Soon, Chad would die.

I blinked and Chad's eyes were locked on mine. The sound of the room rushed back in. My mind was wide open, and the look he gave me in return said it all. He knew what I saw.

A cold chill crept up my spine. More vomit bubbled in the pit of my stomach. I needed to escape the suffocating room, escape the people who stared at me, whispered, wondering what was wrong.

"If you'll just excuse me a moment," I murmured, unaware and uninterested if anyone had heard me.

I pushed Chad off me and thought of the most comforting place I could. When the purple smoke disappeared from around me, I found myself alone in my bedroom at Castwell Castle.

My heart raced but it was stupid to think Ginny's prophecy wasn't coming. I had pushed it aside to focus on other things, and it had become more of a distant memory than a tale of the future. Now, it was so close I could literally taste it.

His lifeless emerald eyes pierced through me again, followed by the glow of white orbs, green hedges, beige parchment, orange fire, and Florence's laugh. They were a hurricane in my head but one thing was certain: Chad was going to die. There had to be a second path—one to avoid the first. I could hardly breathe as I tried to weave through the labyrinth of woe and denial.

Chad appeared next to me in a cloud of his magic, but before I could scold him for tailing me—before I could even open my mouth—he cut me off.

"Azalea, it's all right," he said, his voice calm. But what did he know?

"Don't tell me it's all right," I snapped, panic turning the words into a screech. "How could your death possibly be anything resembling 'all right'?"

"We already know about the vision," he tried. "You've seen it before—"

"I know!" I screamed. I didn't need him to remind me. "But it's coming. It's coming soon, and I have to think," I said, pulling at my hair as I began to pace back and forth. "You could run away," I suggested as if it were the brightest idea in the world. "I could take over for you, just until this passes over. No one even needs to know you're gone. And then—"

"I'm not running away, Azalea," he said with sorrow in his tone.

I stopped my trek abruptly to point a finger in his face. "You don't get a say in the matter if you're not going to protect yourself," I told him sharply.

He took my hand gently in both of his, a pleading look on his face, but I snatched my hand from him.

"Perhaps that's how it all ends," he said.

I gawked at him. I could hardly believe it.

"How *what* ends?" I asked, praying he wouldn't say what I thought he meant.

"Our story," he sighed. Those brilliant emerald eyes were acquiescent as he watched me, awaiting my acceptance.

I wanted to punch him. Why was he giving up?

"Our story ends with you winning the war," I corrected.

"Does it though?" he asked. "You've seen me die multiple times."

"But the stars—"

"The stars tell of two outcomes," he reminded me. "One where we win and one where we lose. Neither says I'll go on to live out the rest of my life."

I couldn't speak. Why was he doing this?

"Look," he continued, "I fucked things up between you and me, so maybe my death is the way it's meant to be—"

"Stop," I managed to let out, but he kept going.

"I can't. I—" Chad tried again.

"Stop!" I repeated, but his voice overpowered mine.

"I love you!" Chad shouted, promptly shutting me up. He took a deep breath but my lungs were frozen as he stared into my eyes. "I love you and I want you to know that," he finished, much softer this time—like he was saying goodbye.

"'Want me to know that?'" I parroted, sadness clogging my throat. "You say it like it's inevitable—like you're accepting death."

"I need you to know, in case—" he corrected, but I cut him off again.

"Oh, that's great," I wailed. "You're giving up. Tell me, what good does it do to know you love me if you won't even try to stay alive for me?"

"It's a war, Azalea. Millions of people have died—more people will die—and if I'm one of them, I need to know you still love me before I go."

My jaw fell. "How dare you say that? How dare you just give up on yourself and expect me to confess my love for you so you can take it to your grave? You don't mean any of this. You're too emotional right now," I told him, the complete hypocrite that I was. My blood tears weren't even dried from my face. We were both emotional, but it was him who was going to die. That would scare anyone. "I just told you that you're going to die soon. You're not thinking straight."

"When I think about you, that's the clearest I ever think," he told me, shaking his head. "And if I die, you need to know that."

I most certainly did not need to know that. In fact, I wanted to hear the opposite—anything to ease the ache when he was gone— *if* he left me.

"You'll go on without me," he said, so lightly it was nearly a whisper. He grabbed my hand and laid it flat as if it were the proof. "Look," he instructed, pointing at the lines on my hand. "You'll have a long, beautiful life, Azalea. Remember? I told you that. You're going to have three precious children and you're going to love them with all of your heart."

I remembered. I remembered those words he'd spoken at the lake as we basked in the moonlight. I remembered every syllable, and how I had rejected the idea.

I swallowed hard before I grabbed his wrist and turned it over, eager to compare our lines.

"Show me," I demanded, staring him straight in the eyes to let him know I was serious. I didn't know how to read his palm, but I needed to find out. "Show me your lines and what they mean."

He shook his head.

"What lines?" he asked sadly, and as I looked at his palm, my heart nearly stopped.

My hand was covered in them—straight lines, curved lines, long, short, thin, thick—and though Chad did have a few thin creases, his hand was nearly blank in comparison.

How had I not noticed after all this time?

"My future has always been unclear, whether I look at my palms, or the stars, or the orbs at the library," he said. "It's always hazy, but maybe this is how it was meant to be. Perhaps this is how the blood oath breaks—how Abigail gets to stay alive."

The blood oath.

The stupid, bloody blood oath.

One of his three secrets.

I hated this. I hated every part of this hopeless feeling—like there was something I could do to save him, and keep Abigail alive, I just didn't know what.

I dared to look back at his sullen expression, depleted of all hope.

"What do we do?" I asked.

"Marry me," he said.

And I couldn't breathe.

I fumbled backwards, eyes locked on his, waiting for him to admit he was joking. After what felt like an eternity, a scoff choked its way up my throat like the very frog that once climbed out of it. "Marry you?" I asked, finally finding my voice. But how could he suggest it? "You're mad," I declared. I blinked and more tears fell.

"No," he said, his sparkling eyes going back and forth between mine as he waited for my answer.

"That's not funny," I said, shaking my head. He had gone from talk of death to marriage, and none of it made sense.

"I'm not having a laugh, Azalea," he replied softly, but for whatever reason, it was tainted with doubt.

I opened my mouth but no sound came out. I could marry him. That's what the stars said to do if we wanted to win. I could marry him, and perhaps some miracle would come and save us all.

But as the thought occurred to me, Chad's face fell, his shoulders following.

"What?" I asked.

He shook his head. "Don't marry me to win the war," he said sadly. "Marry me because you love me—because you want to spend what could be our last moments together completely and utterly in love."

My heart seized. I couldn't feel anything but shock. Thoughts no longer entered my head. What could I possibly say?

"I want all of you—" he blurted out, moving in closer, holding my hand tighter. "I *need* all of you, my love," he told me, speaking quickly as though he was running out of time. And perhaps he was, but I couldn't bear it.

"This is bullshit—that vision is bullshit," I insisted, taking a step back from him. "The big prophecy of the stars says you're supposed to work with a flower, and if I'm that flower, you're going to win the war. That means you can't die!"

"You're scared—"

"And you're not?"

"I'm terrified," he clarified, "but you have to promise me something."

"What?"

He placed his hands on my shoulders, gripping them firmly to relay the importance of what he was about to say. "Promise you won't chain me up like you did the night you went to meet with Florence," he told me. "Promise me you won't do anything rash, especially if it puts you in danger."

I stared at him blankly. Why did it matter what I did? I was the one with lines on my palm—some clear future laid out before me.

If he thought I would let him endanger himself, then he was a fool. I locked my mind from him. I knew what I had to do. I knew who loved him and could protect him in ways I couldn't, and I needed to speak to them now.

"I promise," I said without another thought.

He stared back at me, probably gauging whether or not I was telling the truth since he couldn't read my mind. But then his face softened, and he removed his hands from my shoulders and placed them at his sides.

"You haven't answered my question," he said hesitantly, and I knew precisely which one—the one asking if I'd marry a dying man. "I don't blame you for doubting it, not after this, not after everything I've done to break your trust. But just know that I'll love you and respect you, no matter your decision."

I had to leave. I had to escape before I was forced to think of a future without him.

I stared intently back at him. "I need to be alone right now," I told him quietly, and his face fell as though I had crushed him with my words. "And if you do love me—truly love me—" I pressed, "then promise you won't come to *Ypovrýchio Kástro*. Promise you'll give me space to think all of this through."

"Azalea—" he started.

"Promise!" I yelled sternly, shaking his arm.

He shut his mouth, swallowed, and then opened it once more.

"I promise," he said, but it was barely above a whisper.

"Good," I breathed out, releasing his arm.

I stared into his green eyes—eyes I had memorised long ago—hoping this time wouldn't be the last I'd ever see them. His hand twitched and my eyes flew down to it. For a moment, I let my mind open ever so slightly, and the same timid openness flowed out of Chad. Fainter than a whisper, his thoughts and feelings brushed out against me—sorrow, the longing to reach out and hold me, and fear that everything I saw in the vision would soon come true.

Dropping my gaze to the floor, I closed my mind tight. "Stay here," I ordered, trying to sound firm, but the desperate plea seeped out.

Before his hand could act, before he could reach out to hold me and make me believe everything was going to be all right, I transported away.

I promised him I wouldn't chain him up, and I would hold true to that. But when I promised him I wouldn't step in danger's path...

Well, that was a lie.

Chapter 42: Useless

W hat could you possibly be doing here?" Aunt Mallory
scowled.

She stood outside the golden doors of their castle,
arms crossed, guarding the entrance with her sister. Her back was
as straight as it would go as if she was trying to appear taller than
me. It didn't work.

I never understood how patience truly was a virtue until I had
to speak to the two of them. I took a deep breath to gather myself,
to pretend I wasn't a complete mess inside, and that I didn't
despise them both. But I had to look at the bright side. Chad hadn't
followed me; I could work out a plan to protect him. I prayed he
wouldn't see through my lie. I had thought it through, and I wasn't
going to sit back and watch him die.

The breeze rushed past us, carrying the smell of lilies to my
nose. I refrained from rolling my eyes at the flowers that *still* held
residence in their lawn. Instead, I replied, "I need your help.
Immediately, actually."

Mallory let out a snort while her sister merely glared at the
idea of helping a vampire.

"And why would we do that?" Mallory asked, her eyes
darkening.

"Because it will save Chad's life." And it was as simple as that.

The prospect made them pause long enough to listen. Thankfully, their typical charade of finishing each other's sentences had been snuffed out when Morgan began getting her visions of Chad's death.

"I'm going to track Florence to Lili's lair," I said, widening my eyes as I said Lili's name, to emphasise that they had been working with a vampire-witch all along. "It turns out, the woman you deemed fit to marry Chadwick is actually a descendant of Count Dracula, and she currently resides at his old lair," I informed them, rubbing it in even further. "I'm going alone to scope it out before I bring our army for an attack. The fairies and gnomes have already done so much to help. They have the fortress mapped out, but I need to go there myself. I need to go and see if I can get to Lili and Florence without an army pushing their way in. If they see us coming, they'll flee."

Or worse, they'll slaughter us.

"And why does that require our help?" Mallory asked viciously, drumming her fingers along her folded arms.

I gritted my teeth at her stubbornness. It was nearly tantamount to my own.

"It requires your help because Chadwick can never set foot in that lair." I stared back and forth between the two of them before focusing on Morgan. Taking a step closer to her, my tone and expression softened to a plea. "Please, Morgan," I said, addressing only her. "Your dreams—the visions of Chad—they take place in that vile lair. If I tell him my plan, he'll put up a fight, and after what happened in Egypt, there's no way in hell that he'll let me go without him. He's too protective. But if he comes with me he'll die."

"Is that a threat?" Mallory interjected.

"No, it's not a threat," I snarled, taken aback nonetheless. After all this time, how could they not know how I felt about him? "I want him safe just as much as you do."

"I seriously doubt that," Morgan debated darkly.

A slew of curse words and retched names filled my head. Why were they so hostile?

"He knows me too well," I told them, raising my chin and continuing on—ignoring the harsh words that sat on the tip of my tongue. "For whatever reason, he'll die if he follows me there. You have to distract him. You have to keep him here—safe."

"Safe from you," Mallory sneered.

"You know what?" I asked, giving up as I said it. "Yes, protect him from me. Protect him from Lili, protect him from Florence and anyone else who wants to rip his head off."

I closed my eyes, realising the error in my phrasing. I shook my head to brush the matter aside. Take it as they will, they still needed to keep Chad here.

"Lili is a cross between a vampire and witch like I am," I reiterated. "You once put all your trust in that traitor, yet you still have the audacity to question me?"

"Just because Lili wasn't the prophesied queen, doesn't mean you are," Morgan countered.

A huff left my lungs and escaped through my parted lips. Incorrigible.

"That's not the point," I told them, beyond frustrated that *that* was the detail they were focused on.

"Our sister Madelyn gave up the person she loved for her duty as a queen. Chadwick will have to do the same."

"It'll be hard for him," the other sister said.

"It was hard for his mother."

"The man didn't want to let her go."

My nostrils flared at their continuous dialogue. Apparently, they were back at it—so familiar yet infuriating. I studied the ground, hardly able to look at them. Were they somehow responsible for tearing Madelyn and Chad's father apart?

"Detective Harrison," I said, my eyes snapping back up to them.

"What?" they asked in unison, their eyes squinted at me in both anger and disbelief.

"He has a name and a title," I explained in a domineering tone.

"How is it that you know it?" Mallory asked.

"Not even Chadwick knows," the other witch assumed. But she assumed incorrectly.

"Apparently, we know a lot more than you think we do," I parried. "Your sister's power was the present. She helped save children who were in need of saving—"

"Casters," Morgan corrected. "She helped *Caster* children who needed savings."

I rolled my eyes at her. "Well, for whatever reason, Harrison was focused on the same case she was before she died."

"Probably some pathetic way to win her over," Mallory retorted.

"But it didn't matter," Morgan continued.

"Duty to the Casters and the crown had to come first."

"Not love with a pathetic mortal."

"She got pregnant."

"We thought they might conspire to run away together."

"But she was the firstborn of triplets," Mallory let out, sounding exasperated.

"She was the queen," Morgan continued.

"So we told him she died, hoping it would encourage him to stay away, hoping he wouldn't find out about Chadwick."

I clenched my jaw. They had known all along. They knew that poor Chadwick had ached when his mother died. They knew he had a father out there who would've cared for him, but they decided Harrison wasn't fit to be the father because he was a mortal. Their hate for non-Casters ran deeper than just vampires. They were prejudiced. And Chad was always the one to suffer for it.

"Do you know the pain you caused Chadwick by keeping his father's identity a secret?" I asked, my brows furrowed in disgust.

They snarled back at me as if they didn't give a shit—as if their cause had made their nephew's pain and suffering worth it. Only, it hadn't. Chad would've never been faced with the blood oath if it weren't for his meddling aunts. I needed them to wake up and face reality—to face fate itself.

"You know," I started in, "Harrison stayed focused on that child's case—your sister's vision—until a few months ago when he died. And that child who needed to be saved from her Caster father? That child was me."

I could hear their pounding hearts. I could feel their shock as I stared at their gaping faces. They didn't want to believe it, but the silence that followed proved they knew it was true. Even as Mallory breathed out, "Impossible," I could see it all click together in her mind.

If it were any other day, I would've smiled. But today I had a mission.

"It was," I said, praying it would wake them up from their delusion. "My sister and me."

Mallory shook her head. "This proves nothing," she told me, but little did she know, it meant everything.

So I pressed further. "After Madelyn's death, she visited me as a ghost, singing me songs, protecting me from my father. You insist fate didn't bring Chad and I together, that he's wasting his time with me, but how can you say that now?"

They both squirmed in their spots, the puzzle pieces falling into place while they stubbornly tried to tear the picture apart. Although they infuriated me to no end, I could understand their disbelief. I had trouble facing fate myself. This was all something that needed to be said aloud so the three of us could soak it in.

"Look," I said softly, "I've seen the vision of Chad dying—of me being the one to do it. I know what will happen if he goes to Dracula's Lair, and I know it happens soon. I don't know what drives me to do it—if it's a potion or a spell—or even Lili in disguise. But keeping him away is the only way to stop it from coming true. Trap him here if you have to. Just don't let him go."

I took a breath. "I need to go now," I told them, "before Florence and Lili have time to hurt anyone else. I'm asking you to help me protect him. Will you or will you not do it?"

The silence lasted for two tense beats before Mallory rolled her neck around and breathed out, "Of course."

Sorrow seeped its way in, softening her features just enough to overpower her anger.

"How could we not?" her sister added.

My chest swelled with relief. Emotions caught in my throat, but I swallowed them down, not wanting to break down in front of the witches. "Thank you," I told them as I stared back and forth between the two of them. I hoped they could sense every inch of gratitude I held inside.

"How will you get to her lair?" Morgan asked, ignoring my thanks.

Taking another deep breath, I tried, "I was able to get a few of Florence's hairs. I'm going to track him there and—"

"I know you have a tracking spell," Mallory interrupted as if I were impertinently over-explaining. She let out a small huff before her sister commandeered the conversation.

"But how will you get there? You have to follow tracking spells by foot," Morgan scowled.

"And even with your freakish speed," Mallory continued with a sneer, "it'll still take you far too long to get there."

"I'm not going to track them by foot," I said. "I'm going to transport there."

"That's not how tracking spells work," Morgan sneered.

"Well, that's the way it's going to work," I told her between bared teeth.

They both stared at me, their lack of confidence in me painted on their wrinkled faces.

"But if you so much as hurt one hair on him…" Morgan began, pointing a crooked finger at me threateningly as she advanced towards me.

"That's obviously what I'm hoping to avoid," I retorted, not bothering to hide my agitation.

Without another word, the two of them tightened their lips and gave a nod. I stared back at them, a feeling of dread hitting my stomach as I came to grips with the next step in my plan.

"Bring him here," I told his aunts. "I'll come back once it's all taken care of."

That is, unless I was caught.

I'm Still Unstoppable

Chapter 43: The Tracking Spell

The reflection in the mirror was horrifying, yet sickly beautiful and blonde. Lili stared back at me, blinking as I blinked. I wore a gorgeous pink dress——Lili's favourite colour. And though I was terrified to be in her body, it was only fair. She had used mine more than enough.

I went over the plan in my mind as if it was simple—as if it wasn't suicide. Walk in, kill Lili and Florence before they could poison me or trick me into killing Chad, and take down whoever else got in my way. I repeated the plan over and over until I actually believed I could do it. Chad said I was unstoppable, so that's precisely what I'd be.

My alibi was set. My disguise was foolproof. Chad was with his aunts. And no one, not a soul, was going to get in my way.

With one last look at the reflection, I balled my fists, my nails creating crescent moons against Lili's palms. I relaxed my fingers and picked up a bottle of shimmering teal sparkles that wisped around a glass phial. The gnomes and fairies had used up the tracking spell. They had used it to find the enemy's fortress—to create the magnificent, golden model. However, I didn't need them to transport me there. I had saved some of Florence's hair.

And with those blond strands, I had created a tracking spell of my own.

The Castwell sisters said I had to unleash the spell—follow it all the way to Transylvania on foot. If I followed their instructions it would take too much time—time I could use to kill. But the prophecy was about me. I was the most powerful sorceress—the flower. Perhaps the aunts couldn't follow a tracking spell via transportation, but if anyone could, it had to be me. I merely needed to unlock that door.

Fear sloshed around my stomach like a barbarous storm. I knew deep down I was doing the right thing. Stupid—but right. Only, it wouldn't be a stupid, reckless plan if it worked.

I uncorked the bottle at the exact moment that my doorknob creaked, turning clockwise. My heart pounded as the glittering teal magic lifted from the bottle in a swirl. I grasped onto it and my purple smoke took me—smoke only I could see—and I was gone. Whoever was at my door didn't need the shock of seeing Lili in my chamber. Besides, I wasn't even supposed to be there.

Both fresh and poisonous blood met my nostrils. Screams penetrated my ears. My feet touched down to the ground, only this time, there was gravel beneath them instead of plush rugs. My purple smoke swirled around with the sparkling teal magic before they both dissipated in the wind. The phial was completely empty. Pocketing the container, I looked around, finding no doubt that I was in Transylvania and that my creator—the evil man who had sired me—was nearby.

The pull leaned me forward. Florence's presence consumed me as I stared at Dracula's Lair. The moon glistened down on a large, black castle with flickering lights illuminating most of the windows. It was exactly like the model Fendel had shown us, but without the gold shimmers, it felt far colder. The gravel path wound its way around the castle grounds in what looked to be a large circle. Outside the circle, the plants were fresh, green, and full of life. The plants within the circle, however, drew a stark contrast.

Every plant within the gravel border appeared as if it had been scorched in fire, charred black until it matched the castle itself. The dead winteresque feel didn't fit the warm breeze that blew past, but the stench and the screams that the wind carried did.

From what I could tell, the screams came from underground—too many to count. I knew at once whose mouths begged for help. They were the people whose blood I had watched being drained in my vision. Their screams were hardly muffled by the layers of earth, nor the cheerful voices and laughter that came from within the castle. For a castle that looked so dead—held such death—there was so much joy inside.

My eyes flew around the property, focusing in to see the faint shimmer of magical wards. There had to be a way in without trying to break down the wards—without shaking the whole fortress to its core. If the gnomes and fairies could sneak in undetected, then so could I.

I started to trail the ward's border, perhaps too cautious and fearful they'd hear me. How could they be alerted by the scraping of gravel when their slaves were screaming for their lives? But I continued all the same, carefully placing my feet as I edged the perimeter, looking for a weak spot in the magical barrier.

I'd made it a quarter of the way around the property when I heard a small scuffle. My eyes shot up to the other side of the ward, just half a metre above the ground, to meet another set of eyes.

I stared at the little gnome, his black hat falling over his eyes and resting onto his round nose. He pushed up the brim and then stared back at me.

Fendel.

I raised my hands, trying my best not to scare him, not in this skin. But instead of freezing into his faux-porcelain disguise, he gazed at me with a different type of fear—not a fear for himself but a fear for my safety. Like he knew who I was.

"W—" I started, but Fendel quickly placed his finger to his lips and I stopped. He was right. The Night Crawlers inside would have excellent hearing. I shouldn't blow my cover.

I shifted back into my own form, furrowing my brows at him. Careful not to talk, I shrugged at the small gnome with raised arms to ask how the hell he knew I was here.

What are you doing here? I mouthed to the inquisitive gnome.

He folded his arms against his chest and shook his head, silently scolding me like a child who had been caught sneaking from their bedroom in the dead of night. But I wasn't at Dracula's

Lair to steal a biscuit from a jar. I was on a mission and didn't need a two-foot-tall gnome acting as a parent.

I raised a brow at him, and he quickly placed two fingers on the palm of his hand, walking them across, and then he pointed at me as if it were obvious.

It hit me—the turning of my doorknob—the magical powers he possessed. My small friend was here because he had tailed me.

Only, he shouldn't be here. It should be me risking my life, not him. This was different from the other times he had come. This time he wouldn't be hidden in the shadows, silently mapping out the place. He'd be with an enraged vampire-witch with murder in her eyes—ready to draw Lili and Florence's attention—the intention to kill first and foremost on her mind. He'd be with me.

It was as if my plan was irrelevant to Fendel. It made no difference, because he excitedly waved for me to follow him, running in the same direction I had been going. He hovered close to the ward that stood between us, his small legs running at top speed as I followed him. He slowed perhaps a hundred metres later when we neared a small blackened tree. It was the only black tree on my side of the ward. It stood twice my height and curved woefully, as if it had given up the will to live. There were no signs of leaves or healthy soil at its gnarled roots.

Fendel turned to me and smiled, but I felt as my magic grew weak.

I shook my head, hesitant to go farther, but the gnome gave me a comforting smile like everything was going to be all right. He pointed at the base of the dead tree. I blinked at it. What the hell was I supposed to do at the base of a dead tree?

I looked back at the gnome, ready to ask that very question, but he pointed at me abruptly, shook his head, and then used his pointer finger to mimic his throat being sliced. Just as quickly, he pointed at me again, only this time he pointed at his teeth afterwards, then gave a double thumbs up and a wide, cheery grin.

My lips parted and then shut once more as my brain struggled to piece together his charade.

Teeth. My fangs perhaps?

I stumbled over his gestures, nearly asking if I could read his bloody mind to decipher his clues, but then I understood.

He had told me not to die once I entered the fortress. It was me who should do the killing.

I gave him a firm nod and stepped closer to the tree. Its black trunk was a touch thicker than my torso. My eyes flickered back up to Fendel, and he nodded encouragingly before waving both hands at me as if ushering me to get closer to it. So I did.

I rounded the tree, and like an optical illusion revealing itself, a black hole appeared between two of its roots. It was large enough for me to fit through, perhaps with a bit of difficulty. A shiver caressed my spine as I stared into the pit, which seemed immune to the light. When I focused my eyes, however, I could make out a few shapes down below. Mushrooms.

My eyes snapped back up to Fendel. This is how the gnomes got past the wards. Colourful mushrooms to block the magic—mushrooms that were blocking my magic as I stood above them—magic I'd need to protect myself. But all Fendel did in reply was give a brave nod before he scurried away, off towards the dark castle.

I forced the spit down my throat. A moment ago I wanted him gone. Now, as I looked back down at the daunting hole, I wanted very much for my little gnome to come back.

Another breeze brushed past me. It was late. The sun's heat had left the surface of the forest floor. I could feel the cold through my clothes as I sat beside the hole and lowered my legs down. I'd have to move like a shadow—silent—hidden in the dark until I was clear of the mushrooms and could shift back into Lili. But as I took a leap of faith into the pitch black entrance, taking care not to crush the mushrooms, the smell of both fresh and rotted blood was instantly stronger, and the screams louder as they frantically bounced against my eardrums. Bumps covered my skin. This wasn't a vision nor one of my dreams. This was real.

The fungi snaked its way along a lightless, dank corridor, towards the chaos and sound of rushing water. I trailed my hand against a dirt wall to ground myself to this reality. The pull grew stronger, begging me step closer, yet my mind screamed for me to turn back immediately.

After a few minutes of following the trail, an orange light glowed at the end of the path. The train of mushrooms stopped. As the flickering light of a fire grew brighter, the tunnel's ceiling dropped lower and lower until I was crouched down at a set of solid metal bars in the shape of a small, gothic window.

The dirt around it was crumbled into tiny pieces, looser than the rest. I squeezed my fist, the prickle of magic coming back to my palms. I watched as my hand lightened to Lili's skin tone, and I used her hands to grip the bars of the window. It slid forward easily from its dirt frame, and after double-checking that no one was near, I jumped out onto a cobblestone floor.

The space opened up into a dark corridor surrounded with stone. Several torches were bolted to the walls, which stretched for what seemed like several kilometres in either direction before the paths took a right angle. Even more daunting than its length or the screams of terror was the source of the fresh blood. Lining the far wall was a metre-wide trench filled with rushing red blood—a river flowing throughout the dungeon.

They were bleeding people dry. They were taking more blood than they could possibly need and for what purpose?

My stomach tightened as the blood called out to me, but I pushed the craving away. I focused my ears, beyond the screams, the tears, the whimpers, and the rush of the blood river, away from the crackling fire, and throughout the rest of the underground dungeon. When I couldn't hear Florence or Lili's familiar breaths, I pushed my hearing up and into the castle—past stone, dirt, moans of pleasure, and a chorus of laughter. Beyond all those dreadful things that I had no power to stop on my own, I heard *him.*

Florence's heart beat slowly—far too calm for a man who had caused so much terror in the world above.

I tried to focus on the sounds around him, but it was too hard to tell if he was alone or what I'd find him doing. My mind toggled back and forth between who I should kill first—the man who had murdered millions or the woman who backed him—before firmly landing on Florence. Lili could pretend she was important with her grand castle and scheme, but she couldn't fool me. She wasn't truly the mastermind. She had become Florence's puppet. And the world needed him gone just as much as I did.

I replaced the grate and set off in the direction of the pull, keeping my ears peeled for unwanted strangers who had the potential to get in my way. The blood river ran beside me. Every fifty metres or so, the wall on my other side would open to another corridor, far shorter with a large prison door at the end. Most of the prisoners were attached to red, intravenous tubes, like the slaves at Downy Lair had been—their tubes stretching up into the walls and out into the river. Blood was splattered over the floor as if people had ripped the tubes from their veins, but several people lay on the stones, too weak to move. Those who could manage reached their hands past the bars as I strode by, begging for me to help them. Yet as much as my heart yearned to free them, I forced my feet forwards. I couldn't so much as meet their eyes.

My lungs felt tight, my blood pumping wildly through me with each step. I passed by a cage where the sound of laughter and ripping flesh collided with panic, but I kept pushing on, refusing to look. I'd come back for them. After the greater enemy was gone, I'd bring our army and free them all. For now, I had to be Lilith. I had to hold my head with pride and stride about like I owned the place if I was going to get anywhere near my creator.

Finally, the blood river funnelled into a thick pipe. Next to it was a curved staircase that led up to a rounded wooden door. A tiny barred window revealed the dark night and let in a fresh air that I welcomed amongst the putrid smell of slavery and slaughter.

I flicked my fingers at the door and purple smoke shot towards it. A click of the lock, and the aged hinges creaked as the door swung open.

A deep breath entered my lungs. I could do this. I had the key to any door that stood in my way. All I had to do was believe.

I fought from trembling as I climbed the stairs and ducked through the doorway to find a quiet courtyard. Black lilies filled the centre—perhaps the only living plants on the property. Their soft petals breathed life, unlike the people whose lives had been taken down below.

For a short moment, I fought against the pull towards Florence. The screams down below faded from my mind, the laughter in the castle went ignored. I stood alone, letting the breeze dance along my skin, sending goose pimples along my arms. I watched the moon as it shone upon the towering castle. I listened to the crackling fire from the torches that lined the exterior walls, their orange light flickering across the black stone. It was almost beautiful in a morbid sort of way.

Then a whoosh of magic and familiar breaths ruined it all.

I'm Still Unstoppable

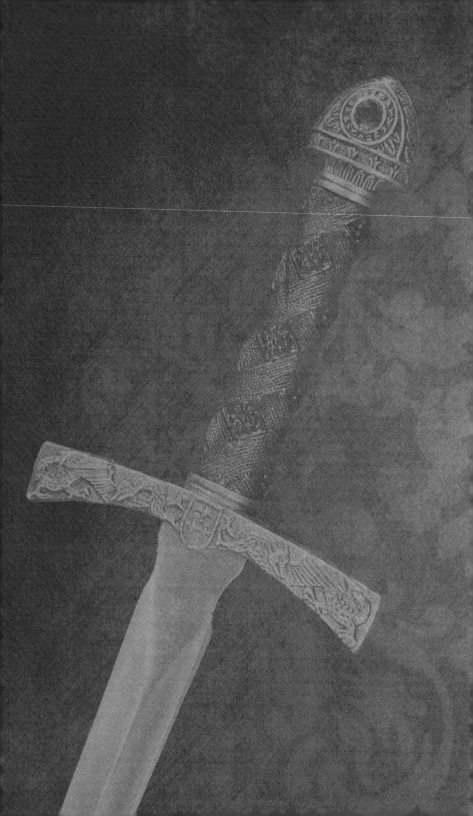

Chapter 44: Mind Readers

How?

How had he wormed his way out of Lancaster? How had he slipped past his aunts and the wards here? And why? Because he had a death wish? To spite me? And to bring them with him?

If I had been afraid of killing him before, now I craved it.

Chad, Connor, Hydie, and Fendel stood against the wall at the south side of the courtyard, draped in shadows, talking in hushed voices. They were lucky—stupid but lucky our enemies were inside.

I skirted along the perimeter, fuming between glances up at the windows—so many windows that didn't make sense on a fortress built for a creature who feared the sun. Ducking behind a pillar, I noted the way their voices stopped, but when I came out the other side, Hydie and Connor were staring at me with wide eyes. The wizard and the gnome had disappeared.

Where— I started to ask my sister, but the word was no sooner in my mind than I was being shoved against a hard wall, the back of my head smacking into the stone, and a shiny dagger pressed against my neck.

I felt the sting of the cool blade against my throat as Chad glared at me with hate in his eyes.

"What—" I started to say, but he shoved me harder into the wall and pressed the blade closer. I could smell my own blood, my skin unable to heal with the dagger still in its way.

Make a sound, he threatened, *and it'll be your last.*

I gaped at him. Of course he was mad I came alone, but furious to this extent? I didn't want to make a sound—to alert the creatures inside the castle—but it wasn't me that was going to blow my cover to shreds. It was him.

Then it hit me. My cover.

I could hear their panting breaths—feel the heat of Chad's hatred against my face as they all looked at me—as they looked at Lilith. I flicked my wrist, faster than any of them could stop me, and shifted back to my own skin, my purple hair back in my peripheral.

It's me, I told Chad, widening my eyes as though it would help him see into my soul.

Tell me who you really are, Chad growled, his eyes lit with a fierce fire. *Tell me or this blade slices right through your throat.*

My breath caught as I stared back at him before I looked over at my sister, hoping she could knock some sense into Chad. She knew me. She could hear my thoughts even clearer than Chad could.

Hydie, I tried, *it's really me. Tell him,* I pleaded, but both her and Connor's eyes darkened with suspicion.

The dagger pressed deeper against my throat and the sting grew sharper. A drop of my blood trickled its way down my neck. Chad was ignited with fury, his body tight against me as if he really believed I could be the imposter, but then a flash of doubt clouded his eyes. He didn't know if it was me or Lili. He did, however, know that he could die tonight.

Yet the bloody fool had still risked it all and come to Transylvania.

My hands rose to wave a white flag but his grip didn't falter.

It's me, I replied, not daring to speak the words aloud—not when our foes lurked so close. A glint of red caught my attention, and after my eyes travelled along the short silver blade, they landed on a sparkling ruby the size of a large coin. I recognised that dagger. He had used it against me before. It was the one from his armoury, the one that had pinned my chains to the wall while he pleasured me. It was only a few months ago yet it felt like a lifetime.

Who are you really? he thought, a mixture of fire and fear in tone. *Prove you're Azalea.*

I grimaced, but he didn't let down his guard. Of course he didn't know it was me. Lili could read minds too.

Prove it? I thought to myself. How? I could hardly think over the sounds of our pounding hearts.

You're an arse, I led with. *You're an arse, a liar and the most stubborn person I know other than myself. Would your precious Lili think the same?*

I don't know, he countered, ignoring my jealous remark and raising a brow at me. *Would you?*

This was ridiculous. I squinted my eyes at him angrily. *Then you tell me how to prove it,* I told Chad. I could easily break free, faster than his eyes could keep track. Either way, I still needed him to trust me—to know who I was. *Never mind the fact that either Lili or me could blast you away easily,* I couldn't help but add.

How about you figure it out before I slit your throat right here? he demanded in a low, dangerous voice, shoving the dagger further against my neck.

Only, I'd heal far too quickly for a slit of my throat to affect me in the long run.

You're right, the eavesdropper responded, though the last thought was meant for myself. *You can heal. I'll have to cut off your entire head to be safe.*

I rolled my eyes and threw up my mental shield until I was ready for him. Stupid mind reader. But we both knew he wouldn't chance it.

A glint of the blade flashed across Chad's face and a thought fluttered across my mind. I smiled up at him. *Let's just say that I had a much better experience the last time you used that dagger against me,* I said slyly, and it did just the trick.

That's disgusting, my sister said, her shoulders finally loosening.

Chad's grip softened before he swept me into a tight hug. Then he pulled away, his hands feeling along my hair, my arms. His eyes scanned every inch of me, checking to make sure I was okay before landing on the spot the blade had cut, right as the wound sealed itself shut. Perhaps the only good thing about being a vampire.

His lips met mine, kissing me like he thought he'd never see me again. *You're safe,* he sighed into my mind, a wave of relief washing over him. *I was so scared they'd capture you—that what I had told you the other day had driven you away. But I shouldn't have said those things. I should've been happy just to have you near, and alive. I should've been content with the way we were doing things.*

I furrowed my brow, trying to comprehend it all. Did he seriously think I ran off to Transylvania because he said he loved me? That *that* was why I had his aunts distract him—why I hadn't wanted him to come with me? Because I was scared of his feelings?

Before I could reply, he asked, *What were you thinking?*

My brain switched back into defensive mode. *What was I thinking?* I flustered. *What were you thinking? And how the hell did you even get here?* I snapped, trying to multitask between yelling into his mind and listening for our enemies. *Your aunts said the tracking spell had to be followed on foot, and you've never been here before. You can't transport right in.*

I could ask the same of you, he countered.

But I glared at him, crossing my arms as I waited for an answer, and immediately, his eyes fell to Fendel, who stood at his side.

Fendel has been here, he explained. *I knew you'd come, so I asked him to transport us. He came by first to confirm you were here and then he brought us.*

My eyes turned red as they raced down to the little gnome, who promptly grabbed onto Chad's leg. Fear flashed across his face before he half-dove behind Chad and turned to porcelain.

How many times had Fendel hidden from Chad behind my legs? Now the tables had turned. Traitors. The whole lot of them.

My eyes flickered over to Hydie, a fierceness behind them. They had to leave.

You know about my visions, I berated her, my chest rising and falling with the betrayal. *You know he's supposed to die here. How could you let him come?*

She flinched before raising her shoulders. *He was determined to come either way. It was between him and Connor coming by themselves and me, coming to make sure they weren't being daft. I chose the latter.*

I pivoted my head back to Chad before shaking it disapprovingly. *Of all the royal guards you could've brought,* I started on him, *you decided on a sarcastic werewolf, a two-foot tall gnome, and my sister?*

Nigel's the only guard I fully trust nowadays, he explained, *and he is otherwise preoccupied on a special mission—one only he has the power to do.*

I blinked at him, expecting a better answer as I didn't give a shit about what Nigel was up to.

Your turn, Chad challenged. *How did you get here? Fendel said you disappeared from your room and showed up here.*

I looked down to see Fendel, unfrozen and peeking out at me, but as soon as his eyes met mine, a wave of porcelain crossed over his skin. I looked back at Chad and shrugged.

I transported, I said simply.

But that's not how—

A tracking spell works? I finished, crossing my arms impatiently. *So I've been told. Yet that's how I got here.*

And now that we're all here, Hydie added, giving a shifty-eyed look around us, *we're helping you with your mission and then getting the hell out. So it'd be great if we could hurry this up a bit.*

Absolutely not, I tried. *I'm doing this without you.*

But Chad held my arms and stroked his thumbs along them. *Look,* he said calmly, *I could feel something was off. My aunts were trying very hard to push me out of their heads, only I could sense you were in danger. I had to find you.*

I let out a huff of air. His aunts were pointless.

So they just let you leave? I asked. What the hell had I enlisted them for if they were so utterly useless as to let him come prancing over here?

Chad shook his head quickly. *They most certainly did not let me leave,* he corrected. *They think I'm still in Lancaster with them.*

And how is that? I asked, folding my arms with a sort of defiant intrigue.

Chad let out a breath. He opened his mouth to explain, but Connor let out a small cough.

"Are any of you mind readers going to tell me what the hell you're all talking about?" he whispered, clearly annoyed, but Hydie, Chad and I shushed him in unison.

Connor widened his eyes, staring right into mine as they grew red again, and he shivered. *Note to self,* he thought in his usual obnoxious tone, *never tell the vampire I'm sleeping with her sister.*

Hydie smacked herself on the head. I didn't have time to feel surprise or guilt for invading his mind without consent, because my body was already lunging forward to attack the werewolf for laying his grubby paws on my sister. I could see the whites of his eyes, fear radiating through him as he realised I could hear him. But as my fingers touched his neck, ready to throttle him, Hydie grabbed onto him to move him away. Chad pulled me back, and Fendel grabbed tightly onto Chad's leg, but a whoosh of magic made us all freeze.

My eyes went to the source of the sound. A few hundred metres away, on the other side of the shimmering wards, ten figures appeared in the distance. A few had red eyes. The rest, I couldn't tell what they were, but three—three had familiar scents and brown burlap sacks covering their heads.

It was instinct that took over—instinct that pulled my hands away from Connor's neck. We all crouched down, hidden from the strangers as they kicked one of their captives in the stomach. The person fell to the ground with a grunt. More slaves to add to their collection.

Chad's face contorted with confusion, then a sort of understanding dawned on him.

"Lilith!" one of the people called towards the castle as they shook a prisoner. "Let us past the wards. We've got a present for you. Three to be precise."

There was a shift in the air and Lili appeared on the grounds, gripping Florence's arm as they appeared in a colourless magic. The pull intensified, pushing me towards him from behind. My feet stumbled but Chad slipped his hand into mine. I could feel

Florence's presence in every part of my body. But Florence couldn't feel me. None of them could. None of them looked in our direction. None of them saw us, or heard us, or smelled us through the light breeze. Yet somehow I could smell Chad, not next to me, not where he knelt holding my hand, but across the way.

A grin spread across Lili's face before she looked to Florence. She turned her body into him, her fingers lightly travelling up his chest.

"A present for *us*." She cooed the correction into his ear, standing on the tips of her toes to reach, and her smile curdled my insides.

She dropped back down to her heels and met the eyes of the creatures who brought these prisoners. Slowly her features shifted, and she morphed into me, but with pink hair.

And as if to prove exactly how special these prisoners were, the burlap sacks were yanked off in unison to reveal Aunt Mallory, Aunt Morgan, and Chadwick.

Chapter 45: Seeing Double

One Chadwick tightened his hold around my hand while the other was forced onto his knees beside his aunts.

Chills coated my skin. What was happening? How was this possible?

Chad's mind was silent beside me as he stared at the scene. If it weren't for the horror stricken on his face, I would've wondered if the distance was too large for his human eyes to see.

Lili pointed a finger at the wards and they lifted enough for her guests to enter. The prisoners were dragged in and shoved to their knees as they struggled against silver chains, the metal clinking as they fought. As the wards fell back into place, Lili bent over to study Chad and his aunts—my face as her mask—her smile never fading. As her eyes reached Morgan, she poked a finger at her nose.

"Time to bring that vision of yours to life," she said, the threat rolling off *my* lips.

And with a swish of magic, each of the figures was gone.

The pull forced me towards the castle with a strong tug. They were inside. It was happening. The dream was coming true but it wasn't how I pictured it.

My eyes snapped to the Chad crouched next to me.

Who the hell was that? I asked him.

I watched his throat bob.

That was Nigel, he said, the thought quivering as he stared at a door to the castle.

Nigel. That was his special mission—one only he had the power to do. He had taken Chad's place so he could slip away from his aunts. Nigel was a shapeshifter, just like me, and just like Lili. And now, he was in her clutches.

This is bad, Hydie said, throwing her thoughts towards me.

And it truly was. Chad's aunts were captured, as was his best guard.

My eyes shifted to Connor, who seemed completely bewildered, and then to Hydie, who looked as if things couldn't get any worse.

Chad's hand went limp in mine. His eyes widened as if to give an apology. He shook his head ever so slightly. *I can't leave them,* he said, his gaze pleading for me to understand. *If Aunt Mallory's visions are correct—if this is the scene Ginny O'Brien sent to you—then Nigel is about to die,* he said sternly. *He'll die and it will be entirely my fault.*

I took a deep breath. It wasn't wise for Chad to stay. It wasn't safe. Just because there were two of him didn't mean he was protected from harm. But he was right. We couldn't leave, not now. His family was in there—all he had left of them. And I wouldn't stand to let Lili take them away from him.

Shit, I thought, squeezing my eyes shut before racking my brain for a plan.

I flicked my fingers and my hair turned pink. If someone were to see me, I had to pull off Lili-vibes in my own body. Perhaps I could pretend to have captured Chad or something, but how was I going to explain my gnome, my werewolf, and my sister?

I remembered Chad's expression when the kidnappers first appeared.

Those people, I started, *the ones who brought your aunts and Nigel here... Did you recognise any of them?*

Chad nodded, staring at the fortress. *One—* he said before breaking off. *One of them is a leader of the Warlocks of the South.*

A chill crept up my back. So it was true. That's why the southern warlocks hadn't come to our meeting. Lili, the master of lies and deceit, had won them over. That must have been how the three of them got captured. They must not have known.

Fendel's skin shimmered with a porcelain sheen as if he was going to hide in his statue form but thought better of it.

We should bring more people, Hydie suggested, an anxious expression on her face as she held Connor's arm.

I looked away, not wanting to think about Connor and my sister—not wanting them to have come in the first place. But it was too late.

You go get help then, Chad said decidedly before he turned away from us and started towards a door opposite of where I had exited the dungeons. *I have to go save them.*

My heart began to pound against my chest. He was going to get himself killed trying to save his own doppelgänger.

I gave my mates a pleading look. *We're not ready to attack,* I told Hydie.

If we gave no notice, who would come? We had the location of their hideout. The second Florence or Lili found out, we needed to attack with everything we had—not half-arse it.

I threw a look back at Chad, all the way across the courtyard as he reached for a doorknob and slowly turned it.

Shit, I thought again. And then I sped off after him.

I slipped my hand into Chad's as he crept into the castle, taking care to step as lightly as we could, but it hardly mattered. The splash of more rushing blood covered our sounds and our scents.

Chad used my hand to draw me close to him, and I could feel his heat through his shirt. He was brave—far braver than I would've preferred at the moment—but if he was going to be here, at least I had him close.

The castle was just as I remembered from my dreams—dark and fit for an evil fortress—yet strangely welcoming. The gorgeous architecture lured us along.

We tiptoed down a corridor with dark red damask wallpaper and black crown moulding, glancing behind us to ensure we were alone. We passed paintings of red-eyed vampires that stretched back centuries, each in an ornate frame of tarnished silver. It felt as though their eyes were following us until we came across a dusty painting with claw marks scratching out its eyes and face. This one was at least doubled in size compared to the others. The words *Count Dracula* were carved neatly into its name plate. Next to it, in a frame of polished silver, and without a lick of dust, was a painting of Lilith. Her blonde hair was nearly lifelike as it draped over her shoulders. The hint of a smile played in her eyes, yet it didn't carry down to her lips. The name plate read, *Lilith, Daughter of Dracula, Rightful Heir.*

Chad and I exchanged dark glances. We weren't merely up against one child of darkness, but two: the son of Hitler and the daughter of Dracula. And what a treacherous pair they turned out to be.

We followed the sounds of the cascading blood, more and more voices gathering near it, and stopped in the shadows when we reached the end of the passageway. A dark doorway led out into a large hall where black paint chipped off the aged walls. Black candles flickered upon cobweb-coated chandeliers. Nearly a hundred creatures stood at the bottom of a large staircase, the gruesome, four-story tall bloodfall crashing into a pool that sat at the top of the first level. I had seen its golden replica on the map. I had watched the rivers flow towards it, but none of that had prepared me for the monstrosity it was.

Millions of litres poured into it, making the fountain at Downy Lair trivial. It splashed out, dotting the floors in red. My stomach turned as I wondered how many veins of tunnels and prison cells were down below to amass this volume.

I could feel it like a chilling memory. This was the setting of my dream—of Ginny's vision. I had been there before. I had been up those exact stairs. Only this time, I was faced towards the blood fall, not away from it.

Chad slipped his arm around my waist, holding me tight as we peeked through the doorway. The small wall beside it was all that shielded us from the crowd's attention. The horde grew steadily as Casters and Night Crawlers flowed down the staircase to stand in the entrance hall.

Nigel and the aunts were nowhere in sight. We watched the disguised Lili lead Florence up the stairs towards the fountain. She held onto his hand as she pulled him with her, and though she stopped to turn to the growing crowd, Florence's eyes remained on her.

He trailed the back of his finger across her cheek as if it were a delicate flower. There was a desperate longing in his eyes as he looked into what appeared to be mine.

"Make a show of the king's death," he purred in her ear. His finger found its way to a strand of her hair, and as he curled a pink lock around his finger, I witnessed a foreign softness in his demeanour. He leaned into her slowly, and I focused my ears to hear him whisper, "Your hair. It should be purple."

The excitement seemed to vanish from her features. Her teeth ground together, sounding in my ears as Florence bounced down the steps and towards a chair that someone in the crowd had placed for him. Despite the scowl Lili wore plainly, as though she'd rather die than obey, her hair shifted to purple.

It was worse than staring at her in a mirror. It was worse than tossing and turning against the nightmare Ginny had sent me, or watching the pain Morgan wore behind her eyes every time she screamed into my head that I was going to kill Chad. It was reality, and it was slipping away so quickly I could hardly grasp it to slow it down.

There are too many people, Chad said from beside me.

I nodded, thinking the same thing. It wasn't supposed to be like this. I was supposed to stop it. I *came here* to stop it, but the goal was to catch Lili and Florence alone, not in a crowd. If Chad and I so much as breathed too loudly, we'd have to transport away and then there'd be no chance in saving Nigel and Chad's aunts. There'd be no chance at a surprise attack with an army. And then all the work the fairies and gnomes had done would be useless.

Lili smiled at the crowd, a smile that froze my insides. The order for everyone to quiet was barked out, and the room fell silent.

"As you all know," Lili began, my voice coming from her lips, as strong as a lion's roar, "I've spent a lot of time in Lancaster, working with the grand duchesses of the Casters, making them believe I was on their side. Today, that pays off. I created a special mirror amongst the thousands they possess for their own vanity, and patiently waited. Now, with the help of the Warlocks of the South, we've captured the king of Casters and the last of his royal line." She turned to a doorway before calling, "Benji, bring them in."

I felt Chad's breathing crescendo against me as everyone's gaze followed hers. A scuffling noise seeped into the room as Benji dragged Nigel in. The sack was back over the guard's head as he writhed across the floor. His wrists and ankles were still bound together with chains that blocked his magic. A warlock and a few vampires brought in his aunts. Their sharp jabs and attempts to break free were nothing against their captors.

Lili sniffed the air as if she smelled the most delectable sweet and twirled a purple curl around her finger as Nigel was drawn closer. Then Benji placed Nigel on his knees.

What do we do? Chad asked.

I shook my head. I had no clue. I couldn't think with the blood pouring down, provoking my hunger and making my mouth water. I couldn't focus beyond the bloodfall, the building crowd, and the pull towards Florence as he settled himself into the chair.

It's your call, I replied, trying my best to rein in all those distractions.

Lili's fingers traced over the sack, right where Nigel's cheeks would be, and then she yanked it off, revealing Chad's face.

He needs to fight, Chad said from beside me. *Why isn't he fighting?*

But what could the wizard do? Nigel's orange magic was frozen in place, his face stuck as Chad's. The cuffs weren't allowing him to defend himself. He could tell them who he really was, but even if they believed him, it was still likely they'd dispose of him.

I looked back and forth between Nigel and Lili, both wearing different faces. Could I time it exactly right? Could I transport to Nigel and take him away? How many of the witches and wizards would tail me? Could I take them on my own? And even if I succeeded, would Lili and Florence relocate, destroying all of our planning?

"Please don't do this," Nigel begged in Chad's voice. Sweat and tears streamed down the king's cheek. "Please! *Please!*" he screamed out, his voice crashing against the walls and straight into my ears.

Mallory and Morgan's scuffles and muffled screams drew my attention. My fragile heart shattered for them, despite everything. Lili laughed, and my eyes snapped back to her.

"King Chadwick," she said in an airy voice before she looked at Florence.

He gave her a single nod, and I knew the worst was coming. I clutched onto the wall. I had to do it now. I had to save him before it was too late.

I looked at Lili, ready to let my purple magic take me—damn the consequences—but she froze. Her gaze flew over the crowd, over every blood-thirsty creature before her, until her blue eyes crashed into mine. They pierced into me, and I could feel her straight down to my soul.

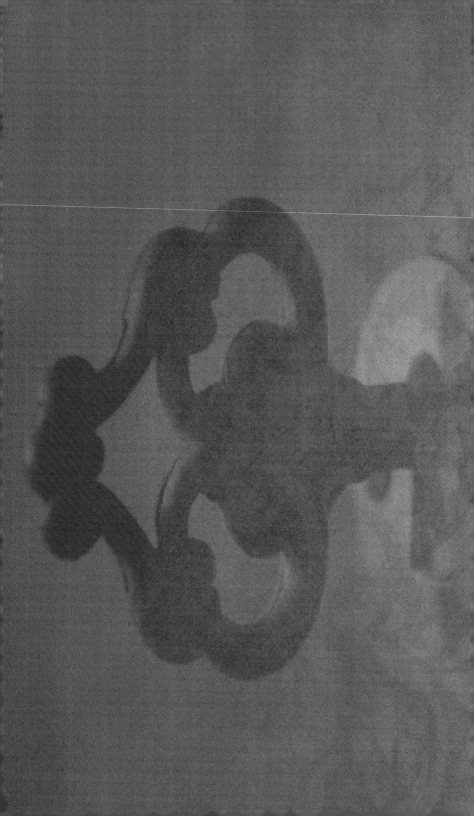

Chapter 46: Unlock the Door

I t was déjà vu.

I remembered this moment from my nightmares, the moment when our eyes met, yet the roles were reversed. It wasn't me threatening to take Nigel's life. It was Lili—just as Connor had predicted—but it still came down to the question of why I was in Lili's head.

My heart nearly stopped as I stood there, paralysed.

"Do it!" Florence screamed, and I jumped.

Instantly, Lili's eyes ripped away from mine. She grasped onto Nigel's head, thrusting it to the side, and her teeth tore past his skin, into his veins.

Chad lunged forwards, but I grabbed his wrists before he could flick them.

She saw me, I pleaded as he looked down at his wrists and then up to me, but I wouldn't let him go. *I won't lose you,* I demanded. I'd let them all die if it meant he was safe.

Every inch of me cringed as I pulled Chad further behind the safety of the wall, completely hidden from the doorway. The sound of Lili gulping away Nigel's life slammed into me. I was forced to hear Nigel's feeble attempts to stay upright—his body shaking against her hold. It tore at my insides until every last drop of his blood was gone. His heart gave one final beat before finding nothing more to sustain it.

Chad couldn't take his eyes off mine as we stared into one another, fighting to give the other strength. I didn't have to send the thoughts into his head. We both knew we had to go. He closed his eyes as we heard the thud of a dead body hit the floor.

The crowd cheered loudly but I could still hear Nigel's body convulse against the ground. I looked back at the doorway, my chest heaving. Lili was going to come. She was going to come after me. There wasn't time to save his aunts.

A hand touched my shoulder and I jumped out of my skin as I whirled around. But it was my sister's brown eyes that looked back at me. Her grip tightened as she gave me an empathetic look.

We have to go, Hydie told me, panic vibrating through her mind. She looked over her shoulder at Connor before turning back to me. *No one's coming to help.*

Morgan's shrieks began to echo and bounce off the fortress walls. She must've broken past her gag because she screamed out, "You killed him! You killed him! You killed him!" like a record stuck on repeat.

I felt Chad's body begin to shake within my grasp. I looked at him. His face was a greenish-white as his legs quaked beneath him. He held onto me tighter to keep himself steady. His eyes darted in the direction of his fallen soldier—in the direction of the two women who had raised him as their own—and he choked. He was in shock. Before I could fight away the sickness that was brewing in my stomach and soothe Chad's worries, a gold cloud swallowed us whole and we landed in the castle under the sea.

The waves outside *Ypovrýchio Kástro* cast blue-green patterns across the white marble floors, and as much as I wanted them to lull me into a false sense of serenity, the anxiety pumping through me simply wouldn't allow it.

My attention shot up to Hydie, and she swept me into a hug.

"I'm sorry," she said into my ear. She held me tight as an odd mixture of panic yet relief flew out of her. "She saw you, Azalea," she let out as she pulled back to look at me. "She saw you and I panicked. I had to get us out of there. It was only a matter of seconds before she turned on you next."

I nodded, my words lost in the blur of visions, screams, reality, and blood. She was right. Nigel was dead. Florence, Lili, the crowd—they all thought Chad was dead. Mallory and Morgan were in danger. There was nothing we could do for them if we were dead too.

My whole body seemed to find Chad at once. My eyes took in his expression—blank as he stared off through the wide window and into the ocean. My ears studied the pounding of his heart and the breaths his lungs struggled to slow. I ached to hold him. Grasping onto his shoulder, I let my other hand soak in the warmth of his cheek. His stubble pricked at my palm, grounding me to this moment as guilt ate away at my stomach.

He was here.

He was alive.

And though I should be aching for the loss of an innocent life, I couldn't stop thanking the heavens for the blood that was pumping through Chad's veins.

But how could he feel even an ounce of relief? His best guard had died in his place, and who knew what his aunts would face next?

"Your aunts are going to be all right," I promised him, but it was empty. "Lili made her point with one death," I told him, but that couldn't possibly be true. Not with the millions who had died in Japan. Not with the lives that had been stolen for the blood river and the bloodfall.

I glanced at Connor and Hydie for help, but they looked just as forlorn as Chad. My eyes scanned the floor.

"Where's Fendel?" I asked, hoping he wasn't still in Transylvania.

"He's safe," Connor replied quickly, shaking the raw feeling of dread from his stance. "He's letting the gnomes and fairies know it isn't safe to go back there at the moment."

I gave a firm nod in reply. "I need to rally everyone," I decided, fiercely trying to suppress the chaos in my mind and allow myself to think clearly. "I need to go to the mirrors at Castwell Castle and let everyone on our side know Chad's still alive before word gets out that he's dead. We don't want our allies losing hope—not when we need everyone to be ready."

I turned to Chad, his face still green, his thoughts still back in Transylvania. "I'll handle the meeting in the mirrors," I told him firmly. "In the meantime, come up with a trade or anything we can do to buy your aunts some time. Is there a way we can get in touch with Lili?" I asked, rubbing my thumb and index fingers along my brow to help me focus. "Like a mirror she can't get through or—" I screwed up my eyes for a moment before the obvious answer jumped up my throat. "A phone!" I exclaimed. She had called him before. They had talked on his mobile phone.

I focused my attention on Chad but it was as if I contained the energy for both of us and he contained none. He nodded slowly and placed my forehead to his.

"Have someone offer a trade, but don't let Lili know you're still alive," I told him.

I turned back to Hydie.

You two go with him, I told Hydie, blocking my thoughts from Chad as I gave my sister a meaningful look. If I couldn't chain him up, at least she and Connor could stop him from doing anything rash. We needed to think logically—to act without emotion if we were going to get his aunts out alive. *Perhaps you could use your magic to try soothing him?*

Of course, she replied.

I reached to squeeze her hand in thanks, and before my heart could convince me to stay with Chad, I transported to the attic in Castwell Castle.

The attic floor creaked under my feet as I stared into the mirrors—a labyrinth of unbearable memories—flames, shattered glass, and reflections that moved on their own. Lili. Only this time, Lili wasn't there to haunt them, nor was Chad's mother, or the ghoul I once believed lurked up there. I was alone. But soon, half the world's leaders would have their eyes on me.

Each mirror stood in its place as if they had never been broken. Since meeting with Eyeron, each had been carefully dipped into magical potions and resurrected.

An eerie feeling crept up my spine. Chad had made us desert our home for a reason. We hid under the cover of the ocean for protection, and as much as I missed this castle, I had to stop coming back.

I pushed back my hair, a fruitless attempt to make myself look presentable.

"Mirrors," I said, addressing them as though they lived and breathed in front of me. "Give me every Caster, Night Crawler, and mortal leader who could see the black invitations."

I trained my eyes on each mirror, focusing on them until I saw them for what they truly were. They were more than reflectors—they were portals—just as Chad had taught me long ago. The glass shimmered all around me, and before I knew it, I was staring into the homes of hundreds, eyes of every shade staring back at me.

Eyeara.

Leo.

Charity.

Koda.

Victoria.

Queen Sadiq.

The prime ministers and more. Beings from every continent.

I took a deep breath, forcing a numbness to come over me, and I told them everything they needed to know.

The Caster duchesses were kidnapped. The king's decoy was killed. I ordered them to prepare for a fight. They only had tomorrow to prepare. The next day we'd strike.

I held it together long enough to watch the last of the mirrors shift back to my reflection before my knees crashed down to the ground.

Every thought in my head was a fleeting blur. Lili had to be onto us by now. She had seen me standing there with pink hair. She was going to ruin everything. I had to see what she was doing—if Mallory and Morgan were still alive—and I knew just the way in.

Though I had only ever been able to see into Lili's past, I knew I had to steal into her present. I had to reach into her mind and let it guide me to her consciousness. I closed my eyes tight, remembering what it felt like to be Lilith—the feel of her skin, her pride, her ambitions, her worries, her pain—until I found the exact words I needed to hear.

My eyes snapped open and looked at myself in the mirror before I uttered the command into my mind.

Unlock the door.

Chapter 47: The Bite

Lilith | Present | Dracula's Lair

*T*he screams in the dungeon made me recoil with disgust—cells upon cells overcrowded with mortals and other creatures who would serve as our meals.

I fled down a never-ending corridor lit with torches, along the river of blood, up a staircase to a door with a small window, and out into the moonlight. The moon painted a glow over my skin and I stopped to lean against the stone wall.

Closing my eyes, I tried not to think of Azalea, standing—unwelcome—in my home. Her, or some bizarre trick my mind was playing on me. I tried not to think about Chadwick. I tried to breathe in the fresh air. Instead, a foul smell wafted in through my nostrils: rotted teeth, greasy hair, and fungus.

I opened my eyes to reveal Benji's hideous form, his dirty blond hair slicked back into its usual ponytail. He was smiling at me with blood-stained teeth, and I wondered how long it would be until Florence's teeth turned the same. Benji rocked a wicker basket in his hands as if he were happy to see me. I did not return the sentiment.

"Let me guess," I said, pushing off of the wall to stand straight. "Florence sent you to watch me?"

His vile breath escaped with a laugh and I held my own. Back when he lived at Downy Lair, I didn't remember him being so disgusting.

"He said you might be needing these," he replied, evading my question. He moved his hand to open the basket and I saw the rotted blood stuck under his fingernails right before he revealed the mushrooms.

That explained the smell of fungi.

I gritted my teeth, understanding what Florence wanted me to do.

"Fine," I snapped. "I'll make sure the wenches are secured in their prison."

I went to snatch the basket from his hand but he jerked it away and wagged a finger at me.

"I think I'll come with you," he said.

I didn't bother to tear his head off. He was worthless—a pawn under Florence's control. Instead, I headed towards the sixth floor, away from the prisoners downstairs to the prisoners we kept in the castle, like a favourite pet we couldn't bear to leave outside. Only, the witches were not favourites. They were collateral. And if they had any information, it was my job to get it out of them.

Thanks to the mushrooms, my invisible magic couldn't deliver me to their room, so instead, I let my vampire half take over, and I ran on foot. A row of what were once brightly coloured mushrooms lined the bottom of the door. Now, they were spotted with mould and black decay.

The mushrooms were powerful for their size—just smaller than my palm. Powerful enough to stop both the duchesses' magic and my own. We were running out of the handy fungi thanks to the stupid little gnomes. They had kept their stocks locked tight ever since they found out we were using them. The rest of our supply would soon be rotted.

I always used to think it odd that my mother kept the gnomes frozen in front of the small cottage my father had banished us to. Now, I was beginning to understand why.

A buzz grew louder until I felt a wind behind me. I turned my head to see that Benji had finally caught up, his eyes glued to my backside. He licked his lips as his gaze slowly moved up me, taking in all my curves, before flinching when his eyes met mine.

Immediately, he bent over and began swapping the old fungi out for the new.

I scrunched up my nose as I took him in, watching him work in a hurry before he stood up straight and looked me in the eyes expectantly.

"You can leave now," I demanded, glaring into him.

He recoiled at the sound of my sharp tone.

"But Florence—"

"But Florence nothing," I finished for him.

It was my castle by birthright—one inherited as soon as my good-for-nothing father had died. Florence didn't get to tell me what to do in my own home.

He had been treating me differently the past few weeks, as though he no longer trusted me. As though I hadn't created him—as if I hadn't helped him every step of the way. Ever since he met with his precious Azalea. Whatever she had said to him, whatever they did during their little rendezvous, had poisoned him against me. Benji's behaviour was merely more proof.

Benji flinched again as my hand dove into my pocket to retrieve my keys, the ancient metal cold against my skin. If I wasn't so angered by his and Florence's secrecy, I would've smiled at his reaction—it meant he was afraid of me. The big, bad vampire—afraid of me. But then again, maybe I wouldn't have smiled. He reminded me of Elizabeth and the pitiful look she had given me.

I turned away from him and thrust the key in the lock. As it clicked, I opened the door briskly and shut it behind me.

The room was grand and dark like the rest of the fortress, draped in elegant maroons, black, and greys, nothing white or brightly coloured like the mushrooms. Two coffins, lined in red velvet, replaced beds in this guest room. It was as my father had left it except for my witchy additions—a large mirror and a floor to ceiling window that let in plenty of sunlight—additions I had installed throughout the entire castle to spite my dead father. Only, the windows ended up serving as a daily reminder that I *shared his blood and an intolerance for the sun's rays. So I'd added a special ward around the castle to block it.*

The witches were already standing. Their hair was frazzled, their eyes were bloodshot, and salty tears glistened along their cheeks. Their arms were folded—more like a hug around themselves than a show of their usual temper, and their backs were crooked from the weight of the devastation they felt. The overly confident witches had shrivelled up after watching the man they had raised as their own die. Yet instead of fear on their wrinkled faces as they watched me walk closer, there was a clear expression of confusion.

"Lili?" they asked in unison. They stared at me, completely distraught.

"Oh, right," I said, slightly taken aback. It had always amazed me how blind they were. "You still think it's the other vampire-witch who's killed your little Chadwick, although I'm sure you've heard how horrible I am. I suppose that's my fault, though. Shapeshifting is a tricky thing to follow," I explained.

I would've been more than happy to demonstrate if I could've used my blasted magic, but the dropping of their jaws signified that changing my form wasn't necessary. They believed it.

I waited, careful to take in every part of their reaction, to see if my hunch was correct—to see if they knew more than they had let on. But their sorrow didn't waver.

"You killed him?" Morgan breathed out, the truth clogging her senses. She closed her eyes and shook her head, sadness swallowing her as she said, "You killed him. You killed him. You—"

"Yes. I know," I interrupted harshly, rolling my eyes at the repetition. I had heard it enough every time she, Azalea, and I were in the same room. "You don't have to repeat it. I was there," I growled at her. "I did the killing."

Part of me itched to tell them my suspicions, if only to cut out their dramatics, but knowing them, it wouldn't help.

"You can't keep us here," her triplet spat out, looking around her as though every item in the room was either filthy or cursed.

A laugh burst from my lungs. It was exactly like Mallory to be a snooty bitch when she was in a cosy room rather than a dungeon.

"You're lucky to be in here. You know..." I drawled out, running my hand across the velvety rim of a coffin as I rounded it. *"I never liked either of you. From the moment I met you in those woods, I knew you would merely be in my way. But truly, you made my job easier. You see, while you were busy doting over me and hating the other little vampire-witch, I was wrapping you around my finger. It was easy to get away with things and find out information when you were making Azalea the enemy."*

Their lips tightened, stubborn not to admit their mistake, but of course, I wasn't lucky enough for their mouths to be shut for long.

"Why are you keeping us locked up?" Mallory blurted out.

"Mostly for information," I said with a calm sigh, making my way to the other side of the coffin.

They both recoiled away from me.

"We don't know anything," one said.

"They held a big meeting," replied the other.

"We weren't invited," Morgan sneered angrily—almost as if she had actually wanted to be a part of it.

"Define 'they,'" I demanded, squinting my eyes. *"Are they trying to rally all of the Casters or all of the Night Crawlers?"*

"Both," the bitch enunciated, heat in her eyes.

Ah, I thought, slightly amused with how clever Chadwick had become. So he had managed to get the Casters and Night Crawlers to work together. Not that it was hard. I succeeded in uniting them for my fight—mostly by force—but still, I was impressed. The little king was more resourceful than I gave him credit for. No wonder his prejudiced aunts weren't invited.

I shook my head at them, holding in a smile. For two women who hated vampires so much, they sure had one hell of a bite.

"Don't forget, I read minds," I told them, not bothering to mention that I couldn't read them now—not with the barricade of mushrooms at the door. I tossed my long, blonde hair over my shoulder. *"I've gotten quite good at it over the years. Often, I can get in your head even if you try to block me out. Sadly, it makes torture unnecessary, but we could always use that as a fun alternative. We won't dismiss that idea just yet. Let's wait and see how big of a nuisance you both are."*

"You're not going to hurt us?" Mallory asked, completely ignoring my threat, but her sister looked too depressed, like it wouldn't make a difference either way.

"I think we'll keep you unharmed. You're worth more to us that way," I decided.

I walked over to the window and let out a long, dramatic breath. My eyes scanned over the dark grounds, searching for movement, wondering if Azalea was out there, trespassing around my property. I moved over to the mirror next, taking in its tarnished frame before I looked at the reflection. My skin was as pale as theirs yet so much smoother—more pleasing. I wondered if Azalea had ever imagined standing next to Chad when he was his aunts' age and she still looked in her early twenties. Did it matter now?

"You wouldn't guess I was older than you, looking at the two of you." I turned around to face them once more. *"You know there are potions to keep regular witches from ageing, don't you?"* I asked bluntly. *"Why would you* choose *to look that way?"*

"Leave us alone, Lili," Mallory said, uncharacteristically soft, almost like there was no bite left in her.

But that was simply no fun.

I rolled my shoulders back, sizing them up before I attacked. *"Did Chad tell you he found his mum's killer before he died?"* I asked.

My words pierced the very air around us with a thousand needles—with venom—with spite. And the horror that coated their faces was delicious. I leaned in slowly, my ears focused on the breaths they sucked in, my eyes trained on the disbelief they wore on their faces, and my heart relished every second of it. For once, they had nothing to say.

"By the looks on your ghastly faces, I'm guessing not," I tutted at them.

Then I knew just how to make it infinitely worse.

"And if he didn't tell you that," I continued, taking my time with each slice into their hearts, *"I'm going to take a leap and bet he didn't tell you that you've met the woman—that you know the killer. Perhaps not by name, but you've seen her with your own eyes. She's a vampire, Azalea's best friend, Abigail. Don't worry though,"* I said, leaning back from them as I lightened my tone.

"Azalea wasn't conspiring with her or anything. In fact, I don't think she knew until I announced it."

They were silent except for their pounding hearts. Where was their bite?

"But to top things off, do you want to know what your nephew did when he found out it was her?" I asked, drawing it out as long as I could.

I waited, yet there was still no reply. I looked back and forth between the two of them, before deciding to test Mallory—to torment her severely. She was more likely to rile herself up than her sister. She sucked in her cheeks, pure hate sparkling in her eyes.

"He did absolutely nothing," I told her, shaking my head.

The witch moved quickly, her hand whizzing through the air to strike me across the face, but my vampire side made me quicker. I caught her wrist and smiled.

There it was. There was the bite.

"That's why he died, you know?" I asked, doing my best to sound innocent, even as I threw her wrist away from me. "There was this whole debacle with a blood oath, which I may or may not have convinced him to do, but either way, he'd be alive if he had just killed Abigail. Instead, he let her live. So really, he's the traitor."

"Go to hell," she said, her nostrils flaring.

But I let out a small chuckle. Oh, didn't she know? I was somewhere far worse.

"Don't you want a world where witches are free to be themselves?" I asked them both before sitting on the edge of one of the coffins. "A world where we don't have to hide from mortals?"

"There is no world without Chadwick," Morgan replied, but this was no longer fun.

"Suit yourselves," I said standing up, brushing the dust from my hands. "You'll be our prisoners then. Oh, and if you think of anything useful while you're locked away up here, feel free to give a shout."

I turned to leave without another word. It was useless keeping them here. They knew shit.

I flung open the door, ready to get far away from those wretched witches and the mushrooms, but came face-to-face with Benji. I shut the door behind me before I internally snapped.

He smiled at me, sensing my distaste for him and not caring.

"Lilith," he said, eyeing me like a tasty treat and not his superior, "when Florence finally gets Azalea, I think I want to have a go with you."

I put on my best smile. "Benji, when Florence finally gets Azalea and this new world has begun, I'm going to chop off your dick and wear it as a necklace."

His face fell right as a buzzing sound came from my pocket. I lifted my phone out to see it was one of Chadwick's guards and rolled my eyes. Probably a pathetic attempt to get me to free my royal hostages.

I smashed the phone to the ground at Benji's feet, and he scampered to the side as a thousand pieces scattered across the floor. Then I shoved past the pervert to leave.

"Disobey my orders one more time," I called back to him, "and I'll turn your ballsack into matching earrings." Then I took off at a run, headed straight for Florence.

He was going to be livid, but after my conversation with the witches, my hunch was still tingling excitedly.

Azalea had been here, I could feel it. There was something in her frozen stance, hidden in her eyes, that whispered a truth. And though the two witches I had just spoken to didn't know, deep down I did.

It wasn't really Chadwick who had died today. Azalea would've come straight for me. She would've raised hell.

No. Chadwick was still alive and well. And Florence was going to be livid when I told him.

I'm Still Unstoppable

Chapter 48: To Break the Curse

Azalea | Present Day | Attic

I snapped back into my own head, absently scanning the ground around me. I'd done it. I'd snuck into Lili's present mind, and she hadn't the faintest idea. Two things were certain now. One was that she knew Chad was alive. The second was that his aunts were too.

He should know, I decided, staring at my reflection in the mirror. Chad should know they were all right, but the question that lingered in my mind was whether or not I should be the messenger.

Chad had been in shock, and though his aunts were alive, our enemies still held them in their clutches. He had just watched his own death—not entirely him, but his most trusted guard. Perhaps we no longer had to worry about Chad dying, but he had an undeniable weight on his shoulders—a weight shoving him down and darkening the world around him. And given what had passed between us these last few months, I was no bright light.

He had asked me to marry him and what had my response been?

He had told me he wanted to spend his last days knowing my heart belonged to him, and I had ignored the proposal because I didn't want to marry a dying man. Surely, I'd be the last person he wanted to see. Had I proven myself as unworthy because I hadn't answered first, before Ginny's prophecy had come to light? Now that I knew it wasn't his blood that left his veins—that it wasn't his soul leaving his chest—was I too late?

What would Abigail say? She was my best friend. It had always been a rare case that she wasn't rooting for Chad and I to be together. From the moment I told her about him, scared she'd cast the idea away—a vampire befriending a Caster. But she hadn't. She had plotted ways to keep him safe from Florence. And after Chad and I shared our first kiss, and I went into full-blown panic mode, Abigail was the one to shove me back in Chad's arms—nearly literally. It wasn't until she found out he was the Caster prince, and she started to suspect who his mother was, that she turned hesitant. She questioned the idea of us moving in together. And who could blame her? Perhaps she feared for my safety. After all, who could be mad enough to love the type of creature who took their mum away from them?

Chad. That's who. After all this time—after everything he and I had gone through—Chad, the High King of the Casters, a man who could read the stars, wanted to marry me. Yet instead of giving my answer, I was back to the trembling, broken shell of a girl I had been after our first kiss. A girl who feared love.

I went back to *Ypovrýchio Kástro* to shower, to dress, to think, but not long after, I gave in. I had to see Chad, and my body led me to him as if my heart could feel his location.

From the other side of our bedroom door at Castwell Castle, I heard the rustling of papers, the shifting of his clothes. I could smell his scent, picture our belongings in my mind, all before I knocked on our door. I knew he was inside, but I kept my mind out of his thoughts in case privacy was what he needed most.

"Who is it?" he called, the sound of turning paper meeting my ears.

I cleared my throat anxiously. "It's me," I replied.

"Come in," he said, his voice lighter, less weighed down than I thought it would be.

I opened the door to find him sitting on the floor between the chaise and the fireplace, our room in pristine order as it had been for months—everything in its place. Everything except for the papers in his hands and his mother's trunk, which sat wide open.

My heart skipped a beat. The last time I had been in the same room as him and that trunk, I was doused in water, scorch marks on the hems of my dress. The chest and I were both safe from the fire Lili had started with a reflection of me and a thousand candles. Chad had hesitated to touch the trunk, his eyes haunted with the memory of his mother. Now, he looked as though there was nothing he'd rather do than riffle through its contents.

My eyes shot away from the chest and to his striking green eyes. He looked at me expectantly.

"I had a vision," I opened, "of Lili. Your aunts were there. They're being kept as prisoners, and though they're heartbroken and grieving your death, they're safe for now. They're in a comfortable chamber. I don't think they'll be harmed."

Chad nodded, his eyes shifting down to the floorboards before looking back at me.

"I can feel them," he said softly, the glee he had previously worn lost in the dark room. "I feel their sorrow, but I also feel hope, like they're safe."

I watched him closely, studying the pain on his face, yet thankful for each of his breaths. He needed hope. I'm glad he discovered some when I couldn't afford to give any of my own. But he had to know...

"Lili knows you're alive," I told him bluntly. His face fell further as he stared back at me. I pursed my lips, pushing myself to go on. "I know we'll figure it all out, I'm just—" I lowered my chin, letting my hair fall around my face. "I'm really sorry about what happened to Nigel. I wanted to do something. I *should've* done something. And I know you trusted him. He gave his life to keep you alive. I'll never forget his sacrifice."

Chad nodded again, slowly, methodically as he took it all in from his spot on the floor. Then his jaw tightened to reveal a brave face. How could he not be terrified?

"Let me show you something," he said, breaking the stark silence.

He reached a hand out to me, and though I took it and let him ease me down to sit beside him, I couldn't shake the feeling of dread for what was to come. I could feel that the end was near. There was always something. There would always be something deathly waiting for us around the corner until both Lilith and Florence were gone.

I smoothed my soft blue dress down around me, anxious to look at the chest. Lili had almost demolished it. Chad had tucked it away until now.

Tilting my head towards him with an ambivalent gaze, my eyes met his, the spark of excitement back within him.

Squinting my eyes, I asked, "Are you all right?" In truth, he looked *too* all right. The shock had deserted him and was replaced by an odd calm. "Did Hydie use her magic to calm you down?" I spewed out. "Did she use too much?"

Chad let out a warm laugh. "Now *that* is entirely plausible," he said before moving on far too quickly. "I've been going through some of my mother's old belongings," he began, "and in them, I found this."

He handed me a journal. It was the one I had seen before, flipped through the pages, and read fragments of the stories it had to offer. Now, the smooth surface felt inviting in my hands, yet I knew what it held—a picture of me when I was a child—descriptions of the haunting dreams Chad's mother used to have of me.

"I don't really know why I took the chest away from you that day," he continued, my eyes snapping back up to him. "You have just as much of a right to read through it as I do, if not more. I think I was scared—like she was less mine in a way if she was also yours. But I was wrong, and for that, I'm sorry."

I shook my head. He had a right to be upset. Why would she visit me as a ghost and not her own son?

"She wrote about my dad," he went on, his eyes flickering down to the journal, "and how they fell in love." He ran his hands through his dark hair and let out a deep breath. "But she never told him about me."

I shut off my mind. Half of me knew I should tell him his aunts already told me that while the other half knew it wasn't the right time, not with them being locked up as hostages.

"She never talked about him," he said, sadness coating his throat. "Perhaps it hurt her too much, but she chose to lead the Casters instead, and to teach me all she knew—to love me enough for the both of them." He closed his lips, pausing long enough to feel the burn—the loss.

I reached across to him and held his hand, rubbing my thumb over it softly, letting him know I cared even if I didn't know the words to properly convey it. He closed his eyes, taking in the feel of my skin against his. When he opened them again, his eyes were clouded with the distant memories of his mother.

"When my mum died, I was never really mad about it—not the way my aunts were. I was sad and lonely, especially after her ghost stopped visiting me, but I knew she was watching over me. I knew that the vampire was out there, but I didn't wish them harm. I merely wished they'd change so they wouldn't take away anyone else's mum, and that's exactly what happened."

He reached over to the journal, absentmindedly running a finger in swirls around the cover. "I know it's not really Abigail's fault," he said. "I want to talk to her, tell her I don't blame her. But if I do, it'll put her in even more danger."

I frowned, not understanding. "How so?" I asked patiently.

"When I'm near her, I feel the urge to complete the blood oath—like finding out it was her fuelled the curse somehow."

Instantly, my mind was back in the tent, during that frosty journey through Russia when he admitted that truth. Then it flashed to Lili, barging into the pub, telling us it was Abigail. I had seen Chad and Abigail together only a handful of times since—the way his body tightened—the way he had turned away from her.

"I wish I could take it back," he said, his volume louder, more assertive than before. "I wish I hadn't traded my father's life so I could find Abigail and kill her. In doing so, I ruined not only my chance at happiness, but yours, Abigail's, and my father's."

"No," I tried, my brows furrowed as my head shook away the idea, but he stopped me with a sulking expression.

"I have," he said, as though it were that simple. "And I've been trying to find a way to undo the oath—to undo as much heartache as I can—but I haven't found one yet."

He let out a heavy breath, furrowing his brows as if readying to tell me something.

"Part of me wishes I had been the one to die tonight, instead of Nigel," he continued, his voice thick with guilt. Shivers sprouted across my whole body as he said it. "It would've broken the spell. It would've let Abigail live."

My throat bobbed as heartbreak tried to push its way up.

"Chad—" I said, choking on the thought. I felt my mental shield drop, letting him in, but I didn't care. I squeezed his thigh. As much as I appreciated his openness, his honesty, my heart ached knowing he felt that way. A red tear fell onto my dress and I watched it soak into the fabric as I sniffled. "I feel like I just got you back. I can't watch you die again. I can't…"

With a slow, careful hand, he lifted my chin and rested his forehead against mine. He looked back and forth between my eyes.

"I'll find a way to break the blood oath," he told me. "Once I do, I'll make amends with Abigail, and I'll tell her how I feel."

I nodded, letting another sob escape. I wouldn't lose him. Thank heavens he hadn't let his guilt consume him. "I think she'd like that very much," I told him, and he nodded.

"I know that breaking the oath won't bring my parents back," he said, nearly a whisper, "but at least then Abigail can be at peace."

I thought about that life—where I could have both Abigail and Chad again. Where I didn't hide from Abigail, unsure what to say, or fight with Chad just to avoid confronting my feelings for him. A world where they were both alive, both mine again, and happy. It would be magical.

I looked up at Chad, to try and search for the right words to say, but his expression sent a jolt to my heart. He needed to say something. I could feel it. Only, I wasn't going to like it.

"I'm going with you, back to Transylvania, Azalea," he announced. "Not because I have a death wish, not because I think I have a better chance at saving my aunts than you do, but because I can't let you face those horrors all on your own."

My heart fell. He wanted a part in the grand plan.

There was no point in saying I wouldn't be on my own—that I'd have an army fighting behind me. He had made up his mind, and I could hardly blame him. I'd feel exactly the same if the roles were reversed.

He pulled back from me as I nodded, though he gave me a very stern look in reply.

"No chains," he said firmly. "No handcuffs, no spells, no tricks, no running off on your own."

I blinked and more crimson tears trickled their way down my cheek, tickling as they fell, but Chad placed his hands along each side of my face, brushing them away.

And despite my better judgement, I nodded once more, hating myself for giving in—feeling like this agreement would take him away from me forever. If I had any bollocks I'd transport him to Egypt, have Queen Sadiq lock him up behind the bars of falling sand.

Instead, I used all my energy to stop myself from blubbering like a fool.

I rested my head on Chad's shoulder and squeezed his hand. "I promise," I told him.

He rested his head against mine again and stroked my hair. A melody vibrated against me as he hummed a song, a song he had hummed before—the same one his mother used to sing to me. My heart caught in my throat. After a few moments, the song swirled into a beautiful end.

Chad took a deep breath, releasing it as a heavy sigh. "I should go rest," he whispered, his chest tight with regret as he said it. "There's a lot to prepare," he added.

He placed a soft kiss above my brow, but I grasped onto him before his magic could take him away.

"Stay the night with me," I spewed out before I could think of the repercussions.

We hadn't slept next to one another since our journey through Russia, the cold winter air forcing our bodies together. But I had been so close to losing him today. I didn't want to spend another night without him in my arms. Regardless of the lies and secrets he had kept, he'd forever be my Chad. He'd forever be the man that whisked me away—the man who showed me how true love felt—the one who'd do anything for me. And after seeing the life leave him, I needed to hold onto him tonight more than ever.

He studied me with those dazzling green eyes of his, his face creased as though he longed to know my thoughts. I didn't shut him out. I let him feel every ache to hold him, to love him, to keep him alive. And as I stared back and forth between his eyes, a plea for him to understand my needs, he nodded. I let out a breath, closing my eyes and I felt his forehead gentle against mine. He nodded again and my heart lifted.

"Of course," he said, softly against my ear. "I have yearned to hear those words for a very long time."

We made love that night, under the ocean, in our temporary bedroom, tangled in the sheets. There was not a single ounce of rage as our bodies connected, as our minds opened fully, letting the other in. I soaked in every move, every touch, every feel of him, memorising him and holding onto him like I'd never let go again. We talked until the early hours of morning, laughing, crying as he told me memories of his mum. Then after he fell asleep, I wound my fingers into his dark hair, and savoured each of his warm, tired breaths. I wanted to freeze the moment. I wanted to run away with him, away from the war, and live out our happily ever after. But it was as if the cruel hand of fate wouldn't let me.

I'm Still Unstoppable

Chapter 49: Emerald Green

No sleep graced me. I spent more time tossing and turning than resting as Chad slept soundly beside me. For me, there was no sleep, no dreams, no peace of mind. Only worry.

When I could take it no more, I slipped out of bed. Taking one long last look at Chad in his peaceful sleep, I snuck away to bathe. I dressed in a pretty gown, hoping it would improve my mood, and transported to *Schloss auf den Felsen*. My arms were crossed as I stared at the map laying out Dracula's Lair. I had been there. I had succeeded in absolutely nothing, but I wouldn't make the same mistake again. Soon, they'd get the fate they deserved.

I pored over the map for hours, studying the layout as if every captured soul depended on it. And perhaps they did. When I could see the map clearly, even with my eyes closed, I went back to my temporary chamber in the ocean. Only, when I arrived, Chad was gone. The spot where his body had laid was now cold.

I swallowed hard, praying he hadn't given up on me—hoping against hope he hadn't thought I'd tried to run away again. But when I closed my eyes, I pictured Chad in my mind, and a warm sensation wrapped around me. He knew I loved him, and I could feel in my heart that he loved me back.

Knowing sleep wouldn't take me, I let a book distract me—for old time's sake. After being curled up in bed, lost in a fantasy book where the heroine fought with a bow and arrows, and the snakes were as white as snow, a light gleamed from the corner of my eye. Across the room, my sage green purse glowed with the promise of a letter.

As soon as I grabbed it, I could feel a soothing heat coming from it. I brought the purse over to my bed, and after pulling the blankets back over my legs, I reached in to take out the pen and the letter from Chadwick.

Thoughts filtered in and out of my head. What was he writing to me about? Part of me wished he was offering me a stamina potion to give me the will to go on with our plan. Another part of me feared he'd decided to go back to Transylvania early. It was neither. Instead, the letter was simple.

Holding up?

Only two words. I gave him a truthful answer.

No. But it would be odd if I was.

I lifted the pen from the paper, pressing it to my lip as I thought of a distraction—a way to lift the troubles that were pulling me down into icy waters.

You never told me my surprise. The one I wasn't going to like.

I don't know why I asked. Clearly, it wasn't meant to cheer me up if I wasn't going to like it. What sort of rubbish surprise doesn't cheer a person up? It intrigued me nonetheless.

His reply was an evasion rather than an answer. But I don't know why I expected anything less.

And you never answered my question. The one about marrying me. Sounds like we're even, doesn't it?

I let out a laugh, wishing he was here, yet I couldn't decide if I would scold him or kiss him. So I decided to dish his snarky wit right back at him.

Sounds like I need to beat your arse...

Meet me in our gardens.

I swallowed hard. *Ours,* I thought, breathing out, longing for anything that was *ours* instead of this wretched, lonely room that reminded me of how we were apart.

Biting my lip, I looked up at my clock. It was nine at night. The sun had fallen again, but it still wasn't wise to go. We had a small portion of precious time before the attack. We should stay underwater until the time was right. But at the same time, I was as ready for the battle as I'd ever be. I could afford to waste away another hour, couldn't I? If it meant being with Chad...

I looked back at the page, the letters disappearing to allow space for my reply.

Are you going to try and seduce me if I go?

No, I wouldn't dare.

Damn. I was hoping you were.

Better luck next time, I suppose.

A smile overtook my whole face before a horrid thought washed it away. *If* there was a next time...

Fine. I'll meet you in the gardens, but I think you could do a better job of convincing me. Could I at least get another snog out of the deal?

That entirely depends on if you like your surprise or not.

Shit. What in the bloody hell did he have in mind?

I tossed the duvet off of me, a bizarre combination of dread and curiosity driving me forward. Checking myself in the mirror, I decided I was quite happy with my choice of dress. It was green—emerald, like Chad's magic. If I wasn't too cross with him after this surprise of his, perhaps he'd enjoy taking it off me.

Right as I was about to transport away, a potion bottle on the vanity caught my eye. I snatched it up and slipped it into my pocket in case Chad had the bright idea of using a pair of magical handcuffs. I didn't want him to have the upper hand. Then my purple magic swirled around me, taking me home.

The lake reflected the vibrant colours of the twilit sky as darkness approached. Around the edges, it glistened with thousands of sparkling lights. As I followed the reflection up to the orbs that created them, I realised they were white lanterns magically floating above the lake's perimeter. They trailed around and then away from the lake and towards the maze, creating a pathway.

At first glance, it seemed as though snow was falling along the path. I gasped as I saw that it wasn't snow, but soft azalea petals. The petals drifted from the sky and landed neatly along the grass to create a mesmerising walkway. My eyes followed them down to the maze, where the tall hedges had parted ways to reveal a straight line to the centre. To the glowing blue fairy tree. To Chad.

My heart leapt from my chest when I saw him, standing in ironed black robes, a white button-up shirt and a shiny black tie. Even from a hundred metres away I could see his smile, reaching from ear to ear, smell the hint of salty sweat on his nervous skin, and hear the soft grass flatten beneath his feet as he rocked anxiously on his heels.

I knew precisely what his surprise was, without reading his mind. Every inch of me could feel it, from the fluttering butterflies in my stomach to the tingling across my skin as I forced my feet towards him.

He was right, I thought, as I drifted down the trail. I hated this. I hated it so much because I loved it—longed for it even. It was our future, or at least what our future could be.

The petals glided down my hair and across my arms, tickling as they went. The lanterns guided me until the blue light of the tree shone upon us, radiant as always. Yet I couldn't stop looking at Chad's green eyes and his contagious smile as he beamed at me.

I fought back my own smile as I tried to give a scolding expression instead, but I couldn't manage it.

He flicked his wrist and at least a hundred pieces of beige parchment flew around me, momentarily stealing my gaze from his. They flapped around like delicate birds, the wind from their flight dancing across my skin.

I gave Chad a questioning look and he merely gestured towards them, telling me to look for myself. I grabbed one of the letters out of the air. I recognized it immediately. It was my handwriting, a letter I had written to him in France, apologising for falling asleep and leaving a drool mark on the paper. His reply sat right below it, his snarky reply. One of the thousand reasons I had fallen in love with him.

I reached up for another letter as I let the first fly back into the air, and I knew that one too. It was the very first letter he had ever written to me, telling me that if I ever needed to talk, he was here for me. He had practically been a stranger in that moment, yet he had been so caring, even then. I reached for another, and another, and another, each a memory that I held dear. An invitation to his Saint Valentine's Day Ball, a quick note of me telling him I was still alive, and more.

I turned back to the wizard in front of me, completely speechless for a moment before I asked, "Are these *all* of our letters?"

He nodded as he studied my face diligently. "Every single one," he said quietly, as though trying to sound brave.

"But how?" I asked, furrowing my brows. "Each letter disappears so we can write the next."

He shrugged innocently, his eyes sparkling with blue light and a suppressed joy. "I have my ways."

I rolled my eyes, biting my lips to try and conceal my smile. Of course he had his ways. He was a brilliant wizard and a hopeless romantic.

The smile fell from his face and was replaced with a much more serious expression that accelerated my heartrate tenfold.

"Now," he started before taking a big gulp and steadying himself, "I know you said you needed time but…"

There was no need to finish, for I knew the end. Time was up, and not by either of our decisions.

He flicked his wrist again, and a faux night sky lit with a thousand stars hovered right above us. I watched in awe as the twinkling lights rearranged themselves and spelled out the question he had asked me before. The one I hadn't had the guts to answer.

Will you marry me?

I felt as he wrapped his hands around mine, and I looked into his eyes, finding both worry and hope there.

"If the stars won't set a clear path," he said bravely, "then we'll rewrite them. We'll make our own destiny."

Tears brimmed in my eyes as I looked away from him and back up to the stars. It was beautiful. Far more beautiful than the last time he had made the stars appear in our tiny orange tent, sheltering us from nightmares and wendigos. I looked back at the man in front of me—the man who held my heart yet still trembled before me.

I shook my head, not believing I was awake. "How did you conjure this all up on such short notice?" I asked, my voice nearly cracking over the emotions in my throat.

A laugh rumbled up his chest and through to mine as he pulled me against him. "You honestly think I haven't spent every day for nearly two years dreaming of this moment?" he asked, giving me a look that melted my insides.

He took my chin in his hands and directed it towards one of the castle's towers peeking out from above the hedges.

"You once stood up there with me, and we talked about how my future was already mapped out in the skies." He turned my head back towards him so our lips were all but a breath apart. "But

Azalea," he continued, his warmth caressing my skin, "your future is written in the stars, entwined with mine. And though we don't know how long that future is, I promise I'll fight to spend a thousand years blowing you away with all of the magic this world has to offer. I'll dedicate every second towards earning your trust, your love, your heart. I'll fight with you against every battle, knowing that you'll always win. And Azalea," he said, turning my palm over so he could run his fingers along its surface. "I want to have these three beautiful children with you, that share your eyes, and your smile, and your bravery, and our love until the end of my days."

A tear fell from my eye as he pulled away and got down on one knee. He slid a velvety black box from his pocket, and with a click, the top separated in two to reveal the most gorgeous ring I had ever seen. A silver band, engraved with swirls, met a set of Celtic knots on either side of a bright emerald cut in a princess style. I stared at it, my breath taken away.

He steadied himself on the ground before his eyes pierced into mine. Then his lips parted. "Will you marry me, Azalea, and become my queen?"

I could not breathe. I couldn't so much as blink as I stared at the ring and pictured a long, beautiful, happy life with him.

As his features began to tense from the anxiety of waiting for my answer, I dropped to my knees in front of him. I grabbed his cheeks, memorising the feel of his prickly beard for the hundredth time and breathed out, "Oh, fuck it."

I crashed my lips against his, and as he wrapped his arms around me, I let his touch erase every nightmare, every vision, every doubt of us being together.

He pulled away from me to look into my eyes, the smile back on his face, right where it belonged. Only, as he did, another pull took over, stealing the glee from my lips.

Dread filled my stomach and was mirrored on his face as a pull pivoted my head back towards the path, past hedge after hedge, out of the maze and towards the castle. And not any pull.

The pull.

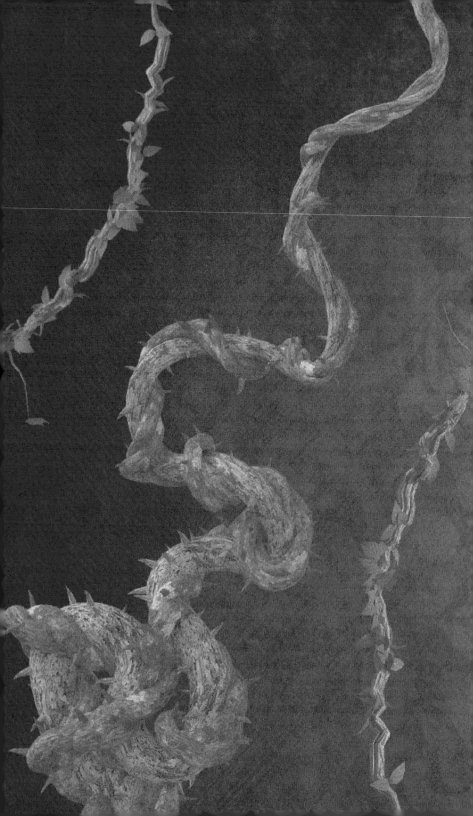

Chapter 50: Four Figures

I see you finally fixed the mirrors," Florence's voice called into the night.

My hands turned cold against Chad's cheeks. I looked back into his green eyes and it was as if I could feel all the sorrow in his heart. He didn't have to whisper into my mind to tell me we had to go. Let Florence take our home. Let him burn it to the ground. It didn't matter as long as we had each other.

I saw the faint shimmer of Chad's magic as it sparkled in the corner of my eye, ready to transport us away, but at that precise moment, something slithered up my arms. I felt the smooth surface wrap around me like vicious snakes, yet it looked like there was nothing there. It coiled its way around me, taking me as its prisoner, and a flood of doubt washed over me. We were seconds too late.

The hold jerked me away from Chad, away from his touch, away from his warmth. The tendril of his green smoke disappeared as I was yanked up from the ground. Something pulled him backwards onto the ground—something invisible— the same thing that wrapped around me. My mind flashed back to the night Florence bit me—the way those same invisible ropes held me down as I screamed for mercy.

Lili. She was here. She was doing this. She had to be close. And if she was, I could wrap her fucking ropes around her neck until she let us free.

A flood of people fell out of the castle's entrance, but Lili's blonde hair and blue eyes weren't amongst the crowd. Florence led his entourage onward, trotting down one of the curved double staircases. There was a bounce in each step before he bent down to look through the straight path Chad had carved into the maze.

"I see you, darling," Florence sang to me before straightening back out. He continued his jovial bounce down the steps and past the statue of Chad's aunts and mum.

I longed to wake up. It was a nightmare—a premonition. It had to be. Any second, I'd wake up and devise a plan to escape this future.

Chad grunted and my gaze flew back to him, panic in my heart. He tried to lunge towards me, but Lili's invisible force was merciless.

A buzz sounded in my ears. I blinked and Florence and at least twenty others were next to us, the blue glow of the fairy tree shining across their skin. Florence sank his claws into my shoulder in a possessive grip. I flinched as the pull snapped into place like a rubber band smacking against every inch of me—so strong, so brutal. My stomach sank as I recognised the feel, and my deepest fear set in. This was no dream. This was reality. Florence was truly here. And I was utterly helpless.

Two men with red eyes grasped onto Chad, pulling him and stretching his arms wide. A woman with a pointed hat pried Chad's fist open until the ring and its box reluctantly left his hand.

"He was holding this," she informed Florence.

Florence plucked the ring out of its box to stare at it, a sneer on his face as if the emerald embodied all the love I put into Chad instead of him. Sucking in his cheeks, he tossed the ring to the ground. The blades of grass hardly moved as the ring vanished into them—a symbol for our lost hope. Still, my heart yearned to find it.

Florence drew closer to Chad's face, squaring his shoulders as his grasp on me dug deeper. "She's mine," he growled slowly.

His cruel voice painted a gruesome picture of his intentions, of all the plans he had for stealing me away and making me his.

Just as he had meant to do the night he created me. Just as he had wanted in the years since Zena's passing. But Chad didn't flinch. He didn't utter a word as his struggling stopped. He stared Florence down, a bold, kingly authority on his face. I tried to slip into his mind, to steal a shred of hope we'd get out of this. But his mind was locked. Instead, hatred radiated from his eyes—a promise to the man who sired me that he'd never have me. Because I didn't belong to Florence. I wasn't anyone's to own.

Florence's red eyes snapped to mine, fire flaring behind them as a look of pure fury lashed at me. He had received Chad's message loud and clear, and there was going to be hell to pay before I would escape Florence's claim over me.

A stranger shoved a dirty rag into Chad's mouth. Florence yanked at my hair, forcing my gaze away from Chad, and I let out a scream. The invisible vines pulled tighter as I tried to turn back—as I tried to tear them off of me, but all I could do was listen as one of them punched Chad in the stomach, and he let out a muffled grunt.

Florence tore me from the ground. I made to reach up and tear off his head, to pluck out his eyeballs, to do anything, but the invisible chains wouldn't allow it. It was as if I were no stronger than a crying infant fighting him off.

Another buzz sounded. Wind blew through my hair, through my dress. The scene blurred and suddenly Florence and I were out of the maze. The double staircase was within reach, the shadow of the grand statue darkening our skin.

Chad! I screamed into my mind, trying desperately to hear him, to feel him, to know he was all right. But his voice didn't echo through my mind. Where was he?

I pushed myself out of Florence's hold but it was as if he let me—as if he knew the hidden chains were enough to subdue my strength—that Lili's power was enough to keep me prisoner. I crashed to the ground and her magic did exactly that, binding my hands so I couldn't use my magic.

Hundreds of people circled us, some still pouring out the doors of our home. Some with red eyes, severed torsos for others, claw marks scarring so many faces. I searched the crowd to find Chad, to find an escape, but every sound, every smell, every jerk of my chains crashed into me, adding to the chaos. A torrential downpour of anxiety flooded my lungs. It threatened to paralyse me, but I couldn't let the fear or the chains conquer me. We had to get out. I had to get to Chad, and we had to leave.

My focus snapped to a witch as she flicked her fingers. Black magic jutted out and four beds of straw appeared before me, tall wooden posts erected from them. But I couldn't understand them. What was their purpose? What was Florence going to do now that we were in his clutches?

My hands started to tremble. Still, I forced myself to stand up from the ground, the invisible chains permitting my back to go straight. I dug my nails into the holds, moving ever so slowly as I tried to break one hand free. That's all I needed. Just one hand to blast them all away.

I took a long, slow breath but as soon as I did, my eyes fell upon a man with fair blue skin and pointed ears.

Eyeron smiled at me, so vivid without a mirror between us. "You told me to pick a side," he said slyly. "So I did, and you were right. It feels so good."

I glared at the elf, thankful he had lost his title—thankful for the way my hatred for him fuelled my urge to break free.

My hand slipped from its chain. Before anyone could stop me, I flicked my fingers, and purple fire crashed into Eyeron and several others around me. Their screams filled my ears. Their panic gave me a spark of hope within my stomach, but that hope was quickly doused as dozens of creatures turned their vile gazes on me. There were too many of them.

Four vampires marched towards me. I faced them head on, ready to strike again and again, but as they grabbed onto me, Lili's magic slithered tighter around me. I couldn't move my hands. Together, the invisible hold and the creatures pinned my arms behind my back—stronger this time, as if my power was a force they wouldn't let challenge them another time.

I screamed at them, a fierce desire to watch them bleed driving me forwards as they retreated from me, but there was a pull as Florence stepped forward.

He grabbed my chin, pulling my cheek next to his so he could whisper, "Not so fast, darling. There are a few among us that you'll want to try and save before you go and destroy us all." He pulled back, his hot, moist breath stuck to my ear, and he grinned.

The fire I had created was extinguished amongst colourful clouds of smoke as several Casters fought against the remnants of my power. Eyeron stomped out the last of the purple flames before his gaze tore into me. That one look said it all. He was ready to witness my demise.

The vampires let go of me to allow Lili's magic to do its job. I tried to turn around, to find Chad, to see if he could get free since I had failed, but Florence's grip wouldn't allow it. Instead, I watched past Florence as the crowd drew closer to the beds of hay. They all turned to face them as if they were the main show. In a fleeting second, I realised what they were. Pyres. Pyres for burning people alive.

Finally, I heard Chad's heartbeat behind me. Florence let go of my chin, and I shot my head around to look at Chad, to warn him to get away at whatever cost. Florence wasn't going to burn me. He'd try to keep me as a pet. But Chad he wanted dead. For real this time. He had to leave, even if it meant abandoning me.

Only, Chad's eyes weren't on the stocks of kindling, but off to the side, fear coating his entire face. I followed his gaze to find people with burlap sacks over their heads, struggling against the bags and chains. It was just as they had done at Lili's fortress when Nigel and the aunts were first taken. This time, however, there were four prisoners instead of three.

I frowned at the figures—two men and two women based on the shapes of their bodies. Florence's followers strapped them to the wooden posts. One of the women fought against her restraints, splintering the post in her struggle. Florence laughed as though it were a game. His words floated back to me. He had said there were people I'd try to save, yet it wasn't Chad's aunts, not by the shape of them—the strength of the one. Who did they have?

"You see," Florence started, his red eyes shifting back to mine, "when I heard your little boyfriend was still alive, it enraged me. I knew I had to attack before you grew foolish enough to think you could beat me. In a few short hours, we started breaking down the wards of his known castles. We tried to visit through mirrors to go undetected. For some locations it worked. For others, we had to use magical mushrooms to block out the magic. Most of his castles were empty until we came upon one in Austria, a castle built upon a tower of rocks. While we were there, we found some dear friends of yours. Only, you weren't there. So we looked in the most obvious castle of them all, and low and behold, here you are."

I gritted my teeth, my fangs lengthening, ready to attack him, but a grunt from one of the pyres caught my attention.

"Azalea!" one of the masked prisoners called out, the woman who had not broken the pyre, and my heart froze.

I knew that voice. It was my sister.

I could feel the world crash down on me. Why had she been at that castle and not in Greece, protected by the ocean? Now they had me, they had Chad, and Hydie. My baby sister. Who else had they taken? Who had they killed?

"Shut her up!" Florence screeched, and one of his henchmen grabbed my sister from behind, using one hand to cover her mouth over the sack, and the other to slow down her frantic attempts to break free.

I had to do something.

Florence turned back to me. A cold sweat coated my brow. My heart felt as if it would shatter all over again. Still, I wasted no time. I smashed my head against his. White light flashed across my vision, but the pain was worth every ounce when I saw his face. He sucked in his cheeks, a yell muffled behind his closed mouth, vibrating in his throat.

He rubbed at his head with angry fingers—bony fingers he always tried to dig into my flesh and use to control me.

"I'll be sure to remember your hospitality when you're at my home," he grunted through his fangs. Then his head turned so quickly it was a blur. He faced the four prisoners. "Unmask them!" he yelled.

Four people lifted the sacks to reveal terrified faces—faces I knew and cherished with all my heart. My eyes scanned over their trembling frames again and again, like my panicked mind couldn't fully comprehend they were here. One was Hydie, her heart racing as quickly as my own. Another was Connor, scratches all down his skin, his clothes torn as if he had been attacked by another werewolf. Next was Abigail, her dark hair in a mess around her as if she had put up a good fight, the post behind her still broken from her strength as a vampire, extra people holding onto her so she couldn't get away. But the last sent a chill down my spine—an odd déjà vu that both confused and terrified me. The fourth prisoner was Chadwick.

Chapter 51: One Burned, One Turned, One Captive, One Free

I looked behind me but my Chad was still there, his brows furrowed, a gag still in his mouth as his movements to break free halted abruptly.

What was this? Why were there two of him? Nigel was dead. The shapeshifting magic had worn off. Yet the Chad that was being roped to the wooden stalk was very much alive. He too had a dirty rag stuffed into his mouth. His eyes were connected with the Chad who stood behind me. Both looked equally perplexed, both with the same pounding heart that I knew better than my own.

My eyes went back to the Chad behind me. Right as his eyes snapped to me, I could feel his presence in my mind.

I don't know what their aim is—what game they're playing at, he said quickly, *but that is not me.*

The other one crashed into my mind. From atop the pyre, he thought, *Azalea, this a trick. They grabbed me when I was behind you.* His eyes darted to his clone. *I don't know who that is or why they're doing this.*

I let out a sharp breath. I knew very few shapeshifters who were still alive, one being me, the other being Lili. But why tie herself up? Why pretend to be Chad?

I turned back to Florence, who held me close. He smiled down at me, enjoying the bloody match.

I heard a *clink* as they placed silver cuffs around Hydie's wrists, magic-blocking chains that closed her mind from mine. She couldn't tell me their auras. She couldn't see them to tell me which was truly Chad. Yet no one placed the chains on either Chad. It was part of the game. Lili wanted both voices in my head. They all wanted to keep me confused.

Hydie let out a whimper, and my eyes flew back to her. I watched Benji take a handful of her hair and breathe it in as she leaned away, as far as the ropes would allow her.

"Don't fucking touch her!" I shouted at him, assertive like I stood a chance, but Benji backed away comically, his hands raised as if to humour me.

I turned back to the Chad behind me. We had played this game before, only it had been me who had to convince him I was truly myself.

Prove it's really you, I told him desperately. *Prove it so we can find a way out of this.*

It's me, he said, his eyes soft, caring. *Fight Florence off and we'll transport away. We know where their hideout is. We need to call for help and then we'll save them,* he said, staring up at Hydie, Abigail, and Connor.

Don't go with her, the other Chad pleaded, and I looked up at him as he shook his head, his hair brushing against the wooden post behind him. *Don't let your guard down. That has to be Lili.*

I was right behind you the whole time, the first Chad said, my head pivoting behind me again to see him. He looked up at the other Chad, narrowing his eyes. *Whatever you do, don't get near her. Don't let her touch you.*

It was whiplash. I couldn't comprehend who was who let alone make a plan for what to do once I found the real Chad.

Florence's head cocked to the side, his mouth parted, his eyes smiling as he watched me battle with my own mind.

"Tough decision, isn't it?" he asked. "They look so alike. I faced the same confusion when I found out the man I watched die right before me wasn't truly who I thought he was. We had his remains dug up to be sure, and Lilith's hunch was right. He was someone else, not a king, so we came to kill him off for real this time."

I looked away from the vile vampire and back to the Chad behind me. He was right. He was behind me the whole time. He had to be real.

The first time we met, I started, drilling into his mind, *you made me a drink at your pub.* I looked into his green eyes, his brows still scrunched in concentration. *What was the drink?* I asked him.

But he shook his head. *I don't know,* he replied grimly. *I've made a thousand drinks. Ask me another.*

It was my turn to frown at him. It was a very memorable drink. Strike one.

I blinked it away, moving onto the next question, one only the real Chad would know.

What colour is my magic? I pressed.

The crowd around me moved, their intentions unknown, but I kept my eyes on his. His face fell, blood rushing to his cheeks. His gaze flickered over to the other Chad before he widened his eyes at me.

We're not supposed to talk about our colours, he thought, but it was like a whisper. *You know that.*

A sense of pride built in my stomach as I realised he was the imposter.

Strike two.

One last question then, I said, testing the waters further. *After our first kiss, I stopped writing to you, but you told me that I had to at least tell you one thing. What was it?*

That Chad lifted his brows, full of hope, but then his shoulders fell in defeat.

Strike three.

I turned to look at the real Chad—the one strapped to a wooden pyre as if he was ready to be burned alive. He stared back at me, a weak smile on his face, past the gag that was shoved into his mouth.

I made you a Bloody Mary that night, he said softly into my mind. *I was trying to read your mind, to cheat at finding your favourite drink, but all I could hear was the word 'blood,' and like an idiot, a Bloody Mary was my interpretation,* he said, his thoughts warm like a hug. *The colour of your magic is purple, and if you were to only write one thing to me, I made you promise to write, "I'm still alive."*

Lili's invisible ropes loosened around me ever so slightly—a sign she knew she had lost, and I seized the opportunity. I elbowed Florence in the ribs and lunged for the imposter.

We fell to the ground, me on top as fear flashed in Chad's eyes. Using the speed Florence had given me through his venom the night I was changed, I pulled one arm from Lili's magic and wrapped her own invisible ropes around her throat. Grey lines started to snake up Chad's neck—lines of cracking stone.

A vampire.

The gag disappeared from his mouth. His lips plumped out, his skin turned a touch paler. His eyes shifted to an intense shade of blue, and his hair grew long and blonde. Before I knew it, Lili was staring back at me, her cold smile pasted onto her face.

The invisible chains snapped into oblivion. Strangers yanked me off of her. As she gracefully stood up and brushed dirt from a pink, low-cut blouse and black leather pants, her smile only grew.

"Ah, so he is the real Chadwick," she commented, directing her chin towards the pyres. "Not another decoy." She leaned over to look past me and up at Chad. "Just wanted to make sure this time."

There was a slow, dramatic clap from behind me, and as his henchmen forcefully turned me to face Florence, I watched as his hands met a final time.

"Excellent, Azalea!" he congratulated me. "You've won our little game. Well—" he added, pausing to draw it all out, "we have another."

I jerked and kicked to get away but these were no ordinary Night Crawlers that held me. Their eyes glowed red but their grips were stronger than a vampire who needed to feed. They were as strong as Florence had become. They had fed off the blood of vampires to build their strength, and they were relentless.

The faintest swish of liquid sent bumps all over my skin as the potion in my pocket sloshed around. These creatures were stronger than me. I was outnumbered and they had me pinned. If only they'd put me in the magical handcuffs instead. If they had,

I could use the potion before anyone had the chance to catch on, and get the help we needed. But they didn't, and we were alone.

I felt Lili sweep into my mind. My eyes flew over to her as she stared at the exact spot in my dress where the phial was hidden. Her eyes met mine, a gleam of pure satisfaction shining in them. She was in my head. She had heard my plan and now the potion would be confiscated.

I could hear Florence talking to his followers, droning on, boasting about how I would finally be his, but I couldn't pry my gaze away from Lili's cruel smile. Yet instead of coming over to me and taking the potion, Lili's mouth stayed shut.

"You have some choices," Florence told me sternly, and my neck snapped up to look at him. He was holding his hands behind his back as he paced the grounds, concentrating hard. "One of them," he said, directing my gaze back to my mates, "will be burned alive tonight. Another will turn into a vampire. A third will be taken captive. And the last will remain untouched." Florence ran his eyes over me, all too happy with himself for concocting such a devious plan. Then he bit his lip, seduced by the idea. "Your choice, my darling."

Lili's body moved in my peripheral, and I watched her stride with power towards the pyres, each step calculated as if she were savouring the moment. *Ah,* she cooed into my mind. *A traitor, a sister, a lover, and a friend. What to do? What to do?* she sang.

Every muscle in my body tightened with rage. *Get out of my head,* I growled, but Florence chimed in, urging me along.

"The faster you choose, the quicker you'll be able to get over it, really," he said, as if it were all so easy.

Oh, Lili butted in, *I don't want to leave your little mind just yet. I've waited so patiently to get back in. It was such a tragedy when you learned to block me out.*

Get the fuck out, I demanded, but the bitch refused.

But I want to hear your process when you choose which of these lovely people gets which fate, she purred, running a finger along Abigail's chin and delighting in her cringe. *Personally, I hope you choose to have the traitor burned.*

Abigail is not a traitor, I remarked, glaring right into Lili. *She didn't mean to kill Chad's mum, nor would she have if she hadn't been in the state she was.*

Perhaps not, Lili said, shrugging her shoulders before she moved on to stand by Connor, *but it's in her head, even now. She can't stop thinking about it. She can't stop withering away to nothing when she thinks of how much her best mate hates her.*

I do not hate her, I corrected fiercely.

Her words, not mine, Lili teased, so light as if it was a friendly joke.

"Well? Which one is it?" Florence yelled.

"Shut up!" I told him. "I'm thinking."

But how could I think straight with Lili in my mind? How the hell was I going to get us all out of this?

There was a loud *thump* somewhere in the distance and Lili stared at the maze before she turned back to me. Her smile grew more cunning as she widened her eyes, egging me on to decide faster.

Choose Abigail to burn, Lili said, scrunching up her nose in disgust. *If only to put my little creation out of her misery. And pick Chad to get bitten. It'd be fun! He'd get to stay young and powerful forever—more time for him to stress over which one of us is his fated mate.*

Clearly, he's made his choice, I snarled, relishing in the way her eyes lit with fury. I imagined the ring from Chad's proposal as clearly as I could to ignite her fuse even more. It was clear who the prophecy was about, and it wasn't her.

One person turned and one person burned, she teased, though there was more heat to her tone this time. It felt as if she was searing a branding rod into my skin with her words alone. *Such a lovely ring to it, isn't it?*

"Time's ticking!" Florence shouted, shaking his head as if he himself were a clock.

I could feel my eyes turn red, my teeth grow longer. "I said I was thinking," I growled between my clenched fangs.

"Hurry up!" he countered.

And which one do you want us to capture? Lili asked, a fake sweetness in her voice. *A bit of torture to any one of them sounds entertaining to me, although, I do hope you choose the werewolf. He was fun to torture last time when Florence got hold of him in Germany. After he got us the love potion that Florence used on you, it was quite hard to let him go. Pity he can't remember any of it.*

"What is your choice, Azalea?" Florence pushed. The amusement of it all was no longer present in his voice. Instead, his impatience cut through the night. "What's the answer to the riddle? Who gets burned?"

"Shove your riddles up your arse, Florence!" I yelled back, hating him with every inch of my body.

But Florence snapped. "Fine, you stupid whore!" he called out, stomping his foot. "I'll choose for you. Benji," he yelled, turning to his red-eyed mate. "Bite the sister."

Benji made no hesitation as he jerked Hydie's head to the side and bit down onto her neck.

I jolted forwards, terror and fury lashing through me. The vampires' hold on me tightened, forcing me to endure Hydie's agony. But Florence didn't wait long before selecting his next victim.

"Lilith," he called, giving her an aggressive nod.

Lili snapped her fingers and Chad's pyre went up in flames. In an instant, his body was consumed with fire. It licked every part of him, flickering wildly, raging around like it was trying to force the life out of him within seconds.

Cries of pure pain filled the air—Chad's—Hydrangea's—mine as my heart crumbled. I had built this heart back together, piece by shattered piece—and for what?

Agony contorted Connor's features as his eyes flickered between my sister and his best mate. His veins bulged, rippling with a power that fought to consume him. His eyes turned yellow before he shifted into his werewolf form, howling and biting at the air in protest. The pyre shook against his weight, but it held strong.

"Abigail will be our captive," Florence announced over the roar of the fire, over the screams, and over a crowd that cheered the devastation on. "She's always been a bitch to me anyway, and this werewolf... Well, do whatever you'd like," he told Connor. "We've already had our fun with you."

The pleas for them to stop, to show any mercy at all immediately followed. Abigail. Connor. Me. We begged. We grovelled. We cried for them to reconsider. I could smell Chad's skin cook and melt and char. But he was going to be okay, I told myself. He was going to survive this and we were going to get married like he promised me the second he showed me that ring.

Benji released his jaw from my sister and took a deep breath of the night air. Hydie went completely limp—the ropes the only thing keeping her upright. Her heartbeat was the tiniest blimp. She was dying. She needed one more ingredient to complete the transformation. She needed the venom in a vampire's blood.

"Please! Please," I begged Florence. I could transport her to Loxley Lair—to a mortal hospital—to anywhere she could get human blood. "I'll do anything," I screamed at him. "Anything!"

"Anything?" He lured me in, a flicker of promise in his intense, deadly eyes.

"Yes!" I shouted over Chad's screams. My breath quivered, red tears filling my eyes as Chad's anguish rippled through me. I could hear his screams in my ears and straight into my mind. He was unable to think beyond the pain.

I forced my eyes away from him as his clothes fused to his body. I couldn't think about the heat, or the feel of the vampires' hands as they dug their fingers into me, or the way my knees were buckling in on themselves. All I could think about was Chad and how he had to survive this.

"I'll do anything, I swear!" I screamed to Florence.

Amusement lit Florence's face. "Swear you'll come with me. Swear you'll be with me 'til death do us part."

I shuddered at his words. Words meant to be wedding vows, but the word "death" tempted me. And for a moment, just one moment, fear left my entire body. Determination took over. I wasn't going to let any of my mates die tonight.

I looked Florence dead in the eye, ready to give it all up, ready to grasp onto the only option I had left.

"I do," I told him, completely surrendering myself to his will.

Their screams echoed out into the night, but Florence zoomed closer to my face, blocking my view. "Then seal it with a kiss," he said softly and I cringed. A request.

I watched as his fangs lengthened—as he sunk them into his own lip and blood began to trickle down his chin. And he waited. He waited for my lips to come to his as if I had the choice. Only, I didn't.

Hurry, a voice begged in my head. *Kiss him and get it over with.*

The voice was right. My mind flew back to my friends. My family. To all the things they'd done. All the things they could still do. I had to save them. Then my gaze met Lilith's as her eyes sparkled merrily, enjoying the show.

A blood oath, Sunshine, she sang into my mind. *A kiss—a clever way of doing it. If only I had thought of it when Chad made his.* She smiled mischievously before licking her lips. *Seal it with a kiss and you'll die if you back out of the bargain.*

But not if he dies first, I thought.

Lilith's eyes glittered with excitement, and I knew she had heard me.

I turned back to Florence and before I could stop myself, before I subjected my family to any more hesitation, I dove in and my mouth was on his. Hard. He bit my lip, but there was a stinging in my heart at the same time. My blood seeped into his mouth as he sucked it out, mixing our blood together. A sharp spark of magic pulsated through me.

A binding promise.

When Florence pulled away from me, the purest joy I had ever seen on his face washed over him. For a moment, he had the innocence of a warm, unruined spirit within him. Like his father hadn't spawned him from evil. Like he could be content with love and family rather than the death and misery he created in his wake. Then he turned back to the four people I'd do anything in the world for, malice contorting his face once more, and he said, "Lili. Do it."

The fire didn't go out. The screams didn't stop. Lilith merely offered her arm to Hydrangea and my poor, confused, drained sister clenched her jaw down on Lili's arm, and the venom began to spread.

My soul had given up the attempt to form words and the shock that radiated through me weakened all that I was. The blood oath. They *had* to stop.

The vampires let go of me. My arms pounded on Florence's chest, disjointed from the rest of me. The words, *You promised! You promised!* pulsed through me, but Lilith's voice rang through it all.

"He didn't promise you anything," she said, her brows poised.

His words. His words. All he had done was pose a question. *Swear you'll come with me. Do you swear you'll be with me 'til death do us part?* I had assumed it was a promise to fulfil his end of the bargain. But I was undoubtedly wrong, and it was too late. Chad was dying. Hydrangea was changing. Connor was roaring in his werewolf form, unyielding chains holding him tight. Abigail's eyes scrunched tight, red tears drenching her face as she screamed herself hoarse.

The creatures around us started to disappear in puffs of colourful smoke. Eyeron's smile carved its way into my mind as a witch held his arm, and he disappeared with her.

But before I could do anything besides pound on Florence's chest, my betrothed gave one last command.

"Sleep," Florence whispered.

I watched as Lili pointed a single magical finger at me, and everything turned black.

Chapter 52: Ghosts of the Past

The chiming of a clock—pounding synchronously with my memories.

One—my aching skull.

Two—the pull to my creator.

Three—the taste of a vile liquid on my tongue.

Four chimes—the way it slid down my throat.

Five, six—fear crept inside.

Seven, eight—I shouldn't drink. I shouldn't trust.

Nine—a distant memory that this has happened before.

Ten, eleven—the sip that remained in my mouth sprayed out as I rejected it. Drinking the unknown was a risky business. But a voice echoed through my mind.

The twelfth chime—Florence.

"It's too late."

My heart jolted, and I opened my eyes, but I was alone. Twelve strikes. It was midnight.

Stone walls and a barred door surrounded the large, dark, musty room. A stench assaulted my nose. Everything that had happened in the front gardens rushed back at once.

I sat up and vomit spluttered out onto a cold, stone floor. Hydie—writhing in pain. The skin of the man who had just promised to spend the rest of his life with me—melting away—and for a moment, the screams of my friends were all I could hear until I took in the room around me. My loved ones weren't here. Only, "alone" wasn't the best word for my surroundings.

A heap of corpses lay around me, covering the rest of my cell. Empty eyes stared back at me. They looked fresh, as if they hadn't been dead long. No external decay, small traces of heat still radiating off some of them, but their skin was pale—withered as if their blood had been drained—and the small amount that was left could only be detected by a vampire's nose. It was the smell of rotting blood—blood that would poison any vampire—that had made me sick.

I stood up, my vampire speed lifting me away from the bodies in an instant, but I slipped in my own sick before I caught myself and started to back up. I turned away from them, holding my breath, and my hands found the barred door. It led down a short corridor that opened into a larger one where the blood river rushed past. I pulled at the metal, but it was immovable. Giving every shred of energy I could, I tried to bend them apart, but I wasn't in a cell built for mortals. I was in a cell built for creatures like me, and I would not be breaking my way out of it.

Screams sounded around me, bouncing off of the stone walls, down the corridors and straight into my ears. My eyes followed along the floor of the short corridor in front of me to find an assortment of brightly coloured mushrooms, just out of my reach. The edges were turning brown, but after several attempts to conjure my magic, the fungi proved its strength. No purple seeped from my palms.

My body shook uncontrollably as I turned around to face the dead once more. I had to look. I had to see, no matter how frightened I was, whether or not the faces on the ground belonged to the ones I loved.

One burned, one turned, one captive, one free.

I closed my eyes and the images came back to me like a stab in my stomach. Pain was all I could see. So much pain. I had to know what had happened. Had the venom taken over Hydie's body? Was she still writhing in pain? Would she survive it? Was Connor really free? Was Abigail being tortured? And *him*…

I couldn't bring myself to think of his name—to picture his green eyes amongst the orange flames. He couldn't be gone. He wouldn't leave me...

My lungs stopped working. An invisible hold was crushing them, and as I choked on a sob, I clawed at my throat. My world was broken. My world was in complete shambles and panic was strangling me. This time there was no mending it.

He had died a thousand deaths in my mind. He had said everyone eventually dies, but even with the score of corpses at my feet—even after watching an entire country demolished in a matter of seconds, I couldn't fathom the love of my life being gone for good.

My vision blurred with blood tears as my chest grew tighter and tighter. I stopped scratching at my throat. I didn't want the air. I didn't want to breathe ever again, only, as soon as the thought crossed my mind, air rushed into my lungs.

Needles pricked my hand as it slapped into the stone floor. Heaves of air came and left as if it had been that easy all along.

"I've always hated you, you know?" an echoey voice said, and my head snapped up to see a ghost, but not my singing ghost. Someone else.

Missouri looked down her scrunched, translucent nose, as if she were tasting something foul. Her young face was half-covered by her hair as her dark gaze bore into me.

I glared back at the ghost who had given me that look since the moment I met her—since she walked right through me—her ectoplasm freezing my insides when I was already weak from my transformation. It had been some time since I had seen her. She had abandoned Loxley Lair not long after Florence. It was no surprise she was here.

"Leave me alone," I growled, but she ignored me.

Floating closer until her pale, grey frame seeped past the bars, she went on.

"The world as you know it's about to end," she said, her voice scarily focused. "As we speak, Lilith's in America, blasting the coasts off the map. It'll be worse than Japan because they plan to leave survivors, and we all know how haunted they'll become. Florence is on the winning side," she told me simply. "Florence always wins."

"Not this time," I said, but screams echoed through my mind, not merely the ones around me, but *his*. Suddenly, my hope trickled away. A shudder of dread crossed over me like a dark shadow, and I couldn't bring myself to block out the doubt—to accept Florence hadn't won. Everything pointed to it.

"And who's going to stop him?" she countered, flying straight towards my face. Fire glistened in her dead eyes as her temper shot through the ceiling. "You?" she asked as if I were incapable of stopping him. "While you're locked away in a cage? You'll always be trapped. For the rest of your long, pathetic life, you'll be locked to Florence. Perhaps not in here, but you'll be stuck with him nonetheless. He's *obsessed* with you. You're all he's ever cared about since he brought you home to Loxley Lair—a home *I* found for us! The day I met him he told me wanted to live somewhere where more than just vampires could inhabit. But then you came, and you were all he paid attention to. Once you were in the picture, not even the blonde could hold his attention anymore."

I blinked at her, taking it all in, but none of it mattered. Clearly, she hadn't haunted Loxley Lair for the moral aspect. Why the hell was everyone so obsessed with Florence?

I turned my head away from her and focused instead on the fabrics of my dress, a lively shade of green compared to the death that surrounded me. The green brought me no comfort, though, instead reminding me of a certain pair of emerald eyes.

"You're a bit young for Florence, don't you think?" I asked her dully, not affording her a glance. She had never liked me? Well, I had always returned the sentiment. "And a bit dead too," I added, merely to piss her off more. After all, why not?

"I'm not dumb," she screeched out. "I know he has needs— needs I'll never be able to reciprocate. I'll never be able to touch him, not the way Lilith does, not that way he wants you to, but I have needs too. I need to be loved! It's my unfinished business. No one ever falls in love with me. Outside the ability to touch adamant objects, what is it you have that I don't?"

My stomach grumbled but there was nothing left in me to throw up. Lazily, I looked Missouri up and down, taking in the sneer she always wore for me. "Perhaps the ability to smile," I taunted, before looking away again. She needed to leave me alone. I was empty.

She floated away from me ever so slightly, but her tone was lighter as it came out.

"Not for long," she said, with the most cheer I had ever heard slip from her lips. "Soon everyone you have left will be dead. They'll be gone—just like that boyfriend of yours—and they'll never come back..."

I swallowed down my hate for her, but there was nothing I could do to her physically. She was immune to my wrath.

"Except for that stupid ghost," she said, her tone going morbid once more, but I didn't want to hear it.

Closing my eyes, I shook my head. I didn't have the strength to hear her nonsense. I couldn't.

The ghost before me didn't bother to accept my body language as defeat. She persisted.

"She was obsessed with you too," Missouri said. "The one who was always singing that *soothing* lullaby," she spat out as though anything calming was repulsive. But she had my attention. My eyes snapped up to her. "But after I told Florence about her, and we set up that trap for you in Germany, she was around considerably less."

My heart raced as I took her in, pounding ten times faster than the blasted clock I had heard before.

The trap.

"It was so easy," Missouri drawled. "I led the ghost to Florence's hideout, and then she led you there after. Of course she thought she was helping. Only, Florence acted like it was my fault when you escaped and all he had was the werewolf. But I did my part."

My singing ghost—Madelyn. She hadn't been against me at all. She had been trying to help.

In the distance, the sound of footsteps drew nearer, and the pull tugged me in its direction. Missouri and I turned our heads in unison towards the doorway. From the corner of my eye, I saw the ghost shake her head.

"Of course he's coming," she whispered bitterly. "He's coming to see his prize."

Then without another word, she flew through a wall, headed in the opposite direction.

The pull filled my lungs like water drowning me in an ocean of sorrow. The thought of seeing his face—the thought of knowing what he had commanded—submerged me, pushing me under monstrous waves. And the thought of what he'd do next swallowed me whole as he appeared in front of the blood river and firelight danced across his wicked face.

I'm Still Unstoppable

Chapter 53: Worn With Someone Else

Florence strode in with four other men, all with crimson eyes, and extravagant muscles bulging from their red and black garb. One was holding a plump burlap sack in his hands. I eyed it warily before I sized them all up, wondering how many of them I could take. How many of their skulls could I crack in the palm of my hand?

Florence ambled across the stone floor, just out of reach, when he pulled to a stop and smirked at me.

"Good morning, my ravishing wife," Florence lured. A phrase that could've soothed another, yet it sent shivers down my spine. "Or at least, soon-to-be," he added, flickering his brows at me.

I would've puked again if I had anything left in me.

Sorrow was squashed from my chest, replacing itself with a heat that surged through me. I hated every inch of him, body and mind. I felt my eyes shift to red.

"You tricked me," I growled. "You made me watch him burn—watch that bitch turn my sister!" But I knew how dumb it sounded before it even came out.

Of course he had tricked me. Why had I expected anything less?

"Oh yes..." Florence drawled. "'Tricked' is an entirely viable verb for the little scene that went on, but the rest is a bit exaggerated, wouldn't you say? You only saw the start of little Hydrangea's change. No one made you watch as she lay on the ground for over three hours, screaming at the top of her lungs, begging for death. Begging for you to save her. No." He shook his head, his eyes gleaming with amusement. "You were fast asleep—in here, if I do recall."

My mind went blank as I blocked the images out. Then slowly, I replaced the pain and heartache with images of Florence's death—how I would tear him apart—how I would make him suffer far worse than anyone had ever made another suffer. But he didn't stop there. He kept going.

"As for the witch-boy..." he said, drawing it out, making my body contract as he slowly announced the fate of the man I loved. "Tomorrow night, on our wedding night, you and I will make love atop his grave."

I lunged at him without thinking. My hand thrust through the bars. Florence was lying. *He* wasn't dead. *He* had to have gotten out. Abigail—Connor—one of them had to have broken out and saved him. It was another trick. But even as fear flashed in Florence's eyes, my fingertips strayed out of reach.

Florence let out a haughty laugh, his shoulders relaxing though I could hear his heart still hammering in his chest. He studied me, taking in my heaving chest, the hate in my eyes, and he cocked a brow at me.

"Denial," he said decidedly. "It's exactly what I went through… once…" he added as his eyes glazed over in a memory, his lips incapable of uttering Zena's name. "It's the first stage of grief." The fog cleared in his eyes and he stared back at me, flicking his brows at me as if he couldn't wait for tomorrow night. "You get over it eventually—when you have the warmth of another to satisfy you."

I felt like I was being ripped apart from the inside. I shook my head. He was trying to make me give up. That's all it was.

Florence's eyes flashed down to the vomit that lay on the floor and he threw a look back to his comrades.

"You," he barked at one of them, "go get my bride something to drink. It seems she's spoiled her supper."

As if pulled by a string, one of the men fled down the dim passageway, increasing my odds of survival—my odds of escaping. It was down to one on four. I had to get out. I had to find my family and wake up from the nightmare.

But the red-eyed vampire was back too soon.

The buzz of his lightning movement announced his return. He swept back in, carrying a tall, thin, golden goblet full of sloshing red liquid. It dripped down his hand and onto his sleeve, but he paid it no mind.

My stomach should've lurched. It should've rejected the idea of any sustenance with the stench of death still so strong—after getting sick all over the floor. I should've been blinded by the possibility of the love of my life's death. Instead, my body yearned for the blood.

One of the burly vampires tried to hand it to me but I merely stared at it, my fingers aching to reach out to it. I should've grabbed onto his arm, broken his wrist, but all I could do was fight the urge to drink it.

"Still prefer it from a glass, I assume?" Florence asked.

It had been a long time since I had blood other than the duplication potion, and if history taught me anything, it was that this blood was not from a potion or a criminal. No, this blood was from someone innocent. The horrific feeling that it could be the blood of someone I loved tore into me before I vanquished the thought. I had not lost *him* to those fires, or Hydie to her transformation.

Sensing my hesitation, Florence took the goblet from the silent man who held it, and presented it to me, his hand finally within my grasp. But rather than attacking my captor, my vampire urges took over. My fangs lengthened, pricking my bottom lip. My stomach was empty. And with the blood sloshing in front of me, radiating a soft heat, my stomach wouldn't let me think of anything else.

My hands lifted past the bars, taking the goblet into my palms, but Florence kept hold of the stem.

"That's it, darling," he said, tilting it towards me. "Drink up."

My eyes flickered up from the blood and into Florence's red eyes. There was an eagerness in them as he watched the rim move closer to my lips.

Sense smacked into me and I smelled the blood. Something was off. I stepped back, letting go of the cup. My heel brushed against a dead body, and I jerked away from it.

"You've poisoned it, haven't you?" I asked, returning to my senses.

Florence's eyes flashed with anger before he allowed his lips to curl into a grin.

"More or less," he said lightly, his tone hinting at innocence— a joke. "You see, Azalea," he said, swirling the blood around the goblet and sniffing it as if it were a fine wine. "Though these lovely gentlemen and I have been feasting on the blood of other vampires, giving us a strength far superior to yours, I know just how feisty you get. The blood you drank from my arm, the first night your life truly began, gave you your speed, and I can't have you trying to run off before we're wed. I should've waited to change you until after you were mine. It would've been easier. But we all learn from our mistakes," he said with a shrug. "The mushrooms and a set of handcuffs will take away your witch powers, and the serum inside this blood will make you as weak as a mortal. You've already had some, but it seems it didn't agree with your stomach," he said, gesturing the glass toward my vomit. "But trust me, drinking this is the easiest option you have."

The hate returned to my core as I pushed away my thirst.

"I'd rather die than give up my chances of getting away from you," I growled, and though the other vampires didn't move an inch, Florence's face turned sour with embarrassment.

He chucked the blood towards me and it splashed through the bars, across the dead bodies at my feet, and the hems of my dress.

"So be it then," he snapped, throwing the goblet behind his shoulder. It clanked loudly, echoing as it rolled across the stone floor and back towards the blood river. "You'll get the injection like everyone else. For now, let's get you ready for our special day."

On cue, the men marched forwards, brandishing a key before they entered. As they advanced, one drew something big and white out of his burlap sack. I pressed myself against the wall, but they grabbed onto me. They were stronger. I'd have to outwit them.

Meanwhile, Florence stood in the doorway, grinning from ear to ear, eager to watch the show. "The night I created you, I made a very big mistake," he said, loud enough so I could hear him over my own useless grunts and kicks.

His men wrapped their large hands around my arms and legs, ripping the clothes from my body. I latched my foot around one of their ankles, but the men yanked me free, my bare skin hot against theirs. Florence's eyes raked my body as I stood in nothing but my undergarments, still held by his incessant followers. Then one of them shoved the white thing over my head, tugging it down, yanking my arms through the long sleeves, and the long skirts fell down to my legs to trail onto the floor.

"You see, I let you around people with a strong moral code," Florence said, methodically running his hands against the bars of the open cell as if baiting me to try and escape. "What was I thinking—keeping you at Loxley Lair of all places? I'll erase your memories again, but this time I'll take you far away, keep you to myself, until you think my way of life is all you've ever known. You won't feel the need to go on some quest to find out more or remember the dead man who once stole you away from me."

His guards held me tight, just as strong as Florence warned me they were. I struggled against them with all my might, giving every ounce of energy towards getting out of their grasp, killing them, and going to find the others, but I couldn't get away. Metal touched my wrists and there was a loud *click* as something locked into place in front of me. As I stared down at the handcuffs, I took in the outfit they had forced me into.

A wedding dress.

The men pulled me towards Florence, towards the door to my cage, half carrying me, half dragging me, until they halted, and I was face to face with Florence. I spat in his face, erasing his smile.

He wiped away my spit with a glare, but otherwise, he was unimpressed. Looking down at the stark white bridal apparel, the smile returned to his face.

"Like it?" he asked, and my stomach jolted with disgust and guilt. "It's a 1940's piece, worn by my father's bride—the whore he eventually married instead of my mother."

But what the fuck did that matter?

"I'll never love you, Florence," I told him, fighting against the hold his men had on me. "I'll never stop fighting to be rid of you, no matter how many memory potions you feed me."

But he grasped the back of my hair, and a scream left my lips, mixing in with the others.

"Oh, you will love me," he said, completely sure of it. "And don't worry, we'll hold off on the memory potion for now. But if you keep refusing to play nice, I'll continue to take away everyone you've ever loved until you *beg* me to give you the potion to let you forget."

With that, he shoved me with such force that the vampires let go of me. I tripped over the dead bodies, falling onto my back and onto the dead as a cushion.

The gate clinked shut and they locked it all in one swift motion.

I lay there, propped up on my forearms, my chest rising and falling rapidly. I watched as one of the vampires walked over to a torch and lit my old dress on fire. With an evil grin, he tossed the dress at the cage. I heard a soft *clink* as it crashed into the bars and down to the floor.

I glared at the lot of them, wishing the magic handcuffs were off me—aching for the mushrooms to be gone so I could unleash my magic on them. But the handcuffs stayed in place and the mushrooms sat unharmed.

Florence turned to leave, to desert me here amongst the dead, haunted with the memories and so many screams.

My heart raced as I watched him storm out, but I had to say it, I had to say the thoughts that crashed through my mind.

"And what will you do after all that—" I shouted, "—when you find out I'm *still* a decent being and *still* don't love you?"

He paused, his hand gripping the stone wall until tiny pieces crumbled off and onto the ground. His eyes flashed up to his men for a split second. Then he looked back at me with his fangs bared.

"I seem to remember a certain love potion that did the trick," he said in a hushed voice—a promise.

And then he left me in the cell, smothered by the screams of tortured prisoners, and in a stupid white dress that I should've worn with someone else.

I'm Still Unstoppable

Chapter 54: Pupil

Every inch of me yearned to tear the wretched white dress off my skin, but the cold floor underneath me urged me not to. I stared at the charred remnants of my old dress. I had watched the fire turn the green fabrics to black for 20 seconds. They had destroyed my dress so easily—just as they had destroyed my life. For 20 seconds, I watched the fire absorb my will to move before I remembered the *clink* it had made as it collided with the bars. Fire scorched my fingers as I reached through the bars and seized the fabrics. And for a second, I wasn't me. For a second, I was the green-eyed man I had fallen in love with—engulfed in flames—dying a most agonising death.

Grounding myself to the present, I gripped harder onto the burning silk and the dark cell returned. I thrust a hand into the pockets, my fingers wrapping around a glass phial, and I pulled it out. My skin started to heal the second I tossed the burning dress back out of the cage and onto the mushrooms, hoping they'd burn, but only a handful caught flame. The rest stayed, dissolving my magic.

The glass bottle was now tucked against my heart, biding its time. Soon they'd come to inject me with serum to temporally take my strength, my enhanced sight and hearing—my healing as a vampire. Just as Florence promised. But soon I'd break free, and they'd regret laying their hands on me.

The clock in the distance echoed off the walls, a single chime that embodied my misery. I sat there for what felt like an eternity. Cold, empty, broken, desperate to block every tragic event out of my brain. Still, the clock chimed on.

Two o'clock.

Three o'clock.

Four o'clock.

The screams never stopped. I tried to block them out. My body wracked with shivers as I covered my ears and tried to focus on the cold feel. I wouldn't allow myself to think about anything else—anyone else. If I did, it would make it all real.

The sound of footsteps drew near—fewer than before. One man rounded the corner and stepped into view, and when he saw me, he smiled with his crimson eyes and matching blood-stained teeth.

Benji.

"Long time no see," he said. He ran his fingers down his dirty blond ponytail before flashing a large syringe at me.

I heard the potion slosh against the edges, saw the light glint across the long needle. Then I met Benji's cold eyes again.

"Yet it's not long enough, is it?" I countered.

Adrenaline started pumping through me, washing away the numbness I had succumbed to. He was alone. I had to get out and find the others.

"You still have that spark, don't you?" he asked, prowling carefully towards the prison cell. "The spark that fuels Florence."

I heard a slight scrape of metal come from his pocket as he stopped a metre away from the door. My heart pumped faster. He had to have the key. If he was going to try and stab that needle into my skin, and push the serum in, he was going to have to get closer than the bars would allow. He'd have to come in.

His eyes travelled the length of me, pausing on parts I'm sure he longed to touch. Lust reflected brightly in his pupils. I kept my lips sealed tight, observing his leisurely stance. He didn't have an ounce of fear for me. He was vile. He had the same predatorial look he had in my vision when he was staring at Lili, and I felt the same rage she had. Another trait she and I shared.

"I was advised to bring a team with me to do this," he said, playing with the syringe, eyeing it as if it were a toy. "They said I wouldn't be able to handle you on my own, but we all know the heartache you've just gone through. Perhaps there's no fight left in you. Besides," he said, pausing to look at me, "I thought we'd have a lot more fun if it was just the two of us down here."

There was something else about the dream. Lili had mentioned that, he too, drank the blood of vampires, giving him incomparable strength, but it gave him a weakness. Perhaps he was stronger, and just as quick as me, but he would heal slowly—even slower when I was done with him.

"It'll take an hour or so for the potion to set in, but don't worry..." he announced thoughtfully. "That's plenty of time to play. It's my job to ensure this one doesn't wear off before the next dose, so we'll be spending quite a bit of time together."

He reached his free hand into his pocket, watching me as closely as I watched him. The metal clinked together as he lifted out a ring of keys. Carefully, he picked one out.

I propped myself up against the stone wall, as far away from him as possible, ready to pounce, but I wouldn't show it. My shoulders relaxed but the thundering of my heart was sure to give me away.

"Florence always gets the pretty ones," Benji commented, his face turning to a sneer as he placed the key into the hole. It scraped against the edges as it went in. "He's rather insistent that he should get you all to himself. Only, you haven't been all his, have you? You've been with others. Perhaps I'll have you and he'll never find out. Not to mention, back at Downy Lair, Florence and I shared more than a few lovers. Perhaps he wouldn't mind too much."

I thought back to my first time at Downy Lair. I had seen Benji there, dragging a human carcass across the floor, entering a room where several vampires and slaves were partaking in an orgy.

My eyes flickered down to the key, willing him to turn it, but he caught the look and its meaning.

"Ah, ah, ah," he tutted, shaking his head at me like one would do to a small child. "If you don't want this and every other time to hurt, then you need to play nice," he instructed. "You need to move slowly, and accept what's going to happen between us." He raised his brows and pursed his lips. "Do you think you can do that for Benji?" he asked.

I looked down at the chains between my wrists as they rested on my knees, my lips still locked.

Why did I live in a world where these men thought they could play with my body? That they could do whatever they wanted, and I was supposed to let them...

I nodded, careful to stare him straight in the eye this time, and not look down at the key.

I heard the click—saw his hand turn from the corner of my eye, his other hand wrapped around the syringe, thumb poised on the back. Ready. The gate screeched open, and I held my breath as he crept closer. He held the potion level to his wide eyes as he studied me, watching me like an animal who was about to pounce, preparing for any sharp movements I made. But I made none. Instead, I let him stalk closer and closer, my eyes pasted to his.

"I won't tell Florence," I promised with a quiver in my lip. I tried to channel the same faux fear Lili had portrayed the first time she had met the prince of all Casters and his aunts. "I'll keep it a secret," I reassured him. "Please don't hurt me."

Surprise flashed in his red eyes right before hunger overtook it—hunger and a vile craving to do unspeakable things to me. But as the torches behind him cast his shadow over me, I took what could very well be my only chance.

In an instant, I was on my feet. I stepped behind him, collecting his raised wrist and his neck within my chain. I placed my knee in his back and yanked the chains. I heard the crack of his spine and the gasp that left his lips—a sweet melody in my ears. His knees crashed into the ground.

I yanked the syringe from him with one hand, grabbing his neck with my other. As I held him steady, his screams blended in with the others. I bent down so my lips were against his ear.

Placing my thumb on the back of the injector, I whispered, "It'll take an hour or so for the potion to set in, but don't worry..." His very own words. "That's plenty of time to play. It's my job to ensure you suffer before this dose wears off."

Then I drove the needle directly into his pupil.

I'm Still Unstoppable

Chapter 55: His Name

The keys hit the floor right before his body did. Liquid oozed out his eye as he blinked at me, but otherwise, he was paralysed. I picked up the keys, trading them for the bottle that was tucked against my heart. Uncorking the phial and using a dash of potion to unleash my chains, I stared at Benji.

For a moment I considered putting an end to him. Instead, I left him there, closing the prison door behind me. His neck was broken. He'd heal slowly thanks to his diet. And by the time his bones fused themselves back together, the potion would be ready to slow him down to a mortal's pace. For now, that pain was what he deserved. Besides, I always knew my first kill was going to be Florence.

I crossed over the maze of mushrooms. Leaving the smell of charred fungi and dead bodies behind, I headed towards the blood river, turned right, and followed its flow. The corridor was the same as before, lit only by the orange glow of the torches. The blood river splashed on my left while new corridors branched off every fifty metres or so on my right. My steps echoed as I stormed away from my cell, towards the next few cells, listening frantically for the sound of my family or those who would dare to stand in my way. Once I found Abigail, Hydie, and even O'Brien if he was down here, then I could set things in motion—create chaos—venture up to the sixth floor to recruit the aunts.

Magic prickled at my fingertips the further I got from the mushrooms. I passed by ten corridors, prisoners shrinking away from me as I went, the sight of me inspiring more screams like a panic-driven wave. But as I passed by the eleventh corridor, my magic started to sputter out and the smell of fungi grew strong once again. I kept moving forwards. A moment later, I came to another corridor. Colourful mushrooms were strewn across the floor—cutting off not only my magic, but that of whoever was inside that cell.

There was a pile of dead bodies within, stacked high. As I stepped up to the gate, my eyes glanced over the pile before they landed on two women in a corner. They sat against the hard wall as one held tightly to the other.

Abigail and Hydie.

Hope blossomed in my chest. Abigail's arms were wrapped around my sister, as if she was comforting her yet protecting her from something all at once. Hydie's red eyes cut through the darkness, portraying such a strong yearning that I had never seen in them before. Together, the women stared at a man opposite them as if frightened he'd eat them.

The man's green eyes met mine. Butterflies fluttered in my stomach for a fraction of a second before they shrivelled up and burst into flames. Because for that split second, I thought the man was *mine*. Only, he wasn't.

I let out a struggled breath, blinded by the hope that had consumed me. It had vanquished itself as quickly as it had come as I took in his clean-shaven face and red hair, and realised what those features meant. This man was a stranger.

He sat crumpled in his own corner with the same fearful expression painted across his face. He looked back over at Hydie and Abigail and I understood. It wasn't this powerless man who was tempted to dine on their blood. It was Hydie who craved his.

I followed his gaze, bottling my sorrows the best I could. Hydie's red irises meant she hadn't eaten, and though Abigail turned to look straight at me as I grasped at the barred door, my sister's eyes stayed pasted to the man.

Before I could reach for the keys, there was a buzz and a vampire slammed into the other side of the door.

O'Brien was face to face with me, glowering with the heat of a thousand fires. "Stay away from 'em, ya useless, shapeshiftin' piece o' shit," he snarled, his eyes red with anger rather than thirst. He shook the bars viciously, trying with all his might to scare me off. It partially worked. I had never seen him so fierce.

I flew back a few feet to make sure he couldn't grab me through the bars, but in all honesty, I was so happy to see him. He was alive. Right behind him, I could see his banshee, Ginny O'Brien, floating in place, her white hair and young face gazing at me approvingly.

I surveyed the cell, ensuring there was no one else before my eyes met O'Brien's again. Though his heart raced, and his lungs worked at a hundred kilometres a minute, he didn't back away from the gate.

"It's all right, O'Brien," I whispered. "It's really me. I escaped my own cell to find you all."

"Prove it," he challenged through his bared fangs.

I let out a soft breath. I suppose I'd have to get used to proving myself when there was another shifter around.

My attention wandered over to Abigail and then to my sister, who was now switching from quick, anxious looks at me and back to the man in the corner again. Her wrists were shackled, with the magic-suppressing handcuffs no doubt, and she was gripping onto one of Abigail's arms. The stranger shook with enough quakes to make him sick, but I took in his green eyes and my heart broke all over again. They reminded me of *him*. I tore my gaze away from the man to address O'Brien once more.

I took a gentle step closer to the bars, and watched the torchlight cast shadows across his face. "Riley O'Brien, you're one of the most selfless men I know, and even though I stepped on your feet a hundred times during our first dance at Loxley Lair, you've shown me nothing but kindness. You constantly make brave, bold decisions like saving me from Florence, and befriending me, and even though Ginny's forewarned your heroic death, you refuse to cower away. Instead, you've told her to watch after me and—" I stopped, nearly saying *his* name. But I couldn't. Hearing his name aloud would kill my soul. So, I eradicated the name from my vocabulary all together. "You've told Ginny to watch after us when you're gone," I finished.

Tears swam in my eyes, but O'Brien's face softened. He reached out and grasped my wrist like only a true friend would.

"I'm glad it's you, Azalea," he said quietly.

I gave him a curt nod before taking my arm away from him. I ripped a torch from the wall and began to light the mushrooms on the floor. If I was caught now, I needed my magic to protect me. They shrivelled quickly, and I replaced the torch so I could use my magic to unlock the gate.

O'Brien nodded at me as I rushed past, my knees crashing onto the floor. I ran my hands over my sister. She flinched at my touch but kept her crimson eyes on the stranger.

I reached into my chest to retrieve the phial and immediately uncorked it. There was blood along her wrists, but no cuts. My stomach tightened as I realised what it meant. She had tried to break free of the handcuffs and her skin healed. They were different from the invisible chains that had held me down during my transformation, but torturous nonetheless. My little sister had been through so much pain in the last few hours.

I'm going to get you out of here, I promised her, but her mind was silent in reply.

"Her transformation," I said to the others, tilting the bottle towards the shackles and tapping the tip to make a splash of the potion come out. "Florence said it was horrid. Is she all right? Will she be okay?"

Hydie trembled as the potion set to work and grabbed onto Abigail tighter as the cuffs released her.

Abigail nodded. "He wasn't wrong," she told me, her eyes slightly dazed as though she was remembering the hours Hydie had screamed on the floor. She looked over at O'Brien before she turned back to me. "We didn't have the right equipment to make the transformation any easier on her, not like we do at Loxley Lair. But she'll be all right."

I followed Hydie's gaze over to the stranger with green eyes.

"Who's he?" I asked.

O'Brien shrugged. "Some mortal," he said.

"They haven't fed her anything," Abigail explained. She nodded her head towards the mortal. "Florence is having her starved so she'll feed on him. She's resisting the best she can, but she's too hungry. If she takes a bite, she won't be able to stop herself from draining him dry."

"There's a river of blood out in the main corridor," I told them. "We can all feed from there to regain our strength."

After a hesitant pause, O'Brien and Abigail nodded. They didn't want to drink from it any more than I did. Of course they didn't. They were true Loxley Lair members with good morals who followed our laws. We knew innocent lives had been—and still were—being taken to fill that pool. But we needed our strength, and we were running out of options.

"What about the others?" I said, nodding my head towards the stack of corpses. "Were any of them alive when you got here?"

O'Brien nodded. "They all were," he said, sadness clogging his throat. "They were all at Loxley Prison when I was taken. This is everyone at the jail that they didn' kill on the spot."

"Anyone at the prison who was still alive after it was raided was turned into a vampire," Abigail said, taking over. "Then Florence and his followers fed on all of them, regardless of whether or not they pledged to work for Florence."

"Noel and Leon's mum was one of 'em," O'Brien said, his gaze shifting over to a body in the pile.

My eyes instantly shot over to her. Fang marks ravaged her skin. It was as if they had drained her so quickly that even her newly acquired vampire blood hadn't worked fast enough to heal the marks before death took her.

I felt a pit in my stomach as I remembered bringing her to O'Brien. It was the night I had been pulled to Noel and Leon. Abigail and I had found her in a tub of blood. She had tried to take her own life—to flee from the children she thought were cursed by the devil, all because they were magical beings. I had lifted her up from the bath and taken her to Loxley Lair. O'Brien had hooked her up to machines to rejuvenate her blood, and for what? For my enemy to feast upon her?

My stomach tightened stubbornly, squashing the pit that had been there only a moment ago. *Good riddance,* I thought. If she thought torturing her children was the answer, then it was a blessing she was gone. Her and my father. I wouldn't waste any tears or regrets on them. There were far purer souls in this world

435

who would love their children in their stead. Her becoming a vampire and my father possessing the very powers that he hated me for was exactly the karma they deserved.

I looked up at Abigail. She stared fixedly at the dead woman, her expression reading that she held the same opinions.

"This is the cell they're keepin' the vampires in," O'Brien continued, his eyes darting around the room. "From what we can tell, all the other cells have mortals or other creatures. Only a few of Florence's followers are allowed ta drink vampire blood. They come in 'ere, pickin' us off one by one."

"Florence told them not to touch us yet," Abigail said morbidly. "He wants to put us through hell first."

Hell, I thought. I tried not to think of Abigail's grief of taking a life, or my baby sister writhing in pain. I tried not to think about my own transformation or the fire that whipped around the man I loved, threatening to consume him. Hell was exactly where we had all been. It's where we still were. But we had to get out of its fiery pits. I merely needed to hold myself together until then.

I looked up at them and sadness drenched their blue eyes. But the closer I looked, the more I realised it wasn't pity for themselves or the torture they had faced in this wicked world. No. It was sorrow for me and the hell I lived in.

Abigail stifled a sob before she whispered out, "I'm really sorry about **CHAD**."

A whisper so broken, so full of woe one would hardly be able to hear it. Yet his name screamed out at me. It pierced into me like the fangs of a vampire. It throttled my eardrums like the high-pitched scream of a banshee. It tore into every inch of me, inside and out, like a werewolf ripping his skin to pieces and shedding it under a full moon.

Why would she say that? She had been awake. She could've seen something I hadn't, some sliver of hope. Connor could've broken free from the pyre. He could've torn his best mate away, and green magic could've healed him, like every damn time I had accidentally blasted my fated mate into a wall. They could be on their way to storm the castle, dragons, mummies, elves, and others at the ready. We could take Florence down. We were stronger together. We truly were.

Yet Abigail sat before me, grief-stricken. Where was her hope?

"Surely, he could've made it," I choked out, hating how foolish it sounded as the false hope coated my tongue like poison. "After Lili put me to sleep, you were still there, Abigail. He could've gotten away. He's strong. He's brave. Perhaps you saw…"

But I was rambling. And I was wrong.

Abigail's jaw quivered. She blinked as a stream of red tears fell from both eyes. She shook her head. I closed my eyes, letting my own tears bleed out.

"Can I see?" I asked, stretching my hand towards her. I wouldn't believe it unless I saw it with my own eyes.

I felt her cold hand slip into mine, and suddenly, I was strapped to a broken pyre, held down by creatures who only wanted to do us harm. I was screaming. I was crying out in Abigail's body as my own form was fast asleep in Florence's arms.

Heat blazed against my cheeks as I smelled *his* charred remains. Ash flew into my lungs. The orange fire was merciless. My soul held onto his slow heartbeat, one aching beat at a time, until no more came. I waited for it, prayed for it, begged for it, but my pleas went unanswered.

I completely fell apart.

My lungs gasped for air as I snatched my hand away from her, and I sank lower against the cold stone floor.

This wasn't the way this was supposed to be. The future upon the palms of my hands—where was it? How was I supposed to live a long happy life? How was I supposed to go on without him? He couldn't be gone. It hadn't been him who had died in Ginny's vision, it had been Nigel. Yet his heart had still stopped beating. It wasn't right. It wasn't fair.

I stared at the pile of lifeless forms beside us, wishing I was one of them, wishing fate had taken my life instead of his. I wasn't strong enough to overcome this. How had I not seen it coming?

Denial. That's how. It was just as Florence had said. Denial had given me hope, but it was a lie. Without it, there was no light. There was only a dark, empty world with no future. No three little children with his green eyes and warm spirit. No happy ending.

There was nothing.

I wanted to die. I wanted to sit there and let the pain consume me until I simply didn't exist.

The clock struck the hour, shaking me horribly with each of its five menacing chimes. The walls vibrated against each strike, shaking sense into me, and letting anger wash away the denial until it became fiery venom in my veins.

No—I would not hear his name. I would not die or wallow until I got my revenge.

I swallowed down all of my emotions and stood up straight.

"Come on," I told my friends, my red eyes shifting over to the cell door. "Let's get Hydie over to the blood river, and then get everyone the hell out of here."

I'm Still Unstoppable

Chapter 56: A Bloody Curse

We left the cell door ajar as we made our way out into the main tunnel, Abigail holding Hydie steady, anger driving me forwards, and O'Brien and Ginny trailing after us. The mortal stayed behind, his haunting green eyes serving as kindling to my revenge. He could escape with the rest of the prisoners when the time came. For now, we needed to get my sister the thing she was craving most.

As we neared the splashing river of blood, Hydie leapt from Abigail's arms, practically immersing her whole face into it. It was like a horror film as I watched her, thirst driving each of her movements, overpowering her senses. I pried my eyes away from her, forcing myself to scoop the red liquid into my hands. Ginny stared ominously at the ceiling. O'Brien and Abigail helped themselves to the fresh supply of blood for several seconds before Hydie emerged, gasping for air, blood trailing down her whole front. I stared at her, realising her brown eyes were forever gone. But now her red ones had vanished too, replaced by bright blue.

For a second, she looked better, healthier—satisfied even. Then without warning, she began to fall. Abigail and I caught her in the blink of an eye.

"What's wrong?" I asked quickly.

Hydie didn't answer. She closed her eyes, groaning, and though my heart raced with worry, Abigail gave me a soft look to tell me it would all be all right.

"She needs rest is all," she told me, "just like you did."

I gave a brave nod, ready to accept it, but then my heart quickened again. How could it be all right? How could anything ever be all right again?

The look on my face must have said it all. Ginny floated next to me, a mournful expression on her face. I looked away, trying desperately to grasp onto my fury instead.

"How often do they come down here?" I asked. It seemed that every time I was in this corridor, *they* were above ground. Not that I was complaining, but I knew I shouldn't rely on it.

"Ginny's been keepin' an eye on their movements," O'Brien told us. "Typically, Florence and his followers come down once or twice a day ta feed. They make a quick game out o' it. Other than that, they stay in the castle 'bove ground."

I gave a firm nod. "I stole the keys," I said, taking them from my dress and tossing them to O'Brien. Then I threw him the potion bottle. He caught both easily. "Use them to release everyone you can, as quickly as you can," I instructed. "Go full speed. The more chaos, the more overwhelmed Florence will be." I turned to Abigail. "When the corridors are filled with the other captives, take Hydie and lead everyone out to safety. I'll show you the mushroom path that the gnomes made."

Fear seeped out of them in the form of sweat just above their brows, but they nodded, accepting the plan. A deep breath prepared my lungs for the challenge we were about to face.

"They came down at midnight," I told them, "so we shouldn't expect them until they hear everyone escaping. That buys you a little time."

"What about you?" O'Brien asked, voicing the elephant in the room. "You say it as if you're not comin' with us."

"I'm not," I said simply. "The duchesses are inside the castle. He—" I dug my nails into my palms. "He'd want them to be freed."

Pain stabbed at my heart—the miserable, useless twinge of denial. Then Florence's other words crashed into my mind. Sex on a grave on our wedding night. And I was back to rage.

The fucking monster.

The prisoners' screams crashed against the walls—more lives Florence and Lili had ruined—and then back to my mates. My distraction. My reason for not crumbling to the ground and letting my grief take me. And though Lili was out of the country, and Florence wasn't expected for hours, time was an illusion. It appeared we had it when, in reality, we only had however long it was before the monsters above realised what we were doing. Whatever we did, we needed to act fast.

I looked up at the others, ready to start plotting our way out, but a soft voice clouded my vision.

"It should be me who's dead," Abigail said, and my eyes snapped up to look at her. Her voice cracked on the words. She looked as if she'd be next to crumble.

O'Brien and Ginny shifted awkwardly and Hydie rested, but they were silent as they waited for my response. I thought about the fire—the blood oath *he* had made—forewarning his death if it wasn't fulfilled. I had been so blind.

"Absolutely not," I blurted out. It was done. As much as I wanted to undo his death, I would never have sacrificed Abigail instead. "The blood oath has been fulfilled," I told her, softening my harsh tone. "He knew what could happen going into it. He was tricked because that's what Lili and Florence do. And though he wanted so much to tell you this himself, he wanted you to know he wasn't mad at you. He understands that you couldn't control it, and you don't have to feel any shame. These past few months, he had to stay away from you to keep you alive, but he was trying his best to find his way around it and break the oath."

Oath, I thought, despising the word. It was no oath, no promise, no joyous vow. No—it was a bloody curse.

Abigail stared down at the floor. "But it should've been me to pay the price, not—"

"Abigail, look at me," I said, cutting her off. I couldn't hear his name again. I just couldn't. Apart from that, I needed my best friend to know she had every right to walk this earth.

She looked at me, but I could tell her mind was already made up. I took a step towards her, and she closed her lips.

"You are alive for a reason, I know it," I told her, meaning every word. "You're here because you saved Cristin from a life of revenge and hatred—you saved me from a life of becoming Florence's property—and you provided the love that Noel and Leon deserve when their own mother wouldn't," I said firmly. I swallowed, pushing past the knife in my heart, past the pain of losing my happily ever after with the man I loved. "He knew how kind your soul was, and you'll continue to share that kindness with the children and watch over them. You'll shed that guilt so it doesn't weigh you down. Do you understand me?"

Her face scrunched up as though it pained her, but she nodded anyway.

I let out a sigh. We didn't need to mourn. We needed to destroy our enemies.

Abigail looked down at my dress. "What about your blood oath?" she asked, eyeing the white fabric as if it was a poisonous snake.

I looked down at my outfit, hate driving me once more, and transformed the dress into proper fighting gear—light and flexible to allow movement.

"Til death does us part," I said pointedly, and Abigail nodded, knowing exactly my plan.

"He's had it coming for a long time," she said, her eyes lost in the past before she looked at me, the hint of a dare in her eye. "Make it hurt."

A laugh fell from my lips. I grasped her arm before looking straight into her eyes.

"And that is why you're my best friend," I told her, and she gave me a smile, one I hadn't seen in a long time.

I met each of their gazes with red eyes, ready to make my first kill. "Let's go," I said, supporting Hydie's weight. "I'll show you the way out."

I'm Still Unstoppable

Chapter 57: Meant To Be

The five of us flew down the corridor, back to the small, barred window that hid the mushroom path. I handed Hydie off to Abigail, then lifted the window from its spot and set it on the ground. Brushing the dirt off my hands, I listened down the pathway. Screams met my ears, but no footsteps or menacing voices.

"All right," I started. "Lead everyone out through here. Once you're out, past the wards, everyone needs to scatter and go anywhere but here. There are bound to be more witches and wizards in the cells. Have them transport the others away."

I looked at each of them, so brave, so alive, but fear bit at me. Would there be enough Casters to get everyone out in time? How many would be left behind?

My sister swayed. She had to make it out. If not, it would be all my fault. I should've killed Florence sooner.

"I'm really sorry they did this to you, Hydie," I told her.

She gave a weary smile before she wrapped my hand in hers. "I'll be all right," she said, her voice hoarse, and I knew she was right.

I squeezed her hand back. "I know," I told her. "Remember when we were small and father used to go out to the gardens during his fits? He'd completely butcher the hedge of azaleas and hydrangeas, yet every time they'd appear in full bloom the next morning. They're like you. No matter how many times life tears you down, you come back, as strong as ever." The words fell from my mouth. She was resilient. I wished the same could be said for me.

Then I wrapped my arms around her and Abigail, pulling them in tight. "Take good care of her," I told Abigail as the three of us embraced.

She nodded, a tearful sniff playing in my ear. "Of course," she replied.

I broke away and gave O'Brien a hug. When he pulled away, worry furrowed his brow.

"Ginny," he said. "You go with Azalea."

"Oh no," I insisted. I didn't want protection, or for my mates to witness the slaughter I was about to do. Besides, O'Brien was the one who needed her, not me. "She should stay with you."

But the banshee ignored the idea. She floated over to me, a stubborn look upon her face as if she might scream if I rejected her company again.

We all seemed to take one big collective breath before we parted ways. Abigail, O'Brien, and my sister headed back towards the cells. As soon as Ginny and I were away from the mushrooms, I clutched my fists, gathering the strength to shift into a disguise— one I needed to pass through the castle above. I couldn't shift into Lili. Missouri had let it slip that she was in America. Which meant I had to shift into the man who was about to pay for all of his sins.

I closed my eyes and pictured Florence's blond hair—the very face where some saw handsome features, yet I only saw evil. I imagined him all the way down to the clothes he had been wearing earlier. When opened my eyes I looked down and saw Florence's hands, not a speck of dirt beneath his fingernails. No. He wasn't the type to do the dirty work. He had it done for him.

"The aunts are on the sixth floor," I told Ginny, Florence's voice coming from my lips, making the hatred in my veins pulse. "Let's start there."

We sped along the blood river, raced up the stairs, and ducked through the courtyard before slipping into the castle. The screams from down below were muffled and replaced with laughter and the clinking of glass.

We entered a grand hall—the same hall where Nigel had taken his last breaths for his king. A wasted sacrifice. I shuddered as the bloodfall commandeered my senses: the sight of it, just up the first set of stairs, as it crashed into the pool below; the smell as it tempted me, regardless of my full stomach; and the feel of it on my skin as tiny droplets flew out in a mist. I buried the idea that I had drunk from its supply only moments ago.

Embodying Florence's cocky stride, I made my way towards the staircase, Ginny close beside me. My foot touched the first step, ready to speed up the rest of them, when a buzz whizzed through the castle, and the pull tightened.

A pair of grand double doors burst open behind me, and I watched as my creator strode out of them. A crowd of at least a hundred others stood in the room he had come from, all dressed to the nines, mingling with glasses of blood or liquor or both. A celebration.

Fuck. Of course he wasn't alone. Not even close.

The glass Florence held sloshed around dangerously as he laughed merrily. And just before his eyes shot over to me, I shifted out of his skin and into another's.

"Benji," he said to me, his voice coming down from its high. "Just the person I was looking for. What took you so long?" he asked, holding his arms in the air to emphasise the question.

The party continued on, the vile creatures behind him sparing me quick glances before returning to their drinks and joyous conversations. Like they weren't shattering the lives of innocents.

I turned around fully, my foot coming down off the step, my lips matching his smile. "Don't tell me you're unaware of how feisty your bride-to-be is?" I asked in the friendliest voice I could manage for someone I wanted to rip apart to shreds. "But the injection seems to be working fine. She'll be nice and easy for you soon enough."

Florence smirked, vulgar thoughts crossing his mind and brushing against mine. He raised the glass to his lips, but his whole demeanour shifted when his eyes fell upon Ginny.

His hand paused its climb. Swiping the glass away from his mouth, a sip's worth of blood splattered against the floor. "What the fuck is the banshee doing here?" he demanded, his voice echoing through the hall at the height of his usual rage.

I froze as several eyes inspected us. The party hushed.

Careful to take slow breaths, I glanced over at Ginny and then gave Florence a guilty look. "All right," I sighed warily. "Now, don't be too cross, but I may have had a small *bite* to eat while I was down in the dungeons—and I know you said you were keeping that Irish fellow alive and all, but I couldn't resist. Apparently, he didn't have a next of kin, so ghosty is all mine."

To my surprise, Florence shrugged and finally took a gulp of his drink. I heard the glug as he swallowed it down.

"At least she's on our side, I suppose," he decided, wiping his mouth on his sleeve. "The more the merrier!" he jeered. Then his eyes darted over to the staircase. "Where were you off to? The fun's about to start. They're about to detonate the first bomb in America." I winced at the thought but Florence didn't notice. "Lilith's not here so she can't have a hissy fit about the orgy this time," he went on. "And you'll never guess who else I've recruited. Two witches and a *manananggal*," he told me excitedly. "And I asked the manananggal what the hell we were supposed to do with her. The sun hasn't risen yet. Her good half is laying useless somewhere else. And you want to know what that cheeky bat said to me?" He paused for dramatic effect, leaning in towards me to deliver the punchline. "She said, 'Oi! I've still got a mouth,' and I just about died!"

Fuck, I hated him.

I forced myself to laugh. "Don't worry," I began, "I'll be there soon." I rolled my eyes. "*Lilith* has tasked me with checking on the hags upstairs. Then I'll be back down."

"That reminds me," Florence replied, holding up a finger as the idea came to him. "After that, I'm going to need to you to do another injection—on that Abigail girl this time. Then bring her up. What good is an orgy without a slave trying to escape the entire time?"

My fists tightened yet I forced a smile on my lips. Not a single person in the party seemed bothered or even to notice his crude words. The itch to kill him urged me harder than the pull towards him. It didn't bother me to know his party would tear me apart if I killed him then and there. In fact, part of me craved it—an end to both Florence and my sorrow. No, what halted my fingers from tearing his heart from his chest were the people down below who deserved long happy lives, and the aunts several floors above who may not find freedom if I didn't give it to them. That, and the idea of Lili walking away scot-free. I couldn't let that happen.

"Don't have too much fun without me," I said, flashing Benji's blood-stained teeth. "I'll be back with Abigail shortly."

Florence gave me a dismissive wink and I took it as my cue to go. I ran up the steps, slow enough that Ginny could trail behind me. As we got further, I could feel the pull yanking me back, and I thanked the heavens Florence couldn't feel the connection we shared.

Up and up we went, my heart pounding at the idea of seeing the aunts. I was going to have to prove it was really me again, and even then, why would they trust me?

On the fourth staircase, a blurred image crossed my mind. I stopped mid step and the vision crossed me again, but this time I saw a set of pale hands hurriedly tossing clothes into an open trunk.

My gaze shot over to Ginny, and she looked at me with squinted eyes, trying to understand why I stopped. I focused on the vision and knew the sixth floor would have to wait.

"Something's off," I said.

Black candles on the floor—in a circle around her.

A pink dress—stuffed into the trunk.

Blonde hair thrown over a shoulder as anxiety boiled within her.

Lili was running away, and in a hurry too. But fate had brought this vision to me. And I couldn't let her get away.

"Change of plans," I whispered to Ginny before nodding over to a door not far from the top of the stairs. "Lili's not in America. She's in there, and I have a feeling in my gut that I need to get her now."

Perhaps my first kill didn't have to be Florence. Perhaps I could settle for the woman who created him.

Ginny's transparent brows furrowed. But then she turned to look back down the stairs and her eyes glazed over in a milky white colouring.

A hollow, ear-piercing scream left her lips. The cry of a banshee.

I rushed to cover my ears. What was she doing? She was going to get us caught.

Her eyes returned to normal but her scream went on. I opened my mouth as her gaze tore into me, only her expression said it all. O'Brien. Something was going to happen. She had to go.

Go, I mouthed.

The sound of her loud shrill continued, yet her ghostly voice played in my head—a line she had said to me once before.

Everything will turn out the way it's meant to be.

Then she vanished, taking her scream with her.

I stared at the spot she had disappeared from and then back to the door. Lili was behind it. The woman who killed the love of my life. I made my decision. They'd have Ginny to help them down below, and I'd have my rage to help me up here.

I shifted back into myself and sped, opening the door as I went. Another door closed from somewhere else in the room, but then Lili's eyes met mine. They sparkled with wonder, right before a shot of my purple magic reflected in the whites of her eyes, and she shot backwards.

I'm Still Unstoppable

Chapter 58: Roars and Rays

Lili crashed down, skidding across the floorboards, and knocking over some black candles. They circled her, spanning from a tall wardrobe to just beneath her bed. She scurried in a blur to reset them, their wicks staying aflame. Then she grunted out in frustration as her eyes snapped up to me.

"Not you again," she growled.

I didn't give her the chance to say anything else. I blasted at least ten balls of purple fire at her. But she had the same speed I did, the same magic to block it, and centuries more practice. As each ball went soaring towards her, she pointed a finger at them and dissolved them with her invisible magic. Sparks flew as she extinguished them, showering down on her perfect bedroom before they too died out.

Lili grasped onto her bed frame as she fought back—the same bed she had used my body to have sex with the murdering bastard she was so in love with.

"Stop, you stupid girl!" she shrieked at me, but I refused.

"You killed him," I screamed back at her, loving green eyes flashing into my mind right before I sent a vibrant flame to her bed. It ignited in a purple fire so furious that I could feel its heat whipping at me. Then I sent another blast towards her so she wouldn't have time to put out the fire.

"It's funny you don't know what you're capable of," she smirked, casting my attack off to the side.

But her smile fell as my foot bumped into one of the candles on the floor, and real fear flashed through her eyes.

"Stop!" she cried out again, fright replacing the humour in her tone. "Don't touch the candles," she demanded, dousing another ball of purple fire with her magic.

I looked down at the candles, not giving a shit about her wishes, and forced the flames to rise. A wall of fire surrounded her, scorching the ceiling in a perfect circle. I panted heavily, watching her through her prison.

"You're going to die, Lili," I promised her. "You're going to die for all the lives you've ever taken. You're going to die for turning Abigail and creating Florence, and not a soul on this earth is going to miss you when you're gone."

That struck a nerve. Her nostrils flared as she pointed a finger straight at my chest, but I blocked her invisible magic with a violet shield. Using the shield against the fire, I jumped into the circle and onto her, knocking her to the ground again. The shield vanished as I wrapped my fingers around her neck. I dug my thumbs into her jugular. Grey cracks sprouted towards her face, but as she grasped on my wrists with all her might, grey cracks began to run up my arms.

I spit in her eyes and her grip loosened in time for me to free a hand and strike her across the face. I kneed her in the stomach and she groaned loudly. Her eyes blazed red as the cracks returned to perfect peach skin. Grabbing her arms, I pinned them down to the ground and set fire to her skin. She kicked her feet from beneath me like a tantrum as she tried to wiggle free.

"You stupid, bloody whore!" she shrieked, right as her knee collided with my back.

My whole body rolled over hers and towards the fire in a somersault before my nails scraped against the ground, slowing me down. The heat of the fire burned my face as I stared at it. I turned around, glaring at the vampire-witch, and I was met with her fury. Her fingers wrapped around my neck, nearly crushing my windpipe. I choked, the metallic taste of blood on my tongue.

My cheeks heated. My eyes bulged. I grabbed at her face, hooking my fingers in her mouth—pulling it so hard her skin nearly ripped down the side of her cheek. She yelled out in pain, and tore her face away from me. Before my eyes could track her movements, she punched me square in the stomach, and I flew through the wall of fire.

Air deserted my lungs. The fire seared my skin, covering what felt like every inch of me as I squeezed my eyes shut. Pain like I was dying. The very pain she had inflicted upon *him*.

A bubble burst from my stomach. I could feel it grow so large that it swallowed me whole. As I opened my eyes, I watched myself fly towards the fire, through it, my neck straight back into Lili's grasp, and I sent a spell across her arms.

She stumbled back, screaming as she stared at the stubs her arms had become—the bottom halves still frozen around my neck as blood drained from them. In one swift motion, I yanked them off of me, and tossed them in the fire. But even as her screams continued, I watched her arms lengthen, growing past her elbows. Then her hands reappeared as she healed herself.

Her eyes flickered up at me with such hate I thought I'd burn to the ground from her gaze alone. But as we each sent a stream of magic towards the other, mine was stronger. It crashed into hers, sending her entire body soaring out of the circle.

She smashed into the ground, her body aflame. Yet even as she waved a magical hand to put out the fire, her head snapped up and she stared over at the door. Instantly, I felt the invisible string that tied Florence and me together. It grew taut. And as I heard the buzz—as I felt the string get shorter and shorter—Lili turned back to me.

She bared her fangs. "Great," she growled. "Now we're both fucked."

But I didn't care if Florence was coming to join the fight. In fact, I craved it. It distracted him from all the prisoners who were escaping down below.

I shifted into Benji just as Florence blasted through the doorway. His eyes crashed into mine, confusion coating his face before he noticed Lili, and his rage started to take over.

"What the hell are you doing here?" he barked at her, turning his body towards her to size her up. "You're supposed to be overseeing the attacks in America." His gaze flew over to the fire, the candles circled on the floor, and then to the bed where her trunk sat ablaze.

I blinked and Lili was up on her feet again, brushing soot off her chest as if she hadn't just been getting her arse kicked.

She opened her mouth, but right as she did, I sent purple ropes around both of their necks. I strung the ropes around my hands, pulling them in closer, feeling my magic radiate like electricity as it pulsed out of me. The sound of their choking—the sight of their bulging eyes—seemed to feed me more strength.

I shifted back into myself, wanting my face to be the last either of them saw before they died. As I wondered which method of death would inflict the most pain upon them, a loud roar shook the whole castle.

My neck jerked towards the tall window in the room, but an invisible vine wrapped around my ankle and tugged me to the floor. My head smashed against the wooden planks. White blurred my vision as at least ten more roars crammed their way into my head. The whole room shook as if its walls and grand towers were crashing down on us.

One of my purple ropes snapped and Lili was free, peering out her window and up at the dark sky.

"My wards!" she shouted out, her face full of anguish until it shifted to malice.

Florence's knees crashed into the ground. He continued to choke against my ropes, his face nearly as red as his eyes.

I turned back to Lili and stood back upon my feet. I sent a blast straight at her head right as a chunk of the ceiling crashed down— the same shape as the candle border below it—adding kindling to the fire. She easily stepped out of my magic's way and the blast shattered the window beside her. A breeze blew in, sweeping a blast of the fire's heat towards me. She covered her face as the glass sprinkled over her and then her eyes darted to me. She hissed at me angrily before the wind from her magic wrapped around her, and she disappeared.

My heart clenched. No. She didn't get to leave. She had killed him. She had *fucking* killed him. I had to go after her.

In an instant, I stood at the spot where she'd disappeared, her invisible magic tingling around me, Florence's chain sweeping him along with me. I closed my eyes, relishing the feel of her magic, and I let it take me to her.

My feet crashed into the soil outside, the sound of Florence's body hitting a split second after. Lili stood mere metres away, glaring at the sky as a hundred dragons, topped with icy-blue riders, blew fire at the wards.

Holes in the faint, golden dome started to appear everywhere, some connecting together like constellations mapped out in the sky. Sunlight poured in through them, but we stood in the shadows. People began pouring out of the castle to stare up at them—vampires, witches, manananggals, and more. Even Eyeron came out to gawk at what was once his own army, now against him.

I studied the cracks in the wards, weighing my options, wondering if I should run from the enemy that was surrounding me on the grounds or if the elves would break through in time. The vampire-witch may be centuries old, but there was no way her magic was stronger than a hundred of those beasts and their riders stacked together.

Florence made a choking sound and Lili's eyes snapped to me, realising I had tailed her.

Suddenly she was in my face. "How dare you bring them here," she screeched at me. "The elves and their filthy dragons will burn it to the ground. This is my home. This castle is *mine!*"

I stared at her for a second, stunned she was bothering to speak to me rather than rip my head off, but then a dragging noise and a voice sounded behind me.

"Don't worry, Lilith," Benji said lazily. My eyes flew over to the vampire as he approached us, pulling a large burlap sack along the ground. He looked up at the dragons. "Your wards are strong. They'll hold off long enough to make our point."

He pulled at the sack with the same weakness as a mortal. The stench of death rammed into me as confusion seeped in. He was supposed to be in my cell—paralysed. The vampire blood he drank should've slowed his healing process enough while the serum took over his bloodstream to weaken him. Yet he knelt down next to the bag, his eyes on me as he tore it open. I could feel the rip of the bag as it simultaneously tore my heart. And when I saw the mangled body—the face within the bag—my heart broke. Tears formed in my eyes as I stared down at O'Brien. Dead.

Blood covered O'Brien—scratches, tears, marks of a wild beast. There were no signs of life—no pulse, no faint breath. There was nothing. My mate hadn't been killed. He had been slaughtered.

I gawked at Benji, trying to piece it together in my head, wondering how the hell he had healed in such a short time, or how he had gotten out and managed to inflict this much harm.

Benji shook his head at me slowly as if I was missing the obvious answer to my conundrum.

"I've never been much for vampire blood," he said tauntingly, his red smile only for me. "It makes you heal far too slowly."

He turned to Lili, whose shoulders rose and fell with every harsh breath—her eyes trying to track Benji, the dragons, and me all at once.

Florence pulled at the ropes, desperation in the tug, seeking mercy as he choked. The heat from the fire brushed against my skin as the dragons worked to break their way in. My breath quickened as the crowd around me drew closer, ready to strike.

Benji's lips parted to speak but he aimed his words towards Lilith. "I caught the Irish fellow breaking the slaves out of their cages. They're all gone!" he yelled, standing to face the whole crowd. "While you lot were inside partying, I was trying to stop them. *He* stayed back to fight while the rest of them got away," he said, tilting his head down to O'Brien. "Him and this one."

He pointed back the way he came. I could hardly hear the dragons over the pounding of my heart as my eyes met with my best friend. Near a stream of sunlight, Abigail was gagged—cuffs around her wrists and ankles—red tears streaming down her cheeks. Her onyx hair was matted with dried blood as she stared at me. Missouri stood behind her, shoving her transparent hand through Abigail's back to urge her forwards—smiling at every shiver Abigail gave in response.

I reined Florence in closer, my purple ropes swirling up my arm. "Set her free," I demanded, "or I'll kill Florence."

The whole crowd seemed to inch ever closer, on the fence between attacking and waiting for the command. Fear filled their eyes as they glanced outside of the wards, and all around us. A laugh broke their silence.

"You think that a quid pro quo is going to work on us?" Lili asked, glaring into me, but then her brow rose with intrigue.

For a second, I was stumped. Why wouldn't she go for the offer? She loved Florence.

She took my hesitation as a weakness.

"Fine," she dared, striding over to Abigail. She grabbed at Abigail's hair and yanked her down to her knees—inches away from a ray of sunlight that streamed in through the cracked wards. Abigail let out a sharp cry. "I created her," Lili continued. "I can take her life away." She flicked her brows at me, insinuating a dare. "Call the dragons off *and* hand Florence over to me, or your little mate gets turned to stone."

Abigail grasped at Lili's hand but my strong, brave, friend had hardly any fight left in her. Lili forced Abigail's head into the light. Abigail's forehead started to sizzle. She let out a scream as smoke filled the air. Her once flawless skin began to harden and turn grey.

Eyes of every shade turned to me, their shoulders drawing near to them, ready to pounce. My soul ripped apart. She was going to die if I didn't fucking do something. I yearned to take the bait, to save Abigail. But a little voice in the back of my mind told me this is how they had beaten me before. It was another trick. If I did what Lili said, she'd still cast Abigail to stone. There had to be another way.

The stubbornness that had kept me alive throughout everything kicked back in. I flashed my fangs at Lili and yanked the rope so Florence was grovelling on his hands and knees. I would not let them win.

"Alright then," Lili tested, her tone as light as a feather. "Let's see which one dies first."

"Get her!" Benji barked.

A shrill buzz crackled in my ears as the vampires advanced. I yanked Florence's chain towards me and gripped onto his head, ready to tear it off. If I wasn't going to make it out of here, then I'd be damned if I wasn't taking him with me.

Hands and claws tore into my flesh as I squeezed Florence's head tight. Fear swam in his crimson eyes. But right before I could watch the light fade from them, his followers pulled me away.

I screamed fiercely, hitting and kicking and blasting my magic at them. While Night Crawlers held me down, Casters blocked my magic with a series of spells and shields. I felt as someone grabbed onto my leg, the snap as pain shot through my entire body. Someone behind me pierced their fangs into my neck. As the world started to fill with fog and tiny white stars, I heard the pounding of fists and three tiny voices shouting my name.

"Azalea!" they called, and the pain was no longer important.

Through the holes in the wards, I breathed in the smell of their lavender bath salts mixed in with the scent of their skin. I froze. I knew those voices—one of which I had just heard for the first time.

The wards thundered around me. They gave one final, ground-shaking crack, and the dome split open.

I heard the quick strides of Kana's eight legs, the rushed breaths as Noel and Leon followed her towards me—hope driving them past their fear. As if they could help. As though they could save me the way I saved Kana in Japan, or Noel and Leon from their mother. As if these weren't the very creatures who had drunk their mother's blood.

And just as a werewolf turned in their direction, his teeth bared, ready to run at them, a bubble emitted from my stomach. But this time, instead of absorbing me, it seeped out, growing and growing until everything around me was immersed in it. The world began to grow lighter until it was nothing but a great, white, blank slate.

And I thought about the one place I wanted to go.

The one person I wanted to hold tight, and have him tell me everything was going to be okay.

Chad.

I'm Still Unstoppable

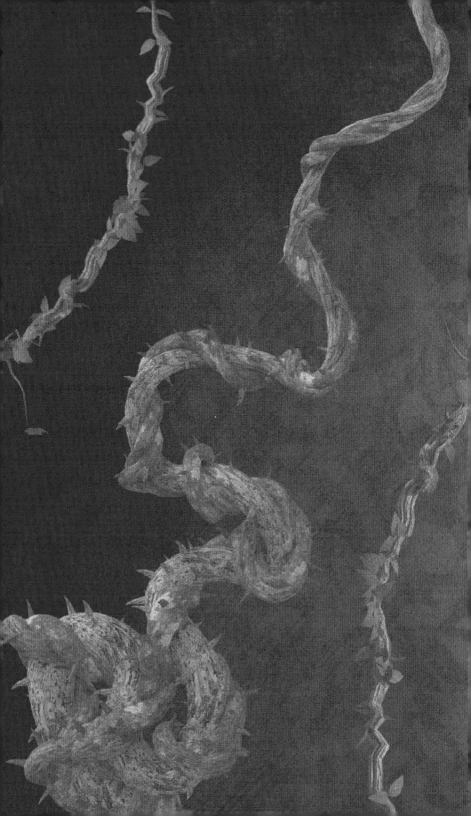

Chapter 59: Déjà Vu

I landed on a patch of grass with a loud thump. I had fallen for what felt like several kilometres. A silent scream left my lungs as I clenched my jaw onto my wrist, desperate to distract myself from the pain. I stared at the green hedge in front of me—grounding myself to the present. The blades of the green grass brushed against me as my body worked hard to heal the broken bones, bites, and scrapes.

Green.

The green of Chad's eyes.

The green emerald he had given me when he asked me to be his queen.

Something glistened in the corner of my vision, and I looked to find that exact ring, nearly hidden by the grass. I grasped onto it and put it in my pocket. As a wave of truth washed over me, I realised where my magic had taken me.

I was back in the maze.

"Time's ticking!" Florence shouted from afar, and instantly, I was sitting up, bolt straight.

His voice rang through my ears. Those words. That command. I had heard it before.

"I said I was thinking," came a growl, and shivers erupted down my spine.

My lips were closed, but I would bet a thousand souls it was my voice that had said it.

I looked down the long, straight path, past the letters that littered the ground, past fallen azalea petals and glowing white lanterns. And I saw a scene of chaos as I looked into the past.

"Hurry up!" Florence countered. Just as he had before.

And there I stood, trapped by creatures stronger than me, facing the dilemma of how to break free while Lili was in my head, and Florence was berating me. *One burned, one turned, one captive, one free.*

I had gone back in time.

"What is your decision, Azalea?" Florence pressed in a harsh voice. I remembered it clearly.

I blinked and looked down at the parchment around me— pages and pages of letters—each filled with love.

How? How was I here? How had I reversed it?

The bubble, I thought to myself. I had produced a time bubble that had covered everything. And it had reversed time.

My eyes flew back down the path in the hedges, right as Florence's voice thundered out, "What's the answer to the riddle? Who gets burned?"

I scurried behind a hedge, hoping no one had seen me. There were two of me. Not a decoy. Not a shapeshifter, but two of *me.*

Hope started to blossom in my chest. This wasn't a dream. This wasn't a nightmare. It was a miracle. I focused my ears, searching for that heart I longed to hear. I pinpointed it in an instant as if it was my very own. It thudded on, strong and fierce. It was a heavenly symphony, lifting my soul. Chad was alive. And I knew exactly what I was meant to do.

"Shove your riddles up your arse, Florence!" I heard my past self yell back.

"Fine, you stupid whore!" Florence snapped. I watched from the protection of a hedge as he stomped his foot like a child. "I'll choose them all for you. Benji," he yelled, turning to his red-eyed mate. "Bite the sister."

Benji acted as quickly as I remembered, jerking Hydie's head to the side before digging his blood-stained teeth into her neck.

I watched myself jolt forwards, my muscles reacting the same now, aching to stop it. My sister screamed out into the night. I was meant to do something. I was here to stop this, but how? I was still outnumbered. There wasn't time to get help. It was up to me.

"Lilith," Florence called, and my eyes shot up to him as he gave her a nod.

Lili's fingers snapped, and Chad's pyre rose with flames.

My body ached to run to him, to grab him, and take him far away from here, but it hit me like a punch to the gut. They had to see him die. They had to believe it wholeheartedly.

I listened to all their screams—watched Connor fight against his chains as he shifted into a werewolf—and shuddered at his howl as he watched his best friend burn alive.

"Abigail will be our captive," Florence announced to the crowd. "She's always been a bitch to me anyway, and this werewolf... Well, do whatever you'd like," he told Connor. "We've already had our fun with you."

I heard myself beg—watched my sister go limp. I heard the words I had shouted out in desperation, hoping they'd follow through on a promise I now knew meant nothing.

"I'll do anything," I screamed at him. "Anything!"

"Anything?" Florence asked luringly.

"Yes!" I shouted as Chad's screams cleaved the night. "I'll do anything, I swear!"

A bead of sweat dripped down my forehead as my heart raced. I gripped onto a branch in the hedge, holding on tight as if it would steady me, but how could it?

"Swear you'll come with me," Florence demanded. "Swear you'll be with me 'til death do us part."

I cringed at his words, even worse as I heard my response.

"I do."

Chad's scream echoed towards me, shaking me to my core. They needed to leave. I needed to save him.

"Then seal it with a kiss," Florence suggested, so quietly I had to focus my ears to hear it.

I forced myself to watch his teeth lengthen. I knew what was coming next. The blood oath.

Hurry, I begged myself. *Kiss him and get it over with.*

And after only a moment's hesitation, I did.

I watched my lips crash into his. I remembered the sting as he bit my lip—the spark of magic binding us together tighter than the pull ever had. Bile clogged my throat as the man I hated above all else got exactly what he wanted.

As soon as his lips tore away from mine, he gave the smug smile I longed to claw off his face. "Lili. Do it," Florence commanded, sealing what I thought was all of our fates, but it couldn't be. Not now.

Chaos erupted as Lili placed her arm to Hydie's lips, and the venom began to spread through my sister's veins. My stomach threatened to spill as I watched myself beg for mercy—as my heart crumbled to pieces for the people I loved. But Hydie was going to be all right. Hydie was going to survive, just like we always had, and she'd have Abigail to hold through her transformation. It was Chad who needed me right now.

Florence whispered the final word, the word that sent me to my slumber. "Sleep," he said softly. It was nearly time.

My eyes crashed into my past self right as my head fell back, and Lili's sleeping charm worked its way through me. In an instant, soft, even breaths flowed through my lungs. I was in their clutches, fast asleep.

Florence picked up my limp body. His smile was soft, almost loving as he watched me sleep in his arms. I gripped the branch tighter. He didn't love me. He was no longer capable of feeling true love. His heart was too ruined.

"Take them to the dungeons," he commanded a few members of the crowd, pointing at Abigail and Hydie. "Put them in the cell with the other vampires. We'll make them watch as we feed on them one by one."

The creatures around them began to move throughout the crowd. Some started untying Abigail and Hydie and throwing them over their shoulders.

They'll be all right, I told myself, squeezing my eyes shut to try and endure Chad's scream—Hydie's cry. Hydie was going to make it out of the dungeons with the rest of the captives, and I had hours before Abigail needed my help.

A witch moved towards Chad, still writhing in the flames, but Lili screeched at her. "Stop!" she demanded, a sneer across her face as if the witch was daft. "Don't take him down. He's not dead yet. I'll bury him," she said, turning to Florence. There was a hint of a question in her voice as if she were covertly asking his approval. "I'll give him a nice little grave on the property so Azalea can see his fate. Then I'll go to America to ensure everything goes smoothly there."

Florence gave her a sour look, apparently under the impression that she was incapable of handling both.

My heart pounded as Chad's yells died down and turned to desperate moans. His lungs, his heart, his everything was failing him.

Lili rolled her eyes. "He's an inch from death," she berated Florence with a glare. "How could I possibly fuck it up?"

"All right," he said, looking down at my unconscious frame as if I were a child that needed to be rocked. "But the plan has to go off unhinged." He looked back at Lili, his face harder. "These bombs mean everything. You have to get this perfect."

"I know," she snapped, giving Chad a bitter look as if his groans and suffering were an inconvenience to her. "That's why I'm going and you're not, Florence."

Instead of scolding her for her attitude, Florence smiled. He handed off my body to the vampire beside him and then walked towards Lili, the crackling fire growing louder. Then he grabbed Lili's chin roughly and pulled her in for a kiss. I ground my fangs together. He was despicable. When he pulled away, a wizard grabbed onto his arm and nearly everyone disappeared, leaving only Lili, Connor, and Chad behind.

Connor howled out, but it turned into a yell as he switched back into his human form.

He screamed obscenities at Lili, raged against his chains, and shook his whole pyre. She ignored the werewolf as she took slow, deliberate steps around Chad's pyre. Every part of me ached and trembled with rage. Yet Lili personified a calm evening, as though she were merely enjoying a cup of tea by the fireside. How could she be entirely tranquil when someone was dying beside her?

The orange glow of the fire danced across her skin. Circling Chad with her cheeks sucked in, she stared at him, lost in thought. But this was my chance to change the future—to stop her from taking Chad's last breath—from blasting America to shreds—from turning Abigail to stone.

I was lightning as I ran towards Lili. The anger within me surged, breaking through the air with a vengeance. I grasped onto the sweet melody of Chad's heart as I went. It beat once. Twice. And then silence. A deafening silence. But I pushed the wretched doubts and despair out of my mind. This time, I wasn't facing denial. I was grasping onto true, tangible hope.

I reached towards Lili, her throat mere centimetres away from my fingertips. Her blue eyes flashed with fear as she took in my deathly stare, and she vanished from midair.

I'm Still Unstoppable

Chapter 60: I'm Still Unstoppable

I flew through the spot Lili had disappeared from and came to a halt in front of Chad. Connor yelled out. I looked around to see if Lili had returned, but he was staring straight at me. Connor wasn't afraid of Lili. He was afraid of me.

I shot a bolt of magic at the blazing pyre, extinguishing it in one go, and aimed another at Connor. His chain shrivelled into nothingness. In a single blink, he was back to his werewolf form, lunging towards me.

I produced a shield, and he ricocheted off it. A quick whimper left his throat before he rolled to his feet, ready to pounce again. He roared out into the night, a threat to tear me to shreds.

"Connor!" I shouted out over him.

I knew precisely his conundrum. He didn't trust it was truly me.

I held my hands up in surrender, moving slowly to gain his credence. The shield disappeared around me. "It's really me," I told him softly, staring into his big brown puppy dog eyes as his snarl faded away. I gave him a smile. "You know?" I added lightly, trying to bring my silly mate back to the surface. "Your friend who most certainly does not approve of you sleeping with my baby sister?"

His form shifted back to his human self, and I staggered back as he wrapped his arms around me in a hug—a hug I needed so desperately after everything I had been through.

I held him tightly. "You were brilliant, and you were fierce," I told him, trying to sound brave past the tears that were threatening to fall, "but now we need to get Chad back, all right?"

He nodded against me and then pulled back, tears streaming down his face. "But how?" he asked, sadness forcing its way up his throat. "His heart, Azalea," he cried. "I can't hear his heart."

"I know," I said, taking his hands in mine. "But I can do this," I told him confidently. "Help me get him down."

I could hardly stomach it as we released Chadwick from his holds, off the stake, and down to the grass. I knelt beside him, pulling his head onto my lap, shaking as I took in a face that was so catastrophically mutilated that I could no longer recognise it. Every spot of him was either burnt, bloody, blistered, or broken. But I could fix him. I had to.

Connor paced back and forth, his hand clutching onto the back of his head in worry, but I had seen Chad's healing powers. I had seen him heal his own broken bones. If mortal doctors could revive a heart with Caster tools, I could do the same with my magic. I just had to unlock the door.

Power built in my core, equal to the surge I had felt when I reversed time, equal to the love I felt for him. A vibrant violet glow washed over Chad's entire body, seeping into him. I waited as my magic encased him, as the flesh on his cheeks, his hands, and every part of him shifted from char and blood to the beautiful, sun-kissed tones it normally was. When his melted robes detached themselves from his skin—when the boiled blood vanished—the char disappeared—and his face became his once more, his hand grasped my arm.

I jumped as he held my arm tight and air filled his lungs. His heart pumped steadily. His brilliant green eyes met mine, and his flawless skin was exactly the way it was the day I met him in the bar and decided he couldn't die. He needed to live.

Chad stared deep into my eyes as we held one another. Connor fell to his knees beside us, his jaw dropped in awe.

I pulled Chad off of my lap and into my arms, squeezing him so tightly I could break his ribs. His chest moved against mine with each of his breaths. The sound and feel of his thudding heart moved my soul. A flood of joyous tears poured out of me like the bloodfall, and I sobbed like a baby—glad to have *my* Chad back in my arms.

Connor's arms wrapped around the both of us, and I let out a wet laugh, praying this was real—praying I wasn't lost in a dream. We all pulled away, just enough to look at each other properly and accept this version of our story as reality.

Chad wiped away my tears, laughing with me as Connor placed his forehead to Chad's shoulder.

"Thank you," Chad said aloud, studying the back of his hands incredulously before feeling his cheeks and his hair. "I can't explain it," he told us breathlessly. "I can feel what happened, only I don't quite remember it."

"Be thankful you don't," Connor replied, shaking his head in disbelief. "I never want to see you like that again. I completely lost it."

"Where's everyone else?" Chad asked, looking around for the first time at the quiet gardens.

Connor's posture crumbled at the words.

I swallowed hard. "They took Abigail and Hydie back to their lair. We have to go get them. Lili saw me. She may not know *how* I got back here, but she knows I did."

"How did you get back though?" Connor asked, panting heavily. "One second you were knocked out cold and disappearing with Florence. The next you were in front of me," he explained, furrowing his brow as he tried to piece it together in his mind. "How did you get away from them so quickly?"

"I didn't," I replied before mentally preparing myself for their reactions. "I was there for hours but then—" I looked between each of them and blurted it out. There was no sense in keeping it secret. "I created a time bubble. It coated everything around me and then suddenly, I was back in the maze."

I placed my head against Chad's to feel the warmth of his skin against mine.

"I don't know how I did it," I said, shaking my head against him. I couldn't look at either of them. I hardly believed it myself.

How were they going to? "All I know is that my heart can't bear to watch you die again. I love you, Chadwick. I love you and need you. I can't do this without you."

More tears streamed down my face, casting the world around me in a red blur, but Chad's soft hands wiped them away as soon as I blinked.

"I'm still alive," he told me, his voice as soft as flower petals as he rubbed his thumb across my cheek.

A laugh bubbled up my chest and out past my tears as I remembered promising to write him those exact same words.

I took his hand and kissed his palm. I had done it. I had saved him. "I'm still unstoppable."

And I was. I truly was. I wouldn't stop until Lili and Florence paid for taking my Chadwick away from me.

Connor scoffed before crossing his arms in front of him. "Well, I'm still completely shattered," he huffed, and I couldn't help but let another laugh choke its way out. "How are we going to get them now? They'll be expecting us."

"Will they?" I asked, furrowing my brows in thought. Perhaps I was delusional but a strain of hope still swirled its way around me like magic.

"You said it yourself. Lili saw you," Connor spat out.

"Yes, but the other me is still living in this timeline," I explained. They both blinked at me and I hurried to explain. "We watched them take me with them. And if that's the case, I'll make the exact same decisions I made the first time. All the slaves will escape, including Hydie," I said, emphasising it to Connor.

My heart clenched as O'Brien and Abigail floated into my mind. I looked at Chad and I felt him in my head.

Do they not make it? he asked softly.

I swallowed and shook my head. *No, but we have time. I'll think of something.*

He nodded without missing a beat, believing wholeheartedly that I could do it, but my stomach fell as I asked myself that exact question. Could I?

"Let's go to the mirrors," Chad said, trying to pull himself up with a grunt.

"Absolutely not," I demanded. I placed a trembling hand on his chest to keep him down. "I can't lose you again," I pleaded. "I won't do it. I won't let you go. I'll stay with you, and you can rest. I'll never let go of you again."

But his kind features told me everything I needed to know. He would not be sitting this one out.

"We're stronger together," he said, his voice like silk. He grabbed my hand firmly and looked deep into my eyes. "We can beat them. And this time, I'm not going anywhere. You have my word."

My shoulders rose and fell in quick beats as I stared into his green eyes, absorbing his faith in me—his faith in us.

"We can do this," Connor said, and my gaze followed him as he stood up. "What do we do first?"

I took a few more breaths, trying to will my lungs to slow down. Then I looked back and forth between the two of them.

"Chad's right," I decided, wiping my face with my sleeve. "We need to get to the mirrors." And as much as I didn't want to say the words that were about to fall from my lips, I had to. "The others will be fine in Transylvania for now. We go where we're truly needed. We go after Lili." To where she'd be trying to blow the American coasts off the map. "We can't let her detonate any more bombs. We have to stop her from killing millions like she did in Japan."

The two men nodded in unison.

"We have until the clock strikes five in the morning in Transylvania," I continued, remembering the chimes of that wretched clock. "Then Eyeara and her people can lead the dragons to attack. Their fire can break down Lili's wards." I shifted my focus to the werewolf. "Have Fendel and the other gnomes take you to the mushroom path that leads beneath Lili's fortress. There will be thousands of creatures escaping, and they'll need our little friends to help transport them away. That's where Hydie will be. She's going to need you."

Connor pursed his lips as if he were considering his role, but then he squinted his eyes as he asked, "Is that your blessing that the two of us can be together?"

Thank the heavens Fendel would be there to make sure that part of the plan ran smoothly. Was that truly the only part Connor was contemplating?

I shook my head at him, a laugh of disbelief leaving my lips.

"If I say no, would it stop you from loving her?" I asked him.

Connor grinned his usual goofy grin and shook his head.

I tilted my head down as I gave him a scolding look. "Then go save my sister," I enunciated, "and I'll kick your arse later."

He kept smiling as he helped Chad and I up from the ground. "Sounds like a plan," he agreed.

Holding their hands in either of mine, I gave them a brave look.

"To the mirrors?" I asked.

Chad nodded. "To end this once and for all," he replied.

I gave myself a moment to watch the life glisten within his eyes—life that I would cherish for the rest of our days. Then we all took a deep breath, and lavender magic swept us off our feet.

I'm Still Unstoppable

Chapter 61: Answers

I gazed into my mind, focusing all my attention on Lili. I saw her, standing atop a lighthouse, wind sweeping through her blonde hair as the moon shone down, highlighting the pink in her cheeks. I penetrated her mind, felt her fear, her worries, her motivations. She had seen me before she disappeared. She had seen me, and she couldn't fathom how it was a possibility. Was it another shapeshifter? Was I the one who had a decoy this time instead of Chad?

She pushed it all down and held her chin up high.

It didn't matter.

She had a job to do.

And we were absolutely ready for it.

A salty mist whipped through the air as a battle roared around me. It had been hours. Somewhere within Dracula's Lair a clock was striking five in the morning. My anxiety was a deranged bat, attacking me from the inside. Though we had done so much within this strange bubble of time, the hours were catching up to me. Time passed like sand trickling out of an hourglass, threatening to spill its last grain if I didn't hurry. I had to get back to Transylvania. But not yet.

"Stun all of them!" I shouted out to an army of our allies. After speaking to the leaders in the mirrors, our support came at the ready, Night Crawlers and Casters alike. "Don't let any of them get away." We couldn't risk them leaving to warn Florence. He had to stay at Lili's fortress, ignorantly enjoying his celebration—blissfully believing the world was in the palm of his hand.

I had ventured through the mirrors, eager to conserve my energy. Now I stood at the edge of the western coast of the United States. Nearly half our forces were spread along the west—more in the east. The indigenous tribes, the American Witch Council, the mermaids, and more were all ready to protect the country from devastation. The elves were still in the south, rallying their dragons for the ride north.

The ripping of flesh stole my attention, sending a shock to my heart. I turned to see a werewolf claw into its prey. I didn't know if the woman it tore into would be turned into a werewolf, or if she'd bleed to death before it came to that. All I could do was cast my magic to freeze the werewolf in its tracks before I turned to a Caster, hell-bent and ready to destroy anyone who neared the lighthouse—the same one where Lili hid.

The buzz of vampires as they sped across the pebbled beach and into the water filled my ears. I sent purple ropes to trap them. Fairies swarmed around a magical device that was meant to blow up the entire west coast, ensuring it would no longer serve that purpose.

Demriam splashed up from the ocean. Her long green hair wrapped around her golden crown before it draped over her back. She glared at more people as they tried to escape into her seas. I plugged my ears in time for her siren's song. At least ten of Florence and Lili's henchmen fell to the ground. They sat along the tide, watching the horizon intensely as if they were going to be there until sunrise.

I grinned at Demriam, impressed, and her eyes met mine. She raised a brow and her cheeks tightened as if fighting off a friendly smile. Then she dove into the water, off to fight the next villain.

Perhaps she could be a decent person—*if* we hooked her up with a proper man for mating season…

I ducked behind a large trunk of driftwood and searched the sky. Spells of every colour flew across it and back down to their targets, but Chad was nowhere in sight.

Where are you? I asked, knowing he was too far to hear. Saga's roar answered instead. A shimmer of a silvery portal flashed in the air, and the beautiful white dragon appeared out the other end. Her purple eyes flashed with a fierceness that weakened my knees. Fire brewed in her white stomach, turning it to blue before a dazzling azure fire was cast out of her mouth. It lit the docks, stopping anyone else from trying to flee to the ocean. The wind from her wings fanned a rush of warm wind over me as she drew nearer, and I smiled as I saw her rider.

My magic swirled around me, placing me on the back of the dragon. As I wrapped my arms around Chad's torso, the deranged bats turned to butterflies in my stomach. Saga flew sideways, her roar shaking me, but the ride no longer scared me. I felt at peace on her back.

I hugged Chad tighter. "About time you showed up!" I shouted through the wind.

Chad's whole body shook with his laughter. "You never were one to be patient, were you?" he teased.

I transported us both down to the beach so the dragon could do her own fighting while we did ours.

I stood back to back with Chad, combining my vampire speed with my witch powers as if my body knew our lives depended on it. The lighthouse stood in the corner of my vision, a bulb flashing in a rhythmic pattern to guide boats to shore. Tonight, however, it served as *my* guide.

Blue eyes flashed as their owner hid in the shadows of the lighthouse, fear etched into them. My mind infiltrated Lili's and I felt her fear zap through me like electricity.

I squeezed Chad's hand. *Lili's here,* I told him. *I have to go after her.*

A green orb erupted from his palm, shielding us from further attacks. From within its protection, Chad spun me around to face him. One of his hands cradled the nape of my neck, and he pulled me in for a kiss. Our tongues didn't hold back as spell after spell crashed into his shield. My heart pounded as I tasted his sweet mouth, relishing the way it felt against mine—like they were meant for one another. Wrapped up in his warm embrace, I nearly decided not to go.

Give her hell, he said, the sweet hum of his voice caressing my mind, and I nodded.

She'd be going to a place far worse than Hell.

The sands of time continued to slip. We were stronger together, but right now it meant we had to divide and conquer.

I pulled back to stare into Chad. *As soon as you can,* I instructed, *go to Ypovrýchio Kástro. Warn Cristin that he has to keep all three of the children there, no matter what happens.*

Chad nodded his promise and kissed my lips again, making me never want to let go. Then he leaned back. *Save your sister, save the children, and kill Florence,* he hummed against me. *And then you're all mine.*

My lips crept into a smile as his brilliant green eyes shined brightly.

See you in Transylvania, I said, steadying myself for the moment his shield dropped.

See you in Transylvania.

The second his shield fell, I ran to the lighthouse, rocks and sand slipping beneath my feet. I launched myself over driftwood and up a spiral staircase that led to the bright light. Lili's eyes widened as she took me in, her chest heaving up and down with raw panic, and she disappeared.

But not without a trace.

Her magic played along my skin as I let it take me. I landed behind her in her bedroom. The harsh noise of the battle was silenced and replaced by the quiet, cruel laughter and clinking glasses as a celebration persisted somewhere below. We were back at Dracula's Lair.

Lili's room was elegant, feminine, and wicked all at once. I hadn't truly taken it in before. There were sheer black curtains hanging from the wide window, every piece of glass perfectly in place. A soft, pink duvet lay impeccably flat across her bed. The smell of fire was gone, the ceiling was smooth and white, and the charred floorboards were back in their place. The black candles sat calmly in their circle, and from the centre, Lili twirled her finger, and their wicks ignited.

She turned around with haste, but as her feet moved towards her wardrobe, her eyes connected with mine and she froze—completely immobilised. Her eyes flickered down to my hands and back up again.

"How'd you do that?" she asked, her fear fading and replacing itself with intrigue.

I raised my brows at her. She was the one who had transported half a world away. Not even Chad could journey that far without mirrors or a dragon—not unless he tailed someone. Lili and I were anomalies.

"I could ask you the same," I challenged.

Her expression morphed into a grin. "Mighty wide jump for such a young witch," she said as if she were teasing me. "*Powerful* some would say."

She strode over to her wardrobe, careful to stay within her circle, grabbed out a large trunk, and placed it on her bed. Returning to her wardrobe, she began riffling through her clothes, quickly unhooking some and leaving others.

"After 400 years of practice, transporting small distances became easier for me," she explained as she turned around to carry the clothes to her trunk. "Soon, I began to crave the challenge. I wanted to test my limits."

I studied her hands as she moved—calm and steady. Not a single ounce of fear left. Anger bit into me like a ravenous vampire. Where had her fear for me gone? The fury that swirled inside of me longed to lash out at her, to kill. But another more stubborn—perhaps more daft—part whispered this could be my only chance for answers.

"Running away?" I asked her, forcing a calm over myself. If she didn't fear me, I wouldn't cower from her.

"Only until the world forgets about me," she drawled lazily.

I rose a brow at her. "How could we ever forget about you?" I asked tauntingly. "You killed Hitler—a man who killed millions—yet you turned around and killed even more. It doesn't add up."

"He was killing my people," she sneered. She said it as if she needed no other explanation.

"Then why not stop World War II?" I asked. "Why not stop Hitler earlier rather than wait years until Florence helped you kill him? Why let Florence kill all of these people now? You could've stopped all of it."

She turned back towards her wardrobe but this time there was distinct vexation in each of her footsteps. "Lives had to be taken—" she snapped, "sacrifices made to get to where we are. It's all part of the greater plan. Fate."

"Is that what Baba Yaga told you?" I asked, tilting my head at her curiously.

The pounding of her heart filled the grand room as her eyes widened.

"How did you know—"

"It came to me in a dream," I interrupted, challenging her with my stare to continue.

She smirked as if her spilled secrets were part of this greater good she spoke of. "All this time I was trying to make Chadwick believe he and I were connected, when it was really you and I with the connection."

"What's that supposed to mean?" I asked.

She stuffed three pairs of obnoxious heels in her arms before letting out a deep sigh. "Potion making is one skill I was never able to master in all my years," she told me. "After your werewolf friend unknowingly stole the love potion for us, I secretly kept some for myself. I had been slipping Chadwick drops of it here and there. Not enough that he'd fall head over heels and throw himself at me. No, he's too smart for that. He'd see right through me. Just enough that he'd feel something—a strong connection perhaps—but as with everything, you went and ruined that too."

The connection Chad felt to her. One of the three secrets he had told me in the snow.

Lili took a deep breath. "When you've been around for hundreds of years, war and death become another part of life. You learn to not get so emotional over it. You'll see," she decided for me before dumping the shoes in her trunk and going back for more.

"Then why did you let Chad live?" I asked, completely stumped. She could've killed him when he was on fire—made sure he died—but instead, she ran.

"What?" she sneered but she was playing dumb.

"One burned, one turned, one captured, one free," I mimicked in her sickly sweet tone. "You kept your promise for each of them, but not Chad. You knew just as well as I did that I could save him, didn't you?"

She smirked, twirling a blonde lock around her finger. "I had to flee," she said lightly. "You would've killed me otherwise."

"Bull shit," I countered fiercely. "You don't strike me as the type to give up without a good fight."

"Perhaps there's no fight left in me," she said dully before her sly smile reappeared. She crossed her arms with satisfaction. "Ever think of that? Or are you too busy trying to ruin my life?" she asked harshly before facing away and fiddling with her trunk. "Chadwick is the king," she announced loudly. "He's collateral. If I let him live, I can use it in my favour."

"I'm still not convinced," I told her, taking a step around her circle, edging closer. "If he was dead, you could've shapeshifted into him—played the part."

She shook her head, her smirk shining on her face as she turned back to me. "Clever, clever witch..." she said, clapping her hands slowly. "Too clever for your own good, some would say." She pushed her tongue against her cheek as she contemplated her next words. "That idea *did* cross my mind but there's no longer a point. Seriously though," she asked, relaxing her shoulders, "how is it that you manage to ruin every single little thing? I can't even curse you without you breaking them. Two years ago, I cursed you to fear love, blood, and all things red, and you broke it. *Then* you broke the love potion. *Finally,* I cursed you to fear killing us, on the off chance that would save me. I was afraid you'd hurt me or even Florence when given the chance. I wanted to keep him alive, in case he proved useful to me. But you broke that too."

I blinked at her. All the times those words had triggered me— all the anxiety and fear I felt from those things—it was all because of her? Back in Antarctica, Eyeara had told me I had been cursed. It was down to Lili. She was the mastermind, interfering in all of our lives the entire time.

"Slowed you down from getting with Chadwick though," she continued, taunting me with her smile. "You were hesitant to fall in love with him for a long time. Not that I knew you two were together yet, but it was still a nice touch."

I shook the ideas away. None of it mattered. She was avoiding the point.

I took a step closer to her, holding my head high, and I asked again, enunciating every word. "Why let Chad live?"

She smiled as if impressed I had realised her game. "Fine," she said. "I let him live because I genuinely like him—because I knew Florence didn't deserve you. Perhaps part of me still has a heart," she hissed. She tilted her head down, a darkness sweeping over it. "*Perhaps* we could call it even, and you could let me go my own way."

At that, I had to laugh. "I'm afraid I can't do that," I told her, and she cocked a brow up at me, daring me to explain. "*Perhaps*," I parroted, "we chalk up you 'murdering millions' to you being *old* and used to death. *Perhaps* you change your ways—see the light—" I mocked, "and never take another life. I could consider letting you go, if only you weren't about to turn my best friend to stone in not twenty minute's time."

Lili let out a harsh breath and rolled her eyes. "Oh, and did you have a vision of it?" she sneered, crinkling her whole face as she looked at me with ridicule.

"No," I said firmly. "I saw it."

"You saw it in a nightmare," she replied darkly—as if I was wrong.

"No," I told her calmly. "I saw it because I was there."

She froze at such an impossible prospect, and blinked her pretty, blonde eyelashes at me. "You expect me to think you saw it, then travelled back in time twenty minutes?"

"A few hours actually," I corrected.

"Lies," she hissed, but I could tell by the pounding of her heart that she believed it.

I grinned, studying the mask of disbelief she wore on her face. She believed it, yes, but she couldn't understand it.

"Truth," I parried, raising my brows to welcome her challenge.

"That's impossible," she tried, her voice airy, far less confident than her usual persona.

"Anything's possible for the woman of the stars, the most powerful sorceress," I said with a shrug. "Even killing you before you get the chance to take Abigail away from me."

Lili stared at me for several beats. I could feel her in my mind, but I didn't bother to lock her out. I wanted her to feel it—to know the truth. Her blue eyes burned with intensity before she suddenly looked away and out her large window.

"What happens after?" she asked, gazing off into the distance. She crossed her arms and I heard the drumming of her fingers as they tapped anxiously against her skin. For a satisfying moment, fear flickered off her tongue. "What happens to Florence? Do you kill him?"

The question jarred me. Florence. She wanted to know his fate but not her own? I took her in, the way her chest filled with air and didn't let go. The way her nails began to dig into her arm as if she was holding onto her last shred of hope. Only her face remained straight as though she felt indifferent.

I shook my head. I didn't know Florence's fate yet. "I wasn't graced with that knowledge," I told her, a bitter expression on my face. I wish I was.

Her jaw clenched as she took it all in. She nodded slowly, lost in thought before pivoting back towards the window, her hands finding a ribbon on her dress to busy themselves with.

"Do you ever think about how you'll do it?" she asked, true curiosity coating her voice. "How you'll kill him?"

She flicked the ribbon before turning back to me, her brows poised high as she waited for my response.

I let out a breath, realising I knew the precise answer. "Every single day since the moment you two created me."

She nodded, apparently expecting that answer.

"How will you do it?" she asked, pure intrigue on her tongue.

The question caught me off guard. Her words. The way she phrased it as if it wasn't simply a possibility. She knew it would come to that. She knew I would do it.

I shrugged. *Burn, crush, poison, or flay. Which one shall it be?* "I haven't quite decided," I admitted coolly. "Every method seems too good for him."

A smile grew in her eyes. It wasn't cold or cruel, but understanding.

"I think of it quite frequently myself," she confessed, her eyes distant again. "I picture driving a dagger into his heart, stabbing him over and over as his blood splashes over us—draining him until his body convulses beneath me, and every last sign of life fades." She spoke each word clearly as if it would make them come true.

I could picture her doing it too—clear as day.

"Why don't you?" I asked, a bit too eagerly, but I was met with a look that indicated I was daft not to see the reason myself.

"I love him," she said as if it were simple, the hostility back in her voice as she scolded me. "I love him, but all he ever talks about, thinks about, dreams about is you!" she added, her voice crescendoing with every word and spewing out like lava. The hate was back in her eyes, harsher this time. "I can hear every single thought in your head—in everyone's head—but in Florence's head it's only you, you, YOU!"

She took a deep breath to steady herself. But as quickly as it had come, the anger was extinguished, and a cackle poured from somewhere deep inside her. I stared at her. She was completely mad.

"Such a cruel world we live in where we can love someone who doesn't love us back," she said, gesturing to me. "Where people can love someone who doesn't deserve to be loved." She clicked her tongue and looked away.

I didn't know which of us she was referring to—the one who didn't deserve the love. Florence. Her. Me. But I could feel the pain as it vibrated up her throat.

I looked around her room, remembering who she was—her father—her past.

"Everyone in this world needs to be loved," I told her, a phrase I had told myself long ago on the night I had been bitten. "Florence wasn't given enough love as a child, and neither were you, and look how you two turned out."

"And you were given loads, were you?" she growled, throwing her hand towards me. "Your father told me himself he never loved you—right before I killed him in his prison cell."

I tried to block out the idea of Lili speaking with my father, and the odd twinge of jealousy I felt at hearing she was the one to take his life for good.

"I had Hydrangea," I reminded her, "and my mother in her own way." Now that I had my memories back, I could see that. She may not have protected me in her frail, depressed state, but she meant to. "And even Chad's mum cared for me in her ghostly form," I continued. "She looked after me as a child. So I was loved."

Lili's face turned stark white. Then she placed her index finger and thumb together, and stalked closer to me, still staying within her circle. "You mean to say," she tried to clarify, narrowing her eyes at me, "that Chadwick's mum's ghost looked after you as a child?" Her repetition of my words came out as though she was completely flabbergasted.

I nodded, grinning even wider this time. "All part of being fated mates with her son, I suppose. Apparently," I said, mostly just to rub it in, "the stars do not lie."

I could hear her breath catch even though she played it off with a small laugh, but for once, she had no reply.

Glancing down at the small flames, I asked, "What's the deal with the candles?"

"Witchcraft," she answered quickly, apparently thankful for the distraction. The fire flickered in her eyes as she took them in. "If I stay within them, Florence can't feel the pull towards me. He won't know I'm here, abandoning him." She shook her head like it was all an elaborate joke. "I visited Baba Yaga again. It turns out fate has picked a side. And the outcome does not look good for me."

I let out a short laugh. "No," I agreed. "It does not."

Suddenly, something tugged at my insides, different than a pull. More like a vigorous push in the opposite direction. I blocked Lili out of my head as I looked over at her chamber door.

I was in the castle. My past self was probably stuck talking to Florence. In a few, short minutes I'd be in here, hellbent and broken hearted over something it turned out Lili hadn't completely done. But I had to let that version of me feel that hurt. I had to in order to go back in time and save Chad. Only, the push made it very clear I shouldn't be here when my past self came in.

My eyes darted over to another door at the far end of the room. "Where does that lead?" I whispered to Lili.

Her brows furrowed as she gaped at me. "My study," she replied, "but—"

"And is there a door in there that leads back out to the corridor?" I asked, the hushed words flying from my mouth.

Lili shut her lips, completely thrown, but nodded anyway.

I strode over to the study door but paused before I touched the knob. I was stupid for wasting time. I should've killed her, I knew it—but something about my dreams—something about seeing life through her eyes stopped me. Besides, I had to get to Abigail and O'Brien before it was too late.

"Where are you going?" Lili asked, a touch too angry towards someone who wished her dead.

"Don't worry," I told her, knowing the arse-kicking I was about to give her. "You'll see me very soon." The push urged me away harder. I had to hurry. "Just—if you only do one good deed for the rest of your life, Lili, please don't kill Abigail," I pleaded. "She doesn't deserve it."

"Is that what did it?" Lili asked. "Is that what gave you the strength to go back in time?"

I shrugged. I hadn't had time to process it thoroughly. "Partially," I answered. Abigail, compiled with losing Chad. But the part that truly sent me over the edge was the idea of the children being in danger.

Fuck. I hoped Chad had gotten to Cristin in time to stop the kids from coming.

Lili bit her lip and studied me as my heart raced. What did she want? What else could she possibly tell me?

"Did Chadwick's heart stop beating?" she blurted out.

I blinked at her, thinking back to the horrific scene in our garden. "Yes. Why?"

"Then their little blood oath is broken," she replied, her voice soft as she said it. "My little creation can live. As can your Chadwick."

A gleam of hope began to shine through, but it faded just as quickly. She hadn't promised it—nor would I have trusted her if she had.

I gave her a firm nod and opened the door, but as I heard Ginny's banshee cry pierce through the air, I stopped again.

"For what it's worth," I started, turning back to Lili, "I'm sorry about your arms. If it's any consolation," I added, my lips creeping into a smile, "they do grow back."

Her face creased as though she thought I had gone mad, but there wasn't time to explain. I heard the buzz that my past self made as I stormed towards her bedroom door. Right as it clicked open, I shut the study door behind me.

Chapter 62: White Eyes

S hit, I thought as I darted across the study. What time was it?

I heard a crash as my past self blasted Lili across the room and I jumped. If I was in there, it meant there were precious moments to get down to the dungeons—to warn O'Brien and Abigail of their fate—to stop fate from happening.

I tried to gauge how much time I had as I strode across to the other door. I'd spent too long with Lili—too long in America. We had saved millions of lives by going, but at what cost?

I turned the knob and stepped soundlessly out into the corridor, but a shrill voice came from behind me.

"What the hell are you doing here?" Missouri asked from behind me.

I shot around to face her, my eyes wide as I stared back at the ghost. Why hadn't I transported? Why had my rampant thoughts distracted me from getting down to the dungeons immediately? But it hardly mattered. What mattered now was if I could stop the young ghost from sounding the alarm, and whether she believed I was Lili or myself.

I squared my shoulders and sneered at her—my best Lili impression without shifting into her. "Never you mind," I told her.

gathering some of the fierce attitude Lili carried on a daily basis. She didn't like Missouri any more than I did, that much was certain from my dreams. I needed to shake her off, and quickly. "Go about your business elsewhere—" I started to command but in so much as a blink, an icy force went straight through me.

My entire body froze from both the cold and the panic, but it was more than cold. I was ice. I was a solid block of ice, in agony.

I tried to shake it off—to move or use my magic—but Missouri blasted through me again. I bit back a scream.

She needed to stop. She needed to leave me alone long enough that I could transport away, but she knew what she was doing. She knew I was immobilised.

"Which witch are you?" she hissed, soaring through me again.

I fell to my knees, choking against the chills. As I clutched my chest, I looked up to see the fury slashed across Missouri's face. She made to blast through me again—to stop me—but this time she was intercepted by a blur of grey that was equally as chilling as her own ghostly form.

I watched as my singing ghost grabbed onto Missouri with her transparent hands—hands that shouldn't have been able to hold onto anything, let alone another ghost. Madelyn placed her hand over Missouri's mouth to stop her from alerting Florence of my escape or ruining my chances of getting to my mates in time. And though Missouri squirmed, Madelyn held onto the bitter ghost tightly, refusing to let her go.

I had to leave. I could hear the clock ticking as if it lived in my brain. Any second now, I'd blast Lili out of her magical circle and Florence would be drawn to her pull. He'd see Missouri, Chad's mum, and me if I didn't flee.

I opened my mouth to thank my singing ghost but urgency flashed through her eyes.

Go! the ghost screamed into my mind. It didn't help free me from my paralysis as shock rattled me. I had never heard her utter a word that wasn't in song, yet I had just listened to her thoughts.

I didn't have time to contemplate it. So I ran.

I ran for precisely two seconds before a fleeting thought in my fear-driven brain reminded me I could transport away. I was a witch, and a vampire, and I was unstoppable.

Purple swirled around me. My feet touched down onto the hard, dungeon floors. Something shoved me hard against the wall. I looked to see hundreds of creatures rushing past. There was so much to see—so much to hear. Mortals and the blur of vampires. The tapping of several legs as jorogumos ran along the walls and ceilings to avoid the stampede of creatures below them. Winged women dragging their detached legs as they flew amongst the crowd. Nearly every face was gaunt, nearly every heart pumped adrenaline through their weakened bodies. I could smell it mixed in with their cold sweat. Groups of gnomes rushed by, carrying the wounded out of the tunnel, six to a person like ants carrying food back to their colony. Others were draped over their cell mates' shoulders—ones who had scraped up enough energy to escape. Magic of every colour swept around us as some were able to transport away, taking with them as many as they could manage, but the rest fled down the dim passageway and towards the tiny hole in the wall.

I looked down to see several children filtering out with the crowd. One bumped into me and instantly, I could hear all of their screams in my head. I shuddered. It wasn't the first time I had heard them. These were the children from Leon's nightmares—children Florence held down here like the dirty scum he was—and they were finally freed from his clutches.

My gaze flew to the opening far down the tunnel, where all these innocent souls made their escape down the path of mushrooms. Ginny was whispering in O'Brien's ear. His brave, focused expression fell as he took in her words. Yet he gave her a nod, his eyes lost in a daze as he began lifting the small children into the hole. Connor was in the mouth of the tunnel, crouched down as Abigail handed Hydie off to him. He pulled my sister into the hole with him. Fendel was behind him, ushering the survivors along the tiny pathway that would lead them to their freedom.

Connor's eyes met mine. Half a laugh escaped his throat as if he couldn't believe the scene around us, and I knew precisely how he felt. All these people—tortured, drained, forced to witness Florence and his horrors. They were going to make it out. That much I knew from my first trip through this timeline. I returned

497

Connor's stare with a nod, and he took my sister down the mushroom-lined tunnel and out to where I prayed they'd be safe.

The same screams from before surrounded me. There was so much fear radiating through the place—far more than I thought there'd be by now.

I pushed my way into the crowd, driving myself towards my old coven mates.

"Azalea," Abigail shouted over the chaos as she placed a hand to her heart, a wary breath leaving her lips. She furrowed her brows at me. "The aunts—" she asked, confused why I was here. "Why are you back? Did you get them out?"

Fuck. That had been the original plan, hadn't it? I had told Abigail and O'Brien to get everyone out while I saved Chad's aunts.

O'Brien studied me, probably wondering the same, but there was no time to explain. I shook my head to clear it.

"Both of you need to leave. Now," I added sternly, grabbing onto each of their shoulders.

But Abigail immediately shook her head, looking down at more frail, dirt-covered children that were climbing up into the hole.

"We can't," she said quickly, her voice panicked over the shrill cries that bounced down the walls. "They're not all out," she replied. "I'm not leaving until everyone is safe."

But I needed *her* to be safe.

I breathed in deep to calm my nerves. There were so many people to worry about. It wasn't just them.

"Fendel," I called behind them, my eyes focused on the dark passageway. The little gnome scurried forwards at full attention. "I need you to go up to the sixth floor and free Chad's aunts. There will be a door lined with mushrooms. Tell them if they harm you, I'll keep them as statues in my front gardens. They'll fit in nicely with the one that's already there."

The gnome didn't hesitate. He gave a salute and vanished in a puff of rainbow smoke.

I tightened my grip on Abigail and O'Brien's shirts, a pit forming in my stomach, knowing what it could mean for those who were still down here if I transported them away. Benji said O'Brien and Abigail freed them all. If I forced them to leave, would the story stay the same, or would they perish? And where was Benji now? Still in the cage where I left him? How long would Madelyn be able to hold off Missouri?

O'Brien gently took my hand off of him and held it in both of his.

"I know what happens," he whispered, but I couldn't bear to accept it, even as the words slipped from his lips. Instead, denial churned in my stomach as he added bravely, "Ginny told me how this ends."

The end. Not merely an end to a story. The end to his life—the sole purpose of a banshee was to protect the last of her line.

"That's not going to happen," I told him. I stared straight into his eyes. I would not allow it.

I felt Abigail's shoulder fall beneath my fingertips, her expression nearly identical to O'Brien's—stubborn, morbid, dawning comprehension.

"I'm not going to let them die so I can live," Abigail said. "Not if I could've gotten them all out."

"And we *will* get 'em all out," O'Brien added, a flood of confidence overpowering any worry he might have felt. "Ginny saw it," he said, nodding over to her. "That makes it worth it. I always knew I'd die a hero."

A tear fell down my cheek. It wasn't fair. Why did good people die while horrid people like Florence walked the earth?

The screams grew louder, but the sadness that filled my core drowned them out.

I would not stand by and let them die, but perhaps I could focus on stopping Benji and Missouri from capturing them instead. A reluctant trickle of acceptance seeped into me. I opened my mouth to tell them my new course of action, but O'Brien's eyes flew down the long corridor. His heartbeat quickened, sweat glistened across his brow, and I saw the reflection of a monster in the blacks of his eyes.

The rush of the prisoners exploded into a fear-induced stampede. The crowd surged faster, some toppling over others and crashing into me. A roar filled the corridor and my head snapped in its direction. Far down the pathway, as far as my eyes could see, a horned creature reared on its back legs, ready to catch its prey, before it bounded down the path towards the last of the prisoners. Though its legs were longer than its arms, it ran on all fours, swiping several people out of its way and into the wall. With a fierce roar, it sank its claws into a helpless vampire, and I found myself sprinting towards it before my mind could comprehend my own actions.

The buzz of Abigail and O'Brien running behind me filled my ears. They were coming to help, but I was quicker. I transported mid-run, grabbed hold of the monster by its horns, and yanked it away. It crashed onto its side but was back on its feet within a blink, growling at me and gnashing its sharp teeth.

Up close, it was even more terrifying. It had a skull-like face, a large, hairy chest, and a crooked back that was massively disproportionate to its thin, sickly legs. I knew this creature. I had seen it once before—smelled the rot it gave off, feared its long horns that camouflaged into the trees branches, its dark features that blended into the night. But mostly, I feared its ability to creep into nightmares—to infect your dreams like a poison and turn you into one of them.

It was a wendigo.

Its pupils were vertical slits, surrounded by mesmerising teal irises. As it opened its mouth, I forced myself to look away from its eyes. Spit and a loud screech assaulted my face as Koda's words played in my mind. *And not even a vampire is fast enough to evade them.*

The creature lunged back to its original target and hovered over him, drips of slimy saliva trailing from its maw as the man shivered beneath it. I watched with shaking terror as the monster's eyes morphed from the beautiful teal to a blinding white. The man beneath it stopped his struggle. His eyes glazed over—stark white—the twin of his attacker's. Even his shivers ceased. He became locked in the creature's trance.

I blasted a ball of violet fire and the wendigo flew back, off its victim. It crashed into a second wendigo that had rounded the corner. They both smashed into the wall and immediately sprang up, my reflection a target in their eyes, even as their white eyes shifted back to teal.

The man awoke from his daze, shaking his head as the two wendigos raged towards me, pure anger on their faces. They were impossibly fast, just as Koda had warned. Abigail and O'Brien reached my sides, their chests heaving in the same rhythm as mine. With my eyes still trained on the monsters, I sent purple flames towards them and then picked the man up from the ground. The smell of his blood seeped from his ravaged arm before blending into the smell of the blood river. He grunted sleepily as I tossed him to Abigail.

"Get him out!" I ordered as the monsters advanced towards me again.

Right as she left, I sent purple ropes at the wendigos' ankles. They tripped, a cloud of dirt surrounding them. I sent ten more blasts of magic. Finally, the spells penetrated their thick hide, and they burst into flames.

"What the hell are those?" O'Brien breathed out as three more turned the corner and crept towards us.

"Wendigos," I answered simply.

But the situation was far from simple. Why were they here? The tribes had said wendigos acted on their own—that Florence couldn't have gotten them on his side because they didn't take sides. What was going on?

More roars filled the corridor, shadowing the screams. I watched for the briefest second as Abigail helped the man and the last of the group pile through the cramped exit. But even if I replaced the grate to the mushroom path, it wouldn't stop the vicious creatures from going after the innocent people we were trying to save. We had to buy them time to get past the mushrooms, past the wards, and out to where the gnomes could transport them away.

Abigail rejoined us in time to watch in horror as a hoard of wendigos skidded around the corner. At least ten of them charged towards the hole the prisoners had escaped through. The three of us and the length of the tunnel were the only things standing in their way. And it was not enough.

O'Brien ran towards the one at the front of the pack. Abigail sped to attack another, and I sent a barrage of purple bullets, aimed at each of the monster's skulls. Some passed through their heads, splattering blood and brains against the walls, while other bullets missed their targets and crashed into the stone, tiny holes left in their wake.

A few wendigos slipped past us, galloping down the long tunnel towards the exit to catch their next victim. I sent a shot of magic in front of them, aimed at the ceiling. The ground shook as stones and dirt fell in an avalanche, crushing one wendigo under its weight and aggravating the others as their horned-heads crashed into the blockage.

A monster behind me screeched before I heard its claws swipe through the air. O'Brien yelled out. The smell of his blood struck my senses. I whirled around to see long tears in his shirt, claw marks slashed against his skin. But as he lunged at the wendigo again, his wounds began to heal.

I turned back to the monsters by the fallen rock in time to see them aim their horns at me and advance. I sent purple rope around them but the one nearest clawed at me, ripping the flesh across my arm. I screamed out. With my free hand, I sent out a spell, but the one on the rope kept running. Suddenly, I was being dragged along with it. I sent a zap as it lugged me across the floor, but it merely screeched and tried to shake me off as it ran. Though my skin tore against the ragged ground, leaving a trail of blood behind us, I tried again and again to stop it from running. It wouldn't slow. We rounded the passage they had all come from. I sent my magic to hit the ceiling ahead of us. The stone ceiling crumbled down, barricading the wendigo's path. It smashed into the rocks, unable to stop itself in time, and then roared in anger. I scrambled to my feet, aching even as my skin began to heal, and yanked the rope to get it away from the rocks. It turned on me, malice plain on its face. I saw my whole body flinch in the reflection of its eyes.

Something slammed into the other side of the barricade. The roar of more wendigos rammed into my ears. We were caged in with the wendigos, several more trying to get in by the sound of it. They slammed into it over and over, pebbles falling with each of their attempts to break through.

The rocks rumbled and a grisly claw burst through. Roars erupted through the gap. Harsh movements beyond the hole became a blur as a flood of wendigos tried to fight their way past the blockage and into where we were already surrounded by the others.

The wendigo beside me watched its friend try to break through. Taking its distracted state as an opportunity, I sped back around the corner. The creature was quick to follow. Its feet skidded across the floor after me, closing the gap between us. I felt its hot breath on my neck, the air as it swiped at me with its claws, and I transported back to Abigail and O'Brien to escape.

Abigail grunted out as she held a wendigo in a chokehold. It trampled around, trying to bang her against the walls and break her hold on it, but she didn't let go. O'Brien broke off the leg of another as its horns became lodged into the wall. Its screeching cry filled the space.

I turned to a wendigo who was still charging at me. I sent a spell at it, narrowly missing right before it crashed into me. My head hit the ground as I went down. The wendigo climbed over me. Its hot, moist breath was revolting as it brushed across my face. It snarled and dug its claws into me. They penetrated my arms, through skin, muscle, and bone. I screamed, pinned into place. The smell of my blood filled the air. Pain radiated through me and my vision blurred. It opened its mouth wide, showing off its razor sharp teeth. Only, instead of biting me or consuming me as its breakfast, it stared into me. Its teal eyes morphed to white, and the dark corridor disappeared.

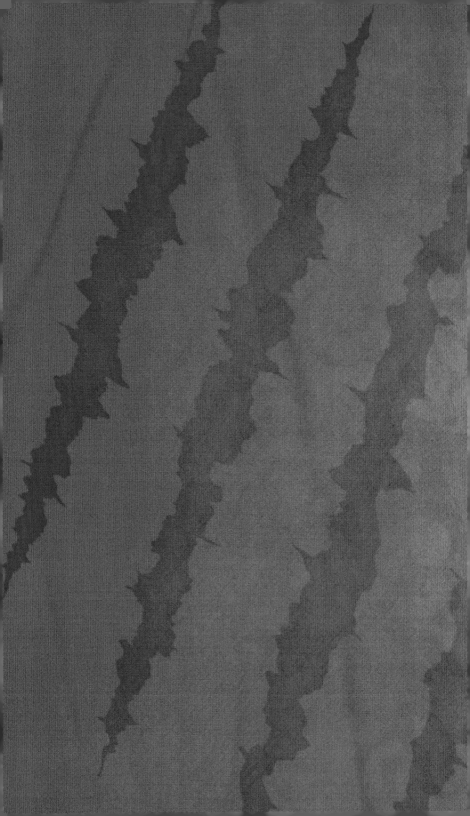

Chapter 63: They're All Dead

I *was falling—through the ground and then through the air. My limbs moved slowly as I plummeted, blackness surrounding me. I splashed into a pool, the liquid swallowing me whole. I tasted the blood as I choked on it—as I drowned—trying to swim to the top or stay afloat. Finally, I grasped something hard and pulled myself up.*

Blood dripped down my eyelashes. I couldn't reach the bottom of the pool with my feet so I clung desperately to the edge, pulling myself up as much as I could. Something bumped into me, and I gasped as I realised it was a body. A flood of dead surrounded me—at least fifty people floating face down in the pool of blood. Fear shot out of every pore of my body. Death and poisoned blood crashed into me like a tsunami. A large mass of blood crashed down next to me, pushing the bodies down, and I knew where I was. I was in the bloodfall.

A small laugh travelled past the cascading blood, and my eyes shot up to see Elizabeth Downy. She was several metres away, reclined against the stone. Both her arms were draped over the edge of the pool as she faced me. Her demeanour was calm, though half her face was ruined from the acid that had doused it—just like the last time I had seen her, before I watched her die.

The current from the crashing fall threatened to pull me under. My blood-covered hands slipped against the side of the slick pool. I steadied my grip, my mouth ajar as I stared at her flesh. She was no ghost.

Poisoned blood dripped into my mouth, and I spat it out in time to see Elizabeth's lips curl into a scowl.

"You haven't done it yet, have you?" she asked. Then she was inches from my face, her eyes swimming with hate. "You said you would kill him!" she screamed.

My whole body jerked away from her. My hand slipped off the pool's edge, and I grasped onto the thing closest to me. It bobbed under the water from my weight, resurfacing as I realised I had grabbed onto a dead body. Only, it wasn't just any dead body.

I saw the deathly, hollow stare of my sister. I let go of her, chills covering my body as I sprang back, splashing violently at the blood to swim away. But the bodies inched closer. I looked around me and realised who the corpses belonged to. It was everyone I knew. Everyone I loved. Chad's eyes stared back at me. Then O'Brien, then Abigail, Fendel, and Connor. I splashed away before something bumped into me from behind. Frantic, I turned to see Elizabeth again, towering over me, covered in blood just like everyone else.

"This is your fault!" she screamed. "You told me you'd kill him and you haven't!"

I opened my mouth to reply—to justify why Florence was still alive—but I blinked and Elizabeth Downy was gone.

I was in a field, standing at the edge of a cliff as the smell of fire and burnt flesh filled the air.

I'm dreaming, *I told myself, trying to shake off the sight of my dead loved ones and Elizabeth's scarred face. This was the wendigo. It was in my head.*

I turned around, looking for the beast, searching for its horns, its skull face, curled claws, and long limbs, but instead, I saw a different monster.

Florence stood upon a pile of burnt bodies, the ruins of a city surrounding him. His red eyes glinted in the sunlight. Though the rays shone down on both of us, our skin didn't smoulder and grey. And when those eyes met mine, his mouth curled into a smile.

As quick as a blink, he was off the pile of bodies and the pull was yanking me around. I turned and came face to face with him. The gravel beneath my feet crumbled. My stomach leapt as I fell off the side of the cliff.

I was plummeting to my death, but Florence wrapped his hands around my wrists, stopping my descent. He caught me, but I wanted nothing more than for his hands to leave my skin—for him to fall off the side of the cliff so I could forever be rid of his touch.

He gripped onto me tighter while I dangled off the edge, one move away from death. The gravel beneath Florence's feet ground loudly as I looked down at the nothingness beneath mine. Gravity yearned to take me as its own.

"They're all dead," Florence said calmly, and my eyes shot back to his. "Everyone you love, everyone in the world but you and me. I killed them all. I killed them so we could be together. I killed them, and now you're mine."

I stared him straight in the eye. I was going to fall, and I was going to die. Only, I wouldn't be going alone.

I yanked at his arm and we both fell off the cliff. My stomach deserted me. I couldn't think. All I could feel was fear. Florence screamed out, but I had no air left in my lungs. Then a song filled the air—a soft, sweet lullaby I had heard a thousand times before—and I was back in the dark corridor.

A body flew over me, knocking the wendigo off of me with a loud grunt before I saw O'Brien wrestling the creature. The wendigo let out a loud roar as he slashed O'Brien across the face and torso. I flicked my fingers and the wendigo caught fire, its deafening screeches bouncing off the cave walls. A second wendigo jumped over my head, its claws scraping me as I ducked down. And as my heart thundered, and my magic grasped at the beast to tear it away, it caught hold of O'Brien. Together, each wendigo grabbed onto him and his body tore in half.

I screamed his name as his blood showered over me.

It couldn't be. Ginny had warned us. O'Brien had a choice. I had told him his choice. Only, I couldn't fathom it. He had sacrificed himself to save me from the wendigo. But he couldn't truly be lost.

I was allotted a fraction of a second to stare at him in horror—blood soaked into my clothes and coating my face—before the wendigos turned on me. One scurried closer, its horns taking the lead, and pinned me to the wall. My head smacked against the stone. White and green lights clouded my vision. Pain seared. Bricks crumbled. And a scream from far away bounced off the walls.

Abigail.

Where was she? Where were the other wendigos? There had been more than this.

The wendigo roared at me and then stared into my eyes, ready to take me into another nightmare. But it would not take me into its dream. It would not turn me into a wendigo. It would not win.

I summoned all my strength and kicked the creature back. The tunnel shook as it crashed into the wall and fell into the blood river with a splash. It shook with rage—blood continuing to ricochet off it, creating a macabre speckled painting. I cast my magic in a circle around me and watched in slow motion as my power filled each creature's body, and they all imploded.

I fell to the ground, catching myself on my hands before my eyes met O'Brien. The cold hand of death had wrapped itself around his heart and stolen his life. But I needed him to come back.

I crawled over to him, pulling his head onto my lap. My heart was pumping wildly, my lungs struggling to match its pace. My eyes roved over the deep claw marks—the gashes that swept over the top half of his body—his lower half that lay a few metres away. His skin wasn't healing itself as it should. He was a vampire. He was supposed to heal. But there was no pulse, no flutter of his eyes, no breath. He was gone.

I cradled O'Brien's head in one arm and flicked my fingers on my other hand. Purple magic seeped out. His legs flew towards us and reattached themselves. His wounds slowly closed, but the blood still stained his clothes, and his body remained motionless.

A movement caught my eye, and I clutched O'Brien in a protective hold, until I realised the spirits of Ginny O'Brien and Madelyn Castwell had joined us. My banshee and my singing ghost.

They both wore a hopeless sorrow on their faces—Madelyn as she looked at me, Ginny as she looked down at what was once her last living relative. My singing ghost shook her head. I looked back at Ginny, hoping she'd have better news—hoping she'd look into the future and decipher if O'Brien could be saved. Only, she too shook her head.

But I wouldn't let death suck the hope out of me.

I grabbed O'Brien tighter and flicked my fingers again. I could reverse time—a small bubble around his body—just large enough to take back his death and give him life.

But as I repeated the motion over and over again, the lavender stream didn't bend to my will. It didn't form a bubble of time. It didn't undo the damage to his halted heart or breathe life back into him. It did nothing.

I looked up to the ghosts who were meant to guide me—to protect me and shield me from harm.

"Help!" I pleaded. I needed them to hurry. I needed them to bring O'Brien back and help me go after Abigail. "It's not working. My magic—it's not letting me undo it."

But I could tell by their sunken faces they didn't believe I could fix him.

"Time is a fragile thing," Ginny said, her voice echoing against the dark tunnel walls. "It's already incredible that you're in two places at once right now. To try and reverse time within an already reversed timeline is implausible."

I felt O'Brien's shirt, the fabrics against my fingertips now soaked from his blood. Ginny's words tried to sink into my consciousness, but they seemed to bounce off my stubborn eardrums and back towards her.

I wasn't one to listen when people told me what I was or wasn't capable of.

So I kept going.

I fired out my magic, filling it into O'Brien, willing his lungs to grasp air, willing his heart to beat and his soul to come back. But as a clock ticked loudly from somewhere in the castle—as Abigail was taken farther and farther away—nothing helped.

A buzz interrupted my heartache. My eyes flew up to Ginny and Madelyn. I knew I had to hide.

I jumped through the hole the wendigos had torn in my barricade and into a short corridor with an empty prison cell. My back pressed up against the cold stone. I held my breath, tried to quiet my heart, but it didn't matter. The buzz passed my hideout and stopped at what had to be O'Brien's body.

I heard Benji's voice as he cursed under his breath. Someone with him coughed on the fumes of death and decay.

"What the bloody hell happened?" the stranger choked out.

Benji yelled out in frustration before pounding on the stone. "Stupid fucks!" he shouted out. "I let out the wendigos out of their cage to stop the prisoners from escaping but *this* fucker and that Abigail girl must've stopped them." He grunted out once more. "I mean, look at this place. It's deserted! Not a single slave left," he griped. A scraping sound followed as though he had kicked at the rubble.

"Fuck," he let out again.

"Well, where's Abigail?" the other person asked, their voice strained as if they were trying not to breathe in the smell of poisoned blood.

"That dreary ghost has her," Benji answered, still sounding pissed off. "Give me that bag," he demanded. A scuffling sound followed as if he snatched the bag before waiting for a reply. "Help me put his body in here. If we don't have the slaves, at least we can show off the dead bodies of the ones who let them out. And then we can go find that bitch that stabbed me with the serum."

I blinked at the darkness. There were rustles as they grabbed O'Brien's body and stuffed him heartlessly into the bag. It stabbed at my chest.

This was how it happened. This was how O'Brien died and Abigail got captured. I hadn't stopped it. If anything, I had caused it by letting that wendigo lull me into a nightmare.

And if Benji had O'Brien's body in the bag and Missouri had Abigail, I was out of time.

The ground shook beneath my feet. Sheer panic coursed through me. The wards were breaking. It was happening.

I transported up into the garden with hundreds of black lilies. The sky was lit with fire. A dragon roared into the sky as a small stream of sunlight burst through the wards—wards that were meant to cast out the daylight.

I heard a choking sound and dropped to hide behind a shrub. As I peered through the foliage, I spotted the other me—my purple rope wrapped around Florence's neck. Lili's eyes were like daggers as she glared at my past self. There was a short buzz and she was in my face.

"How dare you bring them here!" she screeched. "The elves and their filthy dragons will burn it to the ground. This is my home. This castle is *mine!*"

Then came the scraping sounds as Benji dragged O'Brien's dead body across the ground. "Don't worry, Lilith," Benji said lazily. My friend's blood—poisoned with death—filled my nose once more. "Your wards are strong. They'll hold off long enough to make our point."

But I needed the wards to break. I needed our army to cause a distraction, and I needed my past self to leave. If I went out now, it would distract me from reversing time and saving Chad in the first place.

I looked away as Benji tore the bag open. I couldn't bear to see O'Brien's lifeless body—to know once more I had failed to save him. Instead, I looked just past the wards.

An army gathered outside the shimmering barrier, biding their time before the dragons weakened the magic. I saw Charity, Leo, Irma, Ingrid and the rest of the Loxley Coven. I saw Queen Sadiq, Fendel with both Mallory and Morgan—safe from captivity. I saw creatures I knew and even more I didn't—all ready to fight as soon as the wards broke.

Hope filled my chest. How had I not noticed them before? They had come. They had come because they had once seen the writing on the black letters. They had come because they wanted a world where we could all live in peace—Night Crawlers, Casters, and mortals. They had come because I travelled back across time and told them I needed them here.

I looked over at my past self—her lungs aching to take a breath as she looked at O'Brien's dead body. Her head snapped up to look at Benji just as mine did. The red-eyed vampire was going to die. He was going to die for setting those wendigos loose. He was going to die for choosing the wrong side.

Creatures poured out of the fortress, just as they had before. They gathered near Benji, watching and waiting for the order to pounce.

Across the wards, my eyes locked with Chad's. He had been within the wards before, only last time, I had been furious with him for coming. Now, as his green magic appeared beside me, I thanked the heavens for the weaknesses in the wards and that he was able to transport here.

What happened? he asked, folding his hand around mine. His attention flew over to Lili, the exact person I was supposed to have killed already, and then back at me, puzzled.

I looked away, too ashamed to answer. I hadn't killed Lili or saved O'Brien or Abigail. What the fuck had I done?

Chad placed his other hand on my chin and lifted it towards him. *You saved me,* he said, answering the question that hadn't been meant for him. *You saved me, most of America, and arranged for Kana, Noel, and Leon to be kept safe. Since you've travelled back in time, you did all that and managed to save thousands of lives down below—including your sister.*

Tears pricked at my eyes. And as I scrunched my lips to the side, trying to rein the sadness back, I nodded. He was right. And if I hadn't gone down to the prison cells below and blocked the tunnel, everyone else wouldn't have made it out. I had done that. I had helped save them with O'Brien and Abigail. And if hope was lost for O'Brien, at least Abigail still had a chance.

"I caught the Irish fellow breaking the slaves out of their cages. They're all gone!" I heard Benji yell out. "While you lot were inside partying, I was trying to stop them. *He* stayed back to fight while the rest of them got away," he said, tilting his head down to O'Brien. "Him and this one."

I ducked back behind the shrub, dragging Chad with me.

Abigail, I told him. *We can still save her. Missouri has her now but soon Lili will have her. I never saw her actually die. The dragons are going to break past the wards enough to let more sunlight stream in, but we can stop it from turning her into a statue.*

A thought struck me. What if Lili had taken our conversation to heart? And now that Chad had warned Cristin to keep the children at home...

Dread spread like fire within me. What had I done?

"Set her free," I heard myself demand, "or I'll kill Florence."

Fuck, I thought.

What is it? Chad asked, squeezing my hand to let me know he was still there—to let me know we were stronger together.

I heard Lili's laugh. Her voice made me cringe as she asked, "You think that a quid pro quo is going to work on us?"

I grimaced, my stomach churning, my heart threatening to burst out of my chest as I looked at Chad in the corner of my eye.

It's just—I started as my hands began to shake. *What if it's not enough?* I asked Chad quickly. *What if seeing Abigail start to burn isn't enough for my past self to turn back time? The children won't be in danger this time around. So what if it's not enough to send my powers over the edge? What if I never go back? What happens then?*

Chad's face fell as wonder dawned on him. I smelled the fear seeping out of his pores, and he gripped my hand even harder. I heard the spit slip down his throat. His eyes darted to the wards and back to me.

Something tells me you'll have plenty of reasons to wind back the clock, he decided, and he nodded his head back at the wards.

Sure enough, Noel, Leon, and Kana were waiting beyond the doom.

I could hear Lili talking in the background—Abigail's sharp cry as the vampire-witch grabbed onto her hair and yanked her closer to the sunlight—but all I could focus on was the sight of the three innocent children across the way.

My eyes flew to Chad, but he looked just as bewildered as me. They weren't supposed to be here. They were supposed to be safe in the underwater castle, protected by Cristin, the ocean, and a bucketload of wards.

"Alright then," Lili's voice came, drawing my attention back to her. "Let's see which one dies first."

"Get her!" Benji barked, and the creatures that had gathered on the lawn advanced.

My heart was in my throat. I needed a plan, but my anxiety was acid in my veins.

Save the children, Chad instructed firmly, his eyes locked onto them. *You get them, I'll get Abigail.*

I could feel the panic surging through the other me as the creatures began to attack—the vampires, the witches, the werewolves, everyone.

On the count of three, Azalea, Chad told me, his voice quick but steady.

My eyes widened as I heard the tear of my own flesh.

One, he said, kissing the back of my hand.

I went rigid at the sound of my scream as I gave everything I had out there only for the enemy to rip me apart.

Two, Chad thought as my eyes darted back to the children.

I watched them pound their fists against the wards. They shouted my name and I squared my shoulders towards them, ready to run.

Three, Chad said, and I ran.

The wards thundered around me as I sped across the dirt and dead plants. The world moved in slow motion, but my sole focus was the children. The dark around us grew lighter. The very air around us turned white—a great, white, blank slate.

Just as the smell of their lavender bath soaps hit my nose—just as my arms wrapped around the tiny witch, wizard, and jorogumo—I felt the push from my past self evaporate, and my feet left the ground.

I'm Still Unstoppable

Chapter 64: The Battle

We touched down onto marble floors, the blue-green shimmers of the ocean cast across the children's faces. My hands ran over the three of them as I frantically checked to make sure they weren't harmed. Their expressions were stunned though their tiny hearts raced with worry.

"But Abigail—" Noel let out as tremors shook her body.

I placed my hand to her cheek and stared straight into her eyes.

"Chad's with her," I promised, my voice firm and sure. "He's got her, and he's not going to let anything happen to her."

Noel looked unconvinced, but Leon and Kana nodded next to her.

A buzz filled the air, and as the sound came to a slow, Cristin appeared. Worry drenched his face as he crashed down to his knees, his strong, dark arms wrapping around the children as he swept them into a hug.

"Are you all right?" he asked, pulling back to examine each of them as I had. "I was so worried." He turned to me. "Chad came to talk to me—to tell me about Abigail. The children weren't even in the room when he was here. Then as soon as Chad left, they came running in and disappeared right after him."

"We heard you talking," Kana explained, a rosy hue reaching her cheeks as her eight legs fumbled against the slick floors. She was learning more English every day. "We wanted to help."

"We ran after Chad to try and catch him, and then we just showed up there," Noel continued as if drawing the same breath from Kana. "I don't even think he knows we followed him."

Cristin and I gaped at her. They had accidentally tailed Chad. Cristin would've been stuck here after they left. He didn't have magic to tail after them.

"But Sweetheart—" Cristin tried.

"We *know* we were supposed to stay put," Noel interrupted, "but we couldn't let Abigail die. We love her too much. We can't lose her."

A sad breath left my lungs. They had come because they overheard Chad's warning. Only, they wouldn't have been able to come if I hadn't insisted that Chad alert Cristin. Time was a curious thing.

I readjusted my knees on the floor. "Promise me you'll stay here," I said to the children. I couldn't have them risking their lives. The clock was ticking. "Promise you'll stay safe down here, and I promise I'll do absolutely everything I can to bring Abigail back to you."

They took a collective breath. Noel nodded and the other two followed suit. Leon lunged himself at me, wrapping me up into a tight hug.

"Promise you'll come back too," he urged, his face buried in my shoulder.

Sorrow bubbled in my chest. "I promise," I let out before wisdom could stop me. It was a battlefield I'd be walking onto. A battlefield where an army of entitled, blood-thirsty monsters had already trapped me. But it was too late. The words were out, and I knew I must keep the promise.

I looked at each of their tiny faces in turn before I met Cristin's eyes, the same worry etched in his face.

"I'll do everything I can to bring her back to you," I told him.

I watched him nod, his expression one of doubt and pain, mixed with the fleeting desire to grasp onto hope. I rose to my feet and Leon took a step back to gaze up at me. Tears swam in his eyes. I let his sweet voice replay in my head right before my purple magic swirled around me, taking me back to the fortress. Abigail was my best friend. I had to get to her.

As I touched back down to Lili's property, I took in the blur of havoc around me. The wards were broken. Dragons flew overhead. Sunlight streamed in. A war raged around us.

I clung to the stones of the castle, its shadows protecting only a fragment of the grounds. Thousands of people from both sides fought, ready to end the war once and for all. Some bodies moved with precision—sharp and quick as though they had been training their whole lives for this moment. Fear coated the faces of others. They moved as though their intentions were in disarray—hiding, half-fighting. It was only when someone specifically attacked them that their combat became more pronounced. It was no longer the simple task of pitting Night Crawler against Caster. There were no coloured uniforms to mark allies, or to target enemies. It was those who wanted you dead, and those trying to keep themselves alive.

I scanned the battle—a storm of chaos and fury—until my eyes landed on Abigail and my heart soared to the clouds. Her skin was its usual pale white as she flung holy water on a werewolf. It howled out to the sky as it sizzled into nothing but a dark puddle on the dirt. I smiled as I watched my best friend turn to fight off a witch. She was still alive.

Chad stood near her and cast a stunning spell at the witch before she could attack Abigail. The wretched witch froze and fell to the ground with a thud. Abigail immediately poured water on her, and the witch screamed out as it attacked her like acid—another evil soul leaving this world.

I ducked behind a pile of rubble that had been blasted off Lili's ancestral home, zapped a warlock with a purple stream of magic as he ran towards me with a snarl, and assessed the damage. All the vampires were crowded in the shadows—good and bad. Every other creature wasn't confined to the perimeter of the sun.

A dragon blasted fire at a coven of witches who attacked them with their colourful bolts of magic. I watched the grand wings of another swipe at a horde of manananggals, daft enough to think they could take on a magnificent beast of that size. Their severed upper halves crashed down to the ground, more organs falling out of them than usual—their bodies inept for such a fall.

A hand burst out of the dry soil at my feet, followed by several others. They led a trail away from me until one grasped onto a vampire's ankle. The vampire's red eyes popped with fear right before the clothed hand pulled him into the ground—kicking and screaming until dirt filled his lungs and I could see him no more. Each hand reaching out of the dirt clawed their way up to reveal a score of mummies.

My eyes shot up to see Queen Sadiq draped in her golden garb. Gold paint spiralled up her dark brown arms as she pointed to one of her mummies. Her expression was fierce as she commanded the mummies to attack our enemy—her Arabic running smoothly off her tongue like a dark spell. Several foes were swept up in tornados of sand, their screams paving my way toward Chad and Abigail.

I transported straight to them, and felt Abigail's hand grasp onto mine. Her eyes were wide, her stance taut.

"The kids?" she asked at the same time Chad urgently thought out, *Are the kids safe?*

I nodded at both of them. "They're with Cristin now," I assured them. I looked at Abigail, squeezing her hand back. "They promised they'd stay put, and I promised to get you back to them."

A roar forced our heads in its direction. A wendigo reared on its hind legs, growling at Lili.

"You stupid idiot!" Lili shouted at Benji, her hands raised in front of her as though she was projecting an invisible shield around herself. "Why the *fuck* did you free the wendigos? We can't control them. They don't listen to anyone."

A flash of regret crossed Benji's face. The wendigo aimed its horns at Lili and smashed into the invisible force field around her. Its failed attempt to pierce its target angered it more. It crunched into the shield over and over—blackened cracks forming in midair around Lili. Another wendigo bounded towards Benji and pinned him to the ground. I listened to the sound of his struggles as I shot purple ropes around a witch who had aimed her hands towards Fendel and another gnome.

"You've damned us too," Lili screeched at Benji.

Abigail punched a red-eyed vampire square in the jaw. He flew back several feet and she appeared above him with a buzz before pouring holy water onto him. The water boiled his skin. The sound of his sizzles and screams mixed in with the chaos around us, and within seconds, he melted down until all that was left of him was a puddle.

Missouri let out a sarcastic laugh as Chad and I fought against a swarm of other creatures.

"I can control the wendigos," the ghost said, demonstrating her dominance by zooming through one. It whimpered loudly before crashing to the ground. It laid on its side, wheeling around in a circle, overwhelmed by shivers. Missouri looked back up to Lili with a snarky, satisfied expression. "How do you think we got them into their cage in the first place?"

A flood of squeaky battle yells filled the air as an army of twenty gnomes attacked a single wizard. They wrapped a rope around him, pulled him to the ground, and climbed over him before they scurried off to their next prey. I watched Mallory and Morgan pause their own attacks, a disgusted look on their faces as they watched the free gnomes. Then one of them looked in my direction.

Mallory's red magic shot towards me. Out of instinct, I put a violet shield around me. Only, her magic didn't crash into mine. Instead, it shot past, roping its way around a manananggal who was dragging herself towards me—the intent to kill in her eyes. She hissed her long, straw-like tongue at Chad's aunt, right before Chad finished the monster off with a blast of green light.

My eyes met Chad's before they bolted over to Mallory—shock crashing into me.

She had just saved me. On what planet did Mallory Castwell—Duchess of the "Let's Loathe Azalea" Party—come to my aid?

Her sister cast a spell at a vampire who was speeding towards them. Mallory gave me an uncharacteristically nonchalant shrug before she struck another creature with her red ropes, but then she saw *him.*

"Chad," she breathed out, disbelief coating her face. She stumbled, her guard evaporated as she took in her nephew—a nephew she had seen die with her own eyes.

Her sister caught her with one hand, firing back at another witch before she turned to follow Mallory's gaze. Their defensive stances had melted. A spark of magic shot at them from behind but I sent a purple ball of fire crashing into it, causing it to fly into a rotted tree instead. The tree burst into flames, but the sisters paid it no mind. They had their Chadwick back. And that was all that mattered.

Another manananggal screamed, pulling Leo Loxley into the sky, high above the castle. As he yelled out, as the molten rays of sunlight kissed his skin, Charity shouted his name. She ran towards her husband on all eight legs. But as she flung a silvery web in his direction, I heard a buzz. A vampire wrapped her hands around the jorogumo, pulling her back. Her string of web retracted, falling just short of where her Leo dangled in the sky, smoke sizzling from every inch of his body. His skin was morphing to grey stone at a rate far faster than mine ever had.

Eyeara swept in on her dragon with icy blue scales. The magnificent creature chomped its teeth onto the manananggal, slicing through her skin like a hundred daggers. But as the dragon took a bite out of the small winged creature, Leo fell from the sky.

My heart raced as I transported closer. I cast my hands out in front of me, producing a shield around his body. The purple orb shone bright as I lowered him to the ground, soundless as he touched down. The shield disappeared and I ran to him. His skin slowly faded back to its original state. His eyes were wide as his body began to heal. I crashed down next to him, holding his hand to make sure he was all right, but his wife's scream averted my attention.

Charity's hands were pinned to the ground by a female vampire. The vampire's fangs were bared. All eight of Charity's spidery legs tried desperately to fight her attacker off. In a blink, the vampire's teeth were buried in Charity's neck. The smell of more blood wafted towards me.

I stood in a flash, facing one hand towards my target, the other pulled back, collecting a surge of electricity. I flung my power towards the vampire, right at the centre of her forehead. Both she and the Charity blasted backwards, skidding across the ground for several metres before crashing into the foot of the castle. Four sets of decrepit, clothed hands sprung from the ground, wrapped around the vile creature, and pulled her into the ground. I cast a glance over my shoulder, and Queen Sadiq gave me a firm nod before she turned to set her army of mummies after another monster.

Holding onto Leo's arm, I transported over to Charity. She panted, grasping onto the dirt beneath her fingertips. She moved her hand to her neck to clutch the puncture marks. More blood seeped out between her fingers. Though her eyes were wide, she nodded at her husband and me, her breath laboured but prevailing.

"I'm all right," she breathed out, her legs all scrunched in towards her. "I'm all right. She only took a little."

Leo sat beside her, wrapping his arms around his wife, but the sound of more screams and blasts pulled me away.

A hoard of vampires ripped a mummy apart, limb by limb. A team of a hundred or more Casters teamed up against a dragon and its elf rider. A wendigo was bent over a werewolf, trapping its prey in a dream with its white eyes. An entire tower crashed down, squashing at least 50 beneath it. The sunlight rushed past it and a few unexpecting vampires began to scream as grey smoke hissed from their pale skin. I searched through the chaos, trying to follow the pull toward Florence, hoping to find Lili again, but there was too much movement, too much magic and death, for me to find them.

I heard a disheartening tear as a creature dug its teeth into someone near me. Blood sprayed over me. I looked down at my clothes—fresh blood mixing in with O'Brien's blood and blood from the river. It did nothing to trigger my appetite, only my terror.

We were outnumbered.

The stench of death was thick in the air. Bodies covered the ground. People fell over their loved ones as they fought to defend themselves. The sight stabbed into my stomach. I knew whose lives were being taken. Possibly half our forces were still in America. We weren't enough, just as we had always feared. Did we have enough holy water to destroy them all? Did we have the means to take them as prisoners? Or did we truly have to slaughter them as they were slaughtering us in order to have a chance at victory?

I shot my shield up as a blue spark flew towards me. I let it down and struck my attacker faster than they could track my movements. He crashed down to the ground—frozen. A buzz sounded from behind me and I spun around. A vampire lunged towards me. I pushed him back with all my strength, a grunt erupting from my stomach. He slid back, knocking down ten others before he dug his nails into the ground and came to a halt. Sending a blast of purple his way, I felt a tug.

I looked up to see Florence, 50 metres away, tearing into one creature before catching a small fairy in his hand and squeezing tight. I heard the crunch of its tiny bones before he tossed her corpse to the ground. His eyes shot up to mine. Pushing his blond hair off of his face, he licked blood from his lips.

The look in Florence's eye unveiled an emotion far deeper than anger—far deeper than betrayal or fear or sorrow. It was as if he knew this battle was all my doing, and for the first time, it was if he'd rather see me dead—rather beat me to a pulp—than see me in his marriage bed. The look impaled me, burning me to my core.

He became a blur, aimed straight towards me, but as I tensed my muscles, ready to strike back, a wendigo knocked into him, tossing him to the side.

I took a single breath before I began to run towards his new location—ignoring the wendigo that screeched above him. But I was in motion for half a second when an icy force plunged through me.

A loud wheeze escaped my frozen lungs as I tried to force air into them. The blur of two ghosts streaked away from me. I surveyed the area where Florence had landed. Creatures ran past in either direction until a clear-cut trail marked the way to my sire. The chills that immobilised my body began to fade, replaced by the heat that accompanied hatred. I shook off the last of the chills, ready to go after Florence, but Ginny's grey figure blurred my view. Her long hair floated around her horrified face, her eyes wide.

"You die if you go down that path," she said in an echoey voice, though there were no walls for her words to bounce off.

An aggravated huff left my mouth. I glared at her. It wasn't her fault. She was bound to Chad and me now that O'Brien was gone. But I wanted to go after the bloody vampire. I didn't want her to tell me it wasn't time. I wanted to finish him.

There was a scream and my eyes darted over to see black vines pinning a vampire to the ground. Yellow sunshine transformed their face to a hard grey stone. Life left their frame, their lips forever memorialised in scream. The witch with black magic immediately turned to cast a spell at Morgan, but Chad struck her down.

I made to run past Ginny—to go to the stone vampire—to try and undo time around them in a bubble, but my blasted banshee blocked that path too.

"Not there either," she said in her haunting voice. A mummy behind her howled out as a horned wendigo crashed into it. Ginny put her face closer to mine, redirecting my attention to her. "Certain death befalls you if you go that way."

I ducked down as a jorogumo was thrown over my head, through Ginny, and then crashed down to the ground. Missouri's ghostly form floated through the frightened jorogumo. Tiny bumps sprouted across the spider-woman's skin as she froze in place—her only movement the contraction of her chest as she choked on her own frozen scream. A werewolf bounded towards her and tore off one of her eight legs.

I looked at Ginny, anxiously craving the green light. The instant her head moved into a nod, I ran at the werewolf. The beast didn't get the chance to sniff me out.

I aimed a purple flame at the werewolf and set its fur ablaze. The jorogumo fell from its hands, then ran away with a frantic limp as the purple fire began to consume her attacker. A yowl erupted into the air. As heat blasted off of him, licking my face, the desperate cry morphed into a hopeless whimper.

My eyes were wide. The beast clawed at its skin—trying to peel it off him as Connor had done during his transformations. Guilt imploded my whole chest. My heart pounded against my eardrums. The werewolf's irises shifted from yellow to brown, and though I knew it wasn't Connor—though I knew my mate was elsewhere—something crippled me. The smell of his singed fur overwhelmed my senses. Every noise—every smell—every other sound was drowned out. Then a question barged its way into my head.

Did he deserve it?

Water splashed over the werewolf. Droplets met my skin and I flinched, the world around us coming back in a flash. The violet flames were extinguished, but the smoke became steam, and the holy water consumed him with a sizzle.

I stared down at the puddle, his scream still very prevalent as it rang through my ears. My eyes flew up to see Abigail panting beside me. Holy water sloshed around her jug. She was staring down at the werewolf's boiled remains. Her eyes shot up to me, and her shoulders shrugged as if it had been worth the try—worth it to see if the creature merited redemption. Turned out he did not.

Abigail placed a hand on my shoulder. I nodded back at her to let her know I was all right, but her hand went rigid against me. Her face hardened and her hand fell from my shoulder to meet her heart as she stumbled forward.

She could feel a pull.

A fierce yell erupted from behind her. Panic pulsed through my heart as a yellow-eyed creature made to grasp onto Abigail's arm, teeth bared, a hunger for death in his eyes. But as I realised my counterattack was half a second too slow, some force pushed the monster back. He clawed at his chest and legs, wildly attacking them. Something had a hold on him—something like invisible vines.

Abigail and I looked up in sync to find Lili's finger stretched out at the creature, right before her eyes met ours. The concentration on Lili's face instantly shifted into a softer, questioning look, as though she was trying to get a read on us—as if she was trying to get an approval of sorts. We studied her before I turned to look at Abigail. Her shoulders were rising in time with her breaths, scepticism and confusion furrowing her brows. The same questions that were carved into Abigail's face rampaged around my head. Lili had just saved Abigail from an attack. But my eyes turned red. I knew what her aim was. She wasn't saving Abigail out of the kindness of her blackened heart. No. She was doing it to save her own skin. Lili had said herself she had chosen the wrong side. But she didn't get a last-second switch. She didn't get to blame all her actions on her love for Florence, or hold Abigail in the sunlight just to save her now. She was insane. And I refused to play her game.

I sent a blast of purple fire at her. Her eyes widened as she dove to dodge it. It skimmed past her face, a hair away from her flawless cheek. She snarled at me and disappeared in a cloudless burst of magic.

My feet sped in her direction but pulled to an automatic stop as Ginny pulled in, our noses nearly touching. There was a splash of what I thought was holy water on a creature in front of me, a creature that would've been me if Ginny hadn't stopped me. But I knew the creature it landed on. It was a manananggal from Loxley Lair—the one who had convinced me to go to the prison for the first time—the one who saw the writing on the black envelope. She had a good soul. Yet the clear liquid brought a sizzle to her skin.

Acid.

Malia clutched her chest and the side of her face as her skin melted off. Her long tongue hissed out. Her wings flapped with hysteria as if they wanted take her away from the torture but they couldn't. Abigail poured holy water on Malia's attacker. My knees crashed into the ground, my hands grasping onto Malia as she writhed around. Her intestines shrivelled where the acid had touched it. As I pulled her hand away from her cheek, the memory of Elizabeth Downy's face clouded my vision. It was the same substance that had taken her will to live.

We have holy water, I thought, completely traumatised. *They have acid.*

They were throwing their own version of the liquid to ruin us. Only, theirs seemed to be cursed by the devil instead of blessed by a priest.

I spun my hands in a circle around Malia's boiling skin, white puss seeping out. I tried with all my might to produce a time bubble—to heal her wounds—but I could feel the ache in my body. I could feel the wear that time travel had caused and knew that this type of magic was too much for me to replicate. Not after travelling back hours. Not after bringing Chad back. I didn't have it in me. So instead, I closed my eyes, blocking out the raging war around me. I imagined the way the manananggal's skin had been before—the way she looked that night she convinced me to go with O'Brien and the others in search of a prison meal. And when I opened my eyes, lavender glowed over her. Her face was no longer tortured by pain. It was no longer contorted by melting skin. It was her own again.

She grabbed onto my hand, her chest heaving up and down anxiously. She nodded as she came to herself once more.

"Thanks," she hissed out, but her long tongue shrank, slinking back into her mouth and turning normal.

My gaze followed hers as she looked upward. The early morning sky was brighter. Earth's tilt was reducing the size of the castle's shadow. The darkness that protected the vampire's skin—the night that gave manananggals their wings—was quickly becoming no more.

Malia looked back at me, her eyes intense as a few other manananggals nearby paused their fighting.

"It's daylight," she told me, her eyes flickering down to her severed torso. "We need to get back to our legs. We'll be as useless as mortals now."

I looked around, selfishly gauging what it meant for the fight. Were there more manananggals on the other side or ours? Would we be even more outnumbered? Or would the loss of manananggals in the fight benefit us?

A group of gnomes near me caught my attention. I beckoned them over.

"Please," I started as Malia's wings began to capsize in on themselves. "Find as many manananggals on our side as you can and get them back to their legs," I instructed, looking back up at the sky and then down to their tiny faces.

Simultaneously, the gnomes nodded. One stuck his fingers in his mouth and blew out a whistle. On cue, the army of gnomes set to work, four of which grabbed onto Malia and disappeared with her in tow.

Ginny floated higher into the air. Her pale grey eyes focused across the grounds. I could feel in my bones—in the prickles up my spine—that she sensed more danger.

I tracked her gaze. Out in the sunlight, Chad had a bright blue vine wrapped around his arm. His free hand worked tirelessly to fight off a gaggle of five Casters throwing magic at him. I transported next to him before Ginny could advise me otherwise and blasted three of the Casters back, stunning each of them in one go.

The sun burned against my skin. I clenched my teeth together, throwing a shield around Chad and me. The patches of stone began to morph back to brown, but the enemy seemed to multiply around us. More of them advanced forward. It was nearly twenty to two now as they cast their magic at my shield, trying to shatter it to pieces.

A fierce wave of air pushed against our attackers, causing them to stumble back. Saga roared from the sky. Her belly grew dark as her massive wings carried her towards us. A hand wrapped around my wrist, and I looked up to see Chad bracing me for transportation. I could feel the scalding heat from Saga's fire as green magic swept us away from the blue flames. We landed several yards away, in time to see the burned remains of the Casters crash to the ground. The earth beneath us shook as the dragon touched down, roaring and ready to burn anyone else who tried to harm us.

Magic of nearly every colour shot into the air, uselessly ricocheting off a dark grey dragon yet knocking its rider clear off. The elf fell from a height taller than the castle, wind brushing his long icy blue hair around him.

I shot out a purple rope, willing my magic to wrap around him. As soon as it did, it retracted, pulling the elf toward us until his body knocked Chad and I clean off our feet. The three of us fell to the ground in a heap, safely in the shadows. But when I sat up to check if the elf was all right, I could tell by the hollow look in his eyes that he had already passed.

Another lost. We needed something—anything—to turn the tide.

Chad's hand curved into mine as he pulled me up from the ground. A vibrant orange spark flew straight at us, and I had to tug him back down. We covered our heads as the magic crashed into the castle wall, sending stones and shards of glass to shower down on us.

I could smell the dry dirt as I practically buried my face in it, squeezing my eyes as tightly as they would allow. The ground shook as more mummies tore their way out. I could smell the blood of every single creature who had lost their lives on this soil—so many in such a short span of time—and the pain of their loss ripped at my soul.

What were we going to do? How were we going to end this?

Chad held onto my waist and pulled me up from the ground once more. There was a mix of fear and determination in his green eyes—eyes I wanted to lose myself in rather than the death and rubble that surrounded us.

The dirt beneath us started to soften. Our feet sank slightly into the ground as the dry grains moistened, turning darker. A circle of water expanded to at least five metres in diameter, changing the dirt to a thick mud. The earth shook again—violently. In the centre, the mud began to boil. Bubbles burst along the surface as a mass rose into the air. The mound towered at least four metres high, wiggling as though it could breathe, as if it possessed life.

Chad's head tilted back in time with mine as we followed its frame up, trembling as shapeless limbs protruded out of its sides. Holes formed where its eyes would be. A large hole acted as its mouth, letting out a roar that made the very molecules in the air seem to freeze in terror.

"It's all right!" Abigail shouted. I looked over to see her staring straight at me. She glanced back at the monster, surprise coating her face rather than fear. "He's on our side!"

The faintest memory of a mud monster Abigail had once mentioned brushed against my mind. The creature turned around, its front hardly discernible from its back, and swiped at a vampire who was piercing its teeth into an undeserving gnome. The vampire flew to the side, his growl turning into shock as he looked up at the creature. He crawled backwards to get away but at least forty members of Florence's fleet closed in on the monster of mud.

A movement in the corner of my eye drew my attention. Torpedoes of every colour swirled around, revealing more people than I could count, with beautiful dark skin and wearing lavish African clothing. Most had brown eyes while others sported the bright vampire shades of blue or red.

They came, I thought with a joyful sigh of relief.

It was as if every single Caster and Night Crawler on the continent of Africa had arrived, standing on the other side of the gravel path where the plants were rich with life, and stretching out as far as the eye could see. They had listened to Queen Sadiq, just as she said they would. And they were here to help as one united nation to establish peace across the world.

One man with dark skin and red eyes swooped in, the gold paint on his body shining like armour. He buzzed past all of them to stand on the battlefield next to his wife, who was already amidst the fight with her mummies. Though his expression portrayed he'd rather be anywhere else, he straightened his back, ready for combat. Queen Sadiq smiled at him and kissed his cheek. Perhaps the pharaoh hadn't seen the magical ink at first, but at least he had come around.

The mass of them ran onto the castle grounds, hardly bothered by the sun as it touched down on their skin. They descended upon the crowd like a giant wave attacking a ship.

My attention snapped back around me as one of the vampires who had forced me into that putrid wedding dress shattered the bones of a French vampire. I combined my speed with my magic and sent a ball of fire at him before he could evade it, and then immediately went to back up Chad, who was going head-to-head with the former king of the elves.

I shot purple ropes around Eyeron's wrists and ankles. Chad finished the job with a shot of green magic, aimed straight at the elf's stomach. It knocked Eyeron onto his back. The two of us towered over the blue elf as he struggled against my ropes.

"It appears it's your turn to wear the chains," I told him, remembering the tracking bracelet he had once insisted I wear.

And then Chad and I were off to the next challenger.

A jorogumo spun a wizard around several times, covering him layer after layer in her web. Ghosts, on both sides it seemed, flew through their victims, paralysing them with icy insides. Mallory and Morgan were blasting red magic at anyone who attempted to destroy them. Night Crawlers and Casters alike stood frozen solid in a maze around them—a taller version of the entrapped gnomes that used to decorate their front gardens. I had to admit, this version I approved of.

Statues spread across the field. My heart raced as I took them in—each a vampire whose skin would eternally be stone. My eyes scanned over as many as I could take in, praying I would not see a familiar face, but Chad shook his head and I looked at him.

"I doubt many of them are ours," he said, watching the way I stared at the stone figures. "Before I spoke to Cristin, I went back to Castwell Castle to collect some potions I had brewed and then duplicated. I didn't have enough to give it to everyone, but it will protect some."

He pulled a phial out of his pocket and placed it in my hands. The colour was familiar, and then I realised I had taken this potion before.

Chad winced. "Probably should've given this to you earlier, huh?" he asked, guilt taking over his features.

It was the potion that helped protect vampires from the sun. He had given it to me before Detective Harrison's funeral—to protect me from the daylight in his absence. The funeral of his father that Lili had kept him from.

I smiled a weak smile, looking up from the phial and into his eyes. "I believe you were a bit preoccupied," I said, glancing around at the chaos that still ensued.

"Just a wee bit," he replied with a laugh.

I uncorked the phial and tilted its contents into my mouth. The bitter liquid coated my tongue before travelling down my throat. Using my sleeve, I wiped off my lips, and felt the tingle as the protective magic took over.

"Cheers," I let out.

I hurled the empty phial at the back of a vampire's head. It shot through like a bullet, interrupting him from his meal. The vampire fell to the ground, the hole in his head beginning to heal itself, but then hands burst out of the ground. Florence's crony screamed out as a mummy pulled him into the ground and he disappeared.

A fairy zoomed past, a wendigo chasing after it, but several of the Casters from Africa worked together to take the dream-invader down. Saga roared, launching back into the sky. Her white belly filled with fire before she released it over the castle. The dark towers and turrets lit with blue flames, the heat overpowering the warmth from the sun. She landed on the castle, unbothered by the fire, stones crumbling and falling under her weight.

I heard a loud cry of frustration and immediately found Lili staring up at the purple-eyed dragon. She cast an agitated finger up at the beautiful beast, but she should've known better. Saga didn't so much as flinch as Lili's invisible magic buzzed with electricity. Sparks showered back down to the ground.

"Stop doing that!" Lili screamed at the dragon, immediately pushing her magic forward in another attempt. "You stupid—

fucking—dragon!" she called out, her magic shooting out in time with each word.

But Saga's hide was too thick to penetrate—at least for one witch—even as powerful as she was. Lili let out a long, infuriated grunt. Her body shook with anger before she tried a new approach. Rather than point at the dragon, she squared her shoulders towards the castle. The fire died instantly, black smoke darkening the sky. Saga answered by hunching down and blowing more blue fire over the lair, determined to burn it to the ground.

Vampires from Charity's sister coven ran past me, yelling in French. A creature roared behind me and I sent a spark of electricity through it, but at least ten wendigos began to circle Chad and me. I wondered if they remembered me from down below or if they could merely sense we were the real threat.

A pull jerked me, right as a green shield snapped into place around us. Florence's voice called out, too close to be good news, doling out orders to his army.

Chad's hand slid into mine. A wendigo lunged itself at us but the green magic held. I squeezed Chad's hand. Each wendigos' eyes turned white—each monster ignoring Chad to stare straight at me as if they could sense I was the one with a weakness for nightmares.

We can do this! Chad shouted into my mind. *But we need to get to Florence. He's the one in command. We don't need to kill all their forces. If we kill him, perhaps it'll drive fear into the rest of them.*

Two more wendigos launched themselves at Chad's shield. Cracks spread across it like a web. It splintered, threatening to break, but Chad squeezed my hand back and the cracks disappeared.

He was right. We now had nearly all our forces here or fighting on the opposite hemisphere. Most of Florence's number were people who were afraid of him or cowards who thought he stood a chance. They wouldn't come to his aid once they heard it was a losing fight.

We could do this. We needed to annihilate the monster here and that would be the worst of it. If only there was a way to wash all the evil away.

I looked over to an empty jug of holy water, the way it sat, discarded on the ground. I thought back to the meeting we'd had—a suggestion of how to use the holy water. Then I thought back to Japan—the way Lili's magic had made the sky crackle with lightning—the way the mermaids controlled the stormy skies and the sea, bending it to their will. And I knew what I had to do.

Pointing both my palms up at the sky, I flicked my fingers and pushed all my magic up towards the heavens. The sky darkened. An ominous cloud swept in on the winds, pulsing with violet magic. Thunder filled the air. As the cloud grew darker and darker, I could feel the power I possessed.

Lightning flashed across the sky, and my gaze fell, travelling several metres away, as if pulled by an invisible force. My eyes locked onto Florence's panicked expression. Then they flashed over to Lili, who was staring at the sky, backing slowly towards the wall of her castle.

She could feel it. They all could.

There was a strange silence as the fighting stopped. Every head was turned up at the clouds. I watched as the very first drop fell from the sky. It splashed upon my brow, soft and cool. I took in a deep breath of refreshing air. The whole world went still as several more droplets fell, crashing down onto the array of creatures, the earth, and everything the domed wards had once protected.

That's when the silence ceased and the screams began.

The rain crashed down, landing on every inch of Lili's property. It sizzled as it sank into the skin of our enemies.

The vampires were the fastest. When they realised what was happening, their buzz of movement mixed in with the cries. They scurried into the castle, or out into the woods, away from the menacing cloud. The other monsters were much slower. Steam filled the air around us as their skin melted. Night Crawlers and Casters—vampires, witches, werewolves, and more. Anyone who bore evil in their hearts. Their screams began to morph into gurgles. But it left no trace of death. No poisoned blood. The air smelled fresh. Clean. Pure.

A crowd remained, wide-eyed as the villains melted away into nothingness. But it wasn't over. We couldn't let the others get away.

The rest of us moved as one, a collective power, aimed towards those who had run. A dragon roared and then fire burst towards the castle. Chad sent a stream of green magic, blasting off the grand front doors of the lair that held more of our enemy, then reproduced his shield around us. Tornadoes of sand whizzed through the rainless woods, chasing down several targets as the dragons flocked above, burning down more.

Everything was as it should be. Every wicked soul was about to be annihilated. But something was wrong. The pull was jerking me in the opposite direction, away from Lili's lair, away from Chad, and away from the fight—fleeing with the other cowards.

Florence was escaping.

Chapter 65: Beyond Repair

I focused on Florence's frantic breaths as he sprinted away from the fortress. He was far past the border of dead plants to escape the cloud above, and into the forest of green.

"Ginny!" I called out, past the shield that encircled us.

I could see Chad turn to me from the corner of my eye—feel his confusion radiate through our hands as he held on. I pivoted away from him to look past the green dome, in search of the banshee. As I did, she appeared next to me, inside the shield.

I jumped, staring back at the ghost who was apparently impervious to magical shields. Her face was relaxed even though the war was not yet over. Even though hundreds of thousands—if not millions—had died tonight.

"Stay with Chad," I commanded, not allowing any room for argument.

After she nodded, I turned to face Chad. I could feel his fear like the thunderous shakes of an earthquake, but he gave me a half smile. He knew what I had to do.

I know we're stronger together, I told him, *but I have to do this on my own—to heal.*

He nodded slowly, his eyes narrowed in concentration, a thousand thoughts flowing through his mind. His fists tightened as if he considered stopping me. But the war that raged inside of him was subdued by the faith he had in me.

You're going to do brilliantly, he said before he pulled me in close.

He rested his head against mine—gentle, trusting, empowering. I breathed him in—the sweet scent of his skin, his sweat, his blood. I loved every part of him.

I know, I replied. *The stars and I kind of have a plan where I stay alive.*

His chest rumbled against me as he laughed, his voice vibrating against his vocal cords. He placed his nose against mine and brushed it from side to side.

Just... he stopped, searching for the right words. *Just let me know if you want... moral support,* he settled on. *And promise me you'll at least let me help you get Lili.*

I nodded, pulling him in closer. *Don't worry,* I promised. *That we can do together.*

I gave him one more tight squeeze before I released him. Then I let my magic take me to the pull—succumbing to it one last time.

Woods surrounded me. The plants breathed life now that we were kilometres away from the fortress. The trees were thick with leaves—blocking out most of the sun even though it had risen higher in the sky.

With the bulk of the fight behind us, it was easy to concentrate on the sharp sounds of Florence's movement. My eyes locked in on his blurred frame as his limbs worked in overdrive to take him far away. He looked back and I could see fear in his dilated pupils, though it did nothing to slow his stride.

The morning sun sizzled against his skin, shining down between the small gaps in the tree cover. I smelled the smoke—saw the patches of grey across him—but he ignored the burn. He kept fleeing, knowing that the only thing behind him was certain death.

I ran after him, the potion working to protect my skin. A purple vine jutted out of my hand and around his ankle, pulling him to the ground with a *thud*. Leaves and dirt scattered as he crashed down. He turned so quickly, as if ready to strike me down. But when his eyes met mine, they shifted from that of a monster to that of a lovestruck fool.

"Azalea," he breathed out, crawling back towards me instead of bolting.

A dull-witted creature.

I jerked the rope towards me and the fear he should have felt seconds ago seeped from his pores. I smelled the salt in his sweat—breathed in the panic he breathed out. He desperately clutched at the ground, dirt gathering under his once spotless fingernails, and he whimpered. He knew his fate. He knew what I was going to do to him.

Smoke darkened the air as the patches on his skin turned to a smooth, grey stone—satisfyingly slow from the vampire blood that was supposed to make him stronger. But I didn't want him to die that way. I didn't want the sun to get the glory of taking his life—for him to become a statue for his followers to forever commemorate. I wanted every single inch of him to diminish into nothingness. And I wanted it to hurt.

"Azalea," he tried again, but in a blink, I was in his face. He stumbled back, tripping over himself. He slid along the leaves and dirt as he stared at me.

I cast a shield around us, and though the sun stopped attacking his skin, the grey patches were slow to heal.

"You don't get to say my name," I enunciated, the power from my voice making him sink into the forest floor even further. "You don't get to call me yours, or stuff me in a wedding dress, or promise a life of compliance, potions, and slavery." I wrapped my purple rope around both my hands and pressed it to his neck, swinging a leg over him so he was pinned.

He choked, forcing words up his throat. "But you have to be mine," he replied, grasping onto my hands. "I love you!" he cried out, raw emotion coating his voice as if his heart was tearing down the seam. "I *love* you, and all I've ever wanted was for you to love me back."

Magma pulsed out of my hands, flowing through the ropes. It seared his skin. Crimson blisters peeked out beneath my purple magic, but he hardly flinched.

I pressed the ropes deeper into his throat, ignoring the burn of the lava within them, even as it scalded my palms. "You don't love me, Florence," I explained, because apparently he needed to be yanked out of his fantasy world where women like me fawned

539

over controlling, soul-sucking demons like him. "You loved Zena, and I'm not her."

"She's not here anymore, but you are!" he croaked, a vein bulging at the side of his temple.

"Then perhaps you'll get reacquainted with her in the afterlife," I countered. Perhaps she would despise him as much as I did. How poetic that would be...

"But she was *good*," he pleaded, shaking his head at me while stroking the very hands that were choking him. His feet kicked uselessly as he struggled beneath my grasp. "She won't be where I'm headed."

"Sounds like something you should've figured out decades ago," I remarked. That was not my problem.

"She didn't deserve to die!" he screamed out.

"Neither did the millions of people you killed, Florence," I screamed back.

But he stopped. He stopped his struggle, he stopped trying to escape my wrath, and his hands paused. He stared up at the sky, past my shield. His eyes glazed over from a haunted memory, misery encompassing him and stealing his soul.

"But I had to kill her," he let out. A breath. A confession.

My heart stopped. I nearly loosened my grip from the shock. "You had to kill *who*?" I asked him, shaking my head. "Your father killed Zena." I clenched my fingers around my ropes as hard as I could, feeling the anger boil inside me. "You told Lili that your father killed her."

"He did!" Florence screamed, but then his anger evaporated as quickly as it had come. He shrivelled into himself. "It was his fault," he whimpered, tears caught in his throat. "I couldn't refuse..."

My nostrils flared. "What do you mean?" I growled through gritted teeth.

"He *made* me kill her," Florence said, as he began rubbing frantically at my hands. "He made me do it to prove I was his son—then he turned me away after I had done it. The racist bastard said I never would've fallen in love with her if I was truly his son."

The truth stung me like a thousand hornets. I blinked at him. "You mean to tell me—you did all of this—became a vampire, killed innocent people, turned me—all because of a mistake *you* made 80 years ago? Zena could've lived. The two of you could've lived happily together if it weren't for you chasing after your father's approval."

Florence's shoulders lifted and the weight of a lifetime of bad decisions pulled them back down into the ground. "All I wanted was for him to love me," he whispered, staring off into the distance. "But he tricked me."

I shoved the ropes deeper into his neck. This time, he grunted out as the magma seared him. I dug my knee into his chest, and his hands stopped stroking mine. My red eyes reflected in his and he started to tremble. He was scared of me. He was terrified. And he should be.

"'Tricked you,'" I repeated, widening my eyes at the irony of it all. "*Tricked you* like you tricked me?" I asked. "Tricked me by stealing me away in the middle of the night—tricked me by giving me your arm to bite and drink your blood to turn me into a vampire—tricked me by taking away my memories, taking my life, drinking that bloody love potion just to get me to kiss you— tricked me into making that blood oath?" Bile rose in my throat at the memory of his lips on mine—his blood in my mouth.

Never again.

I dug my knee further into his chest, hovering over him like a snake about to strike their prey. "But thanks to that blood oath, you sealed your own fate," I hissed. "And *death* is precisely what will do us part."

My ropes shot back into me. I pressed my hands against the spot where his decrepit heart lay. Pushing all my magic into him, I focused on his venom—his blood—the parts of him that turned me into the vampire I was today.

His blood began to pour out of him, bubbling like holy water. It sizzled loudly as it seeped from his lips, his nostrils, his ears. Though he tried to scream, I covered his mouth with one hand and forced his screams back into his lungs.

He didn't get to scream. He didn't get to call for help.

Purple vines scoured the forest floor, wrapping around him and strapping him to the ground so he couldn't fight his way free. As he shook violently beneath me—his limbs useless, his screams suppressed—I remembered the night that had started this all. The night Lili's invisible vines forced me down, and the burn as Florence's venom worked its way through my veins. I remembered my hair falling out. I remembered praying to die. And I remembered hating him with every part of my soul.

His blood bubbled out, melting his skin. His bloodshot eyes begged for mercy, yet I pushed even more magic into him and stared right back at him.

I watched his red eyes turn blue.

I watched as the evil from his soul was washed away.

For a second, all that was left was the little blue-eyed boy Lili had met in the schoolyard. Innocent. Broken. Yet still beyond repair.

Then those blue eyes rolled back into his head, his frame shrank, the puddle of his remains burst into purple flames.

And Florence was gone for good.

I'm Still Unstoppable

Chapter 66: Run, Don't Cry, Just Get Away

The pull snapped away like a string that had been wrapped around me, pulling far too tight for far too long. It stung as it whipped into my chest. My whole body seized. My lungs gasped for breath as if the reason for my existence had deserted me. Then I stared down at the puddle Florence had become, watching as my purple fire devoured it, and the sting evaporated. An entire ocean of relief swept over me.

He was gone.

He was truly gone.

I had asked Abigail the day Florence bit me how to rid myself of this pull—how to escape the urge to draw near him—how to sever the bond he started the moment his venom ran through me. For two years I had wanted him dead. For two years I had suffered for each of his breaths.

Energy fled my body. I wanted to sit. I wanted to sit and breathe and feel his absence—to let joy consume me. But I couldn't afford it. This was all the time I could allow myself for now. Chad and Abigail needed me.

I transported back, outside the old ward line where green trees lay on one side of a path and dead trees sat on the other. I was lost in a daze, trying to comprehend if I had truly just killed my maker—if I was free. My heart jumped as I took in the sight of thousands standing beneath the green trees, protected from the sunlight and holy rain.

It was as if more creatures had arrived to fight—a mixture of good, bad, our side, theirs. But rather than slaughter one another, they stood docile, stunned as they watched the steam billow up from the remains of my cruel enemies. Not a single one was brave enough to step under the surging cloud of power. Because it was a power that no witch or vampire had ever possessed before.

My feet carried me through the crowd. Each creature backed away from me, creating a path as I went. Vampires with red eyes flinched away from me. Witches glared daggers into me, but none were brave enough to attack. They had either seen me produce that cloud or were wise enough to catch on.

I looked down at my outfit as I edged closer to the fortress, ignoring all the eyes that were on me. I was stained with so much blood. It took everything in me not to scream. Waving my hands over myself, the blood vanished, and I looked back up at Lili's castle.

She was right. Her home was in ruins. Saga's fire had been extinguished by the rain, but most of the castle was now either charred or in demolished heaps across the dead front gardens. Movement outside the castle was scarce. Corpses either littered the ground, were statues, or had been reduced to puddles. O'Brien was amongst them. I clenched my fists as I let that knowledge stoke my fury.

The clatters and war cries echoed through the castle and out through the front doors, informing me that the small remaining battle had moved to the interior. I closed my eyes, the sound of many breaths and pulses filling my ears until I found Chad's. And I let my heart transport me straight to him.

I landed beside the bloodfall right as Chad blasted through a warlock. The enemy went crashing into the pool of blood, and I moved quickly to avoid the splash. Ginny stood near, her spirit floating above the last of the chaos, watching with a wary eye yet not objecting to any of Chad's decisions. Though I felt numb, my body moved towards the fight, knowing it was my duty. I had killed one leader. But there was still another.

I wrapped my hand around Chad's, a look in my eyes telling him I was ready. But it wasn't just him who needed to end Lili. Not just him. Not just me. But one other person.

My purple magic delivered us to Abigail. A red-eyed vampire was pinned under her foot. She glared down at him victoriously as he writhed beneath her. With a shiver of satisfaction, I realised it was Benji—right before Abigail's boot came down hard— shattering his skull. The crack pierced the air. As blood poured onto the ground and she forced her foot from the cavity his head had become, I placed my free hand into hers. I wondered if she ran out of holy water or if she merely believed he deserved this death instead.

"You have just as much of a right to kill Lili as either of us do," I told her. She looked into my eyes, then glanced up at Chad. He gave her a firm smile.

With one collective nod from all of us, I closed my eyes and pictured Lili. I could see her location as clearly as if I were seeing it with her eyes. I saw where she stood—felt her hopelessness— and my magic took us there.

Our feet touched down onto the slick castle floors, the shade from the dark lair casting a coolness over my skin. There Lili stood, soaking wet. We watched as she stared up at the large portrait of her father before she turned to face us with speed only a vampire was capable of.

Chad flicked his wrist and a pair of magic-blocking handcuffs clicked into place, chaining Lili's hands together. She backed up, bumping into the large frame and tilting it at an odd angle.

I stared back and forth between the vampire-witch who despised me and the legendary man who fathered her, noticing the resemblance for the first time. Though his hair was black and hers was blonde, they had the same cheekbones, the same beauty, the same fair, flawless skin. They wore the same arrogance and craving for power. But then Lili's expression shifted to fear and the resemblance stopped. She wasn't powerful or beautiful or a legend. She was trapped.

The three of us let go of each other's hands, drawing in closer to our prey as Lili's eyes darted to the side, searching for an escape, and then back to us when she saw there wasn't one. She couldn't use her speed, her strength, or magic against us. I watched as her throat bobbed—as rain and sweat glistened on her brow from the glow of a torch—and listened to her heart bang against her chest.

She took a deep breath and placed her chained hands out in front of her.

"I have wronged each of you," she said, her voice shaking on the edge between panic and grievance. "In fact," she added, addressing each of us, "I fear you three are the ones I've wronged most of all." The portrait rattled behind her as she pushed further into it—like she was trying to sink through the wall. She let out another breath to steady herself and stood tall. "But I have not wronged you as much as you were led to believe."

That's rich, I thought as an unimpressed chuckle left my chest. My eyes flew to Chad and Abigail, expecting to see similar thoughts cast across their faces, but they frowned at her as though pondering more.

She let out a breathy laugh that rivalled mine. "You see, I've also saved each of you."

"Go to Hell, Lili," I growled out at her.

But she looked softly into my eyes, inviting me into her head.

I can't go to Hell, she told me, and just me. *I'm already trapped somewhere far worse.*

The words stabbed into me so fiercely, they forced my eyes away. I pressed my lips together tightly, staring at the ground.

"You turned me into a vampire," Abigail let out with authority. "And then you left me there to—"

"Would you have preferred the alternative?" Lili screeched out, and my gaze shot back to her as we all jumped. She took a long step towards Abigail, her eyes wide, the chain clinking as she zeroed in on her creation with the utmost focus. "Think of where you were headed," she demanded. "Think of the concentration camp they were taking you to—the horrible death you would've faced!" she screamed. "I gave you a second chance at life. I gave you the chance to find love, happiness—a family!"

"You left me there to fail," Abigail countered. "I was all alone. I didn't even know what I was."

Lili laughed, her jaw tight as she shook her head and rolled her eyes. "I knew you were strong," she answered firmly. "I knew you could survive. And you did."

"You created Florence," I interjected. She was anything but innocent.

"To kill Hitler and create a new world!" she retorted in a desperate scream. Then she rounded on Chad, squinting her eyes as if insulted he had the audacity to be cross with her.

"And your father was dying before we made that stupid blood oath! He was a mortal. All mortals begin to die the second they're created."

"You have a distorted perception of death, don't you?" I asked, remembering what she had told me earlier about her thoughts on death after so many years on this earth.

"No," she snapped. "*You* do."

"You obliterated an entire country of people," Chad said, justifying our intent to end her.

"No," she corrected, her usual venom slipping off her tongue. "You were led to *believe* that was my doing when really it was the Warlocks of the South that orchestrated that whole ordeal. But we couldn't give them credit for it. Not when you thought they were on your side," she directed towards Chad.

"You still let it happen," I replied, and her hate redirected to me.

"So did you," she blurted out. "Florence gave you the option to stop it. He told you the key to stopping the whole affair. Only, you were too slow to take it."

I pursed my lips, crossing my arms tight against my chest and shaking my head at her. It would've been another trick. But what did she expect from us? Were we supposed to let her go? Expected to let her off scot-free? She was evil. She was a villain. She had to pay.

"The rain," Abigail breathed out. My eyes followed hers to the droplets that fell off Lili's dress, creating a puddle on the floor. "It didn't harm you," she pointed out.

My chest tightened. Abigail was right. Lili had been in the rain. She was soaked. But how had it touched her skin and not reduced her to the sorry sack of shit that she was? How had she protected herself from it? How was she immune when the others on her side weren't?

"There's a *difference*," she snarled at me with fierce eyes, "between being battered by centuries of heartache, and being evil." She said it as if it were simple. She stared into me, her blue eyes shining brightly as she studied me—tracked every small movement I made from the glare I gave her, to the way my throat bobbed as I swallowed, and then down to the tight fists I made.

I looked away from her, a bitter taste on my tongue. She wasn't *good*. She wasn't a saint or a heroine. I hardly knew if she was worthy of redemption. But then I heard her in my head and I looked back at her.

Is he dead? Lili asked, her eyes widening with importance.

My stomach flipped over. She didn't have to specify who.

The slightest spark of joy lifted the corners of my mouth. I tilted my chin down as I dared her with my eyes, hoping to cause a blow. *Want to see how I did it?* I asked, pushing my magic into her head since she couldn't use her own. I half wondered if she'd say yes. *I can show you precisely how it happened.*

But she didn't take the bait. She looked away, biting the inside of her cheek as her fingers ran along a tattered part of the wall.

I'm sure I can imagine it on my own, was her reply.

I studied her as she looked back up at the portraits all the way down the wall. She had loved Florence. But Florence wasn't good for anyone, especially Lili.

I turned to Chad and took in his lax stance. His thoughts swirled around my mind like a beautiful symphony—a swift piece of kindness and understanding. Then I took in Abigail, her warm, friendly face, knowing she wouldn't harm a fly unless they truly deserved it, and it was clear by both of their expressions that it was time we gave Lili a true chance.

Turning back to Lili, I let my thoughts pass into her head.

You let Chad and Abigail live. I owe you for that, I admitted. Then my inner tone turned dark. *But you owe the world for the devastation you caused in the name of this 'new way of life' you yearned for.*

Chad placed a hand on the small of my back, giving me the courage to let her go.

"Run," I told Lili flatly, no pleasure from the word.

"What?" she breathed out, shrinking a few inches as she cowered in on herself.

"Don't cry," I said with another step.

"But—" she stammered, looking at the others as her breaths shook her whole body.

"Just get away," I told her, my face less than a breath away from hers. I grabbed the blonde hair on the back of her head. My grip pulled the skin on her face tighter and I stared hard, threats swimming in my eyes. "You get a head start. If I recall correctly, you're good at staying hidden. But when we find you, and we will," I said firmly, "my debt will already be paid. The royal crown will not come to your aid."

She threw another cautious glance at Abigail and Chad as if they'd change their minds any second and stop her. Neither of them moved. Her eyes met mine once more and she nodded.

I let go of her hair and placed my hands politely behind my back before sending one last thought into her mind.

Don't make me regret it, I growled.

She parted her lips, but apparently, she was too shocked to voice her reply, so she shut her mouth.

Wouldn't dream of it, Sunshine, she told me. A smile lit her eyes but it wasn't her usual, cold, cruel smile. It was a smile for someone who was blessed with a second chance. Though I hardly knew if she deserved it.

Perhaps you could work on earning that colour of yours, I suggested, taking a step away from her. *Heal your soul enough so you can see just how vibrant your colour can get.*

Her brows rose before she squinted her eyes in wonder.

Some connection we have, isn't it? I asked her, grinning. I had won, even if she hadn't entirely lost.

She smiled back before eyeing the gap we were creating for her to escape.

Abigail withdrew the phial I had given her earlier, uncorked it, and poured out the very last of its contents onto Lili's chains. The handcuffs clicked open, and Chad flicked his wrists. They disappeared amongst green smoke.

I didn't know what to expect—if she'd thank us or if she'd attack. But with one last shallow breath into the air, I blinked, and the vampire-witch disappeared.

My shoulders fell from exhaustion. I listened to the sound of our breaths. I tried to focus on the feeling in my chest to discern if it was hope or regret, but it was indistinguishable.

"I think that was the right thing to do," Abigail said thoughtfully, breaking the quiet we shared. Her tone suggested that the words were more for herself than anything. "At least for now," she added, a hint of scepticism on her tongue.

I nodded, standing between her and Chad.

"What if she goes on a killing spree?" Chad asked, uncertainty weighing down his voice.

But I shook my head, narrowing my eyes as I stared up at the portrait of Dracula, and then at the one of Lili. "We won't let it get to that this time," I said firmly. I let out a deep sigh. "Besides, I can infiltrate her mind whenever I want," I said with a smug smile. "And if all else fails, I have these pretty blonde hairs for a tracking potion," I noted, taking my hands from behind my back and holding up three long hairs.

Abigail laughed, realising my reason for grabbing the back of Lili's head.

Chad's face split into a grin—one so warm and big and filled with amusement. "Such a wicked witch," he said, shaking his head at me. "I'm so proud."

Abigail took the hairs from my hand and gingerly placed them in her empty phial. Then I grabbed both of their hands and rubbed the back of them with my thumbs.

"Now," I said decidedly, "let's go clean up the muck out there."

I'm Still Unstoppable

Chapter 67: Whole

There was an odd sense of calm and relief, even with death so prevalent. Perhaps it was because most of our enemies were puddles of holy water. Perhaps it was because the thunderous cloud had turned white and was now dissipating in the warm breeze. Or perhaps it was because we knew we had won.

We walked through the courtyard, through the display of black lilies, and down the outdoor corridor that led to the front gardens. Though the sun was shining brightly, Casters were creating shields to protect the vampires who had fought by their sides. We heard the roar of dragons above, watched as the mud monster sank back into the ground, and felt the wind as sand swirled around each mummy before they disappeared. A cage of ever-falling sand bars trapped leftover foes—creatures who must not have been on our side but whose souls weren't tainted enough for the holy water to take its full effect. More people walked out the front doors of the castle, some escorting prisoners—people who had run from the rain—people who actually deserved to be prisoners, unlike those we had freed down below. Amongst them—held captive by two other ghosts—was Missouri, looking just as miserable as ever.

As each person spotted us, their feet stopped in their tracks. Their eyes widened as they took us in. Whispers filled my head, too many to separate, almost as if they were screaming their thoughts at me. But I shoved them all out. Part of me wished Hydie was here to tell me their auras, or to help me block the chaos in my mind. Another part of me was thankful she was with Connor, away from this whole mess so she could rest.

I took a deep breath. The rain had washed away the poisoned blood and the foul stench of death. Instead, the wind carried the feeling of peace and hope.

The battle was over, but it wasn't the end. I could feel a new beginning coming, and we had so much to do to prepare for it.

Fendel stood at Mallory and Morgan's feet. His chest puffed up bravely as he gave me a toothy smile. He was no longer afraid of the witches. No gnome would have to be ever again thanks to the new laws.

The aunts wore tired expressions, but the moment their eyes landed on Chad, they choked on sobs. Red magic swirled around them and they appeared next to us, pulling Chad in for a barrage of hugs and kisses.

A warm feeling filled my heart. The two old witches may hate me enough to poison me, cause a frog to come up my throat, and flaunt a blonde-haired beauty in front of me, but no one could say they didn't love their nephew. He was their world. And I was glad he had them.

Eyeara walked towards us, dragging her father behind her. The chains I had placed around Eyeron's wrists were covered in frost. His nostrils flared as his eyes met mine, but his daughter smiled.

"Most of the lingering enemies have been captured," she informed us, "but if it's all right with you, we'd like to take *this* war prisoner for ourselves."

I gave a firm nod. "I suspect we'll be seeing you soon?" I posed to her.

"Most certainly," she replied, her secret smile bright in her eyes. "We have a new world to create."

That we did.

I watched as she handed Eyeron over to her ice-like soldiers and then strode to her dragon. In one synchronised motion, she and the other blue, pointy-eared riders flew their dragons off towards the sun. A circle of air shimmered in the sky and the dragons disappeared through the portals.

Saga touched down behind us, shaking the earth beneath our feet. She nudged her large nose against me, pushing my whole body a metre forward. I laughed, trying to pet the white scales along her face, but she wouldn't stay still. She pushed me forward again. This time, I looked to see if Chad knew what she wanted, but he and his aunts were staring in the direction Saga was pushing me, pale-faced and immobile. Immediately, I followed their gazes.

My heart stopped. Chad's mother floated in front of Abigail, a sweet look on her face. I felt my knees grow weak as I looked at her smile. Chad made to take a step towards her ghost, but he stopped, his entire body tense against me. His face was a mixture of hurt, confusion, and love—a potion of yearning for a lost one. But the fact that his face read as such meant one thing.

He could see her.

They could all finally see her.

A sob fell from Abigail's lips right before her knees crashed into the ground. She stared up at the woman—the woman who was a ghost because of her—and a red tear fell from each of her eyes.

Abigail tilted her head down. Her long black hair draped over her face, and she shook her head. "I'm sorry," she whispered, tears clogging her throat. "I'm so, so—"

But my singing ghost didn't let her finish.

Madelyn placed a grey hand under Abigail's chin and lifted it up. It didn't sink through Abigail's skin or cause a shiver down her spine. It was like magic—like an enchanted memory of a person filled with a boundless quantity of love.

For a moment, the vampire and ghost stared at each other—an unspoken language passing seamlessly between them. Then I heard as Abigail forced air into her lungs.

"All right," Abigail said tentatively, and though I didn't read her mind to know what was said, I had a feeling my singing ghost had made my friend promise to forgive herself.

Madelyn drifted closer, giving each of her sisters a loving look before she placed her hand against Chad's cheek. He closed his eyes, and I knew he didn't feel the cold hand of a ghost, but the warmth of his mother. His stance loosened as he breathed in the moment. When he opened his eyes, they were swimming with tears.

As she turned to me, my vision began to blur with my own tears—red and heavy. She smiled but I could feel in my bones that this wasn't a hello. It was a goodbye. She was saying farewell.

I looked down at the ground. I had doubted her. I had doubted her intentions for so long when in fact, they were nothing but positive. She had watched over me nearly my whole life—cared for me—protected me more than my own mother had or could. And now she was saying farewell. I didn't know how to thank her.

But as she smiled back at me, part of me knew she could feel my thoughts.

Then a warm, white light shone brightly around us. When I looked up, the bright glow consumed her, taking her away forever.

Mallory and Morgan both sobbed beside us, grasping onto each other, and mourning the loss of their sister—the third piece to their trio—all over again. They had been born at the same time and loved one another so dearly. It was unfair for one of them to be ripped away.

I couldn't think. Though the summer sun was bright, rising in the east and casting a long-awaited warmth over me, chills covered my skin. A sick feeling bubbled in my stomach.

Why is she going? I asked Chad, too choked up to ask the words aloud.

I felt as he slipped his hand into mine and squeezed it tight. *The prophecy of the stars is complete,* he replied. *Of all the children she saved when she was alive, you were the last, and now you've won. You don't need any more guidance.*

I shook my head, not to say "no" so much as to communicate that I didn't have the right words. I took a deep breath, sadness weighing down on me as the words came. *How do you know all this?* I asked.

She just told me, he said, serenity flowing through him, and I knew he had heard her in his mind. *She said the place she's going is beautiful,* he thought in a soft, sad whisper. *She said my father's there and he's been waiting for her.*

I pictured it in my mind, some ethereal, bright place where two people—people who loved each other so deeply but were torn apart for nearly three decades—could finally join.

The sickness in my stomach soothed itself. I had lost Chad—seen him die more times than I could count. I pulled his hand up, uncurling his fingers so I could see his palm. A gasp escaped my lips. New lines slithered across his hand in some intricate pattern that gave a path to his future. A crimson tear fell from my eye, and I kissed his hand gently. Those lines had the greatest meaning of all.

Our future, I thought, looking him straight in the eye. *Our beautiful future that I can't wait to share with you.*

I took the emerald ring from my pocket, delighting in the way his eyes lit up when he saw it.

"How—" he started, but he took it gently from my hands and smiled at me. "Unstoppable," he answered for himself.

I nodded. "*We're* unstoppable," I corrected.

His beautiful green eyes shimmered. He plucked the ring from me and slid it slowly up my finger until it sat in its perfect place. My love for him filled my heart. Then he pulled me into him for a kiss, and the last piece of my shattered heart fell back into place.

I was whole again.

Epilogue: The End

T he crowd was far larger this time. Thousands of chairs were placed in tidy rows on either side of the blue carpet. Blue like Lili's eyes. Blue like mine. But this time, there was a sense of triumph in the air rather than animosity and fear. After all, this was meant to be a joyous occasion. And what better day to hold it than on a holiday when mortals already celebrated our kind?

The hall was adorned with gothic decor, the spirit of All Hallows' Eve bringing a smile to my lips. Candles flickered within jack-o'-lanterns, casting shadows upon the crowd as more and more gathered. Cauldrons bubbled, decadent banners hung from the ceiling, and roses as red as blood gave the evening a distinctly paranormal feel. Enormous spiderwebs were spread throughout the room, courtesy of Charity, Kana, and the other jorogumos they'd befriended since the final battle. Live bats fluttered around, adding to the dark ambience. Enchanted mirrors delivered several of our guests, while dragons and automobiles delivered others. Soon we'd all be in our costumes, free to celebrate the night to its fullest. But first, we had business to attend to.

A camera was aimed at us, ready to broadcast our message to the entire world. This time, I wasn't afraid. And this time, a crown with real meaning was perched upon my head.

I was a queen.

My husband held my hand in his, his green eyes shining as bright as ever. I could feel the excitement rising within him. It was his favourite day of the whole year.

Chad pulled me up from my throne, and we started our speech together in the new world we had worked so hard to build.

"It's been over a year since the battle at Dracula's Lair," I announced. "More than a year since we defeated an army of monsters who chose violence and death over seeking cooperation with the mortals. Though their methods were barbaric and treacherous, the world we've created from the embers and ashes is beautiful."

Chad's voice filled the hall of *Schloss auf den Felsen* as he took a turn speaking to the crowd. I looked down at all the faces. So many colours, so many cultures, so many of my friends. So many secrets unravelled.

"The blackout came to an end," Chad said to the crowd, "as mortals around the world reached out to offer a truce. There are still those who fear such a grand change. Still, the world's a brighter place now that Florence is gone."

I looked down at my emerald engagement ring, a matching wedding band lying neatly against it. He was right. A far better world where Chad and I could be together as one.

"Several of you are wondering about the search for Lilith," I commented, shielding my mind in case there were any mind readers in the room. "To that, we must admit we're still in pursuit." I stared around the room to gather the expressions. Hydie observed them too, taking in the shining colours of their auras, and then gave me a firm nod. "But I have a feeling we'll find her soon," I added, only it was a lie. According to my latest dream, she was off building a new life somewhere in South America, half a world away, but a docile life nonetheless. It appeared Lilith could be harmless if she wanted to be.

Perhaps the lack of capturing her made us look weak. Perhaps the crowd around us—the world watching—thought she outsmarted us by staying hidden. But I didn't care what they thought. I knew in my gut she deserved a second chance, so I moved on before they could dole out any concerns.

"We've decided that the terms 'Night Crawlers' and 'Casters' are of the old ways, so we'd do well to get rid of those. Instead, the beings mortals once thought were myths will be known merely as paranormals, because we truly are beyond normal. Fate gave us each gifts, and we will no longer hide them in the shadows."

"We've been working on a lot in this past year," Chad said. "Several programs have begun, such as the mass production of blood duplication potions, voluntary organ donors to help sustain the paranormals, counselling for people who have survived transformations, potions for werewolves who previously couldn't transform by will, and more."

"With that said," I resumed, "our next grand project is to start a school. A school in an underwater castle where children who have been shattered can heal and learn to grow their gifts to become unstoppable—a school where mortal children are welcome and can make lasting bonds with paranormal children. We'll begin by accepting children in need—orphans—or those whose parents are unfit," I added, knowing first-hand this was all too common. "We've already had several reach out to me in my dreams."

We continued our speech, taking turns to answer questions and broaching ideas for this new world where mortals knew we existed—where we could all coexist. After a gruelling two hours, the meeting adjourned, and the fun began.

I transformed my bright gown into a sleek black dress. The bodice hugged my breasts and hips, before it loosened at my knees and trailed down to the floor. The long sleeves gave the effect of bat wings as they hung past my black nail polish—quite the dramatic touch. My lips were as crimson as the blood I drank, my eyes were surrounded in a smoky eyeshadow, and my long, curly, purple hair was black and bone straight.

Chad nodded approvingly, sporting the accompanying costume, all the way down to a ridiculously thin moustache.

"Morticia Addams. My, do you look scrumptious," he said in an obnoxiously charming voice.

"As do you, my husband," I replied, playfully trailing a finger along his moustache. "Although, part of me wishes I had kept

Florence's hand to really complete our outfits—and as punishment. I could torture that hand in at least fifty different ways."

"Of course you could, my love," Chad replied, lifting my chin to him. "But you did such a brilliant job disposing of him. Don't think of it as a waste."

He leaned in close and placed a gentle kiss on my neck. Oh, my sweet spot.

I seem to remember a ball long ago where you offered a good shag in a supply closet, I remarked, wiggling my brows at him. *Is that offer still on the table?*

For the love of all things good, Hydie interrupted, coming out of nowhere and displaying a look of pure disgust, *save that rendezvous for when my sensitive ears are far,* far *away.*

I looked into her blue eyes, perhaps finally getting used to them, and smiled at my sister. She was elegantly dressed as a lion tamer. Connor, the beast she called a boyfriend, ran up from behind and wrapped his arms around her. Her disgust was wiped clean from her face. Connor was in long black robes, round glasses, and had a fake scar drawn slapdash above his brow.

"Today I get to be a wizard and a werewolf," he said excitedly. "These days, it's not cool enough to only be *one* paranormal creature. You have to be two."

"Yes, because we totally chose to be either," Hydie replied sarcastically, rolling her eyes.

"How's business at the pub?" Chad asked Connor.

"Splendid! Overwhelmingly so, to be honest," he added. "Castle on the Rocks is crawling with paranormals who feel right at home and mortals eager to meet us. I even put out a sign that says, 'Free werewolf bites here,'" he said, using his hands to emphasise each word, "in case the normal folk get tired of their ordinary lives. Think you can make it to Salsa Night this Sunday?"

"Perhaps if we wear a disguise," I replied, gazing adoringly at Chad. "I've been having a lot of fun lately with my shapeshifting powers."

"Perhaps we'll run into Wyatt again," Chad remarked, trying hard not to smile.

I elbowed him in the ribs, doing my best not to attract onlookers. We wouldn't want our guests to know how much of a tosser their king was.

Chad's smile broke through as he pulled me in and then placed a kiss on my forehead. I begrudgingly accepted it.

"So about the pub, Azalea," Connor said tentatively, letting go of Hydie to fidget with his striped tie, "I was wondering if I could ask you a few tips about drink concoctions and the sort."

I frowned at the werewolf who forbade me from going behind the bar. Something about how the drinks I made were complete rubbish. But when I opened my mouth, Hydie interjected.

"Come on, Chad," Hydie sighed, linking her arm with his and pulling him away from me. "Connor wishes to speak to Azalea in private, he's just too much of a sheep to say it out loud."

I raised my brows, fearful of what he was going to say. Connor shook his head at her as they walked away, grimacing like she had told his darkest secret.

"You know, it's really unfair that the three of you can read minds!" he shouted after her. I blushed as a few guests looked our way, but Connor seemed oblivious to it. "At least Azalea gives my brain some privacy—mostly."

He shook his head, exasperated, and looked at me as if to say, "Am I right, or what?" I merely stared at him expectantly.

"So, Azalea," he said, draping his arm around my shoulder and leading me in the opposite direction that the other two had gone. "Have you and Chad given much thought to what you're going to do about the whole immortality thing?"

"As in…" I pressed.

"As in him growing old, and you living forever?" Connor clarified.

"Oh," I replied, caught off guard. "Yes, we have."

"And…" he encouraged.

I thought about the vision of Lili, so long ago now, and how she had pondered that very question. Chad and I had indeed discussed it at length in the time since.

"Well, wizards naturally live longer than mortals," I started, "and there are potions Chad can use to sustain his life. But I suppose neither of us really wants to live forever. So when it's time, we'll both settle down. I think I'd rather like to be a statue, perhaps underwater, in front of our new school. There's already a statue in front of Castwell Castle. I figure, why not have one of the co-founders out in front of *Ypovrýchio Kástro?*"

"What about Chad?" Connor asked. "I'm guessing he's opposed to cremation after that whole pyre ordeal."

I furrowed my brow. "Yes, Connor," I huffed out, annoyed by such a scarring comment. "I'd say he would be 'opposed' to the idea of being on fire again. He prefers the idea of a burial at sea too. But far away from the Bermuda Triangle, so Demriam won't get her fins on his corpse. Now, what is it with these morbid questions?"

"Oh, just figuring out how the kids are doing it these days, being in love with immortal creatures and all," he said playfully, but his eyes flickered longingly to Hydie.

He truly was head over heels for her. I was happy for them, despite my first reactions. I think we all needed each other, and I was glad Hydie and I had found the family we had always needed.

I placed a hand on Connor's shoulder and jostled him. "We're all going to live long, beautiful lives, Connor. Unless you break my sister's heart. Then I'm going to torture you worse than I tortured Florence, right before I murder you. Is that clear?"

He nodded quickly, his puppy-dog brown eyes wide, and I laughed. He really was a sheep.

"Now," I said, giving him a gentle shove, "go dance with my sister while the night is young."

He gave his characteristic goofy grin before he ran off and pulled Hydrangea onto the dance floor.

I turned around to go to my dinner chair and nearly tripped over a flood of gnomes. My hand flew to my heart, thankful I hadn't trampled them. At least fifty of them stood at my feet, Fendel at the front, a present wrapped in orange and black in his hands. As he held it up to me, the gnomes behind him bounced on the tips of their toes, clearly impatient for me to open it.

I smiled down at each of them as I took the present. "You didn't have to get me anything," I said, a tear forming in gratitude. "Thank you."

"Open it, Azalea," Fendel urged in a high-pitched squeal.

I laughed, delighted in how far we had come. From the days where they'd freeze over in porcelain, knowing I was a witch before I did, to Fendel feeling he couldn't address me by my given name, and now, to a free world where mortals, witches, and every other paranormal creature could stand together in one room without a single gnome flinching. We had created that together. These little gnomes with big hearts, helping hands, and ambition had played a huge part in that.

There was something small and soft within the wrapping, fabric perhaps. My fingers slid carefully along the paper, unsticking the tape and unfolding the wrapping as I went. I pulled out a pristinely white cloth and unfolded it to find it was a pillowcase. Quite the colour contrast from the red one Fendel had gifted me before.

"It's a white one," Fendel piped in, "since you won't be crying as much anymore."

As if to prove him wrong, a single red tear fell from my eye, but this time it was a joyous one.

I pressed my lips together to stop a sob from bursting out. "Thank you," I managed to let out, looking at Fendel and then at all of the other gnomes. "I couldn't have asked for a better gift, honestly. This really means a lot to me."

Fendel rushed forward, and I bent down to wrap him in a hug. Every other gnome was eager to give me a hug after. I spent the next fifteen minutes hugging each of them, one by one.

The rest of the night was equally enchanting. Everyone danced around the ball—dresses and costumes flouncing through the air. Floating orchestral instruments played alongside vampires from various covens—perhaps old enough to have lived alongside Mozart himself. I took turns dancing with my mates. Chad spun me around elegantly. Connor added in his own salsa moves to the classical pieces that filled the room. I danced with my sister, Abigail, and even Ingrid and Irma, and we celebrated the death of Florence. Charity complimented me on how much my dancing had improved since my first ball at Loxley Lair, and we shed a tear remembering my first dance with O'Brien, and how I had stepped on his toes.

Before I knew it, it was nearly three in the morning. After being completely shocked that Mallory and Morgan kissed my cheeks goodbye, I sat at a table, watching the party. I held a glass of blood duplication potion against my lips, strategically positioned under my nose to cover the stench of the human food. I took a deep breath, feeling at peace as I watched Chad dance with Abigail, both laughing over something one of them had said. My entire body was warm—comforted at the thought that they could share such a moment after everything they'd been through together—comforted at the thought that they were both still alive. I had my best friend. I had my fated mate. And all the pain and sorrow had torn us apart and stitched us back together. Only this time, we were better than ever.

Far across the ballroom, I saw Connor tuck a curly strand of hair behind Hydie's ear. He held it there, rubbing his thumb across her cheek, a look of utter love and adoration in his eyes. His gaze shifted over to me, and he awkwardly dropped his hand from her, mid-sentence. Panic struck his face as he watched me take a long drink of blood. At least he was taking our little chat seriously.

I laughed as I watched Fendel and the other gnomes dance with the children, partners who were still too tall for them. When Abigail and Cristin went to collect Noel and Leon and take them home for bed, Noel pouted. Though it was clear she didn't want to trade her superhero costume for pyjamas, the little witch obliged and insisted on bidding me goodnight first.

She pranced over and I stood from my seat in time for her to wrap her arms around me. I breathed in the scent of lavender soap as she gently rested her head against my stomach.

"That was a brilliant ball!" she exclaimed happily. "Once people start coming to the school, I'll have even more mates. Your babies can come too—once they're old enough," she added simply, nuzzling her head against my stomach as though there were babies already in there, waiting to get out.

My fingers froze.

"Oh," I let out as my gut dropped. I frowned. "Well—" I started carefully, every bone and the very strength I had used to get through the speech was now as soft as jelly. "It's going to be quite some time before Chad and I even think about having children. It's quite possible that I can't have them at all. I am part vampire. It's rare," I told her, knowing perfectly well she was already aware of that. She had been adopted by two vampires who had never been able to birth children of their own.

Noel scrunched her whole face up at me, confused, but a voice intervened.

"I think that's quite enough out of you," Chad told Noel in a light warning tone, reaching his hand out for her.

She took it and skipped happily in place before Chad twirled her around in a circle, her long cape flaring out around her. But my lips were stuck agape. I blinked at both of them.

"No," I said simply, Noel's words clouding my mind. I huffed out a stubborn breath before I closed my mouth and opened it again. "No, that's not possible. Not so soon anyway. I'm not—"

But the cheeky bastard and the twirling child both smiled at me as if they shared the same secret. Chad winked at her and she ran off to join Abigail, Cristin, and her brother.

Panic pulsed through me. This wasn't funny.

I rounded on Chad.

What the bloody hell are you two talking about? I asked, incapable of spewing the words aloud. My heart was pumping too vigorously.

Chad placed a hand on his chest, feigning innocence. "I'm actually not at liberty to tell," he said, taking a few long strides backwards and out of my reach. "You once said you'd want it to be a surprise."

I blinked at him several more times as my brain scrambled to catch up.

The pregnant vampire and her twins.

The night of Chad's coronation.

He had used his magic to check if her unborn child was all right. I had *hastily* mentioned to her that I'd want the sex of the baby to remain a surprise if I were ever to have one—*not* the entire knowledge of whether or not there was a life inside of me.

I opened my mouth to tell Chad this—to explain that I needed to know whatever it was that he did. The ridiculous smile he gave in return all but confirmed he knew a heap.

I took a few threatening steps towards the snarky man-witch and he winced. He lifted his hands into a shrug and took an equal number of steps back.

"Would right now be a good time to tell you that *triplets* run in my family?" he asked, his brows raised, his lips pursed in some ridiculously adorable way that made me want to whack him in the stomach.

If there was any air left in my lungs, I would've gasped, but there was not. I was in shock. I was going to faint. Then, green magic swirled around him and the adorable git disappeared.

I ran towards the small trace of emerald magic and let my magic take me with him. The sight of our bedroom in Castwell Castle greeted me, filling my heart with warmth. We were home. We were in *our* home, ready to live *our* long lives together and raise *our* children.

I felt the heat of Chad's body wrap around me from behind. I breathed in the scent of his sweet, heavenly blood, and held onto his arms.

"You're quite scary when you're cross," he decided.

"King of the new world," I said mockingly, "and you're afraid of little old me?"

"Of course I am," he replied with a smile. "The most powerful person to ever have roamed this land. You're not like the other witches who only possess the gift of the past, present, or future. You see visions of the past, alter bubbles of time in the present, read minds, and are the only one who's ever been able to go back and change the future. You're a clever combination of a vampire and a witch, the winner of the worst war, and the world will forever be in your debt."

He nuzzled his face into my neck, his breath tickling my skin, and said, "I love you, Azalea Castwell." He kissed my neck and I grew weak in the knees all over again. "I love you, and we're going to live happily ever after in this new world we created."

And we did.

Please leave a review

Thank you for supporting my dream of being an author. I would be honored to know what you think. Please drop a review on Amazon and Goodreads!

Q&A with Jade Austin

When did you come up with the idea for this series?
As most of you know, I began writing the "I'm Still Alive" trilogy back in 2008 when I was sixteen years old. I was obsessed with witches and vampires thanks to the popular books and movies at the time, but I wanted to create a world that had both. I stopped writing and reading as much when I got to college and had my son, but I kept thinking of this storyline and I knew I had to finish it.

Why did you start writing again?
During the dark COVID ages, my friend made me read, "The Right Thing To Do," and let me tell you, I hardly slept or worked or cleaned anything until I absorbed that book! After that, I knew I had to get back into reading and writing. What better place to start than the storyline that had been living in my head for over a decade?

What did you change from the original version of the story?
When I started writing this series again, I changed everything, even down to the main characters' names. I aged them up and it became a new adult series rather than young adult. I stripped it down to the bare bones and it became a world better than it had started.

How long did it take you to write the books?
As far as the first drafts go, the first book took me four months to write and the second took seven months because I had Hyperemesis Gravidarum during pregnancy. (Not fun!) The third book, however, took over a year and a half because writing with a baby is *slightly* harder.

What are your goals for this series now that it's complete?
I have always dreamed of these books becoming best sellers! I want a movie deal (or perhaps a show) and I want to act as the main actress. I'm so excited to finally advertise them as a

complete series, especially since book two's cliffhanger was intense.

What should we expect from you next?

Next, I'll be working hard to get these books into as many bookstores and libraries as I can. I also want to turn them into audiobooks. I have about five side stories floating in my head that take place in the same universe as *I'm Still Alive*. I'm excited to put them all on paper. Some are with new characters and some are with the old ones. But first, I have an excellent idea for a high fantasy. Think fae, a pretty map, and even a love triangle. Stay tuned!

How can your readers support you?

Honestly, keep doing what you're doing! Join the "I'm Still Alive by Jade Austin" group on Facebook. Follow me on TikTok and Instagram @jadeaustin09. Leave a review on Amazon and Goodreads. Help me spread the word about my books. You are all helping my dream to come true!

Photo credit: Emily Hasenleder –
Clear Umbrella Photography

ABOUT THE AUTHOR

Jade Austin resides in the Pacific Northwest with her husband Will, her dog Frodo (yes, she's a LOTR fan), and her sons Bradley and Cooper (yes, her kids are named after the actor, regardless of what her husband claims).

Jade teaches middle school mathematics but aspires to be a full-time author with movie deals. She has the coolest home office you've ever seen, and she loves her friends and family with all her heart.

ACKNOWLEDGMENTS

My readers are amazing. Thank you for reaching out through messages, comments, and reviews to tell me how much you love my stories. I completed an entire trilogy because of you. I survived people attacking my story and giving up on it, all because you connected with the characters and reached out to support me. For every tear I've shed over negative comments, you've given me a hundred butterflies in my stomach and a smile on my face. Without you, my heart would still be shattered.

Thank you Samantha, Steph Adams, T.N. Thackston, and my mom for reading the rough drafts! All of your encouragement, support, and brilliant ideas really made this book shine. You've helped me make this story the perfect conclusion to the trilogy.

Special thanks to Samantha Ziegler for all of your brilliant contributions to this story. You constantly lifted my soul with your compliments and challenged me to make my writing grow. If you all haven't already, stop reading this and go read her books immediately. I need more people to obsess over them with me.

Rebecca Kenney at RFK Cover Design has done it again! This cover ties in with the first two so beautifully. How do they keep getting more and more gorgeous each time?

Thank you to my friends and family members who supported me through this grueling process.

Thank you, Shannon, Olivia, Joe, and more for believing in my work and never once making me feel like I couldn't talk about my book or open up to you about the joys and heartaches of writing.

Thank you, Bradley, for being the sweetest, easiest baby to care for.

Thank you, Cooper, for loving to read and write just like Mommy. I see so much of myself in you.

And lastly, thanks to my husband, Will, because I "better say thanks" to you in the back of my book.